• Stage Fright •

In duos and trios, and solo, dancers surged in a wave of backward and forward somersaults under their horses. They leaped lightly onto the geldings' backs, where they stood, arms open, in a gesture of offering to the audience.

Glennys's Horse Sense was at work. She caught and matched with Whistle, who was starting to lose his nerve from the rapid changes of gait and the unexpected cues calling him to mark time on the spot. Repeatedly she nudged his memory and his confidence to the fore, straightening out his hesitations so Nan, his partner, could think about her next move. Wherever there was a weakness in the horses' understanding, Glennys was there, holding them in time . . .

The audience demanded more spectacular changes so that it might receive more intense thrills. But before the performers dropped dead of exhaustion the orchestra played the finale.

The ovation was led by King Leon from the royal box . . .

*Books by Constance Ash
from Ace*

**THE HORSEGIRL
THE STALKING HORSE**

THE
STALKING HORSE

An Evening-Length Opera Ballet
in Five Acts

CONSTANCE ASH

ACE BOOKS, NEW YORK

This book is an Ace
original edition, and has never
been previously published.

THE STALKING HORSE

An Ace Book/published by arrangement with
the author

PRINTING HISTORY
- Ace edition/June 1990

ISBN: 0-441-77923-9

Ace Books are published by The Berkley Publishing Group,
200 Madison Avenue, New York, New York 10016.
The name "Ace" and the "A" logo are trademarks
belonging to Charter Communications, Inc.
PRINTED IN THE UNITED STATES OF AMERICA

10 9 8 7 6 5 4 3 2 1

It's time to express my deep gratitude
to David Chambers, Karole Armitage, Mark
Morris, Jim Self, the Salt Lake City Ballet
Company, and the generous hospitality of
the Sundance Institute.

A deep reverence and a bouquet are offered
to Ginjer Buchanan, an editor who has so
much good sense it may as well be called
Horse Sense.

And a special thanks to Lissa Hattersley,
backbone of the Lone Star, who during a
hot, dirty, noisy New York City summer,
provided a cool, clean, silent apartment
in which I killed a King.

This book is dedicated to Ned Sublette,
who opened the windows behind the scenes.

The quick handler conceals himself behind another horse or even a figure constructed to resemble one. This is called a stalking horse. The free horses will investigate this curiosity in their field. The handler then jumps out from behind his blind, captures the horses, and compels them to perform his will.

In St. Lucien, they say, there is no man who is not a stalking horse for another.

From: A Horsehandler's Wit

The Stalking Horse

• Act I •

· ONE ·

THE BALLET STUDENTS of Marie Bonheur's School of Theatrical and Ballroom Dance had lost their precision over the summer recess. Every morning since class had resumed the pace had been slow, the execution sloppy. Glennys Eve was impatient for improvement.

Tonight summer crossed over into autumn, according to the Fortune House astrologers. Change was in the air for those who could sense it, and Glennys could. She saw, heard, and smelled more acutely than she'd done all summer. Crossover nights were lucky for her.

Twenty-three voices whispered along with Glennys's the sequence of movements that made up the tendue exercise.

The studio floor was divided into four diagonal rows of six ballet students each. "Pointe tendue side; pointe tendue front; pointe tendue rear; repose," puffed from their lips.

Their words ballooned up to the high ceiling of the old building in which Marie had made her school.

"First arabesque, half-toe," screeched Marie Bonheur. Marie was the ballet mistress as well as the proprietress of the school, and also taught the classes in gesture and mime. She slapped her switch on the floorboards in front of her slippered feet while she counted. The violinist scraped out a familiar tune from a forgotten opera.

Twenty-four legs stretched rear, toes pointed and raised to the height of the hip. Twenty-four arms reached toward a wall of mirrors, supplicating an imaginary audience. Their fingers held air.

Glennys saw only her own image in the wall of mirrors. The sunshine slanting through the windows bisected her body, leaving her supporting leg in shadow. Her foot, on half-pointe, took strength from the floor. Her ankle, calf, and thigh were firm. Behind her, her working leg floated free in the light.

None of the other twenty-three saw Glennys in the mirrors.

They all looked only at themselves. Marie Bonheur watched them all.

The ballet mistress's switch cracked against the floor. Dust motes pirouetted deliriously. The accompanist stopped mid-bar.

"Rowena! Which is the working leg?"

Rowena's supporting foot and ankle wobbled, and she fell out of arabesque. She looked down at her feet.

"The left leg is the working leg, Mademoiselle Marie," Rowena stuttered.

Rowena had been balanced beautifully on left as she was supposed to have been. But Marie had seen that her most talented student was not thinking.

Marie slashed viciously at Rowena's right calf with her switch. "Cretin! Love-stupid idiot! We are supporting with the left leg. The right leg works. The right leg, the right leg, the right leg!" Each shriek was accompanied by an application of the switch.

"What if you become coryphée this fall? What if you lead the corps de ballet and the stage geldings in *The White Revue*? The dancers following you are lost! The horses are lost! Fuddle on stage! Humiliation for me and my school! You must think and count, count and think, always. You cannot depend upon the stupid musicians to count for you! They may be lost too! They may be asleep! They may be drunk!"

Marie pulled Rowena's dark curls hard enough to bring tears to the girl's eyes. Rowena smiled through the drops clinging to her lashes.

Marie stalked back to her spot between the class and the mirrors. "Why have I worked so hard for you, Mademoiselle Rowena, when you reward me like this? No doubt you'll be full of a baby or a disease before Queen's early season opens, and all my work for you will be good for nothing."

Her switch threatened the class. "All of you make me ill! None of you worked at the exercises while my school was in recess. So how do you expect to become dancers? The days are long past when any good walking court lady could dance before kings. Now the dance is an art. And art demands discipline!"

The students stood at attention during Marie's tirade. Their feet and arms were in preparatory position, heel to heel, fingers to thighs. But their blood had quickened and a rustle had passed up and down the four rows, and Rowena's smile had gotten brighter.

Marie's harshness meant that Rowena was certainly going to be auditioned for Queen's Company. Who else would get the chance, the others wondered. Each student promised a gold forient to the Fortune Houses if she got the opportunity.

Nolan's own Academy of Music and Dance had low regard
for a Nolanese ballerina. The First Dancers of Queen's, and
many of the corps de ballet, came from the Outremere Domains
of Tourienne, Langano, and Gondol. But between St. Lucien
and the Outremere Domains the Majis Sea was wide and travel
slow. Marie's school was on this shore, and her students were
ready at hand.

"You are beginning to recall how to work," said Marie, "but
you're weak, lazy, and stupid. Summer is finished. Work!
Work!"

Work the class did. Glennys's attack in preparation for grand
jeté was sure and full of power. In defiance of gravity her body
sailed above the floor. For two breathtaking heartbeats she hung
in the air at the apex of her leap. Marie applauded and put
Glennys in the first place of her row.

"Farm girl, let's see you dance," hissed red-haired Nan,
whose place in the front of their row Glennys had taken.

Marie rapped her switch on the floor and called for slow pirouette combinations.

The adagio's deliberate unfolding was the severest test of a
ballerina's sustained control. Glennys's feet and toes were strong
enough to support her, but her shoulders, arms, and neck missed
the elegant mark of form. She put Nan's taunting out of her mind
and concentrated on what she did best.

The floorboards, springy with age, gave up smells left over
from the building's days as a factory for varnishes, glazes, and
resins. St. Lucien's humidity made the walls sweat a noxious
exudation. Most of the students couldn't afford laundresses, and
the smell of their tunics and stockings proved it. No one noticed.
It was the odor of ballet.

Old Harbor Hide Fortune House rang its bell twice more before class finished. The dancers made farewell reverence to honor
Marie, and then, spontaneously, applauded.

Marie hooked her switch over her wrist and clapped her hands
back at them, a frown on her face. When they had quieted, she
said, "I will deserve applause only if all of you increase the
pace of improvement every class, every morning. Nine weeks,
my loves, nine weeks. Whoever of you goes to Queen's Company class will wish these nine weeks had been nine years. Because at Company class you will have to give all your attention
to learning how to partner with the stage geldings so you can

please your Aristo audiences, who insist on having horses in everything. I cannot teach you that. But I will have done my best for you, and you must do the same for me.''

Marie glanced up at the observation curtain. It was closed now but during combination work she'd seen it open.

A class of boys and girls were clustered around Marie's mother at the studio entrance. Madame Bonheur, who had married, unlike her daughter, taught ballroom dances to the children of upwardly aspiring merchants.

''And never forget this. Love is a symptom of stupidity. It's only for idle Aristos and wealthy Wheels. The only love a ballerina can afford is her art. Out of here now, ballerinas,'' ordered Marie.

Glennys blew the loose strands of her hair out of her face. Marie had put her at the head of her row! She must have a chance for a Queen's audition.

The mothers and chaperones escorting their charges drew them out of range of the women running for the changing room. Ballerinas were professional women of the city, stage women, who revealed themselves in provocative clothes. Ballerinas were King's Daughters, who paid an annual fee to the King's privy purse and had the privilege of selling their bodies.

Madame Bonheur stopped Marie. Some of the students eavesdropped shamelessly but heard nothing. Marie's face was full of pleasure as she went swiftly to the private staircase that led down to her office and the Bonheur living quarters.

The ballerinas walked though the mothers and chaperones as if they didn't exist. Some of the escorts, however, were older brothers, and these the ballet students flirted with outrageously.

We are King's Daughters, they said in the language of the body understood by every man. We don't marry like ordinary women, and we're out of your reach. We get lucrative contracts from Aristo dukes and Wheel bankers.

In the small changing room, redolent of perfume and powder, the dancers' topics of conversation were themselves, each other, Queen's, and Marie.

''Maman wants Glennys Eve to come down to the office, quickly.'' Armand, Marie's son, stood in the doorway, avidly eyeing their corseted, semi-nude bodies. A collective groan issued from the room. Armand, like vermin, was a nuisance. He spied on them when they changed, and was forever putting his hands on them.

"Please tell Marie I'm coming," Glennys said. "But one can dress only so fast in this crush-box."

"You heard her, Armie," Rowena trilled. Her black curls popped out of the street dress she threw helter-skelter over her class tunic. "Out, cockroach, out, out, out." But he didn't budge.

Korla, Rowena's cousin, giggled. "You dress so fast, Rowena. But you'll be undressed to the skin again as soon as you get through the door of your room."

"If Rowena slept a little at night instead of rolling around in bed with that musician, she wouldn't get right and left mixed up," sneered red-haired Nan. Nan danced and dealt cards at Crackfyrd's Gaming House, where only Aristos and Wheels could afford to go.

"If I wasn't the best, Marie wouldn't test me all the time," said Rowena with a smile. "She's never corrected you once since we've come back from recess." Rowena knotted the sash of her dress under her breasts, did a plié to swoop under Armand's arm where it blocked the door, and was gone.

The others envied Rowena, who was assured a Queen's audition and who had love too.

"I think Rowena's pregnant," said Nan. "Her breasts are bigger than they were in the spring."

"She's not! Don't say that again, it's bad luck," replied Korla. "Rowena's just gotten riper over the summer because she's so happy. Lovers eat in bed, you know."

"The kind of eating I do in bed doesn't get anyone pregnant or fat either," Armand said, leering.

Nan, Korla, and Rais, a sweet-faced girl who worked in a marionette theater, advanced on Armand. They put their considerable combined strength to the door and tried to shut him out.

"I'll tell you something good if you give me a chance," he bargained.

The girls looked at each other and shrugged. Korla swaggered up to him in her best Music Hall style, her hands on her hips, one foot forward, her face upthrust at Armand. "What can a rat like you possibly have to tell us?" she challenged.

Armand didn't waste his time looking at the three dressed girls. His eyes roved further back where some of the others had been slower about their clothes.

"I know," he said, drawing it out, "that Catherine Gemma was in the observation cubby this morning. She's downstairs with Maman. She's the one who wants to see Glennys Eve."

Nan threw a pair of worn-out dance slippers in his face. "You lie," she stated flatly. "Catherine Gemma does not want to see Glennys. She's not a dancer, she's a horse trainer."

Korla put a finger over the redhead's lips. "Softly, Nan. Glennys will hear you."

Nan turned swiftly. "Too bad for her then."

The other students caught their breath. But Glennys, still thrilled from being put first in her row, and now hearing that it was the Gemma who wanted to see her, paid no attention.

She bent from her hips, gathered her things and shoved them into the saddlebags in which she carried her day's gear. A pair of spurs clanged to the floor. They were honest Horse Skiller spurs, not the ornaments some of the dancers wore on their boots. In the center of the rowels was an emblem of three trees. The same emblem was stamped in gold on the flaps of her saddlebags, though most of the gold had rubbed off long ago.

"I stand behind my words, and I'll say them louder," said Nan. "She's a horse trainer. She's not fit to dance at Queen's. Her mother is a farmer!"

Glennys heard that, as was intended. The others crowded against the wall, expecting her to fly at Nan.

Glennys's fingers were white as they played with the little chains of her spurs. Her head ached. She stared down at the Three Trees emblem on the spurs, the spurs that proved she controlled war stallions, and fought to control herself.

She balanced the saddlebags over one shoulder and fastened the Queen's stable badge on the other.

"Your mama died of weeping twang disease," Glennys said to Nan as she took her exit.

From behind she heard Nan yelling. "*My* mother was an artist! She danced on Queen's stage!"

On the door of Marie's office was a wooden carving of the Mourning Mother, symbol of the Outremere religion, leaning between the son at her feet and the father who loomed over them both.

Glennys knocked confidently. She forgot her headache and the anger. Her fortune at Queen's Opera Ballet Theater was about to be made.

· Two ·

THE FIRST DANCER and Marie were at ease. Marie's feet were propped on a low stool, her skirts pulled up. Catherine Gemma's maid, Amalia, was wrapping Marie's right knee in a poultice.

"Pull up a cushion to the table and help yourself," said Marie.

A stage gelding had kicked Marie early in her first season at Queen's. She'd never be able to dance on stage again. Instead of sailing back to Tourienne, Marie had opened her school. Her distaste for horses was well understood.

Glad she wasn't wearing her spurs, Glennys sat tailor-fashion in front of the short-legged table. She hadn't expected two St. Lucien ladies on a gossip. She dipped a tiny silver spoon in strawberry jam, then into the tea, and licked up the sweet stuff. The spoonful of jam was followed by a sip of tea.

"Don't be nice, Glennys. Drink it down, and pour another cup," ordered Marie. "Your body needs fluid after it sweats."

Catherine's skirts foamed about her in a froth of silk and lace as she too sank to the cushions.

"I've made quite a study of you," she said to Glennys. "You're the first female horse trainer the Company's had, and also the first to study dance. The Company and the performance horses have never worked better together. Even August Gardel says so, and our Ballet Director never praises anything a woman does."

"Thank you, Miss Gemma," said Glennys.

"Call me Catherine," said the First Dancer.

Amalia finished her attentions to Marie's knee, and retired behind the desk.

"I'm presenting a new, full-length ballet to open the early season," said Catherine.

"Joss Thack has it written in the stable schedule, along with the names of the horses you prefer to work with," Glennys said.

"I'm also choreographing it, and dancing the principal role of Lady Eve, the first stallion queen," Catherine said.

Glennys nodded her head, shivered, and carefully sipped more tea. It was coming now, she thought. She was going to be offered a role in *The First Stallion Queen*.

"I want new duets made for me and the principal horse role, which means a lot of long, difficult, extra work. I would like to engage you as my exclusive horse trainer for the early season," said the First Dancer.

The jam in Glennys's stomach turned sour. She drank tea to fight the retching reflex. Her headache pounded.

It was her old skills that were wanted, not her ability to fly across the stage. There was no invitation from Queen's Company coming to her. This wasn't a lucky day. This was the worst day of her life.

Catherine and Marie waited for her to say something, to thank Catherine, to be enthusiastic, to be curious. Disappointment moved within her like a poison. There was an obstruction in her throat. She couldn't swallow. She couldn't speak.

"I believed, Glennys, that you'd leap at Catherine's offer," reprimanded Marie.

Glennys's pride wouldn't allow them to suspect she'd expected another sort of offer altogether. She had to speak, but when she did, she violated Joss's first rule of Queen's stable. She talked of obstacles to the First Dancer's ideas, instead of how to accomplish them.

"Horses are creatures of habit. When they've learned how to do something, and where, and when, they expect it to be the same forever. New positions, and a different combination of movements, means midnight rehearsals. That seems to be the only time our geldings can be taught new tricks. That would be inconvenient for you, and for Duke Colfax."

Glennys thought herself clever to have invoked the name of the old bloodline Nolanese Aristo who sat on the board of directors of the Academy of Music and Dance. He was also in charge of the Office of Inquiry, where records and registries, including the registry of King's Daughters, were kept. He was Catherine's protector. No doubt he was paying a lot of the bills for this spectacular *Stallion Queen*.

That was how a woman got to be First Dancer at Queen's, Glennys thought bitterly. She had to be born and trained Outremere and fascinate a powerful, wealthy man.

"You instruct me, Glennys, as to what needs to be done. It's in my concubine contract that the Duke cannot interfere in any way with my art. I have a private theater at my house. We won't disturb the routines of the Shop or Queen's Theater. Augie Gardel and Collie both support my ballet completely,'' said Catherine.

Amalia handed over a sheaf of papers. Glennys ruffled through them. They were blockings of Queen's stage. Joss had taught her to read the grids during her first week as a trainer. Designs and scenery were indicated, along with the movements of the horses and other dancers. There were groupings for the singers on stage, and for those who would stand in the cloud boxes above.

"I think you will be lucky for me," said Catherine. "A Glennys Eve to help me become Lady Eve."

Glennys looked up at the First Dancer. "Eve isn't the name I was born to."

Catherine shrugged. "I wasn't born with the name Gemma."

Glennys and Catherine talked through the sheets of stage diagrams which showed the different levels and machinery to be utilized for each scene.

A production so lavish, so large, and so novel required lengthy preparation. The costumes, all new, had been designed last winter. In the spring the bids had gone out and the commission given to a textile factory in Drake. The costumes would be recut and sewn to fit the dancers by Queen's own wardrobers later in the fall.

Nothing already in the Theater's storehouse of scenery, drops, and decor was to be used. New flats and panels had been cut in Newport, the arsenal city further south down the coast. The drops were being painted here by the costly stage secrets guild.

"At the very least," crowed Marie, "Cathy's making the most expensive opera ballet Queen's has ever mounted, and that's saying a bit."

"I'm honored to be part of it," said Glennys.

"I'd like to begin working on my partner dances with the gelding Champagne at once. Will you be able to arrange for a rehearsal tonight at my theater?" Catherine asked.

"If Joss agrees. He's the one who has final word on all arrangements," said Glennys.

"He'll agree. Augie and Collie talked to him about this days ago," Catherine said absently.

Amalia rolled the blue-inked stage grids and slid them into a silk tube. "Each copy costs a silver forient, so don't lose them," she warned, and passed the tube over to Glennys.

Glennys knew she'd been dismissed. But instead of leaving

Marie's office she asked, "What compensation am I getting for working double duty?"

Behind Catherine, Amalia gave Glennys a tiny nod of approval.

Catherine looked over her shoulder to her maid. "What did you discuss with Joss Thack about that?"

"Your usual quarterly wage from Queen's stable will be paid to you, of course. But Duke Colfax is doubling that out of his own purse. There will be a bonus after opening night if all goes satisfactorily," Amalia said.

It was another luxury of success, Glennys realized as she went out the door, never to have to discuss money yourself.

On the street Glennys whistled for Baron, her bristlehair mastiff. He was her bodyguard on the streets of St. Lucien. But not even the huge dog could protect her from the ambush set up by Nan, Korla, and Rais. They'd been loitering on the other side of Catherine's carriage.

"So, are you going to dance in *The First Stallion Queen*?" Korla demanded.

"Not exactly." Glennys sighed and accepted her fate. "I'm going to teach Catherine how to dance with her stallion."

"You're the teaser horse, then," crowed Nan triumphantly. "The one who gets the mare excited so the stallion can do his job. A teaser horse!"

Glennys's headache was ferocious.

• THREE •

SO FAR THE only stage experience Glennys had was as a horse trainer. However, the streets of St. Lucien were another sort of stage, one on which the city dwellers displayed themselves every day.

For the teamsters who drove the heavy drayage, Glennys played the Coquette. Around the roving bands of jagger boys she was the Rug Diviner, in touch with the future, too loco to be assaulted. As the Guttersnipe, poor and dangerous, the Fortune House alms beaters left her alone.

This morning on the bridge at Bank Street she stopped. She felt like a foreigner in the hustling crowd scene. It made no sense to her, and she was left without heart for the spirited practice of mime and character. She wanted to scream at everyone to get away from her.

Not even in her first days in St. Lucien three years ago had she been so dismayed. She leaned far over the bridge's parapet, paralyzed by misery.

Baron, confounded because Glennys had broken her usual morning pattern, whined. His tongue lashed the hand that hung listlessly at her side. He dropped on his haunches to guard her saddlebags.

Baron had been with her since he was a puppy, almost as long as she'd been in St. Lucien. Glennys wondered what would happen to him if she threw herself into the water rushing to meet the Majis Sea.

No one cared if she lived or died except her family up north. And all they cared about was the money she sent them.

"Preposterous!" she announced firmly to Baron.

She was no Romantic who believed the world so cruel that all it deserved from her was an early, lovely death. It was as though she'd become host to impulses not her own. She'd evict them. Smarting still from Nan's teaser-horse gibe, Glennys imagined she sent the alien vapors off to her redheaded classmate. That made her feel fine. She set off at her usual rapid pace for Queen's stable and work.

Glennys entered the stablemaster's office carrying the silk-wrapped tube of stage plots as a baton of announcement. Anyone connected with the Theater knew what a tube that size contained.

"Good morning, beautiful," said Lloyd Kerrit, the under-stablemaster.

"About time you got here, Glenn. What's the word from the Gemma?" asked Joss Thack.

"Catherine's word is that everything's been cleared, even with you, so that I can be her exclusive trainer. And midnight rehearsals begin tonight," Glennys said.

Lloyd groaned.

One by one each plot grid was unrolled, backed, and put into a frame. Lloyd hung them on the wall, and saluted when finished. "The new season begins," he said. He was the one who had to recopy the duty rosters so drivers and handlers and grooms would be available for an extra night shift.

As the stablemaster, Joss was the one who had to find the overwork money that paid the horse car drivers, handlers, and grooms for their time.

Glennys, Lloyd, and Joss discussed the list of horses Catherine wanted cast exclusively for her *Stallion Queen*. Champagne had been slotted into the role of the stallion, Torgut, first sire of the Nolanese war horses, the Lady Eve's equine partner. Champers, as they called him, with his silver mane and tail, was the favorite of all the dancers. Every Theater gelding had personality, but even so, Champers stood out. His behavior was that of the complete gentleman, and he was young enough to learn new combinations. They allowed Catherine to have him.

She'd also asked for Cognac and Dainty, the two oldest, most experienced geldings, for the corps. She couldn't have them both because the two were needed for teaching the younger horses and keeping them in line on stage. For the sake of justice they only allowed Catherine Cognac.

Catherine had not thought of an understudy for Champers. But the chance of illness, injury, or exhaustion made it imperative there be one.

"She's refused an understudy for herself," said Joss, "and that's her business. But the horses are our business. Training an understudy into the new routines is going to make you work twice, Glennys. In the afternoons you're going to have to teach Vanity and me what you, Champers, and the Gemma work out in the midnight rehearsals. It will be good for Champers's memory, and he'll help us with Vanity. Maybe that way we can get away without midnight rehearsals for the understudy as well.''

They gave Catherine Flotsam and Jetsam, the two black geldings. ''They're young and eager, not set in their ways,'' said Joss. ''They'll look good behind Champers. When her rehearsals move into Queen's, the Gemma isn't going to care about anything but appearance and ability to keep place.''

They studied the plotting of horses, dancers, and singers along the grids. ''Don't get attached to any of this,'' Joss warned Glennys. ''Sure as taxes it will change before opening night.''

Stableboys had set up trestle tables in the office courtyard. A variety of bread, meat, cheese, and fruit, plus applejack to drink, was put on boards for the stable people. Provision of the noon meal, and, during the season, supper, was one of the rewards of working for Queen's stable. Joss's own chair was set at the head of the tables outside.

Glennys fed Baron his rabbit behind the Pipe Vine arbor, where no one else would have to see his unattractive eating habits.

When the weather was fine Joss practiced his fly-rod casts while people ate. It meant he was available for complaints, suggestions, or conversation. Sitting with his back to the lads and grooms, he flicked his line across the office courtyard.

''Sit with me before you take your string to work in the park,'' the stablemaster ordered Glennys. All of his attention seemed to be given to his line and to his wrist. But Glennys knew he was studying her. She nibbled on a piece of cold fowl and a stem of black grapes.

''Did the Gemma engage you for a part in *Stallion Queen* besides that of trainer?'' Joss asked. ''You were convinced that she would.''

''No,'' Glennys said.

''Are you able to do your best for her, then? I recommended you strongly,'' Joss said, ''and if you fail, that means I fail too.''

''When I first understood that Catherine wanted me only as trainer, I felt full of poison,'' Glennys confessed.

She turned her most theatrically ardent expression on the stablemaster. ''I believe this is a fair chance. I won't fail. I have an opportunity to learn from the best dancer in Nolan. I'm going to make a study of *her*.''

Joss's regard turned from Glennys to a point behind her.

"Pud-lice cadets!" snapped Joss. "Not a one of them on the walls or at the gates."

The cadets from Nolan's Equine Academy provided the security for the Theater's stable and menagerie. It was a constant complaint of Joss's that they took their duty too easy.

"I suppose she's another one wanting to see the elephants," he grumbled. "The bloody cadets have all ridden over to Duke Albany's stable to see that horse his rangers brought in."

Duke Albany's name caught Glennys's attention. She'd met him years before when he'd spent an autumn at Three Trees. Even now, on the occasions when the Duke would come backstage at Queen's he always acknowledged her.

Then, with a start, she realized that the young woman coming toward them wore the plain dress and apron of an Alaminite. It was the first time she'd seen that since she'd left Soudaka County.

According to Alaminite custom, the stranger wore a headscarf to indicate she was unmarried. Glennys assessed her with the eyes of a dancer—alert for feminine rivalry, weighing the other's attractiveness, form, and age against her own. The stranger's face was lovely, her body untrained but naturally graceful, her walk unclumsy. She seemed about nineteen, Glennys's own age.

"She's looking for me," Glennys said, controlling her instinct to run away. "A friend of my mother's, most likely sent to bring me back home to the farm."

Glennys touched the uncovered braids of hair clubbed on the back of her neck. Most Alaminite girls had been married long enough at nineteen to have several children. That was how she knew it had to be Thea Bohn.

The letters Glennys's mother sent monthly by post coach always had praise for the young Alaminite healer who had refused all marriage offers. The Bohn clan supported Thea's declaration that she could better serve their Lord God, Alam, as a maiden.

Joss's tongue went into his cheek. "One innocent farm lass seeking another in the big, wicked city. Your county certainly produces fine-looking women." He patted Glennys's behind. "You're on duty, so don't be too long."

He hooked one of the applejack jugs and retired into the arbor to smoke his pipe until a problem came up for him to tell someone how to solve.

Glennys thrust out one hip in her most provocative stance and attempted to look as debauched and world-weary as possible.

Behind, in the Pipe Vine arbor, Joss mocked her. "This is Glennys Eve, the sluttish jade who ran off to St. Lucien to be a

King's Daughter. She has terrible secrets that she doesn't want to come out, such as—she's never played a King's Daughter once in all the time she's been here!''

"Smoke your pipe!'' Glennys snapped. But Thea's lips were twitching. She'd heard it all, and was politely attempting not to laugh.

Glennys was courteous in turn. "Welcome, Thea. Mother writes of you in every letter.''

"Thank you. Stella talks of you often. She begged me to see you so she could hear from my lips that you're healthy,'' Thea said tactfully.

Glennys knew that Thea really meant that she and Stella prayed together for Glennys to forsake her wicked life and return to the farm.

Thea filled in the silence. "I've never forgotten how you looked in the old days, riding over the county on Three Trees' stallions. All the girls in Dephi congregation were fascinated that an Alaminite girl, no different from us, could be so wicked and get away with it!''

Glennys heard Joss snorting with laughter in the arbor. Everyone at the tables was listening too, though they pretended otherwise.

"Wickedness had nothing to do with it,'' Glennys said quietly. "I was different.''

Thea touched her headscarf. "I am too,'' she said simply.

"I have to get to work soon,'' Glennys said, "but let me show you around. The horses are on this side of the Yard. Across the way is the menagerie and the elephants.'' Finishing with the elephants was the quickest way to ease out visitors who interrupted Yard work.

"You've heard racing called the sport of kings, haven't you?'' Glennys asked Thea. "The Opera Ballet Theater is the Aristo spectacle.'' Hoping to bore Thea into a speedy exit, she reeled off the breeding of the geldings. She described their refined training, which derived from the same acrobatics that war stallions were taught. She gave the cost of their feed, their gear, and the wages of the hands that serviced them.

Thea ran her fingers over the silver plates hanging over each stall. On each plate was etched the astrological sign under which the horse had been born. Glennys realized that Thea was adding up the figures in her head as rapidly as Glennys mentioned them.

"Let me sit down and catch my breath,'' Thea said. "You're

telling me that what I'm seeing represents more than what Soudaka County can produce in a year!''

''That sum doesn't include the Theater, the stage secrets guild, the musicians, dancers, singers, the Academy, and all the rest of the production either,'' said Glennys.

''And all for amusement!'' exclaimed Thea. ''There are folks in Soudaka who are starving. The boys can't marry because there's no more land, and the girls have no dowries because taxes were increased six percent again.''

''I'm lucky to be a part of this,'' Glennys said. ''Because of my position here, Stella can pay *her* taxes. Now what brings you here?''

Thea answered, ''Money. What else?''

The more prosperous families of Soudaka County, such as Thea Bohn's clan, had found that the price for their wool was higher here than in Soudaka County or even at the textile mills in Drake. The profit was enough to make the long journey to the city worthwhile. Additionally, the profits from the lovely lace made by the Bohn women, when sold directly to the dressmakers and drapers of St. Lucien, paid all Thea's expenses with a handsome amount left over. And her expenses were low, since there was now a tiny Alaminite congregation in St. Lucien that could board her.

''That's how I was able to travel here. But smallpox is the real reason. So many of the poorer brothers and sisters have had to go to Drake, to work in the textile mills or the munitions factories. They're coming down with smallpox. The Fortune Houses have a procedure that defends against smallpox, and I want to learn it.''

At least she hasn't tried to get me to go back to Soudaka County yet, Glennys thought.

''I want to heal the world of its miseries,'' Thea said. ''That's my besetting sin, you know, pride in healing. I pray with Stella about my sins, far more often than about yours,'' Thea finished shrewdly.

Champers whinnied impatiently to Glennys as a lad brought him through the central stable aisle.

''I'm really out of time,'' Glennys said. ''But come into the Yard and take a proper look at my horses before I go.''

The nets had been pulled off that protected the geldings' manes and tails. The long hair cascaded from their necks and haunches, thick and heavy as cream.

"This is his costume, as much as a ballerina's skirts are hers," Glennys said, letting Champers's mane pour over her hands.

Even if it was an audience of one, it was an audience. Champers pranced, and flirted his tail. Without urging he made reverence to Thea, his nose bobbing over his kneeling legs, displaying all the charm of his nature as he had been bred to do.

Thea admired him extravagantly. That, as much as the unmarried girl's headscarf, proved her different from Alaminites as Glennys had always known them.

Glennys popped to Champers's back without using the stirrups.

"There's something else, Glennys. Stella and your sisters need money." Thea blushed.

Glennys was as impatient as Champers to get to work. "I can't talk anymore."

A stableboy ran up to Glennys. He handed her up a sealed message, which she opened and read while Champers fidgeted and Thea waited for an answer.

I got back to town last night. Meet me at the Seahorse for supper and you will make my return perfect. It was a difficult, though valuable, summer working for Thorvald on one Aristo estate after another. But now I'm my own man again at night, and I'm very eager to see one that, in the spring, led me to believe she was willing to become a very dear friend.

—George Sert.

At the bottom he'd drawn a caricature of himself, back burdened by a pack out of which brushes and rolled canvases stuck out like porcupine quills.

"Meet me at the Seahorse Tavern in Old Harbor Hide, about seventeen bells," she said to Thea as Champers began to step. "I'll have some money."

Champers curvetted through the Yard's private gate into Velvet Ridge Park. That's what she loved about St. Lucien, Glennys realized. There was always something different in her life. George Sert. His family supported him generously. He could afford a King's Daughter. She wondered what it would be like with a man that young. Her shiver came as much from trepidation as from anticipation. Since her Baron Fulk had been murdered, there had been no man at all. And she'd done her best to forget that he'd ever been her lover.

· FOUR ·

AT THE TOP of a cascade of marble stairs George Sert waited for Richard Thorvald. From the portico of the Fine Arts Academy he had a fine view of Circle Gardens and its magnificent modern buildings, less than a century old.

Nolan was very proud of Circle Gardens. Both political powers, the Spurs and the Wheels, had poured subscription and tax money into the King's Playhouse, the Queen's Opera Ballet Theater, the House of Assembly, and the High Fortune House where the pedigrees of the Aristo bloodlines, man and horse, were recorded.

But George was more modern than Circle Gardens, and he was not satisfied. As Thorvald appeared, George ground the core of the apple he'd eaten against the equestrian statue that stood between two columns of the Arts Academy. Others of his fellow students had set the precedent, some with more obnoxious material than apple pulp.

The statue represented King Albany, the first to unite the Nolanese tribes. With his Blood Chief, Gordon, they'd conquered the Outremere Domains of Gondol, Tourienne, and Langano. But it seemed to young Romantics like George that after two hundred years, the Outremere Domains had conquered Nolan.

The statue had been commissioned by Duke Albany from a sculptor out of Gondol, not a native Nolanese. The horse's reins were bunched into a blob that was supposed to be King Albany's hands. You couldn't distinguish one finger. The horse threw out its legs in angles no equine had ever accomplished in the history of the world.

"Melt it down and make chamber pots out of it, then it would serve some purpose," George muttered.

"Appreciate it," chided Richard Thorvald. "Every time our Duke Albany sees this folly his ignorant youth made of his distinguished ancestor he suffers another fit of generosity toward the Nolanese Academy and Nolanese artists."

They soothed their offended eyes by looking at the lush green

trees in Circle Gardens. Gold, orange, and red were beginning
to tint the green boughs.

"Pick up your case, George. I'm taking you to the depths
today," said Thorvald. As head of the Academy faculty and
favorite artist of the Aristo bloodlines, Thor had entry to places
in the building that no one else did.

George had never been underneath the Academy before. Thorvald led him through gloomy vastnesses where curiosities and
canvases that no one wanted to look at were stored. Then it was
pitch dark. Rodents rustled inside the walls. Their lamps revealed a dusty passage where roaches, silverfish, and waterbugs
were netted in spiderwebs.

Outside a door that gave evidence of contemporary carpentry,
Thorvald halted. "Shutter your lamp when I call for you to come
in," Thor instructed. He closed the door behind him.

George waited, partly exasperated, partly amused.

"Now, George," ordered Thorvald.

He opened the door, and was overwhelmed by a herd of
charging boars, bears, elk, wolves, panthers, falcons, and ser-
pents. Thor's lamplight was caught in their empty eyes, which
wept long, black shadows. George threw himself sideways before he recognized the beasts as masks once worn by stallions
going to war.

Thor had hung the masks on silk lines from the low ceiling.
Their wood, bone, beads, bronze, fur, and feathers danced with
vitality in the dim glow of light.

George was thrilled. These were the collections out of the
burial kurgans under the Rain Shadow Mountain counties. They
had belonged to old bloodlines mostly extinguished in the inter-
tribal battles before King Albany's unification.

"No one wanted the kurgan robbers to have them, but no one
wants them at home either. The bloodlines think destroying these
old things will bring curses and bad luck. Duke Albany collected
them in a fit of enthusiasm and then dumped them down here
thirty years ago," Thorvald said.

Turquoise and silver jewelry for horses and riders was heaped
in burial baskets. Braided grass containers held mane sheaths,
whip handles, tentpole tops, eating utensils, and incense burn-
ers. One corner was a pyramid of different-sized drums. Next to
them were pouch amulets filled with horse hair.

Anything that had the shape of an animal was filled with other
animals that twisted and curved back on themselves. The legs
were drawn up under the belly and the head and neck were

twisted back. The shape of a deer contained many smaller deer running in patterns inside itself, and those again were filled with tinier deer.

The horse designs were an exception. They were filled with the bodies of all the other animals, not smaller horses.

Thorvald shook his head and shrugged when George asked for an explanation. "Even if the Fortune Houses knew once, they've forgotten. Like the rest of Nolan, they're so busy running after money they don't care about the past."

The painting master went to a leather-and-wood sarcophagus. "We'll do this only once. The contents turn into dust after they're exposed," said Thorvald.

He opened the sarcophagus and unwrapped the mummy resting inside. It was a woman, though how George knew that he couldn't quite say.

He mastered his living body's instinctive recoil from the dead. As carefully as he could in the lamplight, he examined the parchment skin, the rags of hair, the ivory-colored bone. He lingered over the skull, which had been neatly trepanned for removal of the brain. Large parts of the lady's thigh muscles had been removed.

George's sense of the macabre was tickled. "Catherine Gemma's ballet! *The First Stallion Queen* indeed. This is a true stallion queen, probably one of the last. Our Langanese First Dancer who loves to flatter her Aristo masters ought to see this."

Thorvald joined him in the laughter. "I wonder how many thigh muscles this old queen ate in her time?" he mused.

George replaced the wraps over the dead woman's bones without touching her with his fingers. "I suppose our colleagues upstairs don't like to think we were eating each other, even in ceremony, not so long ago."

"Broke-dick dogs licking the spittle of Outremere's glory days, thinking it shows their refined taste and artistic imagination." Thorvald's stumpy body was eloquent with contempt. His nose couldn't turn up, since it had been splattered all over his face several times in his youth, when he worked the fishing boats. He'd been a brawler and a roisterer, and still was, to the best his elderly body could stand up to it.

Thorvald said, "I've unwrapped equine mummies on my summer tours when I was younger. Horse's blood and body are still part of Nolan's ceremonies among the back-country Aristos in the south. And who knows what the highlanders under the Rain Shadows do to this day?"

George swung his lamp around, illuminating the room. "These are our antiquities, not the statues Langano digs out of her ground. This room is so full of art I can't breathe."

Thor nodded sharply in agreement. "King Leon's own grandfather carted everywhere the skulls of enemies he and his ancestors killed in battle. My old dad saw them once when he was a boy. First came the old King on his white stallion. Behind him were the wains filled with Outremere booty. Two of them were filled with skulls, packed as sweet as eggs going to market."

Thorvald had saved the best for last. "Come to the table. This'll make your trousers as tight as a pretty piece of twang. Have you gotten any yet, since we've been back?"

George's tongue stumbled. "Tonight."

The table was covered with small painted stones. If George needed any more reason to despise the equine statue on the portico, these stones gave it. The finesse of the technique provoked his jealousy. His brush hand itched to duplicate on large canvas what the long-dead artists had accomplished in miniature on these stones.

There were many kinds of scenes, but George was most interested in the group devoted to hands. The fingers were alive with flesh and blood, flexible with sinew, rigid with bone. The hands grasped short bronze swords, clasped one another, cradled infants, nocked an arrow, milked a mare's teats, held reins.

Thorvald left George on his own among the treasures of Nolan's dark ages. One stone fit perfectly in his hand. On it a man held up an infant to a horse. George knew it was a girl baby, though only the artist's invisible skill told him that.

The man's hands, and the baby's, were disproportionate. The fingers and palms were larger than the expectation set up by the wrists. The man had the reins to the horse's bridle in the fingers of one hand, while the other held the baby around her middle securely to his chest. The girl and the stallion were breathing each other's breath. He knew all this simply by looking at it. He knew how hot it was where they were. He knew a small breeze was flowing over them.

He looked at the scene for a very long time. It reminded him of something, but he couldn't remember what. The oddly sized hands were at the center of it.

He opened his case and took out ink and paper. He cleared a spot on the table and sat on the stool. He began to copy the scene, looking for the secret of the artist who could paint weather so vividly.

Though Thorvald had made the basement chamber as dust-free as possible, it was not a good place to work. There was no ventilation except from the passage. George's eyes ran from the fumes released by the lamp. Soon he was sneezing more than he was breathing.

It seemed he had barely begun when Thor returned. "Time to come up for air, my boy. Come back whenever you like. Just don't spend more than a couple bells at a time or you'll suffocate."

On the portico, the old man and the young one talked about what the subterranean room could mean for a native Nolanese art. There were other students in the Academy who were talented, experimental, and rebellious against Outremere artistic dictums.

"You know even better than me, George, who they are. Take 'em down," said Thorvald. "Duke Albany won't mind, and by rights, what's there belongs to him. He's mad on horses again, by the way. It seems he's finally caught one of those wild ones from the other side of the Rain Shadow Mountains. I'm about to trot over to his house and take a look at it. Everybody else is, it seems. You want to come along?"

"I have plans," said George. "Thank you, though."

"That's right!" bellowed Thorvald. "A little twang to celebrate the fall season!"

The wind had freshened. It blew the dust and lamp fumes out of George's head. He dodged through the well-dressed, well-mounted element preening itself up and down the boulevards. Now that the autumn season was upon them, the Spurs appointed by the King to the House of Assembly were returning to St. Lucien. The population to whom this part of the city belonged had increased even while he'd been under the Art Academy.

In mid-step, on the first bridge across the River Walk, he remembered. Those hands on the stones were like Glennys's hands. Her body was so light and her limbs so flexible that it was always a surprise to notice such long fingers and wide palms coming out of her sleeves.

George ran his own thick, strong fingers through his hair, which he was losing already, though he was only twenty-one.

On Bank Street a man sang while he rearranged the candles, kerosene, lamp reflectors, and lamp glasses that he sold from under an awning.

The fishmonger sells fish and mussels,
The gunsmith sells things that go bang,
The draper sells ribbons and bustles,
And the King's Daughter sells you her twang, twang,
The King's Daughter sells you her twang.

"You get yours now, you hear?" the street merchant called.

Everyone seemed to know his plans, even strangers. Did it show that much on his face?

• Five •

GEORGE TOOK INFINITE pains over stripping off the skin of a greengage. He'd already done three, and had no plans to eat any of them.

If he'd brought his sketching materials with him to the Seahorse Tavern, he'd have had something better to do with his time while Glennys stood outside, occupied with that oddly dressed female. He'd left his case in his lodgings, believing that gallantry called for giving his entire attention to Glennys.

He tore the plum to bits and waited.

Glennys swept into her seat at his table in a flurry of skirts. Her dog sat on his haunches behind her, his jaws as high as her shoulders.

Her big blue eyes looked imploringly into his. "A thousand pardons. That girl is a friend of my mother's and doesn't understand our manner of saying that time is short."

Glennys ran her little finger over George's brush hand.

"And before that," Glennys continued, "Catherine Gemma engaged me to be her personal horse trainer. She only hired me today, but midnight rehearsals begin tonight."

Before he could stop himself, George wailed, "You can't work tonight!"

"I'm so happy to see you again, George, I'm sorry too. I've no choice," Glennys said. "But I am free now, until twenty-two bells."

So she wanted it too. George swallowed the saliva that filled his mouth.

"Now Catherine's search for talent has reached outside the Academies. Last year she asked Thorvald to contribute designs for decor. She and Thor had several discussions about it at her house, but in the end all he had time for was a few sketches. He didn't take any payment for it either," George said.

"Why didn't he take her commission?" asked Glennys. She looked at him as though he knew more than anybody.

Proudly, George said, "Thor's not a decorator, but a gentleman, a painter of noble subjects."

He became aware of how loudly he was talking. The Seahorse had gotten much more crowded since he'd first come in. It was suppertime, and the Romantics, who now were the principal residents of Old Harbor Hide, were beginning the social part of their day's work.

He found he was leaning across the board between them and that Glennys was leaning toward him. Their faces were almost touching. He was holding her hand. One of the maids was attempting to position the jug of ale he'd ordered between them.

George swallowed again, but this time he lowered his voice. "Thor won't go so low as to take Duke Colfax's money. Colfax is so thick with the Wheels that he's a traitor to his estate. He's trying to show himself a good Aristo Spur by underwriting his concubine's *Stallion Queen*. Meanwhile the Duke works hand in glove with the bankers in Drake who are backing Baron Fulk's ammunition factories. That Fulk's another traitor to the Spurs."

Glennys asked, "Do you share Thorvald's attitude? About Colfax and ammunition factories, and—the young Baron Fulk?"

George said, "A pox on them all. Wheels, Spurs, what does it matter? Both think artists are no better than Shoes. In any case, the Gemma's ballet is only another piece of Outremere frou-frou."

While they waited for their food, and then while they ate, George waxed rhapsodic over his discoveries under the Art Academy building.

"Until you explained it to me," Glennys said, her eyelashes fluttering, "I had no understanding of what makes the atmosphere of a ballet. I've only attended to the dancing and the horses, and imagined how I would perform if I were the ballerina."

George watched her eyelashes and her lips move. He heard the sound of her voice, not her words.

She loosened her fingers and withdrew her hand from his. She picked scraps from the platters and threw them behind her to Baron, who snapped them out of the air.

George narrowed his eyes against the newly lit lamps. His focus blurred. Glennys became a composition of strong color values: golden hair, orange-red breast band, dress of midnight blue.

"Why don't all the women without bodyguards and families to protect them in St. Lucien have a dog like Baron?" he asked.

"Because most King's Daughters are only trained to train men." The composition he'd made of Glennys jumped back into focus. She was smiling at him.

Her teeth bit lightly at her full lower lip. She tossed her long plait of hair over one shoulder. "Well, what should I have said? It's true. Don't you think so?"

George thought he'd gotten into deeper waters than he was prepared to swim. Then he realized she was coquetting with him.

Her brows furrowed into a tiny frown and she said, "A bristlehair mastiff is dangerous in St. Lucien unless it's very carefully trained. The breed's expensive to feed. You've got to know from the beginning what you want with one and how to get it. Since I'm a Horse Skiller, unlike the other dancers, training animals comes naturally to me."

She rose from their table. "Excuse me, George."

He watched the outlines of her flanks appear and disappear on the back of her skirt. She went down the long corridor lined with ale casks to the dank latrine. Baron trotted behind her. Her long pale braid hung in the furrow of her back. Orange-red bows climbed the tail of her hair to the crown of her head. George thought how he'd pull the ribbons out of her hair and feel the silky stuff slide through his fingers.

For a moment he wondered if she'd come back.

Now Glennys was at the bar. She was paying her own tab for the meal, in the manner of a King's Daughter.

She stood at the bar for what seemed a very long time. She was deep in conversation with a tall, slender woman, dressed in the height of St. Lucien's current masculine fashion. It was the Lady Leona Boarheel, a cousin of King Leon. She and Glennys seemed to be well acquainted.

Thadee Maywood, the head claquer for Queen's Theater and writer for *Town Topics*, was with the King's cousin.

George felt more than ever like a student in the presence of adults. He watched Glennys laugh with them and then shake her head in negation. She turned to speak with Copely, who owned the Seahorse and tended bar.

Lady Leona and Thadee headed for the door. George's table was right there. If Thadee acknowledged him, the rest of the night would be a success. If Thadee ignored him, he'd kill himself. George was a Romantic.

Lady Leona stalked past. Maywood stopped. "Don't tell me." He put finger and thumb to his temple, then snapped them.

"George Sert. Richard Thorvald's fair-haired boy. Is old Thor back in town?"

By way of reply the flustered George said, "I've got more ale here than I can drink alone. Will you help me finish it?"

Everyone knew that Maywood never turned down a drink and never paid for one.

Thadee considered, and then giggled. "Lady Leona's carriage has taken off without me. Pour me a bumper! I'll drink a salute to the Lady anyway."

The claquer-journalist drank off the bumper without stopping for breath. "So, Sert. Got any tips for me?"

George said the first thing that came to mind. "Before the early season has even begun, none of us can think of anything but Catherine Gemma's *Stallion Queen*. The young woman dining with me is her horse trainer."

Maywood put one hand over his heart, the other on his hip.

Drunk or sober, in *Town Topics* or in the streets, Catherine Gemma was the woman Thadee Maywood adored. No other woman, certainly no other dancer, could be compared with her.

"Very gallant of you, dear Sert, and absolutely true. No one dares think of anything else. *The First Stallion Queen* will change the face of art forever," Maywood declared with a perfectly straight face.

"You see how easy it is," the journalist said, turning the ale jug upside down. "Your drink is disposed of and now I must dispose of myself. Many risers on which to roost before I go to write my next *Town Topics*. Toodly, my dear boy."

George was pleased that most of his own bumper of ale remained. He'd been too nervous to drink while the *Town Topics* writer had been there.

Glennys returned but didn't resume her seat. It seemed as though Glennys's peplum jacket had been pulled farther apart to better reveal the orange-red breast band.

One of her hands was on the chair. Her legs, one after another, assumed attitude and arabesque under her skirts. King's Daughters aspiring to Queen's stage were always doing that. It was a silly mannerism that usually annoyed George immensely.

She said, "Night's down. Would you like to walk on the wharves and look at the water and the sky?"

After he paid his score to Copely he hesitated. She put her arm through his and smiled. It was her smile, he thought. That's why he, more fastidious than most of his friends, had waited for so long. He'd always wanted that smile first, that smile that filled a woman with light.

Baron paced behind them. The waterwinds cleared George's head. He appreciated Baron's attendance here.

The moon was coming up. The warehouses, boarded up by day, had turned into pawn shops, gambling hells, and brothels staffed by no one entered on St. Lucien's City Registry. This was the market and the pleasure garden that served the greasy tenements on the mud flats at the mouth of the Setham River.

Tar and creosote had last been applied to the splintered wood eighty years ago or more, but those sharp odors still cut through the smell of sewage. The piers' loose planking rattled under their boot heels.

The two of them leaned against a massive timber that overlooked the silted harbor. They were sheltered from the wind, which drove away the garbage aromas of St. Lucien as soon as it brought them.

George wondered if he could kiss her now, and then found that he was.

His hands began to find what he'd looked for all night under her clothes. His breathing was hard.

Glennys pulled back from him slightly and said, "Isn't there something at your lodgings you'd like to show me?"

His first impulse was to tell her to be silent, not to interrupt him any longer. Groaning, he said, "What would you like to see?"

"Whatever you want to show me," she whispered. Then he understood.

In his own lodgings he was filled with confidence, knowing he could have everything his own way. He lit lamps and candles quickly. He knew exactly where each flame should sit.

"I want to see you," he said.

The light flickered over her skin and ran into shadowed hollows. The skirt of her overdress, the underskirt, and long-sleeved peplum made a puddle of shadows at her feet. George couldn't wait for anything more.

Her body was a palette of hues and textures. Impressing himself, George rode the waves of her body and fell over the crest three times.

Panting a little, Glennys asked, "Did you see what you wanted?"

"Light," he said. "I saw into my future. But it's gotten dark again already."

Her fingers played with the thin strands of his hair. "I saw the country that I never see except when I'm matching. It's not the same as the Horse Sense, but it expands my senses, and deepens them, and . . ."

"Horse Sense?" George asked.

Glennys was dropping swiftly into sleep. "I was unworthy. I forfeited my gift."

Her words were slurred from drowsiness. "Sometimes it seems like it takes forever, and then with your friends it takes no effort at all."

Her whole body stretched and wiggled luxuriously. She was asleep.

George puzzled over her words. Then he fell asleep briefly, and snapped awake again. His bed was too narrow for two.

The flare and fall of his lights discovered and hid the contents of his studio randomly. The sounds of the other residents in the old merchant marine's townhouse anchored him to time and place.

He got up and trimmed the candle wicks. His body was a pale glow in the reflecting surfaces hung all over his walls.

He moved his lights around the bed where Glennys slept. He sketched her sprawled form, over and over again, as she lay half-covered by his bedclothes.

She woke up, instantly alert. "I have to get Catherine Gemma's horse partner to her theater."

Dropping his sketch pad on the floor, George protested, "Not yet. It's nowhere near midnight bells. We have hours yet."

Glennys ducked under his arm and gathered her clothes. She stroked his hairy, plump chest. On their bare feet she was slightly taller than he was.

"Much to my regret, dear George, I must stop at my own lodgings, and then get to Queen's Yard long before midnight. I've to supervise the load and transport of a mettlesome gelding—and you—you are no gelding."

"Take me with you, then. One more body among the groom and driver won't be noticed at Catherine's theater. I'd like to see what it is you do," George pleaded.

"But you're an artist of noble subjects," she teased. "You despise the ballet."

"I'd like to keep longer in your company," George said.

"I've never taken an outsider to work," she said doubtfully.

"I won't get in the way," he vowed.

"Well then," she said, "put on your spurs, if you have any."

· Six ·

GLENNYS LODGED IN the garret of Petry's house. An old woman now, Petry had been a member of the ballet corps in her youth. With the assistance of her younger relatives Petry kept a clean, decent house, provided hot water out of the kitchen from dawn until late at night, and allowed kitchen privileges. All of her lodgers were King's Daughters, and she had strict rules about men visiting. No business was allowed under her roof. George had to wait outside.

Dressed in Queen's livery, Glennys leaped out of the doors of her landlady's house as though taking a stage. Her face was a shifting mask of silver and shadow painted by the moonlight dropping through the leaves.

They made a shortcut through the kitchen garden, the flowers, and the trees. A bramble-hedged wall defended Petry's premises from the narrow lane. Glennys had a key to the gate.

"Why don't you put your spurs in my saddlebags? We've got a long way to go and we don't want to make any more noise than we have to," she said.

"First I think I'd better give you something," George said, feeling very urbane. "Are three silver forients right for this evening?"

"I'd clean forgotten," she said, clearly delighted at the sight of money, the same as any King's Daughter. "Thank you for remembering. Thea Bohn—that girl I was talking to when you arrived at the Seahorse—cleaned me out of all my money to take back to Mother and my sisters."

The moonlight gave her face a pure, chaste loveliness that made it possible for George to forgive the sweet King's Daughter lie. He was sure she didn't really expect he'd believe that she gave money to her mother, but the falsehood spared them both embarrassment.

"I can pay my water bill to Petry now," she speculated. "Thank you, thank you, George, for remembering, and for what went before. Everything's so turned around today, with Catherine wanting me at midnight at such short notice.''

Glennys, George, and Baron headed for the bridge. "Why do you live in an attic?" George asked. "I thought Queen's trainers got paid enough to have quarters on a lower floor."

"Women with Horse Skiller licenses are rare birds, and we get only half of what men get. The Queen's Yard is subject to the same wage scales as the rest of the Theater's staff and performers. Wages are increased the longer you're with Queen's, and I've been with Thack only two years. Besides, as I said, I've a husbandless mother and two sisters entitled to my assistance.''

This time George believed her. He tried to imagine what style he'd be living in if his family's Gordonsfield business didn't pay for his lodgings, the Academy fees, his clothes, and provide an ample allowance. He couldn't.

The flares on the bridge made it a pool of light. "Will you return to Soudaka County one day?" George asked.

"I'd rather give birth to a porcupine presenting backwards," Glennys declared.

"What's it like there?" he asked.

"Very, very cold for a very, very long time every year," she said finally. "Sorry, I can't talk about it. My mind is on the here and now.''

After West Street, the way became narrow and twisting, and as dark as the muck under their boots, though the moon was bright. She set the pace along routes George had never taken.

She warned George where not to step as they tramped along pools of sewage. Baron cleared off foraging dogs and swine. They cut through back lanes and across private properties.

At first George tried to regale her with descriptions of the Outremere cities in which he'd tried to study art. Once again she warned him to be silent.

This was Dead Well Hide, built up along cowpaths and deer tracks before the Nolanese horse riders had taken the city, even before the Outremere colonists had made it a colony. It was a St. Lucien George had never seen, a city of old stone and ancient mud. Oaks and sycamores touched him with their overhanging branches. Here and there through the smell of the offal came the scent of roses, show-pink, jasmine, and mint. His lantern's light reflected in the eyes of raccoons washing potato peels in the water of the canals. Tiny bridges, barely wide enough for a man's feet, crossed trickles of water long gone, and took them to circles where the wells were so contaminated that no one used the water. Around one George thought he glimpsed the ghost of a drowned child.

Baron suddenly returned and froze in Glennys's path. He'd been ranging silently around, ahead, and behind them. The moon glinted off the knife she wore loose at her hip. She signed George to stop, and crept away behind Baron.

George concealed himself in the shadow of a huge gate hanging off its hinges. Behind it was a ruined fortification from the middle ages of St. Lucien.

Glennys and Baron came back. In his ear she whispered that a troop of jagger boys lay in wait for prey ahead of them. They followed Baron along another route.

George found that the thrill of danger had turned into throat-closing fear.

"It's all right. We know where we are and we know what to expect and how to avoid it," she assured him after the detour was completed.

"You do this all the time?" he asked.

"It's the shortest way. I can't afford to keep a horse. Baron's food about breaks me as it is," she said.

They hit Irongate Prison Yard, but they smelled it first. "This is the safest place in the city after dark," Glennys said. "We can rest here, if you want."

Baron's hackles went up. He growled.

"It's all right, boy," she said, hand on Baron's head. To George she said, "We've never encountered anything more dangerous than weeping women in Irongate Yard."

But it wasn't a woman weeping who stood in the brightly illuminated prison yard. Three men twisted by their necks on an oaken gibbet.

A man in rags and tatters that marked him as one with the hanged men stood by the gibbet.

Baron crouched, protecting his charges.

Another bristlehair crouched between Baron and the man.

Glennys and the vagrant ordered their dogs out of the stiff-legged circling walk that came before a fight.

The man gestured to the hanged trio. "Have you come also to meditate on King Leon's justice?" he asked.

"I'm passing through. I'm already late to Queen's Theater Yard," Glennys replied boldly.

George knew she wasn't late. The Fortune House bells hadn't

tolled twenty-three times. He pulled out his timepiece before he
realized she'd told the man she would be missed and looked for.

Glennys and the vagrant talked about training bristlehair mas-
tiffs. George could only think both of them were moonstruck.

The dogs sat, all their attention on each other.

"My name is Noel," said the ragged man courteously.
"Would you favor me with yours, lady?"

"Don't tell him," George whispered.

"Glennys Eve, at your service, sir. I'm on my way to Catherine Gemma's to do a midnight rehearsal for *The First Stallion
Queen*. So I must go."

"If you train horses as well as you train dogs, the First Dancer
is fortunate to have engaged you," the man said gallantly.

Then he and his dog departed Irongate Prison Yard.

The stench changed character. The other side of the river levee
was lined with butchers' shambles, tanneries, and breweries.

Then they were on King's Highway. The walls protecting the
Theater's horses and menagerie loomed before them, a mass of
old stones on which light from torches and flares trickled down
like oil.

Inside was a crowd scene. The manure carts had come to take
away the day's muck heaps. The horse car was backed to the
stable. Grumbling flew back and forth between the stable hands
and the menagerie keepers as to who was in whose way.

When the team pulling the horse car set out for Catherine
Gemma's theater, Glennys pulled George inside the car with her
and Champagne. They squeezed up to stand at Champers's head.
It was dark. George paid a great deal of attention to the movements of the gelding's feet on the padded floor.

"You're the most reckless woman I've ever known," George
said. The only women he'd known so far were his nurturing
mother and gentle sisters. "That man in Irongate Yard, aping
the manners of a gentleman, was likely to have robbed you,
killed you, or worse."

A low chuckle escaped from Glennys, invisible now in the
dark. "Not him. You've heard, haven't you, that King Leon is a
noctambule? That late at night he prowls through the city in
disguise? And now he knows my name. What the Eidel Kings
hear they never forget!"

George said, with a sniff, "And you're the one who says she's
not a Romantic?"

Glennys was sure. "He wore a wig to conceal his blazing red

hair. And his white war stallion was tethered back there in the shadows. I could feel him.''

She went silent, the silence that indicated she'd had another thought. But she said nothing else.

Catherine Gemma's house was off the Circle Gardens Promenade, backed by one of the Setham River's channels kept clear and clean for water excursions. Her private theater reflected in miniature everything necessary to a professional stage. There was even a pit for musicians in front of the stage apron.

Neither Catherine nor the little orchestra plotting her music cues were happy. Rambert, the music director of Queen's, hadn't assigned composers for the last two acts yet. Catherine moved about the stage to the music they did have. She didn't actually dance, but counted off the measures, sketching figurations lightly in the air with her arms and legs.

''Welcome to Queen's most expensive disaster!'' was Catherine's greeting to Glennys. ''We can't even read through the first act because the lyricists aren't back from summer recreation. If they aren't ready very soon, Rambert will write the lyrics himself, as his final accomplishment before I have him dancing on the gibbet.'' Her lightness of voice and movement belied her angry speech.

Glennys reached for a deliberation of mind and body to replace her lack of assurance. Champagne would match her unconfidence otherwise. Glennys had learned during her work with the Theater that there was always ample opportunity for histrionics; that it would always get much worse before it got better, and that there were always new problems to replace those solved.

Glennys led Champers to the downstage left wing and listened while Catherine talked through the first act. The musical and choreographic figures were to return and develop in the second act, which was when Torgut, the First Stallion, made his entrance.

At Catherine's signal the music began. ''I'm Eve, the mother of Eve, the First Stallion Queen. I've left home in search of the girlchild I must have.''

It was, of course, exceedingly sketchy and hesitant, but even so, Catherine, before Glennys's eyes, became Eve, starved for a baby.

The dancer moved slowly and gracefully across the stage. Glennys knew very well how difficult it was to execute the movements that Catherine appeared to make effortlessly. Though

Catherine was not yet certain of her choreography, Glennys could see that she was already forming sequences of the most complex character, ornamented with extensions and elevations much longer and higher than the standard execution.

Without warning a flower of pain opened between Glennys's temples. It died as abruptly as it had bloomed, leaving a dull, throbbing ache in its place. Glennys sternly ignored it and the sense of displacement and confusion that accompanied it. She focused entirely upon the First Dancer, admiring how Catherine had breath to spare for narration while she danced.

"Eve's quest takes me first to the wide-horned cow, who runs off without speaking. The sow-boar gives me truffles and then attacks. The wolf pretends she's a dog and deceitfully sends me to the panther, who distracts me with her beauty and grace. The eagle in her nest suggests I go to the serpent in his tree.

"The day is coming to an end. The snake tells what the other animals feared humans would learn. He, shunned by all his sister creatures, takes his vengeance upon them and advises Eve to seek out the hornless deer with a hairy tail."

At times Catherine dropped her commentary to count the time of a combination out loud. She requested the musicians to repeat a phrase while she tried a variation.

The conclusion was a sinuous development of the preceding dances. Out of that Eve–Catherine sank to the ground and fell asleep.

Catherine sat up and put her arms around her knees. "As you can see, the first act is entirely the menagerie trainers' show. I think that will work out very well in practical terms. The hunting animals can be gotten out of Queen's before the horses come to stage level at the end of intermission."

The maid, Amalia, brought her a damp towel and a dry one.

The pain surged and ebbed inside Glennys, making her shaky. It was a pain driven by despair. If she didn't know better, she'd have thought there was a horse somewhere, frantic to escape something. But she had no Horse Sense to know such things now.

She unnetted Champagne's mane and tail. He danced, his hooves shining black with varnish.

"You are very beautiful, Champagne," Catherine said gravely. She extended her hand, palm open under his black nose, so his whiskers could touch her fingers.

He made reverence to the ballerina.

Catherine breathed into Champers's dainty, clean nostrils. He snorted back at her. He arched his neck and set the layers of his mane and tail swirling about his fetlocks. He lipped her chin. She touched his lower lip with her tongue.

That was gallant of her, Glennys thought. Though she tried to conceal it, Catherine obviously found the gesture repulsive. Some trainer in Shop equine class, as a mean-spirited joke, must have told her it was required.

Catherine moved slowly around Champers. She supported her weight on pointe with his body. She didn't tense up behind his quarters.

That true confidence won Glennys's unadulterated admiration. It had been a kick from a gelding's hindquarters that had shattered Marie Bonheur's knee.

At Champagne's forehand, Catherine stroked his withers. He leaned into her hand. His tongue lolled out over his lower lip.

Glennys had always found the geldings' willingness to take pleasure at anyone's hands slightly contemptible. But that was the purpose of stage horses' breeding and training. They had to belong to anyone they were given to, and care deeply for no one. Her war stallions, the horses she still regarded as the only true horses, had been very different.

Catherine described what she wanted out of Champers for their first pas de deux. When she danced toward him on a diagonal, he must retreat. When she reversed the direction, he had to pursue. A series of turns to stage right must be mirrored by him to stage left. They would reverse and meet center stage. He'd kneel to her while she performed pirouettes on pointe, adjusting her balance out of each one with his stationary partnership.

"The duet will take on so much more the true nature of flirtation with the retreat and pursuit, which is what pas de deux is about," Catherine said.

Glennys's heart sank. For all that Catherine understood the true nature of flirtation, she didn't that of horses. There had to be some physical guidance.

Diplomatically, Glennys suggested using long lines attached to Champers's bit, on two reels that Glennys would keep in her own hands behind strategically placed scenery.

"Tonight we can begin with the leather lunge lines, and see how that works out," Glennys suggested.

"No," Catherine said. "He must be nude of all but flowers. Eve needed no tack with Torgut. I shan't have them either. It will impress the Aristos as not even *my* dancing will."

For the first time since she'd been working at Queen's Yard, Glennys wished she was what she'd been. If she hadn't lost her Horse Sense, Catherine's demands could be fulfilled.

"Then we'll try to walk him though it twice tonight. The music will have to provide his signals, and we'll have to devise something you can do that will cue him," Glennys said. "But we must begin with the lunge lines."

While the groom who'd driven them over went out to get a bit and the lines, Thadee Maywood let himself into Catherine's theater. He nodded to George and sat down next to him in the audience gallery.

Catherine, Glennys, and Champers walked through the first duet of Eve and Torgut. They began with his entrance while Eve slept. Coming across stage to a solitary dancer was something Champers had performed hundreds of times. But his reversal along the diagonal, backing gently away from her, even with Glennys working him in hand, was contrary to what he'd always done. Champers began to sweat.

"That's all we can do tonight. He's getting anxious," Glennys said.

The front doors of the theater swung open wide. Duke Colfax strode in.

"Enough for tonight, Cathy. Duke Albany wants the trainer in his stable, and I want you to come with me to Crackfyrd's," he ordered. "I brought Albany's carriage here. It's waiting for the trainer now," he added, without acknowledging Glennys at all.

"Tomorrow night, then," Catherine said, before she walked away. There were tiny lines of exhaustion around her eyes.

· SEVEN ·

COMMANDED BY AN Aristo or not, Glennys's first duty was to Queen's. She had to see Champers loaded safely into his car.

By the time the gelding's car was in position, Champers's blanket was sweated through. He swung around on his quarters. His nostrils were wide open to smell upwind. In a character unlike himself, Champers kicked and bit. He wasn't only resisting confinement, he was attacking.

Patiently Glennys coaxed the gelding out of his bad temper and up the car's ramp. After he was tethered she slammed together the tailgates. He screamed and plunged, behaving more like the war horses in the background of his breeding than like a stage horse.

Glennys was hit by wave after a wave of a panic that was not her own. She hung on through the vertigo to the tailgate latch so hard the bar piece cut her hand.

The panic became rage, then abruptly closed off. She was herself again, and Champers was quiet.

"He didn't injure me or himself in that fit," the groom said, his head sticking out over the tailgate, and visibly shaken. "I don't know what's got into him."

Glennys knew. The deepest part of Champers's nature had awakened, that part that hated mankind for making him its slave. It was in all animals, and she'd touched it vividly because the gelding's senses had flowed into her own.

Her Horse Sense had come back. It had flowered in her once and then died by a seasonal cycle of its own. Tonight it had put out new growth, quickened by that wild Saquave stallion, whose kind had lived free of men's demands all their generations.

George repeated, "Glennys, you must get into Duke Albany's carriage. His men are saying they'll take you by force. Glennys! Albany's an Aristo! You must obey him."

George must not know about the Horse Sense, Glennys

thought. He'd think her inhuman. She accepted his hand and
allowed him to lead her to Duke Albany's carriage.

Baron settled on the floor. George took the seat across from
her. She hadn't invited him, but she was grateful for his fully
human, friendly support, which assured her that she too was
still human.

Then she saw Thadee Maywood in the carriage's opposite
corner.

"What are you doing here?" she snapped. She felt exposed
under his curiosity, as if a stranger looked upon her nakedness.

"The Duke and I are old friends. He won't mind me. I'm
curious, Miss Eve, and curiosity is my trade," Maywood said.

"Albany's lived almost a century. On the scale of years by
which he measures things, I hardly think he would consider *you*
an *old friend*," Glennys said coldly.

"You know him better, then? Curiouser and curiouser. Tell
me all about it," Thadee said eagerly.

"Ask his parrot Gustave. He was there and likes talking better
than I do," Glennys said rudely. She tried to find an anchorage
in the roil of smell and sound invading her from the senses of
each encountered horse on the way to Albany's. The Horse Sense
had returned but her ability to shield against what horses sensed
hadn't yet. As a child she'd never had to think about it, for
everything she'd learned, she learned as naturally as breathing
or walking or talking. An adult in a large city, where people
judged each other by signs and signals that had nothing to do
with earth, wind, or water, she was lost in a stomach-wrenching
heave of sensation.

The carriage rolled through Circle Gardens and across the
Promenade, into the private drive of the Duke's townhouse.

In the stable yard the carriage door was whipped open by
someone in the Albany livery.

Glennys was thirsty. The birth pangs of the Horse Sense made
her sweat as hard as class. Marie's next class was only hours
away now, she thought, feeling another sort of panic about missing it.

She drank out of the decorative fountain splashing in the center of the stable yard. She plunged her hot, tight face into the
fountain pool. On the tiles at the bottom was a womanly figure
who wore a cloak that shimmered underwater light and dark.
Glennys's senses focused there, her eyes open under the illuminated water. She thought, I move the darkness here, and push
the light over there. The part of the Horse Sense entwined with

horses coming into her quieted. She pulled her head out of the water, and shook drops like tears out of her lashes.

"Dry yourself with this," said a Duke's man. He offered a huge linen handkerchief bordered with lace. "Lenkert Deerhorn, at your service, Mistress." He bowed.

Deerhorn said, "You've grown up since I last saw you in that bleak northern County. My Duke has often mentioned seeing you since you came to Queen's Theater. He says you're the most talented Horse Skiller he's encountered in all his days, which is why he's called you for the task at hand."

"What is it?" Glennys asked.

"He expects you to get that stallion from the other side of the Rain Shadow Mountains on his feet, and put heart into him so that he'll live."

Aggressively Glennys said, "No Horse Skiller can defeat death when the animal is truly dying. Why not allow him to go in peace?"

"My master's will is otherwise," Lenkert said.

In the stable Albany was crouched in the straw by the downed stallion's outstretched neck. Gustave, the parrot who was his familiar, was on a perch nearby. The gathering changed constantly as the Duke's peers, Fortune House officiates, and horsemen of all degrees came and went.

The stallion was old. His approaching death was natural.

The Duke looked up at her, and made her feel he was looking down. "Make him live so I can learn his secrets," he ordered.

Maywood and George moved closer to each other. This was a face of the urbane Duke Albany that they'd never seen before.

The stallion's hide-bound coat was lighted in the soft glow of the stable lanterns. Reluctantly, Glennys took the Duke's place at the Saquave stallion's head.

His eyes were turned back under his lids. His ribs seemed not to move. For a moment Glennys thought fortune had rescued her from this wretched Aristo command. But a mirror beneath his nostrils hazed faintly as evidence that the stallion lived still.

His body was scored everywhere with the marks of fangs and claws of predators. It had been torn by the hooves and teeth of other stallions he'd fought, and mares who wanted their way, not his.

Her fingers traced lightly over his body. With them she read the story of the life led by a horse that had never been protected or used by men.

All his life he'd fought to live. Now he was fighting for the right to die. As long as he fought her, the stallion would live.

She matched her sense of hearing and touch to his.

She stroked his ears. They were large, heavily furred, with several hairs longer than usual among the protective inner hairs. She talked into his ears with her own mind, for him alone. She forced awareness of her upon him. He roused. The smell of her, the touch of her, a human, an alien, was terrifying. He was old, set in his ways. There was no time to seduce this horse into thinking she was of his own kind. She'd become too human while living in St. Lucien.

He went away from her, no longer listening. His neck went back into the straw.

Glennys began again. This time she matched with his sense of smell. She searched through the stallion's storehouse of scent memory. It was so rich she nearly lost herself. At the bottom she discovered the odor of his mother's udder and stimulated it. Her hand pressed rhythmically on his throat. The reflexes of a foal sucking and swallowing moved under fingers. Perhaps this wasn't going to be so evil after all.

"Bring me a nippled bottle full of water, with a little milk, more honey, and a quarter-grain of strychnia," she said.

After he'd swallowed the bottle she teased up other smells that had drawn the stallion all his life. She brought up grass warm under the sun, the lure of water when he was suffering thirst. They weren't arousing enough to get him on his legs.

She found the smell of mares' urine when they were in season. It was close to the surface of his memory and very powerful. But more powerful, more enduring, was the scent of other stallions, younger, stronger, who had stolen his mares away, and driven him out of the herd and safety.

She pressed hard on the smells that were frightening and repulsive—rank carrion stench, wolves, bears, scavengers.

The stallion scrambled his front legs under his chest and shoveled up his hindquarters. He swayed upright on all four legs. Glennys flowed upright to support him. She'd won.

He screamed, aware of what had hemmed him in, and lashed out with his forelegs, scraping them raw against the stall's enclosure. She screamed too; she couldn't help it. The stallion pulled away from all that was so hideously strange, and went down.

The battle between them was now engaged.

Each time he went down, his fear and rage seeped into her.

She was angry at him, at herself, and most of all, at Albany. Each time she got him to his feet it was more depleting to her and to the horse than the last. She used hatred, anger, and fear, the horse's and her own, as her tools. The nature of what she used showed on her face.

The stall where the Saquave stallion fought to die was fouled. Discharges came out of his mouth and nostrils. Thin streams of piss and excrement dried him out, no matter how many bottles she got him to suck and swallow. The other horses in Albany's stable were getting wild. The smell of death was all around.

Dawn can't be far off, thought George.

Glennys said, "His body won't stand up to this much longer. Let him have a peaceful passing. You won't get your way with him, Duke Albany."

Albany's eyes were bright as sunrise. He looked much younger than he had when George had first entered the stable. He was more interested in Glennys than in the stallion, George thought.

Albany ordered, "Continue until the end."

Glennys couldn't stand up to this ordeal much longer herself, George thought. He had wild thoughts of killing the Duke so she'd be released from his will.

Glennys went against death again. She pinched the dying horse's flesh. She bit him, clawed at the horse's most ticklish, sensitive, delicate places. Tears rolled down her face, runneled the coat of slime on her arms and cheeks.

She pushed at the stallion, yanked his mane, pulled his tail, and kicked him. She went back to his eyes and nostrils to make him hate her so much he'd get up. The weak jaws and legs connected upon her body more frequently.

She threw water on him. Once again the stallion got up. The choked, ragged, bellowed gasps dragged in and pushed out.

The Saquave stallion began to cry.

The other horses joined. It sounded like the keening wail of death in a bloodline Big House. George heard the horses strike their hooves against stalls and mangers. He loathed horses, all horses, because they could sound like this.

Specters of bears, wolves, wide-horned cattle flowed in exhausted hallucination through George's vision, obscuring the body of the Saquave stallion.

Deep within the horse Glennys felt that other self, the Horse Sense self, caught in the withdrawing tide of the stallion's life force. She was so tired, so ashamed. She lay back upon the current and gave herself to it. The current was pulling them into a deep cave. She could rest when she went over the threshold.

A woman, who looked like her mother as she should have been, crowned with stars, was enthroned upon a rock before the cave. At her feet were all the animals of the world. She put out a hand into the current. "This place is not for you, not yet. You have recompense to make, and work, a lot of work to do. Don't be so lazy!"

Glennys clung to the outcrop of the rock upon which the woman sat. The face was implacable. Glennys remembered how to move her arms and legs, how to breathe.

Blood gushed out of the stallion's mouth and nostrils. She looked down and saw her chest and arms splashed with bright crimson. Glennys covered the stallion's eyes with one of her large hands.

George saw that Glennys's lips were chewed away. This woman was training a pretty gelding like Champagne to go on-stage with flowers in his mane so Catherine Gemma could pretend to be a stallion queen? Catherine should see this.

Lenkert touched Duke Albany on his shoulder. The sun had been up for three hours.

Glennys stumbled outside. George followed, but didn't dare approach her. Somehow she'd beaten Duke Albany, that sorry Aristo, and her face was full of light.

She washed herself in the fountain. The air was cooler this morning, and drier. Autumn had come during her battle with the Horse Sense. She stared through the water at the woman in the tiles, but she looked not at all like Glennys's mother, or the woman before the cave.

Duke Albany came to her. "You are strong in your Horse Sense. The Saquave stallion couldn't take you down into the pit." He kissed her hand.

She looked at him, trying to make this Duke Albany into the one she'd known on Three Trees, and she couldn't. The sun hurt her eyes. That the image of the woman on the rock was fading hurt far worse. Her legs crumpled.

Lenkert Deerhorn wrapped Glennys in the Duke's leather cape and carried her to the Duke's carriage. He was able to coax Baron to ride on the box with him and the driver.

Glennys woke up. A bath of hot water gently steamed in her attic. It was tended by a girl wearing the Albany badge.

After her bath she went downstairs to cook herself a meal to satisfy her ravening hunger. In Petry's kitchen she found Lenkert Deerhorn making her a hot supper. Baron was at his feet, and had obviously been well fed.

Deerhorn said, "The Duke went in his person to excuse your absence from Marie Bonheur's class and from duty in Queen's Yard. Sometime soon, but after you have found your balance, my Duke wants you to come to dinner privately with him and talk."

Glennys clung to the vision of the woman on the stone. She didn't want to lose her. The woman made the patterns to which animals and all life were subject. But in the modern world men and women created their own patterns.

More than ever Glennys wanted to get on Queen's stage as a ballerina, not a horse trainer. Only artists could make patterns that transcended those of life and death, she thought.

Duke Albany knew she had the Horse Sense, but he would keep her secret. She had seen his face at the fountain in his stable yard. For him, knowing what others didn't was the supreme pleasure to which he aspired.

She had a midnight rehearsal with Catherine Gemma. She would be there with Champers.

The Stalking Horse

• Act II •

• Eight •

THAT AUTUMN NOBODY seemed to need sleep. The Romantics issued manifestos about everything that interested them, and everything was interesting.

SPURS AND WHEELS ALIKE RIDE ON A WILD HUNT AGAINST THE POOR!

WOMAN IS THE GROINED ARCHWAY OF INSPIRATION!

CONQUEST BY GENIUS GIVES THE ARTIST RIGHT TO ARBITRATE AMONG CLASSES AND DOMINATE OVER ALL!

That season the Elstob University of Mathematics released *Principles of Population* for general publication. Written by a mathematician named Reed, the pamphlet proposed that with a fixed food supply and a birth rate greater than the mortality rate, employment would expand more slowly than population. The pamphlet's conclusion was that since inoculation prevented the thinning of generations by natural means, the smallpox procedure should be prohibited among the classes with income less than 70fs per annum.

The bloodiest riot was a protest against the execution of Midnight Raven, the celebrated highwayman. His gallows speech declared his crimes vengeance done against the tax-exempt, land-enclosing Spurs and Wheels. The Midnight Raven escaped in the ensuing melee.

A woodcut made by George Sert was chosen to grace the ballad sheets that spread the Midnight Raven's story.

Thadee Maywood gave his *Town Topics* almost entirely over to puffing Catherine Gemma and her ballet. The first write-up had included a mention of the Saquave stallion, Duke Albany, and Glennys. He commissioned George to do the engravings.

It was stupid work, but the recognition got George other illustration jobs. He needed them because his allowance didn't stretch to cover King's Daughters. The money allowed him to bed Glennys regularly through the fog-hazed days of autumn. He never got as much of her as he wanted.

His great bouts of work either preceded or followed an assignation with Glennys. He'd already finished the preliminary sketches for the canvas he'd be entitled to hang in the Royal Gallery next spring. He was occupied now with color experiments for this big, but so far, secret, work.

George was the center around which formed a circle of likeminded students rebellious against the Academy's curriculum. His illustration work proved he could earn money. These days he felt himself less of a student.

It had become habit that he'd go with Glennys to the midnight rehearsal if she'd spent the earlier evening with him. George had to acknowledge that Catherine's work was superior to his earlier impressions of the horse ballet.

He got familiar with the ride in Champers's car between late night and early morning. Towards the end of the midnight sessions he said, "This ballet is succeeding because of you. It's because you're a country girl. You've provided a fresh and unspoiled vision, so this time the shopworn attitudes have been avoided. You are—an enchantress."

Glennys said, "You've kept company too much with Thadee Maywood. Jump off, please! An enchantress! Country people would call it witchcraft."

"I call you an enchantress," he continued stubbornly, "because you're not displaying whips, spurs, bits, and all that other Horse Skiller dash."

Glennys hated him to undercut her belief in Catherine's genius as much as she hated her to disabuse him of his Romantic notions about the country folk. "It's my training at work," Glennys insisted. "I've got the contrivances to make Catherine's vision about the horses clear."

George believed he'd won the argument. "Then why so thorny whenever I praise you for your horse skills?"

The horse team pulling Champers's car seemed to stumble in a hole. Champers's weight shifted abruptly. A hoof came down hard on the artist's foot.

That conversation was never properly concluded, George realized afterwards, like so many others about Glennys's past, her training methods, or anything that happened during that night with the Saquave stallion.

Glennys allowed him to draw her nude when they got back to

his studio. That was an effective way to keep him from asking inconvenient questions. And after that, there was the most effective way in the world.

She couldn't tell him about the Horse Sense. He'd love it too much, and let the cat out of the bag. Then the wrong person might learn of her and she'd die. In the county of her birth there were those who would consider her a witch.

The part of autumn arrived that the old folks called Shadow Summer. The skies were blue and the nights were bright. Catherine, Glennys, her geldings, and Joss Thack moved their work into Queen's Theater. Catherine arrived early in the morning and went home late at night.

Catherine fought with Rambert, the music director. She flattered the conductors. She bribed the composers to finish the music for the final scenes.

When she rehearsed the other dancers in their roles, her tact was on the level of a sergeant training impressed foot soldiers. When she cajoled, coquetted, and threatened homicide to the headmaster of the stage secrets guild, she was a general.

Glennys and Joss Thack seemed to live at Queen's. They kept Catherine's hours, except for those Glennys gave to Marie Bonheur's classes. Joss understudied the cues and signals for Champers and the other geldings, in case Glennys become ill.

Joss praised her loudly and often. Glennys had gotten Champers to perform without the aids of bit and reins. She'd also taught the routines to Vanity, Champers's understudy, in record time.

No one, not even Joss, found it strange that the horses went exactly where Catherine's trainer chose them to go. In the atmosphere of the Theater, miracles were accepted as a matter of course. Glennys worked tirelessly and, Joss thought, with a becoming modesty about her accomplishments.

Seats and boxes at Queen's were inherited along with other property from one generation to the next, so few Romantics, dance students, or music students would be there for opening night. But most of them were more interested in learning how *The Stallion Queen* was made than in the performance, and nearly everyone in St. Lucien's half-world knew someone who worked on the production. Friendships and alliances got them inside Queen's for rehearsals. Their attendance spurred a word-of-mouth reputation for the ballet.

Catherine and August Gardel played the favor of entry into rehearsals with the same dedication they showed when they played whist for 20fs a point. Thadee had no trouble lining up a claque for *The Stallion Queen*.

According to theatrical laws, which allow nothing to happen in the way planned, Catherine's costumes and scenery both arrived, after long delays on the road, one radiant Shadow Summer morning.

Catherine had new battles to fight. The seamstresses from wardrobe had too many costume fittings and alterations already for other programs. Catherine had major miracles to perform with the stage secrets guild to get her scenery unloaded. There was damage to be repaired. The drops and cut-outs had to be put onstage so lights and effects could be synchronized with the music cues.

Catherine had no time for dancing, much less horses. Joss took his rod and reel and declared a holiday.

Glennys and George rented a buggy and horse from the Seahorse. They took the rig up to the Palisades where the vintners casked the new wine. Down in the Alluv Bottoms, Glennys bargained with farmers for their produce.

"This proves, Glennys, you're not an artist at heart," George said.

The day was so lovely Glennys didn't pick up the gauntlet.

George couldn't let it lie.

"Tonight we're dining with Duke Albany. But you made us spend the day haggling over the price of roots and sausages. Nobody else in our position does this."

"So," Glennys said. "You dine with the highest in the land. Then you go home to poor lodgings with not a copper in your pocket for breakfast. Apples and cheese stored away means no one can take advantage of you for the price of filling your belly."

George said, "Albany wouldn't make one of Thor's guests, on the occasion of celebrating Thor's painting, sleep with him to pay for her dinner."

Glennys slapped the reins over the fat back of the pony pulling their buggy. "I'm not the guest of you and Thorvald. The Duke invited me himself."

With Petry's permission George helped Glennys haul her purchases up to the attic. The vegetables were stowed in a cold locker he'd helped her build against the north wall, insulated in layers of dirt and straw. The onions, garlic, smoked sausage, and cheese were hung on strings from the central beam.

George said, "Thor's sending his carriage for me. He says

you can ride with us. We'll get there before the other dinner guests so we can spend some time together. You can help me set up Thor's canvas for the unveiling.''

''Thank you for your thoughtfulness, George, but the Duke's sending for me, as he's done before. His man will see me home as well,'' Glennys said.

George's throat went tight. As casually as possible, he said, ''I didn't know you'd been visiting Duke Albany.''

''It's not what you're thinking, George. We eat supper, and I can never stay long, since there's always Catherine's ballet to return to,'' Glennys said.

''So what do you talk about?'' George demanded.

Glennys shrugged. ''Nothing that would interest you. The ballet. The Saquave Desert.''

Before dinner, in Duke Albany's library, Cimi Terrazo exclaimed, ''All the men here, except for you and Master Thorvald of course, are Dukes! Duke Albany, Duke Colfax, and Duke Crail, who, of course, is also a Prince, Prince Roald, since he's brother to King Leon.''

''That's at least three Dukes too many,'' George said sourly, ''for a gathering of this size.'' He swallowed a yawn. Cimi was a pair of Lungs, like ballerinas were a pair of Legs. Artists couldn't hope for intelligent conversation from Lungs or Legs. Their function on these occasions was to provide another sort of stimulation.

This was a kind of family gathering. All of the Dukes were related to each other in one way or another. He told himself his lack of enjoyment had nothing to do with Albany's clear intention that Cimi was his dinner partner and Glennys was Albany's.

''I understand that you're interested in old things and new art, that you want to turn everything around so painting will reflect native Nolanese traditions,'' Cimi said, trying valiantly again.

George didn't respond.

''Do you Romantics at Fine Arts ever discuss how far that can go?'' she asked. ''Outremere traditions have given us the technique and vocabulary of music and dance. If I understand things rightly, the Outremere traditions have also given our painters their system of emblems and symbols.''

George kept the door within sight. Glennys still hadn't arrived.

''Well, do you think less of me, George?'' Cimi asked. ''I changed my name to indicate my Langano training. I was born

Cimi Feathers,'' she confided. "Singers are always expected to be from Langano," she said.

George stared at Cimi's mouth. She had simpered. He waited to see how soon she'd do it again. He feared she believed he found her fascinating.

Cimi preened, touched the massive ropes of golden hair braided into a crown on her head. A great sigh pushed out her chest.

George did find her chest fascinating. He took his fifth glass of Tourienne wine off the tray handed round by a footman.

"Your lungs must be tremendous," he said. "You talk at such length without taking a breath, yet you carry mountains effortlessly."

He'd addressed her chest. Her décolletage turned interesting shades of red and white. He shifted his vision a little higher and saw that the colors of Cimi's face and neck matched her décolletage.

"I wouldn't drink much more of that if I were you, Mr. Sert," she said, "before we go down to dinner." She put one hand to her cleavage, heaved deeply, and left him standing alone.

She was right, George thought. He attended to Thorvald, who sat on a divan with Catherine Gemma.

Yesterday, at the Theater, the dancer's hair had been matted to her head. All of her had betrayed exhaustion. Surely today hadn't been any easier for her. But tonight none of it was visible on her face. She looked immortal.

Glennys hardly opened her mouth these days without invoking the First Dancer's name, and George was sick of her.

It hit him like a thunderbolt when the butler announced Glennys Eve.

Albany greeted her immediately with a kiss.

Her supple leather skirt, tinted a dusky rose, hung straight to her ankles. A short jacket of the same went over a severe white linen shirt and revealed her waist, cinched by a wide, heavy belt of silver. The buckle of the belt, and each oval segment, was a horse in the same animal style George knew so well from the Fine Arts basement.

He wondered how she'd gotten hold of jewelry like that. Then he looked again at the ancient silver samovar service presided over by another footman as the trays circulated about the library. It made him sick to know that Duke Albany had given it to her.

Catherine rose from her divan and followed right on the heels of Albany. She made it clear that she was delighted to see her horse trainer among them.

"Collie," Catherine called, while she kept Glennys in hand, "you've never formally met our trainer. But remember our vow not to speak of dance. This evening is in honor of Thorvald's art, and the opera." She nodded gracefully to Thor and Cimi.

Dinner began with a cold turtle soup on a bed of crushed ice. Cimi didn't dare eat much since she was to sing later. That left her a lot of time to fill. She generously forgave George his earlier crudeness, and entertained him with a detailed history of her training at the Teatro Urbino in Langano.

Reluctantly George refrained from drinking. Thor was having refills between each course. He was going to have to see Thor home and put him to bed.

Threads of Duke Albany's drawling chuckle and blasts of Thor's belly laugh came down frequently to George's ears. Glennys's full-bodied merriment floated on top of theirs. Prince Roald snickered so deeply that he blew wine all over Wendala Span, the actress.

The Duke's man, Lenkert Deerhorn, whom George recognized for a eunuch, gave Glennys solicitous attention at every course. By the time the dessert wines came around George was deeply despondent.

It was a relief when the ladies retired. Thor and George exited soon after. When Thor had refreshed himself they were attended up to the picture gallery on the fourth floor.

George lit the lamps positioned around the canvas. He made sure the footmen understood that for this reception none of the other paintings on the walls were to be illuminated, except those by Thorvald.

They were brought coffee and brandy. Thor refused the brandy. "You go ahead and drink, George. I would like to be alone with my painting for a last moment before the horde arrives."

Thor's work was not yet hung. It was mounted on a dais in the center of the spacious top of the staircase, where viewers could cluster around it without choking the hall that made up the picture gallery.

George and the footman set two chairs in front of the double windows at the opposite end of the gallery. There was a small balcony outside overlooking St. Lucien. The draperies were pulled back. A huge half-moon poured silver light over the glistening floor.

George sat looking out the balcony, his back to Thorvald and the painting. He watched the moon and wondered if Glennys had bedded with Duke Albany. In the silence he heard Thorvald pull away the satin sheet that covered his painting.

He knew that Thorvald was seeing what no one else, except perhaps another talent as great as his own, would see. Thor celebrated the places where his execution had served his vision well. He surveyed the places where he'd had to start over. He grieved over the parts that were wrong and that he never did get right.

The satin fell back into place with a whisper. When it was pulled away again the painting would belong to Albany and the world, but no longer to Thorvald.

The master painter dropped heavily into the chair next to George's. The footman silently placed coffee and brandy by him and retired.

"When I was your age I worked the fishing boats and I drank like a fish. I worked, I painted, and I drank. I had to give up the drink or the art. When I could give up the fishing fleet I couldn't take back the drink and still paint. I'm old. I don't have the power to make again what's back there. I can drink all I like now," Thorvald said.

"If I were an old bloodline Aristo like Albany, it would be different," he added. "My years would weigh little and my vigor would be unimpaired. I'd be what I was when I was fifty. Aristos are born at the top of the Wheel of Fortune, and when it turns, it never turns them under."

George declared, "If you'd been an Aristo, you'd never have been an artist."

Thorvald turned and looked over his shoulder. "Do you know why they're so long downstairs?" he asked the footman.

"The Duke wanted to give you time alone," the man said. "Also, I believe the gentlemen were joined by the Baron Fulk, who had been detained by other business. I'll send word that your preparations are complete and alert you when they and the ladies are coming up."

Thorvald downed his brandy. "So, George, your rosy skirt didn't need my carriage."

George sat, a picture of misery.

"Not bad work, George, for a boy still at Fine Arts to have a King's Daughter that Duke Albany's got his eye on. I don't want to push into your private affairs, but don't try to hang on to her," Thorvald advised.

George's hand pushed away Thorvald's words.

"You've got important matters to occupy you, George. Don't let this trip you up. There's so much twang in Lucien that a man can drown in it if he wants," Thor said.

In spite of himself, George's eyes began to tear.

"I see. You think you've already drowned. But you'll come up again," Thorvald predicted.

No. He would never recover if Glennys deserted him, George thought. No one had ever suffered like this before.

· Nine ·

SINCE THE LADIES all were King's Daughters, the conversation in the ladies' room was of the men downstairs. Among these older, successful women, away from male attention, Glennys feared she might not fare as well as at dinner.

"What can any woman, no matter how brilliant, how seductive, how talented she is in the art of conversation, make of Prince Roald?" Wendala Span asked. The saturnine beauty collapsed on a sofa in a parody of tragedy.

"As usual," said Catherine, "he made three remarks during the meal, and those were so turgid, so long-winded, that one couldn't prevent turning one's attention to anything else!"

The actress gestured into the air extravagantly. "He's always like that! The Prince just doesn't—play. Even when one of those three remarks concerned the most fascinating matter in the world, myself! He ruined my dress when he sneezed all over me. You should pay for a replacement, Glennys. You were the one who told the story about Cayetana de Alba's wager to walk naked from Circle Gardens to Crackfyrd's Gaming House."

The ladies' room had the best of dainty arrangements. There was a neat-handed housemaid to sew them back into their ribbons and corsets, and to repair damages. She worked skillfully over Wendala's wine-spotted bodice.

"How clever of you to have worn such a dark color," she said to Wendala. The maid expected a generous tip out of the Prince's sneeze.

Catherine squeezed Glennys's arm. "Albany will pay for your dress, Wendala, and that's almost the same as Glennys doing so, isn't it?" she predicted.

The others laughed. Glennys felt it was bad luck to allude, even as a joke, to what Albany's attentions might mean for her future. Nor did she know what she wanted those attentions to mean, because the Duke's ways confused her so much.

Cimi spoke Langanese fluently, so Catherine could relax into her own language. Wendala and Glennys were left to each other.

Glennys didn't know much about Wendala's world of King's Playhouse, or the Wheel banker, Rakel, whose concubine contract the actress had recently broken. So Wendala returned to the subject of the Prince.

"Sometimes he does talk, you know. About war strategy, my dear. Or else about the old Queen, his grandmother, and he calls her perfectly dreadful things. How can two brothers be so different? The King is fascinating, and so good-looking. Now there's where I'd adore trying my luck. I'd even pay him!"

Wendala lowered her voice, and glanced over at Catherine. "But that's impossible. The King's perfectly devoted to Duchess Colfax. She's carrying again. This will be the second Colfax child provided by King Leon."

Wendala was getting bored with feminine company. She went to the mirror and made minor adjustments in the bodice sewn to the waist of her overskirt. She began to talk directly to her own image. At first Glennys thought she was working over a part for King's Playhouse. Then she understood that Wendala was carrying on a dialogue with herself.

"I won't even try. I have my own carriage waiting and can leave as soon as I like. Everything I've heard is that he's unable, simply unable. My spirit is willing but what good's that when the Prince's flesh is weak, weak, weak?"

Wendala took a candelabra in hand, paced the floor, and turned suddenly to stare at her own expression in the mirror. She put the light back on the mantle.

"Why are the gentlemen so long? It's not like Albany to keep the ladies imprisoned like this, even if we are artists," she said to the maid.

"Baron Fulk of Soudaka County only arrived after the ladies' retirement," the maid said.

Without thinking, Glennys blurted out, "Baron Fulk is dead!"

"Oh, no, Mistress, he's downstairs big as life," said the maid. Her face was placid but something in the angle of her chin stated Glennys was out of her class. "I believe he and Duke Colfax wish to present a subject for discussion in the Assembly, and want to enlist the support of my Duke and the Prince."

"The new Baron Fulk, of course," Glennys said, fumbling to cover her outburst. "How stupid of me."

"You're from up there, aren't you?" asked Wendala.

"That's why, even now, when I hear the name Baron Fulk, I think of the new one's father," Glennys said slowly.

"Indeed?" Wendala responded without interest.

The maid announced, "The gentlemen would be pleased to have the ladies join them to view Master Thorvald's work."

Glennys extended her hand politely to Baron Stogar Fulk when they were introduced. He made all the meaningless remarks that a man does on such occasions when the woman interests him not at all. Stogar didn't recognize her, Glennys thought with relief. If he didn't know who she was, she didn't have to be that person for him. She knew her appearance had altered. And her name was different now. Eve was an unknown one among Soudaka Alaminites, and common in Old Nolan.

Thorvald's painting was called "The Three Kings." The subject was the most noble one a Nolanese could paint—the conquest of the Outremere Domains.

The Kings of Langano and Gondol were on their knees. Halters twisted their necks back so they were forced to see their fate, which was being enacted behind them.

Blood Chief Gordon and King Albany drank from a skull with shreds of hair and skin clinging to it. The King of Tourienne's crown was closed around the bare bone. The headless body had been shoved down the slope. A huge cauldron of water boiled over a fire.

An ancestor to the Eidels held the leads to the halters of the defeated kings. An ancestor of Duke Colfax was at the anvil. Under his hammer the crowns of Langano and Gondol were opening. Soon they'd be fitted around the skulls that would be severed from the two haltered necks. Slaves stood ready to remove the brains and eyes and throw the heads into the cauldron. By a flat rock, an ancestor of the Fulks held a huge axe.

Over the Kings of Langano and Gondol the sky was dark with clouds. Over the heads of the Nolanese the sun shone. The background was a mass of Nolanese warriors and their stallions. The horses' heads were a sea of beast masks. Captives and booty spread under their hooves.

The paint was so thickly applied that in places it almost protruded beyond the massive gilt frame. The effect was to make the barbaric spectacle intrude into the gallery of the urbane Duke Albany. Red, orange, and yellow leaped from the fire under the forge and cauldron, reflected off the golden crowns, and sparked from Nolanese weapons. Everything else was a gloom out of which faces glimmered and scarlet blood glowed.

The eyes of everyone were fixed on the painting, but those of

Thorvald and George were on the Duke's face. Until Albany
approved or rejected the painting they couldn't breathe.

Without taking his eyes off "The Three Kings," Albany
squeezed Thorvald's shoulder and moved in closer. One hand
held back the two thick braids that fell beside his temples. His
face went right up to the paint. Some minutes later he stepped
back to the head of the staircase and looked at it from there.

"The feathers of the horse masks are moving, like the flames,
with the direction of the wind. You show the wind blowing from
the west, as indeed it was at that moment in history, when the
horse warriors came to the Domains from the west," said Albany.

He came back to stand directly before his picture. "I'm
speechless, Thor. The vitality of each figure is beyond admiration. And the direction of the wind, such a witty commentary."

Albany indicated the axeman. "See, Stogar, in those days the
members of your bloodline used weapons everyone could see,
and wielded them with their own hands."

Glennys felt compelled to look at Stogar's face. It had no
expression but polite interest.

Stogar said, "Like everyone else, we've come a long way
since then."

Glennys thought that Stogar looked at her as he spoke. She
avoided his eyes.

"This is magnificent," declared Albany. "I'm grateful our
ancestors are prisoned within that frame and not in this hall.
They'd cut us down quicker than we can sneeze. A remarkable
achievement, Master Thorvald, worth every gold forient you
gouged out of me, and even worth the eight years' wait."

General congratulations broke out. Albany dropped back from
the painting to where Catherine stood.

"I didn't invite you to the unveiling to insult you, but to honor
you," he said gracefully. "When the Nolanese tribes drank the
blood of Outremere they drank in the greatest and best of her
achievements. That's how I interpret the skulls and crowns, you
see. And because my forefathers were cruel I have the greatest
good fortune to have my hall graced by a First Dancer."

Albany called for champagne to ease her discomfort, and to
drink to Thorvald.

"I want the old stuff! What I grew up on," Thorvald demanded. "Give me Esker!"

Very quickly Deerhorn saw to it. Esker was rough, burning
liquor, not at all what society favored. "This is the drink,"

Thorvald crowed, "that makes a man remember he's alive when his fingers are burned to the bone by the cold of the sea and cut by the scales of fish."

Stogar drank Esker like he was used to it. Glennys saw Catherine take a tiny taste and put it aside. Glennys did the same.

Tonight was the first of Albany's celebrated open houses of the season, where different ranks and conditions could freely mingle. Soon other guests began to appear.

The music room opened. Glennys was conducted there by Albany to hear Cimi sing. Then he left her to attend to his duties as host.

The music room audience was mostly made up of Spur and Wheel women. They nudged each other when Catherine Gemma and Wendala Span entered. The audience chattered so relentlessly that the singer, loud as she was, could hardly be heard.

When Catherine made her exit, Glennys did the same. Catherine skimmed down the wide, winding stairs to the foyer of the garden floor. Glennys caught up with her while Amalia fetched the ballerina's cloak.

"Thank goodness you followed me," said the First Dancer. She took Glennys's arm and bent her head as though they were discussing weighty matters. "Thadee Maywood has been stalking me ever since he arrived. Be my shield. I won't talk about my bloody ballet tonight, not even to him. Didn't you think Thorvald's painting the most hideous thing you ever saw?"

Catherine's public mask dropped. Glennys could see how tired she was.

"I get to sleep tonight. Collie's with Prince Roald and Baron Stogar to discuss the free trade bill coming up in the Assembly. He says he's going to his own house tonight to sleep with his Duchess. But I wager they'll all go to Crackfyrd's. Neither the Baron nor the Prince has a concubine."

Glennys's fingers brushed the dancer's cheek. "It's unfair that you're the one who works the hardest and I'm the one who got a holiday. I wish you lovely dreams and the sweetest sleep."

Catherine's smile returned. "Everyone's dying to know. Are you, or are you not, sleeping with Duke Albany?" She touched the heavy silver links on Glennys's waist.

Glennys's eyes darkened. She whispered into Catherine's ear. "He gave me the belt, and some other things as well. But what he wants in return from me isn't what you think."

Catherine's footman told her that the carriage had made its way through the jam of horses and vehicles choking the drive.

"The old bloodlines believe they've all the time in the world, they live so long. He will ask you to be his concubine, I know it," said Catherine. "Make him pay very, very well for it. It's your right as a King's Daughter."

The two of them stood there a minute, smiling at each other. Then Catherine went off, eager for sleep.

Glennys took her time going back up the staircases. At each floor there were faces she recognized, though most of them had no idea who she was. She was out of her ordinary milieu, the one in which she worked for them.

On the third staircase she met Lady Leona and her tail, which tonight included Rowena, Korla, and Nan, all of whom had been taken into Queen's ballet corps.

Lady Leona tapped Glennys's cheek with her fan. "You've been avoiding all your old friends this season, Glenn."

"*The Stallion Queen* allows no rival, my lady," she said.

"And we all know there's no opportunity for girls' games when one's been taken over by Catherine Gemma," said Leona.

Nan slipped her arm through Lady Leona's. "What tail did you hang on to get here?"

"I came in Duke Albany's carriage," Glennys said.

Nan reached out to touch the lapels of Glennys's jacket. "Leather's the cheapest thing in St. Lucien. It suits you very well." She swished her satin and lace.

Glennys guessed Leona had provided Nan's clothes, but doubted the lady would get much return on the investment.

Thorvald's canvas was surrounded by artists and students of all degrees. Their arguments were shouted in support of their judgments.

"It's ugly!"

"It's alive!"

"Beauty is finished and dull. Ugliness is open to vision precisely because it's active, not finished. It's potent, virile, and therefore beautiful!"

George was in the middle of it all, directly in front of the painting. He caught sight of Glennys. He was enjoying himself so much he forgot he was suffering. He winked at her.

She blew him a kiss and moved on. She accepted her first glass of wine that night and wandered bemused through the crush.

The alcoves along the gallery were all occupied. Away from the painting, the end of the gallery and the balcony were de-

serted. She swept down the passage toward the balcony, looking
for a place to be by herself.

Albany's house was on high ground. On the other side of it,
terraced gardens led down to the river gates. From this side she
could see much of St. Lucien spread out beneath her. A rush of
autumn leaves fell about her, pattering like rain. The balcony
became her stage, and the leaves a shower of flowers rained
upon her as tribute to her performance. Albany could give that
to her, if he would. But he had no interest in sponsoring another
dancer-concubine. He'd done that beyond satiation.

Below, the bridges' flares were mirrored in the water. Lights
danced on barges moving downriver. The huge fortress kurgan
crouched between the Old Harbor and the South Harbor, a grif-
fon that guarded St. Lucien from eastern attack. The Promenade
and the Circle Gardens were outlined in torches. The Fortune
Houses had illumination, and so did the larger Mourning Mother
cathedrals. By itself, in a poor hide of the city, was a tiny,
eternally tended flame, which marked the Alaminite kirkyard.

If she lived in Albany's house St. Lucien would be hers, as
much as it was Catherine's. Perhaps the city would belong even
more to her since half of her blood was Aristo enough that it
was represented in "The Three Kings." What if she made that
fact public?

Resolutely she put the thought away. It was too dangerous.

Occasional strains out of the music room reached her. The
musicians continued to play after Cimi had concluded her performance.

Giddy with the choices the future seemed to present her,
Glennys rose to half toe in her suede slippers. Her arms opened.
She drew up one leg to unfold it like a wing out of her hip. Her
skirt was too narrow. She stumbled, and grabbed for the balus-
trade. Her glass dropped out of her hand.

A huge palm shot from behind her and neatly caught the goblet. A finger flicked the rim and a crystalline note rang out.

"You wore this color the night my sister Thurlow made your
coming-of-age jubilee at Three Trees." Baron Fulk looked down
at her.

Glennys's vision cleared with the dying of the crystal note and
it was Stogar who regarded her, not her murdered Baron. The
hand with which he offered her her unspilt wine was shaped like the
cold one with which she accepted the glass, though hers was
concealed under a wide cuff that came to her knuckles.

"What's the news of Thurlow?" Glennys asked.

"Contented enough, I imagine. It's rumored that the two heirs she's presented to Baron Waterford are not his, though certainly of the Waterford blood." Stogar's smile showed all of his strong teeth.

The young Baron continued to flick the edge of the glass Glennys held lightly between her long fingers. The music and the light in the crystal pointed her attention to Stogar's voice and hand. The hairs on the nape of her neck prickled. Her Baron, Stogar's father, had the same habit of playing with crystal.

"I'd heard my old dad's horsegirl had come to St. Lucien. But I didn't expect to catch you—here," Stogar said.

His chin indicated Albany's gallery and Albany's guests. The surge and ebb of conversational groups revealed many who blazed with badges of distinction. Others, like Stogar, wore the traditional Aristo headdress of twisted satin and neck veil.

The glass in Glennys's hand vibrated and sang.

"It's traditional with the Fulks that the apprentice step into the old Stablemaster's boots when the time comes. We haven't found a satisfactory replacement for Powell, and he's determined to retire," the new Baron Fulk said. "I think you should come back to Three Trees." His voice was full of the urgency to have his own way that she remembered from the old days.

Glennys said, "St. Lucien's climate has made me soft. I'd be of no use in the ice and snow of Soudaka's long winter." ¯

"I wondered where you'd put yourself, Stogar," said Duke Colfax, strolling up to them.

"We invested a great deal in this Horse Skiller's training up in Soudaka County," said Stogar. "I'm asking her to come home."

Glennys shivered. His statement was a request for a favor from the man in charge of the city's registry. If Colfax ordered her to leave St. Lucien she'd have no choice, other than to become outlaw.

"My home, Stogar, is in St. Lucien, not Soudaka County," Glennys stated.

"She can certainly go nowhere until my Catherine is finished with her," Colfax replied lightly. "And I think our host finds her amusing," he added.

Her eyes searched through the gathering for an acquaintance to rescue her. These men wielded too much power, and were too dangerous, for a horse trainer to fence with. Duke Albany was the only person who had an interest in her who was an equal to them.

"Think it over," Stogar said. "It would be to your mother's benefit if you went to work on Three Trees."

That was both a threat and a bribe, Glennys thought. "Queen's Theater geldings have spoiled me, I fear, for the honest horses of Three Trees' bloodline."

"My old dad was blind as a mole about changing times, but when it came to horses there wasn't anything he didn't know. The confidence he had in you is enough for me," replied Stogar. "I don't believe you've lost *any* of your old skills."

The ponderous figure of Prince Roald charged into their company. With no preliminary courtesies he grabbed Glennys's hand. "Stogar, I want to talk with you about that famous charge of your father's into the Sace-Cothberg cannon emplacements at Nemour. But Duke Albany wants Miss Eve to come inside. He thinks this balcony too unprotected for her light dress."

The Prince's voice was preposterously high for one so big. He conducted her in the most awkward manner possible through the crush. His hand in its pearl-sewn glove clutched hers uncomfortably.

He sat her down in an alcove from which the other occupants soon departed. The Prince plunged into a detailed account of a campaign in the Cane Archipelago, which took place in his great-grandfather's time.

She seemed to give him the closest attention. The monotone of his voice was a defense behind which she could turn over disturbing speculations of her own.

Stogar must suspect that she knew he had been the one who murdered the old Baron. Nothing else made sense. Too many Horse Skillers had gone begging for work in the last few years for her to believe she was the only acceptable candidate for Three Trees' stables. So many accidents happened around war stallions. One could happen to her too. . . .

In light of that, Albany's interest in her meant more than advancement in status and livelihood. His protection would be that in truth, not a polite veil drawn over the nature of their relations.

Glennys managed to ask one or two pertinent questions about the Prince's subject. She loathed war but knew something about its theories. She'd grown up with Stogar's younger brother, Hengst. Even then he'd been destined for a military career, and had studied war assiduously.

Under the circumstances the Prince's total unawareness that he was conducting a monologue and not a conversation began to appear amusing. After all, he was only different in degree, not in kind, from most men. George and his friends lectured her most of the time. If she presumed to make an observation or dared to disagree, she was interrupted by them before she could complete a sentence—even on subjects about which she knew more than they did.

Prince Roald surrendered her to Duke Albany reluctantly. "I'd like to talk with you more. Not many women know the difference between tactics and strategy."

"It was only a lucky surmise on my part, Prince. I really know nothing at all about this fascinating subject," she said.

Albany took her away.

Glennys felt he'd rescued her twice, once from danger and once from death by tedium.

· Ten ·

In an alliance with the Wheels, Duke Colfax and Baron Stogar convinced Prince Roald to support a bill for free trade in the Spur House of Assembly. King Leon was opposed, and the proposal was defeated. There'd be no export from the Drake ammunition factories to the Outremere markets.

In exchange, the King allowed duties on import goods to increase, as well as the prices of flour, oil, textiles, wood, and coal. The wage floor of day labor was lowered.

Then the members of the Spur Assembly rode away from St. Lucien. It was the Season of Ghosts, and government business was postponed in favor of hunting. Those born to the saddle were eager to risk their necks, and those of their horses, chasing over their own lands, and those of any hapless farmer, in pursuit of quarry.

Glennys worked the stage geldings hard. She and Joss finicked with the horses' feeding schedules and their diet. They could only improve the timing of certain facts of nature, not change them. A horse couldn't be trained to have the domestic habits of a dog. Binding horses' delicate digestion with doses and too many emetics interfered with their health.

Opening night was six days away.

Champers cantered on the treadmill, Catherine on his back. It was the day's second rehearsal of the middle act's opening.

Champers didn't like the treadmill; none of the geldings did. But Champers was doing very well. His keenness for display made him willing. His canter was sure and smooth, his action clean. For once the backdrop landscape on the rollers worked faultlessly.

The layers of gauzy scrim rose one by one out of the stage on a system of weights, pulleys, and wires. The floor lamps slowly dimmed. The jars of colored water in front of the lamps tinted the stage rose, lavender, and blue to indicate twilight.

Cimi's solo voice soared above the chorus as the brass en-

tered. That was the cue to the stage secrets' operators that
Champers was about to step off the treadmill and onto the platform that would hoist him and Catherine above the stage in a
billow of clouds.

It all happened so fast.

One of the scrim gauzes slipped free of its moorings. It fluttered in the current of air rapidly as a hummingbird and nearly
as invisible. Somewhere a door was slammed shut. The silk
came down on Champers's face.

The horse threw back his neck and the top of his head
slammed into Catherine's nose. Champers's hooves scrambled
under him. He skidded to the head of the treadmill rollers and
fell on one knee. Glennys felt the bruising pain on the bone and
the twist of ligaments.

Catherine desperately shifted her balance. Glennys and Joss
were there. Glennys held Champers's head still and removed the
silk from his eyes. Joss clamped the gelding's knee in his hands
and slowly straightened the leg. Champers did not want to put
his weight down on that leg and walk. He was also determined
to get off the treadmill surface.

"Why am I riding a bloody horse? Is Champers injured?
Bloody Nolanese audiences! I'm a dancer, not a rider! What am
I doing on a horse?"

Catherine's nose was erupting blood.

"You're the best sort of rider," Glennys said quickly. "One
who didn't fall off and break her neck."

The orchestra and the singers were oblivious to the accident
and continued their business. "Shut up!" Catherine screamed.
"Who fastened this scrim? Do I have to do every bloody thing
myself for it to work properly? I'll kill whoever did this. Kill
everyone, now!"

In a moment the stage was crowded with hands and operators,
protesting innocence in at least four languages at once. Catherine strode about, a pitiable creature whose life had been put in
danger by others' carelessness, showering blood from the torrent
out of her nose everywhere. She shook off everyone's attempt to
staunch the flow of blood.

By the treadmill, ignored by the rest, Glennys and Joss min-
istered to Champers.

"It was in the cards, it always is," Joss groaned.

"Why did it have to be Champers? Why couldn't it have been
his understudy?" Glennys complained to the forces of luck.

They stayed up with the gelding all night. Hot and cold packs alternately were administered to his knee. They massaged the leg to keep fluid from collecting and putting extra pressure on the injury. It was a bruise, not a break. Vanity, Champers's understudy, did the rehearsals alone for the next four days.

But Queen's had been lucky. It was Champers who had the leg injury, not Catherine. The gelding was replaceable. She wasn't.

When Champers was brought back to the Theater, it was a sore trial to get him back on the treadmill. Glennys opened her Horse Sense wide and wrapped the gelding's will with hers. She got him back on the machine. She hoped the forgetting she put into his danger memory was permanent. If it wasn't, he'd refuse to run on the canvas again unless she was there to coerce him.

Then it was opening night for Queen's season and *The First Stallion Queen*.

It was quiet on the lower level, where the stalls and the animal cages were. Those who handled the wolf, bear, and panther kept careful track of the time, administering soporifics at intervals to keep the animals awake but docile. The python's handler fed him baby rodents instead of doses. The handlers were responsible for the health of their animals and the safety of the performers and audience. The balance between the handlers' skill and the potential danger delighted the Aristo audiences.

On the stage level, at the wings of stage right, the tangle of secrets' guildsmen, seamstresses, singers, and dancers was so tight Glennys had to fight her way through the passages that led up to the tiring room and the dressing rooms.

Up there she dodged out of the way of arms and legs stretching and limbering. She squeezed her way around the backstage beaus who'd bribed their way in. From the orchestra room came the squall of brass and woodwinds warming up. Everyone shouted, and the singers warmed up their voices, their forty operatically trained throats making the walls vibrate.

A retinue in Colfax livery stood in front of Catherine's dressing room. "The Duke says no one can go in," said one of them, blocking Glennys's entry.

The door flew open and Amalia, red and perspiring, grabbed Glennys's arm and pulled her inside. "The Duke means well, but that means she's been left too soon to brood undistracted. Like any amateur, Colfax has no sense of timing," Amalia criticized.

Catherine's stage fright was in proportion to her responsibility. The First Dancer had a cold. Her nose, bright red, ran like a river.

The dresser followed Catherine's pacing. "Unless you be still, Miss Gemma, I can't sew you into this bodice."

Catherine threw herself into Glennys's arms. "It's a shipwreck! The colors are ugly and make my red nose red, red, red. Everyone hates me. I'm sick! No one will come," she wept.

Amalia raised her eyebrows at Glennys across Catherine's head as they rocked the ballerina between them like a baby. They caressed her. They told her she was the most talented person in the world, the best dancer, that everyone adored her.

"There's not even standing room in the audience," Glennys said. "The King and his sons are already in the royal box, and the opening diversion hasn't yet begun."

"The King has to be here. It's the first night of Queen's season. I despise them all!" Catherine wailed. "One half is here to chase debauchery with my singers and dancers. The others will sit like lumps of lard and snore."

"That's not true. No one is snoring, and they all wait for you and the marvels you've devised for them," said Glennys. "The set of fashion, the swells and journalists love you, Cathy. Thadee Maywood is your slave."

"They adore Cayetana de Alba more! They understand what I do less than my spaniel dogs! I spit on Thadee Maywood!" Catherine cried.

"I brought you a gift, Catherine," said Glennys.

Gifts could usually be depended upon to catch the attention of a King's Daughter. "It's not a luck gift," Glennys said carefully, so as not to offend the forces that ruled performance. "It's a little thing to show how much I admired your horsemanship the day of the treadmill accident."

It was a tiny gold spur, a traditional birthing gift made to an Aristo's heirs. The jeweler had attached the spur to a fine gold chain, and blunted the rowels so it could be worn as a pendant.

Catherine held it up in front of her eyes with one hand, while the other went to her abdomen. She whispered to herself in Langanese while she stared into the mirror.

Suddenly she was calm. She blew her nose loudly, and asked everyone to leave her alone with Glennys. She turned back to the trainer and said, "How did you know?"

"Know?" asked Glennys.

Catherine pointed to her belly.

Glennys's mouth fell open. "You're pregnant? You're sure?"

"There's no doubt, and now I'm glad. I can't get rid of it and dance out the season too. I'd be in bed for weeks. Your gift is an omen that this is the right time for me. It happens to every real woman."

Glennys was doubtful. "It's your role as Eve searching for the Eve daughter that makes you think that way," she said, thinking she was very wise.

"I think," said Catherine with a grin, "it was Collie's third leg between my two and the old jigaboom and jizzabum. It left him empty and me full, and I fell asleep too soon to take care of it because he was talking about Baron Stogar and Prince Roald."

Amalia made a firm return. "No more delay, now. Marie Bonheur has arrived to help you with your shoes and you've not done your face."

Glennys's farewell was counterpointed by Marie's and Amalia's prayers to the Mourning Mother beseeching her favor on behalf of Catherine and her ballet.

Glennys struggled back to the menagerie level. One by one the beast cages rolled up the ramp, and, one by one, they returned. The first act was over.

Next was the comic interlude between acts. The groom, whose task it was to fix the flowers that were to shower from Champers's mane over the ballerina, swore as the gelding shook his neck, and ticked his hooves on the boards restlessly.

Glennys led Champers out of his stall. The horses knew this was the real thing. Vanity squealed in protest that it was Champers, and not him, going to the stage level.

Champers danced up the ramp. The crowd in the wings melted aside to let him through. Catherine glided to his neck and stroked him. Her nose wasn't red and had stopped running. She didn't see Glennys at all. Champers's ears were pricked forward as Catherine laid herself down in a graceful attitude of sleep in front of the waterfall pumped up to the stage. The hiss of cues to curtain, lights, and music came from all sides.

The curtain went up with the dawn music and the dawn lights. Glennys counted along with the music for fifteen measures. Then she touched Champers on his shoulder with her fingers, and touched his will with hers, and the horse pranced over the stage boards to the sleeping woman. He shook his mane and twitched his tail. Flowers scattered over Catherine. He towered over her, and then lowered his head to the right level. The sleeper woke. In wonder, Eve put up her hand to touch his cheek.

Cimi's soprano inquired, "What are you?"

The basses answered, "I fly without wings and on my back riches repose."

Torgut extended a foreleg. Eve put her hand on it and rose from the ground. They began their duet to the acquaintance aria.

The audience demanded an immediate encore to the pas de deux. The applause was thunderous at the new step Catherine had devised, called the pas de cheval, which suggested a horse pawing the ground. The movement passed back and forth between Eve and Torgut.

In the wings, Joss squeezed Glennys's shoulder. She didn't feel it, so intently was she matched with Champers's senses.

After Eve returned to her tribe and gave birth to her daughter Eve, the audience cooed with delight. Catherine nursed a real baby.

The house roared with laughter during the comic character dance featuring August Gardel. The ballet director had gotten himself up as a tribal crone. He brandished a huge carving knife when the stallion Torgut brought his tribe of horses to do homage to his human daughter, Eve.

"You are new meat!" was the chorus of the crone song. Cognac, the old gelding, took the crone by the padded hump on her back, and shook the knife-brandishing character in the air.

The child Eve had a short simple dance in which she introduced Torgut to her friends. The little girl in the part was the daughter of Duke Colfax. The audience applauded the child to show honor to King Leon, who was the child's actual sire.

The applause startled the little girl so much that she hid her face in Catherine's skirts and peed all over the dancer's feet. At least one element of the audience liked that as much as anything else.

The ballet was interrupted often by applause and demands for encores. It ran two bells over the time it would have taken without audience participation.

When it concluded, the curtain calls went on forever. The audience made itself a part of the performance. The stage performers glutted themselves on the love feast. No one remembered that August Gardel, still in his crone costume, had threatened between acts to rip the music director, Rambert, from gizzard to stones because of orchestra miscues.

The stage was knee-deep in flowers. Champers ate up the applause and some of the bouquets. Amalia watched jealously to see that the gelding didn't eat the rings and bracelets, intended for Catherine, attached to the bouquets.

The members of the Music and Dance Academy's board of directors got on stage and made speeches to applause. Duke Colfax got a round of applause for himself. He brought up his Duchess, which was a piece of aplomb that made the audience gasp and applaud some more.

Toasts were drunk in honor of the dead Queen who had given the first endowment to the Theater. King Leon came on stage. He and Colfax embraced.

It was long after midnight when Glennys and the horses got back to Queen's Yard. A spread of food and wine was in Joss's office. There were receptions all over the city, but no one from the Yard—except Champers—had been invited.

It was just as well that they didn't go to any parties. There was a matinee tomorrow, as well as an evening performance.

• Eleven •

IT WAS LOW tide when Thea Bohn picked her way over the sandy coast below South Harbor on her first day back in St. Lucien.

The Majis Sea gave Thea thoughts as big as God. The sound of the sea, the biggest sound in the world, and the look of it, the endless roll of water, mesmerized her. The waves shivered silver and grey in the new year's cold. The expanse of heaven here was much closer to earth than in Soudaka County.

The sky was clouding over. Thea thought it might snow. But she couldn't trust her nose about the weather as she could back home. Everything about St. Lucien was so different, right down to finding someone.

Thea had gone to Queen's Yard looking for Stella's daughter. Joss had told her that since the Theater was dark tonight, he'd sent Glennys out to run one of his own horses on the sand.

She trudged along the water's edge in her thick-soled, fleece-lined boots. Her clothes, layers of good Alaminite wool, should have kept her warm. At home this weather would have been considered a good day to hang the washing out to dry. At home, though, the air wouldn't be damp like this.

Finally she saw a dog in the distance, running up and down the cliffs. Behind it, a horse was running towards her, its mane cresting and falling like the waves of the sea. Under the mane a head was bent along the horse's neck. Then she heard barking, and the beat of hooves pounding on this part of the beach where the sand was packed hard. She felt a flutter inside.

Then she could hear the horse's breathing. He passed right by her, then swung in a wide circle, and returned.

Glennys was extending a hand and a foot to her. "Get up behind me. I can't let this horse stand now. He's too warm."

Thea had no idea what to do. She grabbed hold of the gloved hand. Somehow the extended foot, free of the stirrup, gave her a boost. Her shoulder ached from the wrench, but Thea's legs were astraddle the horse's back under her skirts and petticoats. She was riding a horse for the first time in her life.

It was as the rest of her clan had said, when Elder Bohn gave his permission for her to study healing at the St. Lucien Fortune Houses. In the capital of the heathen, she was breaking every Alaminite commandment.

They ran over the sand. Her eyes swam with moisture. The sea was a shimmer of glass. She buried her head against Glennys's strong back and shoulders.

Glennys worked the horse out of his gallop into a canter, a lope, and then a trot. They went back and forth over the sand. When the horse had cooled down enough Glennys made Thea unloose her grip on her waist.

"I've got to put the hood and sweat rug on him now," Glennys said. She threw one leg over the saddle and was on the sand. She helped Thea off.

Thea's legs were wobbly.

"I recognized Alaminite winter clothes. What brings you back to St. Lucien?" Glennys asked while covering the horse. "I suppose Stella wants more money."

"I wanted to see you," Thea said.

"Well, this is no place to be sociable. I'm taking Otter here," she said, patting the horse, "back to the Seahorse. You can come with me, or we can take you somewhere—as long as it's not the Alaminite kirkyard."

"I'll go with you," said Thea.

"On horseback?" Glennys's eyes crinkled from the smile concealed by her hood and face mask of wool and fur.

"On horseback," Thea agreed firmly.

This time, as she grabbed Glennys's gauntleted hand, and put her foot on Glennys's spurred boot, Thea's heart glowed rather than pounded. Once in Dephi, she'd seen Glennys boost up the old Baron Fulk's daughter, Thurlow, in just this way. Thea thought she'd passed some sort of test.

The horse ramps to South Harbor's docks were icing over. By the time Otter trotted through Circle Gardens, the sky was entirely overcast. Fat wet flakes fell. Young Aristos and Wheels, out in their rigs or on their fine horses, called gaily to each other as to where they might meet at one or another of the evening's entertainments.

Snow accumulated quickly on walls, branches, and undisturbed open ground. The feathery powder smoothed out the hard lines of cruelty on the city's face, and St. Lucien became a serene, chaste city of shining white towers and lacy balustraded bridges.

In front of the Seahorse a group of George's friends from the Academy were sculpting a snow effigy of Master Copely. The proprietor of the tavern stood at the entrance, drinking a mug of mulled wine and jovially criticizing their efforts.

Glennys pushed her riding mask into the neck of her jacket. The young artists recognized her and greeted her with a raucous hail of soft snowballs. Otter shied, and then swung upwind, his nostrils opening wide with interest.

Glennys matched with him and smelled what he did. "Watch out, boys! A cohort of Equine Academy cadets are riding this way. No doubt your art will be a joy for them to trample."

Whoops of glee greeted her information. Copely put the shutters over his windows in case the fun got out of hand.

"You go in, Thea, and tell Joss to send one of his boys to the stable out back to rub down her horse."

Glennys was a trainer. Today she'd played jockey as a personal favor to her boss. But she wasn't about to do grooming chores. Leading Otter, her feet had no sensation of the ground over which they walked. She remembered the scent of Copely's mulled wine. It was likely that Joss would treat her to something hot and spiritous. She hoped so. Joss could easily afford it; Copely always discounted his old crony's bill. And she had no money to buy for herself.

Baron sat on his haunches directly in front of her. He put up one paw. That was his way of saying he was hungry. He'd missed his usual breakfast two days in a row. Out of her saddlebags Glennys took some chicken pilfered from the Queen's Yard luncheon and fed him the last of it. The spread at the Yard was generous, but taking food home was against the rules. She couldn't keep feeding Baron that way much longer before it was noticed.

Joss was three sheets to the wind.

"Glennys, sit your pretty ass down here and tell me what you think about Otter. He's a great horse, isn't he? What took you so long to get in here? Your hot brandy's probably cold by now."

Joss put two fingers in his lips and whistled for the nearest tavern maid's attention. "Hot brandy all around! Yes, for you too, you sweet little Alaminite thing you," he insisted to Thea. "When with the wicked Nolanese, you do as they do."

Glennys wondered again what it was about Thea that put at ease those who most likely would have contempt for her.

Glennys dutifully began telling Joss about his race horse. Otter was smart, and very strong. He wasn't afraid to jump, and had good judgment on how to approach a leap.

"He's not the fastest horse I've ever ridden," she said, "but he's fast."

"Bottom, smarts, and go are more important for a kurgan-to-kurgan event than flat-out speed," said Joss. "I've got a winner! You hear that, Jay?" he greeted his son, who had returned from the Seahorse stable. Joss's eyes were getting a little red. There were several empty tumblers in front of him.

The doors burst open. Drafts of cold air and snow blew into the tavern. The artists were using the entrance as their last line of defense from the attack of the cadets. The rowdiness showed signs of turning ugly any minute.

Copely, his sons, and the burliest of his regular customers pulled the students inside. "That's enough. We'll have the city guards here soon if you don't quit."

Romantics one and all, the students protested. "We'll never yield to the rooty toots!"

"Come on, boys," Joss ordered in the voice that could get all of his employees' attention at once. "Some of those cadets out there will grow up to be your patrons, if they don't get blown up in the next campaign."

"I'll never take money from that sort," one of the Romantics claimed stoutly.

"When your dad doesn't give it to you anymore, you will," Joss laughed.

He called for drinks for everyone, then stepped outside and called to the cadets, most of whom he recognized from guard duty at Queen's Yard. He invited them to join in the drinks he was standing for the company.

Copely winked at him. Peace in his tavern was worth a round of free drinks.

Every one of the Seahorse's great hearths had been fired. The tavern's doors opened continuously to let in the Hide's residents, driven out from the cold of their lodgings. The noise became a roar of conversation, argument, singing, and flirtation.

"Sir," Joss's son addressed him, "the wind's come up and the snow is getting fierce. What are we going to do? Otter shouldn't be taken out in this."

"We'll just have to sleep in my office at the Yard," Joss said. The number of his empty tumblers had increased.

"Otter shouldn't go that far either, I don't think," Jay replied respectfully. "And I don't think you can make it either, sir."

"Well then, old Cope will have to find room for us upstairs," he mumbled.

Baron was restless. He didn't care about the noise and the crowd, but he was hungry. For once, so was Glennys. In Joss's condition, food was the last thing he was thinking of, so there wouldn't be any coming from there. Why was it when she didn't want to eat, everyone tried to buy her meals, and when she would have welcomed an offer, nobody made one?

Her pride wouldn't allow her to ask Copely for a tab. She wished Thea would leave. She must be hungry too. By rights, since Glennys had brought her here, she should stand Thea a meal. And how was the Alaminite to get back to wherever it was she slept?

Glennys went to look out the front doors. A real snowstorm was blowing. She couldn't send Thea across the city alone in this. She was going to have to put Thea up for the night.

An artist, one of George's friends, came over. "I guess old Georgie's either out in this, or didn't get started back at all. Do you know when he planned to get in from Gordonsfield?" he asked.

"He went to visit his family for St. Lucien's Eve," Glennys said. "I don't keep track of him, you know."

"Oh. Another fight, I see," said the young man. "I did hear his family had lined up a marble-quarry owner's daughter for marriage."

Glennys turned her back on him.

Jay said, "The cadets' stallions are out there in the snow. Shouldn't they take them back to the Academy stables?"

"War stallions can handle snow. At least, *mine* could." Glennys hadn't meant to be so sharp.

"Anything born and bred in Soudaka County can handle this piddling snowfall," Thea said, "including me. I must be getting back, Glennys, even though there's been no chance to talk with you."

Glennys hadn't asked this Alaminite girl to seek her out, but since Thea had done so, she felt responsible for her. Thea's company in the attic was preferable to getting drunk and stupid in the tavern, where no one was ordering anything to eat.

"I can't allow you to wander blind over streets you don't know," Glennys said. "You'll have to spend the night with me. A sea-born snowstorm is more treacherous than you think."

Glennys wrapped herself in her outdoor gear. Ignoring Thea's protests, she tied the Alaminite scarf over the girl's bright hair, pulled the wool hat over that, and threw the muffler around her neck. "You're coming with me, and I can't stand to sit in here another minute."

The heat from the hearths and the close-packed bodies had made the Seahorse a furnace. The first moments outside were a relief. Then the numbing damp wind reached through their clothes.

Glennys's icy attic seemed warm, compared with what they'd come through. It was blissfully quiet after the roar of the crowd and the wind.

"You can relieve yourself behind that screen, and wash your hands too, if the water in the jug's not frozen," Glennys said. Her words turned to vapor as she spoke.

She lit two oil lamps, and then fired the braziers that were fixed on a bed of stones under her sleep platform. She drew on the pulley lines running over the central beam. Sausages, cheeses, garlic, and onions appeared out of the darkness above Glennys's head and disappeared into a basket. Apples, carrots, and potatoes came out of the food locker.

She muttered while stuffing the basket in preparation for going down into Petry's kitchen. "And George called me a squirrel because I bought provisions! What does he know about not having money, growing up with it, and going to marry it too? A marble-quarry owner's daughter! At least my quarterly rent's paid up, and so are Mother's taxes. Petry's not going to bother me about using her kitchen, though she will about the water. I haven't paid the water wagon bill. Marie's classes are due for payment. Mother wants more money out of me, why else did *she* come looking for me?"

Thea couldn't help it. She began to giggle. "Oh, Glennys, do you know you sound exactly like Stella muttering?"

Thea tensed, fearing she'd spoken too freely. But instead of turning on her, Glennys stood in the gloom under the center beam, and laughed for the first time in many days.

"You're right, that's exactly how Mother goes on. But I am different from Stella. I can still cheer up. See what I've got to cheer us up with supper."

Glennys opened a wicker hamper and pulled out several bottles of wine. "From the Palisades vineyards. We're going to have a good time, even though it never gets warm enough in here during weather like this to be comfortable anyplace else but in bed. Make yourself at home while I make us supper. Chase the cats off the sleep platform.''

Thea leaned back against the warm chimney wall which made up the far side of the sleep platform. Two heavy-bellied queen cats leaped out of the covers spitting and hissing. Then they crept back into their sleep tunnels under the bed quilts. Warmth and comfort beat out cold and hostility every time, Thea thought.

No, not every time. For example, warmth and comfort meant nothing to Hans Rigg. If she'd gone back to the city's tiny Alaminite community, Hans would have been waiting for her. He'd talk again of how Alam meant her for him, to be handmaid and comforter to him while he accomplished Alam's Millennium.

To take her mind off Hans Rigg, Thea got off the sleep platform and went about investigating the place where Glennys lived.

A window had been cut into the far wall, shuttered and guarded by a heavy crossbar. The floor was covered with old, worn carpets and cushions from Rummage Street. A small clothes-press and a smaller wardrobe stood together. Next to them, under the highest part of the roof, were several shelves and a mirror. That was about it, except for a stool and small table.

Thea opened the wardrobe and was greeted by the smell of bootblack and leather. Pairs of riding boots in different styles kept in their proper shape by boot trees stood on the floor, next to a boot jack. From pegs hung little bags containing pairs of slippers made of kidskin and satin. Bits, spurs, whips, and lengths of leather hung from other pegs.

A bag bulging with dirty clothes was tucked next to the screen in one corner. Thea had spent enough time in St. Lucien to learn that laundry was a difficult task for those without a house and water supply of their own, or cash.

The tabletop boasted a lamp and writing materials. On a nearby shelf were books on horse medicine. Next to them were journals written out by Glennys recording the horses she had worked, going back to her days at Three Trees. Above the table hung a framed license from the Horse Skillers Association and the Fortune House Registry.

There was one more thing on the tabletop—a letter. Thea knew the handwriting as well as she knew her own. It was Stella's. Thea had a good idea what was in the letter; by it lay a flat money pouch.

They ate sitting on the sleep platform from the table pulled up to it. ''Except for the garlic, this is almost like what we'd be eating at home in weather like this,'' Thea said.

''Garlic is something a healer should know about. I've grown to like the flavor, but more important, garlic's very effective with infections. You can use it externally or internally. We use it all the time at the Yard in poultices on cuts and open wounds. It's one of the few things about treating horses I learned here that my Three Trees training hadn't given me. But then, garlic's not cultivated in Soudaka,'' said Glennys.

''I work with people, not horses,'' Thea said, a little doubtfully.

''I'm people, aren't I? For all the Alaminites want to call me a witch. Garlic works on my cuts and gashes,'' Glennys said.

Thea wasn't used to drinking wine, and Glennys usually drank little since her days began early, ended late, and demanded her to be alert all the time. But by the meal's end, most of two bottles were gone. The attic's ventilation was provided by draughts through the boards; even so, the coal fumes accumulated.

The two young women began to tell each other the stories of their lives. It was a delight for Glennys to talk with someone to whom her background didn't have to be explained. Another two bottles of wine were opened.

''Now Hans Rigg wants to marry me,'' Thea said, coming up to the present. ''And I don't want to marry *anyone*, but especially not him. He's part of the reason Father gave me permission to come here for the winter—along with studying medicine and doing lace brokerage for the clan. But Hans followed me here. He's telling the brethren that my soul and Father's are in danger. He says we won't survive the Millennium, unless we see the light—his light.''

Alaminites never stopped squabbling with each other, Glennys thought, and they never quit trying to force everyone else to believe like them. ''How much support does Hans Rigg have?'' she asked.

''Reverend Tuescher had a revelation in favor of the Millennium prophecies. So it's nearly everyone in the congregations, except for the odd ones, like Stella, and us Bohns,'' Thea said. Her tongue was rather thicker than it was earlier.

It was just like Stella, Glennys thought, with a shudder, to get herself on the wrong side of the Reverend once again. Alaminites who didn't agree with revelation and doctrine were heretics, and women who didn't do what they were told were witches.

Alaminites burned heretics and witches sometimes, even though it was against Nolanese law.

Glennys said, "And with all this going on, Stella still wants me to come back to Soudaka and work as Stogar's Stablemistress, because it will save her from taxes on her farm."

Thea poured them more wine. A teardrop glimmered at the corner of each of her eyes. "The only man I could have even considered marrying was Ezekial Tuescher. I cried for days after the old Baron Fulk's war stallion killed him. Nothing can make me believe Ezekial murdered the old Baron. Ezekial was a truly good man, like my father. He wasn't a killer."

Reckless with wine, Glennys exposed one of her long-kept secrets. "Ezekial didn't kill Fulk. I know. I was riding Deadly when it happened," she confessed. "I know who did kill Fulk, though, and so does Mother! And Mother's still willing that I put myself in danger and come back because that murdering Stogar promises he'll give back her farm's tax exemption. If she can't keep that bloody piece of ground without bleeding me white of every bit of cash I get, why doesn't she move here? We'd all be better off. That's why I'm so bloody broke. Stogar killed his own father. I know it, and he knows I know. I wouldn't give much odds on living long if I went back to be his Stablemistress. But does Stella think of that? No! Only the state of my soul and the fate of her farm. She's probably managed to forget that Stogar killed Fulk. Knowing her, I'm sure she forgot on purpose."

She'd done it again; she'd gone on a resentful rant, just like her mother, and said things she didn't want anyone to know. Why did she drink all that wine?

"Thea, forget what I said. It could get all of us in bigger trouble than we can handle. Duke Colfax is Stogar's crony. Duke Colfax is so powerful that he makes Reverend Tuescher and Hans Rigg look like mice."

But Thea was tipped back against the wall, her empty glass loose in her hand, fast asleep.

Glennys took Baron outside for his comfort and to clear her head. Before leaving the attic, she arranged the bedclothes comfortably around Thea. They were friends now, she realized. And there was nothing either could get from the other but friendship, which, in St. Lucien, was a rare condition.

The wind had quieted, but the snow still snittered. Baron and Glennys had the supreme pleasure of tearing up the unsullied snow on Petry's sward. They romped and wrestled. It was a good way to get rid of the wine and coal vapors in Glennys's head.

She and Baron shook themselves vigorously to get rid of the snow on their coats. She'd been lucky that Thea had gone under when she did. If she hadn't, they'd have drunk more and then Glennys would have told her about the Horse Sense—and every Alaminite, not only Tuescher and Hans Rigg, would think that witchcraft.

No doubt she'd have gone on and spilled that Baron Fulk had been her first lover. Almost at the moment of his death, Stella had told him—and Glennys—that Fulk was Glennys's real father.

Her father had been her lover. No doubt her mother had managed to forget that, too.

• Twelve •

THE BLACK AND the chestnut approached each other across
the sawdust floor walking on their hind legs. High-pitched whis-
tles came from their nostrils. Their great mouths were already
open, their teeth exposed. The crowd tensed, anticipating the
shock of the fighting stallions' first connection.

Stallion fights were against the law except on the estates of Spurs.
Most of the audience was outlaw, or, in the language of the ruling
classes, unentitled. They drank, shouted, cheered, and pumped
their arms in the air to catch the bookmakers' attention.

Glennys divided the penetration of her Horse Sense in two
and matched herself with both stallions.

The opponents went head to head, throwing the force of their
fourteen-hundred-pound bodies into battle. Their cutting hooves
flew in every direction over each other's body. Their powerful
jaws ground on whatever part they could grasp.

One of the black's wildly flailing hooves tore the chestnut's
right eye. Glennys's scream of pain and rage was drowned in the
great roaring swell of the crowd.

Albany had gone for the winter without making her an offer
of concubinage. Until he'd left, Glennys hadn't known how much
she'd depended upon that offer, though she still told herself she
wouldn't accept it.

George had come back after the new year full of the marble-
quarry owner's daughter and still expecting Glennys to ignite in
ardor. She had no money and her next quarter's wages wouldn't
be paid until the end of Marche. Betting on the stallion fights
was a dirty thing, but not as dirty as sex with George, when she
was furious with him, for the sake of three silver forients.

The bookie accepting Glennys's new bet raised an eyebrow.
She'd taken long odds on the chestnut against the tide of wagering. He looked her over.

"I remember you from the stallion fights in Dead Well Hide,"
he said. "You won that time too, on long odds. A lucky one,
ain't you?"

Glennys shrugged, discouraging further comments.

It was risky, using her Horse Sense to win wagers. Nothing would provoke the house more quickly to murder than a regular who won too often or a suspicion that a means was employed that put the house at a disadvantage. Glennys didn't influence the outcome of the fight, but matched to learn which horse had the most endurance.

For an hour the two stallions fought. The black and the chestnut were locked in their deadly mutual grip for minutes at a time. The chestnut, handicapped by his half-vision, often overshot and missed his hold on the black's body.

Before the house froze the wagering there was a flurry of last bets. Glennys didn't change hers.

The black's teeth slipped off the chestnut's hide where he'd taken hold. His jaws snapped together with a sound like the report of a firecracker.

The horses pulled apart, gasping great bellowing breaths, their sides heaving, throwing off bloody froth and sweat.

The crowd fell silent, reaching out with senses of its own.

Glennys and Baron squirmed to the back of the room.

The chestnut hurled himself against the black, and the black stallion was thrown to the blood-soaked sawdust. The black was kicked, stamped on, and lacerated by the mad victor's teeth. The black never got up again.

The house never paid out cheerfully to a winner, no matter how many losers there were, and no matter how small the winnings. Glennys made sure she was the first one in line to collect from the tallyman who sat behind his barricade. She was glad the two disguised cadets from the Equine Academy had also won. Everyone could tell there were weapons under their cloaks, and that they were impatient to get on to their next amusement. Tonight Glennys's winnings were large. She and Baron were outside before the cadets had put out their hands.

Now she could eat and buy coal. But she was going to have to find another means of getting through the winter. The bookies and tallymen recognized her now.

The next night at the Theater, Prince Roald was backstage before *The Stallion Queen*, as he'd been almost every night since Albany went south. There was no time for sparkling repartee backstage, much less the rambling monologues that the Prince believed were conversations, so he often pouted.

Invariably the Prince chose the most inconvenient place to

stand, where the traffic from the animal ramps and the tiring room converged with that of the performers preparing to take the stage.

"Glenn, tell the Prince he's got to wait until after final curtain tonight to come around the wings. The prolonged cold has fouled the stage machines, and we've already got more bodies back here than we can squeeze in," said Gardel.

That night Glennys's spirits were so low that she would have defied King Leon himself and not cared for the consequences. "I'm a horse trainer. You or the stage manager manage the Prince," she snapped.

"We have," the ballet director sighed. "We've hinted as broadly as we can to a Prince. But he doesn't get the hints."

Glennys oversaw the geldings' loadout after the performance as usual. All she and Baron had to look forward to was the freezing trudge through the back parts of the city to her frosty garret.

One of the rats, the girlchildren that ran errands around the Theater, called to her. "Miz Eve, Miz Catherine want you in her dressin' room. She get you and that dog home in her carriage, she say."

There weren't many bouquets tonight in the dressing room. But Amalia checked them carefully in case there was a gift attached or a note Duke Colfax shouldn't be bothered with reading. "Nothing worth mentioning tonight," the maid declared.

Catherine was lying down, her ankles, legs, and knees propped up by satin pillows. "After every performance now I'm all swelled up," she said. The dancer ate a hothouse peach with the unaware greed of a child.

"Have a peach, Glenn, if there are any left. Nothing edible is safe around me these days. I haven't enjoyed eating like this in years. At any rate, there's tea," Catherine said.

Glennys refilled the dancer's cup.

"You've been in evil spirits all month, Glennys. Perhaps we can cheer you up. Listen to Amalia," said Catherine.

"Prince Roald wants to buy your King's Daughter favors and will pay handsomely," Amalia said.

This wasn't entirely a surprise, but it was entirely unwelcome. She wouldn't compound the perversion of wagering on the stallion fights by taking money from a man whose body repulsed her.

Glennys lapsed into her dumb country-girl drawl, as she did whenever she refused someone and didn't want to offend. "Nay. You're mistaken, and so's the Prince. I'm not worthy of that kind of attention."

Amalia rolled her eyes toward heaven.

Sharply, Catherine said, "Cut out the country-girl act, Glenn. Amalia's not mistaken. It's her business to be sure of these things." Now the First Dancer was eating chocolates and oranges.

"I don't work like that," Glennys protested.

"You, Miss Eve, don't work at all," Amalia returned. "How old are you? Twenty? If you're ever to get somewhere on the road of King's Daughter, you'd better start now."

"It's not my fault that Nolan classes female Horse Skillers in with female artists and calls us all King's Daughters. I never planned to be one, you know. And I do work. I'm a horse trainer, and—I do work," Glennys said.

"That painter boy wasn't work. You did that because he pleased you, not for the sake of your purse," Amalia snorted.

"No. Not the Prince. I don't mind spending time with him," said Glennys, "but I can't . . ."

"Stupidissima! We are talking of *work*! What matters is that you make that thing between his legs stand and that he's willing to pay you for it," instructed Amalia.

"Ladies, I'm truly grateful, but I think I may still have a chance with Duke Albany, and I can't throw that out the window for a little of the ready," Glennys said.

"Don't you know anything about Aristo men yet?" smiled Catherine. "Albany knows what being a King's Daughter means, Mourning Mother knows he's enriched enough of them in his time! He's been slow to the mark and now he's earned a richer rival. Nothing makes an Aristo hotter than competition. If you have someone richer, like the Prince, and give him up for the Duke's sake, then the Duke will be all the more generous to you, if only to flaunt his victory in Roald's face."

"Why me, then?" Glennys asked. "Except for yours and Albany's patronage, I'm nobody among the King's Daughters in St. Lucien."

Amalia clasped her hands. "Mourning Mother, that's precisely why the Prince fancies you. I mean, that along with your obvious other charms. You've made yourself agreeable to him. Because you're a nobody he thinks you've never heard about his—little trouble."

"His little trouble?" Glennys repeated, puzzled.

Amalia pursed her lips. This was real business now. "That's what he calls it, according to those who've tried to give the Prince his pleasure."

Amalia sighed. She'd been too subtle for Glennys to understand. "More bluntly, your Prince has difficulty maintaining the stiffness of the princely rod—unlike his brother, the King."

"I think what you're saying is as preposterous as the language in which you couch it," Glennys replied.

Amalia and Catherine glanced at each other. The fish refused the bait.

"Sweetheart, why not give the Prince your favor? For once he'd be the leader, and not a follower. He'd be so grateful to get in before the Duke Albany that you'd make more lovely money than your penny-pinching heart can imagine," cajoled Catherine.

"No," said Glennys.

Catherine broke into tears. "If you won't do it for yourself, then do it for my sake. It will please Collie so much if you give his friend happiness, and he'll be so disappointed in me that I didn't persuade you."

"Your Duke is interested in this business?" Glennys asked sharply. There was no trace of rural drawl in her words now.

Catherine looked, tears dewing her satin cheeks. She placed her hand over her heart, her face beseeching Glennys to understand the depth of her feelings.

She whispered, "Not my Collie, but the Duke Colfax, head of the Offices of Inquiry and Citizen Registry—a powerful man in Nolan, with many powerful friends who ask him favors." She spoke the last words slowly and carefully.

Glennys said nothing for a long time.

Amalia began to whisper angrily. "If you had used your registry as a King's Daughter the way you should have, you wouldn't have forced *cara mia* Catherine into such subterfuge and made her cry with your low thoughts about us playing bawd."

Glennys walked to the mirror and looked at the faces behind her. "You mean that if one of Duke Colfax's good friends, like Baron Stogar, wanted me taken out of St. Lucien, but another of the Duke Colfax's friends, like Prince Roald, wanted me to stay, then the favors would cancel out and the Duke Colfax would need take no action about me," she mused.

"And as it happened, there *was* someone," snapped Amalia, "who suggested that the Prince was hot to trot with the silly little horse trainer requested by Baron Stogar, so the silly little horse trainer could remain in St. Lucien with the friends she doesn't deserve, and not go back to the middle of nowhere."

It was silent up on the level where Catherine's dressing room was located. All the performers had gone. The only people in the Theater were the cleaning women and those of the secrets guild working on the stage machinery.

"Why does Baron Stogar want you to go back to his horse farm?" asked Amalia.

"Because he hates me," Glennys said. That was enough to satisfy Amalia, whose background for a thousand years had been urban. For such a person to be exiled to the country was a dreadful punishment.

"I too would prefer Albany's favor over that of the Prince," Catherine whispered, aware of how words carried when the Theater was deserted. "He is the only Nolanese Aristo I've known whose nature does not war with itself. You are a fortunate woman to have caught his favor, even slightly."

Glennys tried not to let her face show the distaste she felt. "What shall I wear to my royal assignation, and when should it be? And how much commission out of my fee are the two of you entitled to?" she asked.

"I think twenty-five percent is reasonable," Amalia said. "You will make a lot. I'll see to it in the negotiations."

"Take half," said Glennys, "as an expression of my gratitude for your efforts to keep me out from under Baron Stogar's thumb." St. Lucien had taught her that even friendship should be paid for.

Catherine's carriage and horses were waiting in front of Queen's Theater. It was warm inside, with fur throws and hot bricks. As the carriage rolled through the poorer streets outside Circle Gardens, voices of women and children begged for charity. Glennys pushed back the heavy velvet curtains over the carriage's window on her side. The postilions' flares lighted the shivering and starving groups in the doorways that flowed past them.

The lantern inside the carriage bobbed and weaved in obedience to the holes and rough places of the streets. The expression on all three women's faces was the same. Amalia searched in the side cubby and lifted out a jar of Esker that had been left behind one night by Richard Thorvald. She opened it. Pregnant though she was, Catherine drank a bitter toast in the rude Nolanese spirits in the age-old complicity of women who knew what they had to do in order to survive, and were lucky enough to have the means to do so.

· Thirteen ·

ON A NIGHT when Queen's Theater was dark and the Wolf's Moon was new, a carriage flying the banners of Duke Colfax approached the Eidel Kings' winter palace. A Colfax equipage, with two women inside, was so familiar an occurrence that it was waved through without a challenge.

Once inside the royal grounds, the carriage swung away from the approach to King Leon's private wing and toward Prince Roald's entrance.

The guards leaped to the saddles of their horses and galloped under the frost-rimed trees. They surrounded the coach before it reached the marble-roofed portico which was its destination.

"Who goes there? Who's inside?" the guards demanded.

Prince Roald's butler and his underlings poured out of the Prince's wing of the palace. "This is the private business of the King's brother!"

The butler tongue-lashed the captain of the King's Guards. "This carriage is loaned to the First Dancer, Catherine Gemma. It was on the list of visitors given to you this morning!"

The captain of the drive checkpoint was furious. "Yes, a Colfax carriage was listed. But the Colfax carriage always goes to King Leon's drive!"

"The concubine Catherine Gemma has friends that she allows to use the carriage that Duke Colfax has given her," shouted the butler. "These are friends of the Prince!"

Prince Roald's breath blew out in great plumes of mist over the frozen park. He slammed shut the glass panels of his astronomical observatory and drank a generous snifter of brandy. He was enraged once again. His assignation had been ruined before it began. His brother's guards had nearly taken off the girl's head.

The stairs to his observatory were built within the trunk of a massive dead oak. The Prince stumbled down them to his bedroom below. The warmth calmed him.

The carpets, thickly padded, climbed the walls to the ceiling.

Hearths and stoves, tended by servants in the wall passages so he'd never be disturbed, threw out waves of heat. The Prince's quarters in King Leon's palace were so warm that most people felt suffocated, as if they'd been shoved into a down-stuffed pillow.

Prince Roald, brother to the King of Nolan and the Outremere Domains, was always sweating, but always feeling cold. He pushed his limp pinkish-orange hair off his damp forehead. His brother had done this to him on purpose, but he wasn't going to allow this opportunity to die as so many others had. He fastened upon the position of the constellations. They'd promised him satisfaction.

The Prince preened in the mirror on the far wall. He was big, much bigger than Leon, even though he'd been born a year later. He was taller than his good friends Duke Colfax and Baron Stogar. He was much bigger than the Duke Albany. And he was smarter than anyone.

Mistress Glennys Eve was announced. She curtsied low before him, easily, as if it was the most natural thing in the world for her to do.

Roald caught a glimpse of her breasts when she rose out of her curtsy. Her silky hair brushed his face as he leaned down to her hand and kissed it. She looked up at him.

"You're so tall, Prince. I always forget how big you are when I'm not in your presence," she said. "You're bigger than any man I've ever met."

Her voice caressed the words that described his size.

The Prince stood dumbly, very pleased by her voice, but not knowing what to do next. She rose to stand next to him. Coming off the soft carpet, she glided against his side. Before she'd stood at her full height her breasts had pressed against him, and she'd turned his palm over and kissed it. His blood leaped at the touch of breasts and her lips. He saw that her eyes were looking to his boots even though her head was up. She had left her hand in his, waiting for his guidance.

He led her to the central hearth and offered her whatever she'd like to drink. Her eyes looked up at him, this time open wide on his face.

"If you don't mind, some Esker and a glass of water. I love to flick drops of Esker into the fire and see the colors," she said.

The Prince's chest expanded while he saw to her request. How delightfully simple she was. Her low voice told him of how amazed, but most of all, how honored she was, that one of his degree had looked down to her, one so lowly and humble. Roald listened so carefully to her words, and his eyes paid so much attention to the slow degrees with which she removed her heaviest layers of clothing, that he didn't notice how she'd dimmed his lights to a few candles.

After he'd given her the Esker he didn't know what to do. He knew what he wanted to do, but he didn't know how to move to do it. He was mightily tired of the blue sparks crackling on the hearth from the Esker. He was tired of showing her what could be seen in the clear winter sky above St. Lucien with his telescope.

Roald took her back down the oak-trunk stairs and planted Glennys, once again, in a chair next to his central hearth.

He brought out a big bound volume, grinning as he put it into her hands. That would get her excited, he thought. It contained one hundred and fifty-two engravings of erotic postures. He boldly insisted she examine all one hundred and fifty-two and tell him which she liked best. That took some time.

After the twentieth engraving he offered her some Gondol chocolate. Stogar had presented him with the secret of putting centers of fruit mixed with the ground powder of the little Gondol greenflies into chocolate confections. Stogar had promised that the greenfly powder turned any woman mad for love.

After her third chocolate Glennys had drunk down an entire pitcher of water. The servants in the passages replenished the water constantly, invisibly, without intruding upon them.

While Glennys ate chocolates and drank pitchers of water, Prince Roald drank a lot of brandy. He talked brilliantly about wars past and future. He talked seriously about the constellation that promised his destiny. He talked fiercely about the bitches, his mother and grandmother. But nothing happened.

He was throwing entire glasses of brandy into the flames of the large fireplace, unable to think of anything else. He swayed back and forth in frustration.

"Oh, Prince, I've never been where someone like you lives. Can I see the rest of it?" she asked. "Most of all, do you have a conservatory? I've always wanted to walk in a place where plants could grow in winter."

Rather befuddled, Roald said, "But the conservatory is Leon's and the gardeners'."

"So?" she asked, her lips pouting, her eyes worshiping him. She giggled.

Roald giggled too. It was an adventure. He'd never thought of intruding into that part of the winter palace since he'd been eight and broken down all the peach trees, imagining they were hordes of soldiers from Sace-Cothberg.

"It's all on your big shoulders, my Prince. I have no idea of how to do anything here," she said.

"We need this decanter of brandy to scout our way into enemy territory," the Prince proclaimed with high seriousness. Roald followed his decanter with the greatest of stealth. It led him to the steamed glass door of the warm, moist, glassed-in section of the palace.

"Pipes of water heated by coal in the floor and the walls," he told Glennys solemnly. "Only royals and bankers can have green in winter."

Once inside the hothouse conservatory, Glennys stood on tiptoe and kissed the Prince hard on the mouth.

"If you want more, you must catch me!" She dashed off. "I've never felt this way before," she called over her shoulder.

When did she take off her boots? he wondered dimly, as he glimpsed the soles of her bare feet.

She was right around that stand of blooming roses. When he pushed back the thorny branches she had darted away. The rushing stream of manufactured waterfalls hid the sound of her movements. He heard her voice from the other end of the conservatory.

"Find me, Prince of Nolan! I can't give myself to you unless you catch me!"

She wanted him to catch her! He cornered her in a mossy grotto where orchids sucked moisture and nourishment from damp tree bark and the rich air. Her breasts were bare.

"You are everything and I am nothing," she whispered up to him from her knees.

Oh, that was true. She was nothing at all. He could do whatever he wanted with her.

Her hands were at his waist before he understood her purpose. His manhood was standing free and hard.

His pleasure was so intense that the release began at the base of his spine. It was so quick he felt cheated.

"We must get back to my rooms," Prince Roald whispered harshly.

He feared being seen by his brother, yet he hoped he would be. He put his arm around Glennys's shoulders possessively. He pretended it was carelessness that kept part of her bodice bunched up under his fingers so that one of her breasts remained bare.

It pleased the Prince very much to have a lovely woman, one

breast bare, under his arm, and a decanter of brandy hanging from the fingers of his other hand.

Inside his rooms it was nearly as hot as in the conservatory but terribly dry. "Now," he said, pushing away the layers of clothing that guarded her loins. "Now for the real thing."

For a very long time he went all over her body. Every time he thought she was a cheat like all the rest, she talked to him, presenting herself in another manner that he'd never thought of before. She really wasn't like the others, the Prince thought finally. But by then he'd been grinding his member into her groin for almost a bell. Her muscles squeezed him, her fingers tickled him, her voice excited him.

The Prince of Nolan and the Domains erupted royally, then fell asleep.

He had no idea what time it was. His rooms were always dark in winter to keep them warm. Then he woke completely.

"I want you to stay here," he said to Glennys.

"Sleep, my dear Prince. We'll talk of this later. Thank you so very much."

Roald curled his big, lumpy body around one of his pillows. His long, fat arms spread over the bed. Even if Glennys had wanted to spend the rest of the night with him, there would have been no room for her.

She retraced their cavortings through the halls and into the conservatory, picking up items of her clothing where she'd concealed them. Then she went to the tiny chamber where she'd last seen Amalia.

Amalia looked at Glennys with a question she didn't have to voice.

"Twice," Glennys said. "Once on my knees, and once in the usual manner."

"By rights you should have a supper waiting for you. All they have here is wine, and not the best."

"All I want is water. I burn. Oh, do I burn."

"Did you have anything at all to eat?" Amalia asked.

"Nothing but some chocolate," Glennys said.

"Chocolate?" asked Amalia.

"Some chocolate from Gondol," said Glennys.

"The Prince gave you Gondol chocolate and now your nether parts burn?" Amalia demanded. "Are you sure you ate nothing else?"

"I ate nothing but the chocolates. I drank water and a very little Esker," Glennys said.

"I believe you. You are a good girl," Amalia said. "This sounds very bad. The Prince gave you no respect."

Glennys wondered what Catherine's maid meant while she waited for Amalia to return. Glennys walked up and down the tiny room. She couldn't sit still. She rubbed her crotch. She hoped no one was peering at her from the wall passages. The itch between her legs commanded her to pee, and to drink water, and to fuck all at the same time.

Dawn wasn't far away by the time Amalia rejoined Glennys.

Glennys was distraught, clutching her private parts, whispering, "Kill everyone now. He's given me a disease!"

"What he gave you was the little greenflies that swarm in Gondol, where Cayetana de Alba comes from. His butler tried to cheat us out of the fee negotiated by me, a registered go-between and personal maid to First Dancer Catherine Gemma, contracted concubine to Duke Colfax, head of the Offices of Inquiry and Registry of Citizens!" Amalia raged. "I'll have him gelded!" She began swearing in Langanese.

Amalia leaned out of the carriage window and shrieked down the drive toward the palace. This time she used the language of Gondol.

Glennys was miserable. She'd been battered and rubbed raw. She was burning. And she despised herself.

"*Puta, puta su madre* that butler," Amalia cried. "Never in my career as a go-between has a client of mine been cheated. *Truffatore!* It is the Prince who is responsible! He doesn't order his house properly, and he's stingy! The King is very wise to give his brother no power, since he can't even do a piece of twang properly." Amalia spat out of the window into the clear winter morning.

Out of the mouths of whores and bawds, Glennys thought wearily.

"We shall go back and make the Prince give us our money," Amalia declared.

"No," Glennys shouted.

"You are stupid. The Prince doesn't know you were cheated. Money is money, filthy or not, and you should never throw it away. You'll never make a successful King's Daughter. You're too Romantic," Amalia said pityingly.

"I am *not* a Romantic," Glennys declared through clenched teeth. "All I want is for you to come up with relief for me out of your bag of tricks."

• Fourteen •

THE FESTIVAL OF Hearts was an Uncommon Day begun long ago to celebrate reconciliations between feuding bloodlines. Its colors were red and white, the colors of the Eidel throne, its emblem a twisted thorn wreath that impaled hearts and roses. It now was celebrated more for the sake of Romantic love, that idea introduced from Outremere and so attractive to the provincial youth that flocked to the cities each generation in ever-larger numbers. St. Lucien's Festival of Hearts was the gayest and the most enthusiastic in Nolan.

Leon Eidel, Headman of the Tribes, First Rider in Nolan, King of Gondol, King of Langano, King of Tourienne, Protector of the Dominions, etc., was, for the day, also King of Hearts. When the parade, which began in Circle Gardens, concluded, the King of Hearts would choose a young woman to be Queen of Roses during the public entertainments in Velvet Ridge Park. She who wore the Rose Crown would preside over the elite Midnight Ball at the King's Winter Palace.

George Sert and some of his Fine Arts friends had staked out a good parade-watching position at the intersection of Garden Avenue and King's Highway.

"Such frou-frou." The one who said that had carefully made his voice haughty and lazy. "Why do these clods care about Rose Queens?"

"I know you're trying to impress those girls next to us with your urbanity, Brendan, but you're being an ass." George's voice was low, but his impatience was evident. He'd been working on his spring painting to the exclusion of almost any other form of recreation or employment. He was in a highly nervous state, and wouldn't have been there at all himself, except that his closest friends had insisted.

Those in the forefront of the spectators were families much like his own, and that of Lark, the woman in Gordonsfield whom he was to marry. They were prosperous artisans or shopkeepers,

or part of the comfortable class of large freehold farmers on their
yearly visit to St. Lucien.

The parade began with a flourish of flags, trumpets, and
drums. The young boys began to jump up and down, pushing
as close to the velvet ropes as the mounted King's Guards allowed. Applause broke from the balconies as everyone peered
down the Avenue toward Circle Gardens. Even George grunted
with satisfaction.

The elephants came, each one carrying a long-stemmed rose
at the end of her trunk. Members of the opera company and the
orchestra of Queen's swayed in pavilions on the elephants' backs.

The elephants seemed to smile under their nodding red and
white plumes. They opened their mouths and curled their trunks,
waving them gracefully back and forth between their tusks. They
walked in pairs and sometimes the couples clasped trunks as
human lovers clasped hands, yet they never lost their roses.

Behind the elephants came the cage cars. Cougars, lions, ti-
gers, leopards, and wolves paced back and forth, or regally re-
clined, ignoring their admirers.

How clever of our rulers, George thought. We Nolanese, who
are animal lovers beyond any other people, grow up with such
happy memories of exotic animals, and those memories are associated with our masters.

From behind the front ranks of spectators came a rumble of
human voices. ''Where's the food?''

''There ain't none until after the fat ones get their eyes full,''
returned another voice.

There were Spurs and Wheels watching the parade, but there
were also Shoes, and those lower than that.

Feasting and ale for one and all at the expense of the city had
been promised. But the boards wouldn't be laid in the Park until
after the Rose Queen had been properly honored with ballet and
music. The rabble didn't care which upper-class twang got the
coveted crown. They wanted a meal.

Then the ballerinas came into view, all gauze, shoulders, and
cleavage as they rode past on tassled, braided performance geldings. In the center, on a horse-drawn platform, was Cayetana de
Alba, First Dancer and, today, the figure of Love. Like most of
the men in the crowd, George sucked in his breath at the sight
of her. Last year it had been Catherine Gemma's honor, but this
season she was in retirement with a big belly, leaving all the
First Dancer honors to Cayetana.

Catherine's representation had been one of purity and yearning. Cayetana's magnificent, opulent figure, her masses of raven hair, her dark eyes, and her superb air of danger and disdain provoked a different face of love. Honey-sweet romance wasn't what men thought of when they looked at Cayetana de Alba, the hellion from Gondol's gutters who had risen to the position of First Dancer in the capital of the Domains.

The corps de ballet threw roses and heart-shaped chocolates wrapped in pretty papers. With each scattering of sweets the dancers leaned out from their mounts, generously displaying their curves. The men along the Avenue clapped and whistled.

Suddenly, at the end of the ballerina display, George saw Glennys Eve, for the first time since their final quarrel. She was riding next to Joss Thack in a line with the other horse trainers of Queen's Yard.

Glennys leaned toward Thack. Her face turned up to his, and she listened to him raptly. Thack's face was smug. George wanted to throw a stone at it. Glennys laughed at something Joss said, turning her face to the sky in merriment, exposing the curvature of her throat. She turned back to Joss, a look of mischief on her face, and touched her horse, which bumped into Thack's, breaking its stride, while hers never faltered in his gait.

George felt betrayed. That was how she had looked at him when she gave him her attention. She'd never loved him. She was incapable of loving anyone. Lark had loved him, and no one but him, since she was a little girl. She was worth a hundred Glennys Eves who smiled at anything in britches.

Then they were gone and the drill team from the Equine Academy came on the scene. They halted their forward march, marking time with their drum-and-fife corps. They turned their war stallions forward and backward, then sideways, the horses raising their legs on each side alternately. The riders swiveled in the saddle, hanging down to the street, switching mounts, tossing their swords in the air and catching them.

After them came the platform carrying the thirty contenders for the Rose Crown. Their mothers had weighed them down in layers of the most expensive gowns and jewelry possible. With few exceptions these Wheel and Spur daughters sparkled with money, not personality. Sharissa Ely, from Blue Fields in the Yemmessee, was one who stood out. She was having so much fun her smile was contagious.

Hats, caps, turbans, and even wigs soared above the crowd. The ladies dropped into curtsies.

"Leon, Leon, Leon!" was heard on every side.

The King and his two sons rode alone, without a guard, on matching white stallions. A bevy of pretty girls from the crowd ducked under the restraining velvet ropes and dashed into the Avenue. Shrieking and giggling, they pelted the King with flowers and love notes. Leon reached down and circled one girl's waist after another. He pulled each girl up to his face and kissed them all.

Much to the disgust of the little boys, kissing and embracing went on throughout the crowd. "We are all related!" rang up and down the Avenue, the traditional phrase of greeting and farewell in Nolan.

The jubilation continued, following Leon's progress. It died out as Prince Roald was driven past in his open carriage. Behind the Prince came a complement of Spurs and Wheels. Some, like Roald, were driven, but others, like Baron Stogar and Duke Colfax, were on horseback. Scattered voices booed Colfax, whose office had the power to decide who could live and work in St. Lucien.

George and his friends left before the parade was over. George led them across King's Highway to Queen's Yard, through its private entrance into the Park. They came up behind the King of Hearts' platform at the top of the Straightaway horse track and settled there, waiting for the Rose Crown entertainments to begin.

Trestles and cook pits were set throughout the enclosed hills, groves, and meadows of the Park. There were boats out on the lake serving food and wine as well, but only to those who were well dressed and could afford the rowboat men's fee. Gamesters, fortune-tellers, buskers, and balladeers plied their trades along the bridle paths. The weather was favorable, as the astrologers from the Fortune Houses and the astronomers from the Universities had both predicted, for a long day's pleasure.

The open area at the head of the Straightaway was roped off by red and white velvet cords suspended from stanchions. Carpets had been laid over the sand to make a performance area in front of the King of Hearts' dais. Behind the dais were tent pavilions set up for the convenience of the privileged, and for the Queen's Theater people. Food and wine already circulated among those behind the ropes.

It was a matter of honor to George and the other artists that they too be behind the ropes. It didn't matter that they hadn't been invited and had nothing to do. The trick of it was to get in, which they'd done slickly since George knew the Yard's gate-keepers from his liaison with Glennys.

The artists had enough friends among the Queen's people that no one challenged their presence. It didn't hurt that several of the cadets from the Equine Academy's drill team had gotten drunk with them at the Seahorse Tavern either. They ate and drank and waved with good-natured derision to the Romantics on the other side of the ropes who hadn't found a way back to them.

Flirtation was the rule of the day. The softness of the air encouraged sensuality. The cold would return, to be followed by the torrential rains of Marche, but today the earth smelled open and fresh as spring. George's heart turned toward Glennys, who had left on a night of bitterest cold. His memory of her thawed and then melted, and was replaced by the picture of her riding past on horseback, her throat turned to the sun. Glennys hated the cold so much! Lark faded into nothingness.

He bargained over a tiny but exquisite wreath threaded with ribbon roses and crystal hearts. He'd give it to Glennys and they'd become friends once again. She'd looked carefree and happy in the parade. Duke Albany had been a false friend to her. She'd forgotten him by now, as he deserved, the swine.

The wreathseller's work was attractive to everyone. He was surrounded by cadets, ladies, King's Daughters, gentlemen. The Duchess Colfax fell to the edge of the group while one of her friends bargained for nine of the wreaths. George also fell back, waiting for the Aristo woman to finish.

He heard the Duchess Colfax's friend say, "The true meaning of the Festival of Hearts has been lost. Now it's only flirtation and worse. Think of our poor King having to bore himself silly with those vapid little girls. They all think their virginity is enough to catch a monarch."

"Catching a monarch in order to be Queen depends upon virginity," the Duchess Colfax said. Her eyes never strayed far from the dais where Leon was surrounded by thirty contenders, none of whom was older than eighteen. Graciously he gave his attention to them all, one at a time, or all together. He showed no sign of boredom that George could detect.

The Duchess Colfax was far along in pregnancy, but even so, in the false spring, George felt a stir of desire when he looked at her proud walk. Her beauty was strong enough to capture a king, but only a king was strong enough not to be burned to cinders by it, and by what her beauty enveloped, he thought.

The gossips said that she and Leon had been in love since he'd first seen her. When Leon's Queen died bearing his second son, the Duchess Colfax went to him and had stayed at his side ever since, as securely as though she were the Queen. But she wasn't Queen, and never could be, not even if the Duke died. And, said the gossips, Leon's councilors were pressuring him to give Nolan a proper Queen. This year's Rose Queen might have the opportunity to manipulate her honor into becoming Queen of Nolan.

George realized how this day must make the Duchess Colfax suffer. But she smiled and her words were light.

Those behind the velvet ropes were so busy eating, drinking, flirting, and laying wagers on whom King Leon would choose that they noticed the other audience not at all. But the performers did.

Cayetana ran back to the performers' tent after doing a simplified solo from *The Magnificent Lovers*. She was sweating, but not from exertion. The crowd's mood was turning ugly.

"I won't go out again," she declared. "Some artists and country families in front applauding don't make an audience, not with so many of another kind behind them."

"If you don't go back and do your solo after the *Garlands From the Heart* dance, you'll be in breach of contract," warned August Gardel.

"Those people aren't an audience! They're a mob," Cayetana said.

"You must dance. It's part of your contract to perform during Uncommon Days in Velvet Ridge Park," said Gardel, his administrator's mind incapable of understanding what Cayetana was saying.

"I've dressed as you decreed. All day I've frozen my *coño* for my contract. But I'll not risk my life. Have you ever been caught in a hunger riot, Señor Gardel?"

"If you don't perform your solo I'll suspend you without salary for the entire spring season."

Cayetana narrowed her eyes. She spoke quietly. "Real trouble is about to chew that *culo gordo* of yours, Gardel." She tossed her hair over her shoulders, turned her back and began to take off her dancing costume, exhibiting her own magnificent *culo* to his disinterested eyes. "I am going home, and so should you."

The ballet director snatched her crimson velvet costume. "I'll give this to Rowena in the corps de ballet. She can dance your solo. You'll regret this insubordination, Cayetana.'' He exited the performers' tent.

"And where will you find another First Dancer for the season that begins tonight, eh Gardel? You going to get Gemma to dance? The cow? With her big belly?"

"Whoever dances tonight, Caya, it won't be you. I'll wager a hundred gold forients on it," Gardel said.

"*Puedes chupar mi verga*, Gardel, and I know you have lots of experience doing that," she hurled at his back from the tent entrance.

Aristo admirers of the Gondolese First Dancer applauded her near-nakedness. They didn't know exactly what her words meant, but knowing Gardel's reputation they had a good idea.

For the moment there was silence behind the dais. The King's speech leading to the coronation had begun. All wagers were frozen now.

". . . and I am sure that all of her worthy peers will agree that no one has embodied more fully what this day means to all of us in Nolan. We are all truly related. I crown Sharissa Ely, of Blue Fields, in Yemmessee County, Rose Queen!"

A daughter of an Aristo old bloodline, a Spur, not a Wheel, got the prize!

The corps de ballet hurried past to enter the staging area. The dancers, attached to their gelding partners by flower garlands, began the Heart Dance around the newly crowned Rose Queen. George raced after them. Glennys would be standing at the entrance and wouldn't have anything to do right now. This was the time to give her the wreath.

The applause given to the corps de ballet's entrance was cut off by a roar.

Glennys and the trainers hadn't been in a position to see the audience gathered in front of the dais of the King of Hearts until the Heart Dance was to begin. When they saw the mob pushing forward their faces blanched. Behind the first few rows of commoner-gentles, the sanded width of the Straightaway was packed by ragged, dirty men, women, and children.

"Bread, not whores!"

"Where is our food?"

"Take the horses! They have silver shoes!"

At the first cry of "Bread, not whores" the ballerinas wisely dropped the garland leads to the geldings' headstalls and exited faster than they'd ever left the Theater after a long night of work.

The families who'd thought they'd been lucky to get places up front were panicking now. The mass was surging against them full and strong.

Before King Leon could give an order, the first line of the audience was shoved into the staging area. The velvet ropes, whose only power was that of common consent, gave way. The front line sprawled over the carpets laid on the sand. Those behind fell over them. Families and friends were forced apart, and then lost to each other.

The King's Guards leaped to their war horses to stand between the mass and the throne, but the cadet drill team from the Equine Academy, still mounted, beat the King's Guards to stand between their lord and chaos.

Leon bellowed, "Cadets, dismount, leave way for the Guards! Sharissa Ely, to me, to me here at the stairs! Help her, Guards!"

The stage geldings reared and plunged, confused and lost without music and their dancers' signals. Sharissa was trapped in the center of the barricade of flailing hooves.

Many in the mob were mere boys. Some were men gaunt as winter wolves. A momentary hush came over them, then an inarticulate growl rumbled towards the front. Wooden clogs, the heaviest missiles at hand, were flung at the horses, and at anyone who looked well fed and warmly dressed. The hunger storm broke.

The Queen's Yard people were caught in it while they tried to reach their geldings. The King's councilors weren't allowing him to rescue Sharissa, but they weren't able to reach her either.

Glennys flowed along the familiar currents connecting her to the geldings, seeking the one who could best help her reach Sharissa. She found Cognac, the elderly, crotchety gelding, and grabbed his flowered line. Her fingers found his ribboned headstall, and she vaulted to his back. Cognac wasn't frightened or filled with panic. He was enraged. This wasn't how a performance was supposed to be.

Profoundly insulted that his well-practiced routines had been disturbed, he kicked out and bit. He shoved against the crowd that was so inexperienced it didn't know enough to leave him room. Instinctively much of what he did was what war horse training honed and reinforced. Glennys encouraged him and pushed forward to the place where she'd last seen the Rose Queen standing. Baron was right with them. He threw his weight and jaws into cutting them through the crowd. He liked this.

Glennys caught sight of a round white arm, still adorned with flowers. Two grinning men were grabbing at Sharissa's breasts.

The Rose Queen ripped off her crown and jabbed the thorns at the men's eyes.

"Baron, strike!" Glennys ordered, her hand signal telling him the target. Baron hit the two men low. His jaws slashed at their calves, and then he was away before they could touch him. Glennys pulled Sharissa with a shoulder-wrenching heave against Cognac.

As the daughter of a stallion-breeding Spur line, Sharissa didn't need to be told what to do. She yanked up her skirts, caught Glennys's hand, used the outstretched foot as a mounting block, and hopped up behind Glennys on Cognac's back. She hung on to the Rose Crown with its long, sharp thorns.

They saw the Duchess holding her gravid belly, running up the throne dais's back stairs. The King was standing on the throne giving orders to his Guards, while lords and other Guards stood behind him.

The Duchess Colfax screamed, "Fall, Leon! Drop to the ground!"

And Sharissa screamed in Glennys's ear. "The King, the King! Someone's killing the King!"

The King's body, long used to instantly gratifying any wish embodied in Duchess Colfax's voice, dropped to the boards. The knife in the hand of a uniformed Guard ripped the air where the King's lungs had been a moment ago. The Guard toppled and bled bright scarlet himself as Baron Stogar pulled his own dagger free from the assassin's back.

Cognac bucked and kicked and bit, his dignity outraged in every way. But the clearing made by his hooves and Baron's jaws had filled up, and they were pressed hard all around.

Blades that were thin and straight, blades curved and wide, blades short, blades long, darted at Glennys, at Sharissa, at Cognac. Sharissa whipped wildly all around and in back of them with her thorned wreath, from which yet a silk heart dangled. Glennys mercilessly used Cognac as a shield, making him lean away from their attackers, keeping him moving as fast as possible.

The mounted Guards plunged into the mob at all points. Their lashes, lances, and war horses loosened the cohesiveness of tangled bodies, and broke it into parts. Aristos who'd gotten to their own horses galloped through the Park to prevent the riot spreading into the city.

A small group of Aristos had made a wedge, the point headed

for Cognac. "It's daddy and my brothers," Sharissa squealed into Glennys's ear. "They're coming for us!"

Right next to Baron Ely at the point was Duke Albany. The Duke guided his horse by knees alone. A short sword was in one hand and a whip in another. His eyebrows were raised in his usual expression of faint quizzicality. He was as cool as when walking the floor of his house. The lash of his long whip snapped in a steady rhythm, wrapping around the necks of blade-wielders.

After Glennys was safely behind the King of Hearts' dais she pulled herself out of Cognac. Waves of delayed fear washed through her, along with hatred for those people out there who had tried to kill her. But underneath the fear and hatred she also felt a sympathy for them. A few people had too great a share of the world's goods and far too many had nothing. Where did she fit in?

Glennys slid off Cognac, leaving a trail of blood behind her. Sharissa had been better protected by her many layers of skirts woven with silver and gold threads. Baron's chest was raw meat and his muzzle slashed. The old gelding had been hit by knives in a dozen places. He snapped at her, for his life had been so upset in the last few minutes he no longer trusted anyone. His muscles were already stiffening. He was too old for the abrupt strain of violent kicking and striking, when all his conditioning had been for graceful movement.

After going over him, Glennys said, "This horse will never work again."

"Then he'll have honorable retirement, like our tired-out stud stallions do, down on Blue Fields," promised the Baroness Ely. "Oh, darlin'," she said to Sharissa, helping her to the ground, "I'm so proud of how you behaved out there, I could burst. Your daddy knew you were safe, so he and the boys are gone to ring in the rabble. I declare, now that you're out of the way, your brothers are havin' the time of their life."

Sharissa clutched her mother. "Did you see? Someone tried to kill the King! And Stogar saved him."

Duke Albany joined them with bandages ripped from petticoats and a bottle of wine to cleanse the wounds of those who'd rescued Sharissa. "It was the Duchess Colfax who saved Leon," he contradicted gently. "Too bad that Stogar struck so accurately so fast. Now we'll never know why a King's Guard became a King's assassin."

Baroness Ely looked sharply at her old friend. "Still as acute in the wits as ever, I see."

* * *

Under Duchess Colfax's direction a makeshift field hospital
was set up. The slender wands that supported the tribal pennants
were pulled out of the ground and broken into splints. Mantles,
shawls, and overskirts were donated as stretchers for the gentry.

By unspoken consent the gay red-and-white-striped bunting
remained fluttering bravely in the breeze.

The Duchess Colfax looked out onto the Straightaway at the
flash of white light that was Leon's stallion. Then, over all the
other noise, she was heard shouting. "Why aren't you riding as
shield to your brother's back?"

"I have no horse," Roald stammered from within his open
carriage where he'd retreated.

"A horse is not what you're lacking, I think," she snapped
pointedly.

Roald glared at her, his face splotched with angry red.

Glennys found the Queen's Yard people by the performers'
tent. The attempted assassination was the main subject of discussion until Joss Thack joined them.

"Bad luck," he swore. "Vanity was gutted. Champagne
hamstrung. I had to give him the death stroke myself. Flotsam
and Jetsam have disappeared with no trace. Maybe someone's
eating them somewhere," he said sadly.

George sat on a cushion taken from the Queen's Opera Ballet
tent, a bit above his friends so he could see all the action. The
Romantics drank wine steadily while he filled the pages of his
sketchbook.

Albany strolled over, squatted next to him, and observed
George's work. Albany was an old, old man, but his body seemed
impervious to the ravages of age. He was vigorous, and ele-
gantly handsome, and his hair was thickly abundant, George
thought enviously.

"Why aren't you with your peers?" George asked sourly.
"Big sport hunting down folk who've got nothing."

"I have no interest in punishing a mob set off by others who
were paid to incite it," the Duke replied mildly. "Whoever was
responsible has interests that I don't share."

George warmed to the Duke's notice of him, even though he
understood that was Albany's intention. He offered the Duke his
wine. Before drinking Albany said, "We're all related."

George's friends were sitting with open-mouthed amazement
watching. The Duke's notice was raising his prestige, George
thought.

The young man and the old watched Glennys moving about the geldings with the Queen's Yard people. Through the talk of the missing, injured, and dead horses was the shocked discussion of the attempted assassination.

One of the King's own had tried to kill him. Others had wanted to murder Leon because they had nothing to eat. Two seemingly unrelated impulses had come together for reasons no one could puzzle out. What could the penniless underclass have in common with a King's Guard to make a conspiracy?

The knife wound on Glennys's thigh broke red through the bandage. George leaped to his feet, but Albany restrained him. Lenkert Deerhorn caught Glennys before her leg gave out from under her. Gustave, the big gray and scarlet parrot, fluttered to Deerhorn's shoulder. The Duke's man put the parrot's perch under Glennys's arm as an improvised crutch.

The Duke said to George, "Miss Eve has a destiny much higher than the scramble of an artist's life." He gave George back the wine. George knew he'd been dismissed. He got up from his cushion and walked away.

George buried the little heart wreath he'd bought for Glennys behind the performers' tent.

As she was conducted to George's vacated cushion, Glennys began to weep. "Horse Skiller," said Albany gently, "everybody's disaster is somebody's good luck. One day you'll be old enough to understand that."

"How dare I cry about horses when children and their mothers have nowhere to live? How can I want to spend my life dancing even if this stupid leg of mine heals true enough for me to dance?" she questioned passionately. "People are dying in the richest spot in Nolan because they have nothing to eat. Explain that to me!" Glennys demanded.

"Listen to me," said Duke Albany. "You can have your chance on stage, and use your Horse Sense too, to help far more people than you did today, but you'll have to listen to me."

Glennys made an impatient, dismissive movement.

"Your luck," Duke Albany said, "was strong enough to keep Stogar from *your* back. Your rescue of Sharissa was worthy of a Stallion Queen. You can accomplish a great deal if you follow the path I've laid out and accept my protection."

He was making her an offer of concubinage, at this time and in this place. How dare he, Glennys thought first, jolted out of her previous train of thought. A King's Daughter deserved a more lovely wooing than this. But she knew she'd accept.

"I am most honored to accept your offer," she said cooly.

The Duchess Colfax, the Ely ladies, Joss Thack, and a ballad group came over to them. The Duchess examined closely the bloodstained girl and her injured bristlehair mastiff. When she saw Duke Albany's hand placed possessively on Glennys's shoulder, the suspicious glint went out of the Duchess's eyes.

She spoke in her most gracious, charming manner. "I have a message from Leon. He remembers you and your dog from a meeting some months ago in Irongate Yard. When your leg allows, you are to join the Queen's Opera Ballet Company, since you'd told him that was your fondest desire. And further, he'd be most honored for you to attend tonight's Midnight Ball, and hear 'The Rose Queen's Rescue,' which these balladeers will compose for the occasion."

"How wonderful," Sharissa cried. "You'll be able to see me dance with the King!"

An expression flitted over Duchess Colfax's face that suggested she, at least, would have been most happy if the Rose Queen had been left to the devices of the mob.

The Stalking Horse

• Act III •

· Fifteen ·

THE OFF REAR wheel on the Jerick Brothers' private coach jolted up and out of another hole winter had opened in the King's Road. No sooner was the rear wheel out than the near front wheel fell into a deeper one.

The three passengers inside had given up apologizing to each other on the first day, even when they ended up in each other's laps. Four days and nights, with only brief stops while the horses were changed, had left courtesies behind. The rattling of the coach, the screeching of the wheels, and the horn blowing at each hamlet and post house had left them nearly deaf anyway.

Bones, bones, bones, Thea thought. I'm not Thea Bohn anymore, only one miserable aching bone.

Thea bounced against the well-padded body of Dorn Jerick, the youngest brother and the only Jerick traveling in the coach. The Jerick Brothers Textile House had sent him to find out the truth about the rumors coming out of Drake, and he'd been kind enough to take her along.

The one piece of information everybody knew was true was that a gunpowder works in Drake owned by Baron Stogar had exploded. Thea had been called by her Alaminite brethren to give her healing skills to the many burned and injured.

Who the other passenger was, it seemed not even Dorn knew, other than his name—Volstead Gridban. Whatever he'd said to the older Jerick brothers had been sufficient to commandeer a place in the Jerick coach.

Volstead's body was hard and lean, and, though polite enough, he kept to himself.

The jolting gradually stopped, and the coach came to a halt. Volstead Gridban untied the leather covering over the window on his side. The air was freezing but the fresh draught was welcome.

"By the deuce, it's still winter up here," he said.

He leaned out the window, and craned his neck to see whatever it was that had been responsible for the stop.

"The under-coachman and the postilion are out with the lamps. Some sort of obstruction on the road," Volstead said.

Dorn Jerick peered out of his window in turn. "We're not far from Drake, though. I can smell it—the smell of money, but much fainter than it should be. It must be true; the other factory hands have joined with the Alaminites from the gunpowder works and shut down the mills. No wonder we can't get finished goods from Drake. Bloody Lighters," Jerick grumbled.

Thea shifted uncomfortably on the opposite seat that the two men had gallantly given to her alone. "I think it was the flood of untrained, unfit, sick, and starving folks from St. Lucien that caused the shutdown," she said softly.

Dorn Jerick repeated what Wheels had said many times in the aftermath of the Festival of Hearts Hunger Riot.

"They'd lost their old way of life. They had no work and no place. They starved in our faces no matter what we did. They'd made St. Lucien unpleasant and dangerous. It was a generous solution to parcel them out up here among the factories and down south to the fields and plantations. In the old days they'd all have been impaled!" he declared.

The untrained farmers brought to work in the factories and mills had lowered the wages of the older, more experienced hands, and, as those workers had warned, had endangered everyone's lives. The Alaminites, who had handled until then the dangerous delicate operations in Baron Stogar's ammunition works, had led the protest. The explosion they'd prophesied came to pass.

Thea wondered if she might be able to help in some way to clear the obstacle in the road. In the darkness of the coach she heard Volstead Gridban moving about. He must be going to help, she thought, though, somehow, she wouldn't have expected it from him.

Before she could act on her thoughts the coach doors on both sides were torn open.

"Hands over your heads! Everyone out! Now!"

Thea and Dorn Jerick blinked like fools in the sudden brightness of lantern light.

Volstead Gridban dived out his side of the coach, rolled over his shoulders, and came up standing, a whip-thin rapier in one hand, a wicked throwing knife in the other.

"Don't close with him; pour your light into his eyes!"

The pulse in Thea's throat beat madly. She knew that voice all too well. It was the voice of Hans Rigg.

She was pulled rudely out of the coach and shoved into the frost-bitten grass at the side of the road.

Thea heard hoarse breathing and saw, flickering in the lamp-light, the masked figures of young, brawny men.

They were laughing.

"I recognize your voice, Hans Rigg," Volstead's words were cool and steady. "I remember it from the Hunger Riot. For your own sake, call off your men. Otherwise I'll surely get two of you before you murder me."

Hans said, "We've got flintlocks and pistols and we know how to use them. Guns don't take years of practice like your Aristo blades."

A bubbling scream followed immediately after Hans's words.

"The fornicating heathen's knife got Daniel in the throat!"

There was a crack, sharper than a bullwhip. Under it was a roar, something like the lingering roll of a thunderbolt.

It had happened too fast for Thea to take in.

"Don't kill me too! I can pay," Dorn cried rapidly, his voice trembling. "He was forced on me, I didn't want to bring him. I brought one of your own at no expense. She's come to help you!"

Thea got up from her knees. Unthinking habit made her brush at her skirts with her ungloved hands. A lantern was trained on her, and she saw her hands were blackened from the soot that for thirty years had fallen out from Drake's smokes onto the surrounding countryside.

"Don't murder him too, Hans, or the others. Take him and his coach drivers with you into Drake," Thea begged.

Hans Rigg stepped out of the darkness.

"Thea, I knew you'd come when we called, but what are you doing in this company—with a Wheel master and an Aristo spy?"

"How else should I have answered the call in the shortest time possible?" she asked.

He reached to embrace her with the intention of putting the Alaminite kiss of peace on her lips. Thea stepped back.

"I won't take the kiss of peace from a murderer," she said.

Hans Rigg's men had opened the boot of the coach. Hans looked through the luggage until he found a small case which he broke open against the milestone. The contents were nothing but tattered old clothes, of the sort worn by factory workers.

"He *was* coming to spy on us. It was no murder we did, Thea. He was a spy from the Office of Inquiry. They've closed Drake so no food can get in. They wanted him to search out our private, secret ways, to take away the little liberty we have left. Then the masters never need negotiate with us at all," Hans said.

Abruptly Hans made his decision. "Butcher the horses and dispose of the coach. Let the drivers and postilions walk back up the road. We'll spare their lives because they're only stooges for the Wheels. And we'll take their master into Drake with us, to share our way of life."

He hoisted Thea's trunk on his own shoulder. "Come, follow me."

The lanterns were dimmed. They stumbled over the icebroken fields, gritty with cinders, black with soot, perilous with roots and stumps of the woods that once stood there. The trees had long since been cut down to feed the cooking fires of the mill laborers. Now there were none.

The party stopped in a pile of broken, jagged stones. Hans stamped hard three times.

A trap door swung up. The barrel of a flintlock pointed at them.

"The Rain Shadow Mountains," Hans said.

"The Millennium," the watchman replied.

"The City of God on Earth," Hans said.

It was a tunnel that had been dug under a dry streambed that ran under the walls of Drake. The water had been diverted many years ago to feed a mill wheel. They came out into the darkness of Drake on the other side of a rusting grate.

The smell of cats was overpowering. The bones of dogs and other refuse were underfoot. They followed the old water channel until it merged with one of the gutters that made the central part of each street, lane, and alley in the tortuous sprawl where Drake's workers lived. Every kind of slops were thrown into the gutters. Dorn Jerick gagged, barely holding back the bile that welled up in his throat from such unaccustomed filth.

"Is the smell too strong for you, Mr. Wheel? It would be worse if the winter hadn't been so dry," Hans said impatiently. "Keep moving."

The bitter black frost held Drake firmly in its talons. The sharp east wind whistled and whooshed like ghosts keening in the tenement entryways. The dust was like powder ice, and their faces burned as the wind blew the particles against them.

It was midnight, but here and there women labored to break the ice on pools and puddles so they could melt it into water. Because of the dry winter, the only free water was that of the poisoned Devil's Falls River. Most of the city's wells had failed, or were too contaminated to use.

Soot hung down in festoons from the roofs and filled the cracks of the old brick buildings. Garbage had raised the street levels several feet above the original plot.

Thea expected they'd finally reach a spot where the air was clearer, cleaner. Hope sprang up at each corner. But when the corner was turned, as they came out into another dirty square, it was no better.

Under a rotting bracket, supporting a flume of burning pitch, Hans suddenly stopped. He grasped Thea's hand.

"Surely you see the Light now. Drake is the sure revelation of Millennium. The merchants of these things that are made in her, that make them rich, stand afar off weeping and wailing, for her riches are made no more, and no man buys their merchandise anymore."

The Prophet of the Millenium led her into the Alaminite quarter of Drake.

The air was as dirty where the Alaminites lived as it was in the rest of Drake, but nothing else was.

The Alaminites lived better than the other workers of Drake because they shared their Prophet's vision. They worked for a purpose beyond keeping their bodies alive. Their families and their community were still in place. They had their kirk, their deacons, their elders, and their Reverends. Until the closing of Drake, food had come in from the congregations in Soudaka County, so they hadn't had to spend so much of their wages at the inflated city prices. Those with multiple wives could leave one wife out of the factories to cook and clean and mind the youngest children. Their garbage went to feed pigs and chickens penned in the courtyards. Their slops were carried outside the Alaminite quarter.

All around her Thea saw the strength, the real good, of her people and their shared belief. But with her was Hans, and his vision of the Millennium which would burn the heathen and the heretic, and who did murder in Alam's name. That, too, had come out of the belief of her people.

Men Thea knew, men who'd sat her on their knees while they talked with her father and older brothers back home in Soudaka County, greeted her kindly. Women she knew, from charity visits and the kitchen work at Gatherins, surrounded her. They commiserated with her weariness. They blessed her for coming.

She accepted the bed they'd made for her only after she extracted a promise that she'd be awakened at the first light of morning.

She rose before anyone came for her. She looked around the tiny room she had slept in. The floor was canted. The ceiling was low, but freshly replastered. A neat curtain, embroidered with the first simple patterns all the girls were taught, filtered the first rays of the sun. Morning was the only time of day that light could reach in, she realized.

When she got out of bed a small, braided rug of rags was under her feet. Her things were on the floor at the foot of the bed, next to a clean slop bucket. A basin, soap, and towels had been placed on a narrow clothes chest. There was a big pitcher of water, and a bucket filled to the brim with clear, clean water.

There was no mirror.

She washed and put on a clean head scarf. After she made up the bed, she knelt next to it on the rag rug to pray.

She asked Alam many questions this morning. She concluded her prayers with requests for an endless store of patience and compassion, and for strength to do the work God called her to do.

Thea forgot everything but the awful need that was about to call on her tiny powers. She forgot that the Spurs and the Wheels were the masters who caused misery, and that they were heathen. She forgot Hans and the murder, and the madness of his Millennial prophecies and the faith that so many of her people had in the prophecies.

She thought only of what the teachers in the Fortune House in St. Lucien had taught her. One by one she named to herself the properties of what she'd brought with her in the big trunk that Hans had carried so easily on his shoulder.

There was fresh bark of alder, since the leaves weren't to be had in winter. She had ointments made from the flowers of pettimug. The dried and powdered pettimug was an essential ingredient of a decoction that helped heal from the inside. Burdock leaves bruised and mixed with the white of egg relieved pain. The leaves added to hog's lard, nitre and vinegar kept putrescence from spreading. Endive seeds made a tonic that cooled fevers. She had dried bark, leaves, flowers, and berries of the dwarf elder. She had dead nettle in all its varieties, yellow, red, and white. There was willow bark, and bark and leaves of the elm.

With her mind cleared of everything but her materials she began to be filled with the light of Alam. Her fingers tingled. She was ready to do what was in her power to do.

Thea didn't hear the knock on her door.

A young woman by the name of Judith, who'd married out of the Kolkiss family into that of the Fenskers, boldly entered though there'd been no answer to her knock. She carried a baby on one arm, another in her belly, and a big cup of bitterberry in the other hand. A small boy, not older than two, hung on her skirts.

Her eyes, the pupils of which seemed to fill the irises, opened even wider. Judith saw Thea kneeling, a pure white nimbus of light playing about her body.

She backed down the passageway to the kitchen.

"Come and see! Thea Bohn's talkin' to the Lord just like Reverend Tuescher or anybody! Come quick," she cried. "It's more than wonderful."

But Thea appeared at her shoulder. She served herself out of the big pot of oatmeal on the hearth, and sat down with the other women at their table. With a look of reverence Thea didn't understand, Judith came forward with the cup of bitterberry.

Thea behaved as modestly as any good, childbearing Alaminite woman, for all that her waist was still slender and her back straight. The only questions she had concerned the injured.

"We put all our hurt ones into the kirk," Judith said. "Once it was a wool goods storehouse, until it was given up. But we've made it the house of Alam."

Puzzled, Thea said, "I know a storehouse must be big, but surely not big enough for everyone who was hurt in the explosion. Where are the rest?" she asked.

Judith said, "We gathered in our own. The heathen ain't our burden. They were the ones made the blow-up, with their clumsy, shaky hands. There were more of them there than us when Devil Stogar's old works went up. Most of 'em died right off." Judith's satisfaction was great.

Thea felt a dimming of the radiance that filled her.

"Water seems to be a problem," Thea said. "We need huge amounts of clean water, boiled and strained, and boiled again. Where can we get it?" she asked.

"We got water. We got a good well in our quarter, and we guard it so the heathen don't steal what's ours," Judith volunteered again.

Thea felt another wavering in the radiance that buoyed her strength and spirit.

"I'd like to go now to the injured before all the benefit of prayer has left me," she said softly.

She followed a young man carrying her chest out of the kitchen to the front of the six-floor tenement. She carried a case of instruments. Forged out of silver and steel, the contents were more expensive than anything she'd ever known an Alaminite woman to own. She blew a silent breath of gratitude to her father in Dephi for giving her the money.

Before they crossed the threshold of the front door, Thea heard her patients in the kirk across the street.

· Sixteen ·

THEA'S SENSE OF time had begun to unravel during her four-day-and-night journey to Drake. Soon after she began ministering to the Gatherin of burned and broken ammunition workers in the Alaminite kirk, she went out of time all together.

So much precious time had gone by since the explosion. Many had died who might have been saved. Others were dying now, who might have lived if they'd been treated earlier.

Alaminite women were cleanly, but they didn't know about boiling water to cleanse the open injuries. They didn't understand that burns shouldn't be wrapped closely.

She had to tear suppurating bandages off all her patients. Thea painfully picked out every thread of cloth caught in the burns so there'd be nothing around which fresh infection could gather. It was dark in the kirk, and there were few with hands steady enough to hold the light for her. She did this work for an endless time, only too often to find it undone. A wife, a brother, someone had come and tightly rewrapped the burns.

She propped open the doors and pushed open what windows there were, so air could circulate. The good Alaminite housewives came behind her and closed the apertures so that the soot and cinders circulating endlessly through Drake wouldn't dirty the floors and bed covers. Thea couldn't make them understand that fresh air, even dirty fresh air, was better than closing up all the vapors of infection within the kirk.

She'd brought a large supply of opium with her, which hadn't been necessary. Opium was readily available and very cheap in Drake. Alaminites did not approve of its use. Opium was for teething babies at best, and at worst something the heathen laborers used. Again and again Thea argued that opium would allow her worst injured patients to rest. During their sleep, drugged or not, their bodies could gather strength to recover.

Even with all these extra troubles it was whispered that Thea was an angel, just as Hans Rigg had said. So many who'd been thought at death's door didn't cross the threshold.

The gratitude of Drake's congregation didn't prevent the all-too-usual Alaminite rivalries. Every patient's jealous relatives believed she shortchanged her attention to their charges in favor of someone else. And none of them could see any reason why she wasted so much valuable time writing about each patient in her record book.

The women watched her narrowly to see which patients she grieved over losing the most. Thea had to hold back all her sorrow and not show any.

She slept in snatches on a pallet in the kirk. Knowing her people, she also pitched in with cooking and hauling water, so the other women would have no reason to accuse her of being above herself and too good to do the woman's burden ordained by the Lord.

One morning, very early, when Thea had forgotten what it was to sleep, she went to fetch water straight after a death. Judith was with her, as she was any time Thea wasn't engaged with the injured.

The stones of the little square were cold and gritty with cinders. But there was a breath of rejuvenation coming up from the south. Spring was coming even to the grim life of Drake.

"What is that sound I hear?" Thea asked.

"I don't hear anything," Judith said sullenly, turning her head away.

"But I do! It's coming up from all the lanes leading into our well square." Thea dropped her buckets. She put off the hands that tried to hold her back.

"Thea, leave it be," Judith pouted. "It's only the heathen, wanting water from our well."

The grief that Thea had held back for so many dead turned to anger.

"I cannot abide this congregational selfishness one more day," Thea cried passionately. "If I have to carry every drop of water myself in my own two hands, they shall have it."

She marched up the lane. "Give me what you have to carry water," she demanded of the ragged group huddling outside the square.

Two battered pails were thrust at her by dirty, broken-nailed hands. Back at the well she put down the first pail on the chain, turning the winch by herself. She repeated the action and carried the pails to the women who waited, and to two more.

This time the two Alaminite brethren guarding the well tried to refuse her.

"Brother Neffer, Brother Smalt, if you won't allow the No-lanese to have water from this well, we won't have it either. Any time one of us pulls up a bucket, I will kick it over."

The heathen were allowed to use the well.

After that morning, Thea parceled out her time between her people and the Nolanese who'd been hurt in the explosion.

Hans Rigg backed Thea, much to her surprise. Soon she learned why. Whatever cellar, whatever damp room that Thea went to, he and his Prophets visited soon after. They brought a morsel of food from the dwindling Alaminite stores. After presenting the precious gift, they'd sit and talk with the beaten-down evicted farmers from central Nolan. Soon the prophets were testifying for Alam and the Light. They told of the burning that was to come for the masters of Drake, the Aristos, and all the heathen of the world. They told how the Alaminites alone would escape the fires of Millennium, for only those with faith in the Lord were chosen to survive.

As the days passed, the little there was to eat became less and less. Thea worked harder.

Thea walked through the silent night streets in blessed soli-tude, away from the Nolanese household where a future Drake hand had been born. Strikes, explosions, sieges, hunger, it didn't matter. Babies had been conceived and they insisted upon com-ing into the world. The baby's father had joined the Alaminite congregation some days ago, at Hans's urging. Even though the mother had died, the man wasn't alone with an infant now.

The moon broke through the cloud scud above Drake the mo-ment before Thea entered the square, now called Lighter Court, where the well was. It had rained all through the long hours the Nolanese woman had suffered in labor. The air smelled good for a change. The skies above Drake had been cleansed, not with fire, but with water, and the factory chimneys had been dead for weeks.

Thea savored her rare privacy, her heart lightening. She looked up at the moon and sighed. The clouds were moving so rapidly it appeared as though the moon were galloping madly over the sky fields. She remembered that wild ride behind Glennys Eve on the seashore of St. Lucien.

Her nose caught the scent of growing things. Boxes of vege-tables that could grow from seed had been placed all over Lighter Court. She recognized the early shoots of lettuce, radishes, and carrots. The Court had been scrubbed clean of ash and soot.

Thea's heart swelled with renewed affection for her people. Unlike the rest of Drake's idle working force, the Alaminites had used this time outside the factories to improve their quarter. No matter what happened, an Alaminite would never stop working.

A rickety ladder leaned against a wall. Thea sat on the bottom rung and threw back her head to the sky. The overhanging building, old and skewed on its foundation, put her in shadow but she could see the moon perfectly.

She heard a baby cry.

Judith, carrying her infant, her pregnant womb round as the moon, came into Lighter Court. She moved over the flagstones slowly, as though drifting in a dream.

Careful of the baby, Judith lowered herself to sit on an upturned bucket, her back braced against the well. Out of her clothes she took a little pot. Judith opened her bodice and took out her breasts.

She anointed a nipple with what she had in the pot and lifted her baby to the nipple. The baby's wailing stopped.

Unaware she wasn't alone, Judith dreamily circled the other nipple, coating it with opium from the pot. She licked her fingers clean and nestled her baby closer to her.

"You've no more milk?" Thea asked quietly.

Judith turned her head slowly on her soft, white neck that glimmered between the strands of her hair.

"It's you, then. No, no milk, not for so long, now that another's coming. But when the one inside comes out, I'll have enough for them both."

Dreamily Judith added, "I had more milk with my first than he could drink. It was all those sheep Fensker's dad gave us, and my grandma's garden."

She swayed from side to side, rocking her baby.

"Fensker, my man, he was the first to die after the explosion, before you got here. I was able to stay home, you know, while he worked. I guess I'll be a hand now when the strike's over and they let us go back to work." Two tears slipped down her cheeks.

Thea asked, "Why are you out on the streets at this time of night?"

Judith's eyelashes fluttered slightly as she gave Thea a sideways look, as if to remind herself that she truly wasn't by herself.

She pouted. "I was following the pale horse of the masters.

I heard him clattering over the stones. The horse comes out at night and licks the breath of little children with his long white tongue. I saw him bend his bony knees and kneel on the breasts of our men all winter before the strike. They cough, and then the pale horse comes so they can't catch their breath. I saw him go into the kirk, but he came out fast this night. You've done your work too well for him to get what he wants there now. He's getting plenty tonight, just the same. I followed him and he went among the heathen."

The baby licked and sucked avidly at her nipple.

"Do you remember when we all were at kirk and Queen's schools together?" Judith asked.

"I don't think anyone ever forgets their childhood," Thea said. She felt as if everything had slowed down. She didn't even feel hungry. "Schoolmaster Muran gave it hot and heavy to the boys who couldn't read and Reverend Tuescher did the same to the boys and girls alike when we didn't know our catechism."

Judith shifted one of her shoulders, and the baby lost the nipple. She guided it back into his mouth. "I meant, Thea, do you remember me from those days?"

"There weren't that many of us in Dephi's kirk school and the old Queen's school that I could forget you," Thea said.

Judith looked at the healer slyly. "You didn't remember it was me who went to school with you. I could see that right off. But I bet you remember that witch Stella's oldest girl, Glennys, and she left long before we did. Remember how we all followed Glennys and Stella in the Defiance Ceremony with our sticks and they carrying the stones of their sin?"

"I didn't have a stick," Thea said.

"Remember Glennys parading around the County in pants on the old Baron's devil horses?" Judith asked viciously.

Oh, my people, my people, Thea cried to herself.

"That was a long time ago," Thea said gently. "Glennys and Stella have done no harm."

"You've been in St. Lucien. I hear that's where Stella's bitch is, still parading around on horses and showing herself off to anybody. Have you seen her?" Judith asked.

"Yes," Thea said, feeling as though she were in a queer sort of catechism class.

"That Glennys, does she have any children?" Judith asked.

"No," Thea said, adding, "neither do I."

Judith reached down again for the opium pot. She switched

her baby to the other nipple and anointed the one it had been sucking.

"Mother's Mercy, a penny a jar. It makes our poor babies believe their bellies are full." She licked her fingers clean again. Her head nodded over her baby's. She jerked up her chin.

"I feel sorry for Stella's girl, with no children, but she don't deserve to have them. She's never been hungry, any more than Stella's other two brats are now. The get of witches don't hurt in the belly like the righteous's children do. Stella's farm is where I should be living. She never had men-children that live, like I do, even with nothing to eat. She killed the men-children she bore, and ran off my brother with her wickedness, and he was her proper married husband. She dallies with the heathen on the Baron's Three Trees and hangs onto that farm no matter what! You don't see her girls, my cousins, working in the Devil Stogar's factories to burn in fires and starve in strikes! She don't even pay taxes!"

Thea was mesmerized by the intensity of Judith's testifying. It was opium reason, Thea told herself, invented by a girl born into a ne'er-do-well family where the men would rather drink and hunt wild dogs than work. She'd caught Fensker, the youngest son of a better family, but she'd lost him too. For all the malice that the woman had in her, Thea pitied her.

Thea said, "Stella pays very high taxes on her farm. She's able to pay them because Glennys works very hard in St. Lucien and sends her mother money."

Judith roused. "They're all witches, and they'll burn in the Millennium, if not before. I don't see anybody from your family working here in Drake, either."

Thea caught the baby when Judith's eyes dropped shut.

"I'm here," Thea whispered. But Judith never heard.

Back in the house across the street from the kirk the other women found Thea in the kitchen holding Judith's baby. While they poked up the fire they sang an Alaminite hymn, a new one.

There's a City we'll build in the mountains,
A bright shining City of Light.
We'll build it with our holy labor
And defend it with God's deadly might.

In the City of God
The righteous will flower,
The bright shining City of God.

We'll watch the world burn
From the walls of our City,
The bright shining City of God.

While in the darkness our masters lie sleeping
Their dogs and their whores by their side
Our sisters are working and weeping
· O'er the bodies of those who have died.

In the City of God
The righteous will flower
The bright shining City of God.
We'll watch the world burn
From the walls of our City,
The bright shining city of God.

Though in slav'ry the heathen may bind us
And befoul Alam's holy name
Yet rejoice! For the Prophets have promised
They'll all be consumed in the flames.

In the City of God . . .

Oh, my people, my people, Thea thought. The only fires she believed coming were those made by men—the Wheels and Spurs, and the Prophets.

Judith stumbled into the kitchen, disheveled and confused. Her two-year-old son clung to her neck. Over his fair-haired head Judith's dilated eyes darted around the room, searching for her baby.

"Give him to me! I was so afraid the pale horse had stolen him in the night." Judith didn't remember their passage by the well in Lighter Court at all.

In the little room given to Thea off the kitchen, before taking her morning rounds, she gripped the bedcovers while she made her communion with Alam.

There was only a couple of spoonfuls of oatmeal for each of them today, but the strike was almost over, according to the Alaminite representatives that had been holding talks with Baron Stogar and the Wheel masters of Drake. Soon the soot would rain down from the skies over Drake once more. The little box gardens in Lighter Court would sicken and die.

She should stay in Drake. Unless Alam gave her a different direction, it seemed that this was what she'd been called to do with her gift of healing. Hot tears poured down her face. She didn't want to live out her years in this terrible city.

The roses and oaks of St. Lucien filled her inner eye. The sharp, wicked repartee of the Seahorse Tavern filled her inner ears.

The Light of Alam didn't come to her now. She'd used it all to save the bodies of her people. There was nothing left. Was this what it was to be a heretic, Thea wondered.

The bustle in the kitchen turned into pandemonium.

"Alam save us!" a woman's voice shrieked. "The Devil Stogar has brought cannon from the King's foundry in Newport. The masters are going to shell the walls!"

· Seventeen ·

STOGAR FULK, BARON of Soudaka County, was the cavalry chief Colonel Acker was pledged to follow into war. The origins of the pledge were a tangle of breeding and alliances that reached back to the dark years of the Saquave Desert and the Crossing over the Rain Shadow Mountains into Nolan a thousand years before.

But Colonel Acker saw himself as an individual as well, with the right to choose the depth of his loyalty. During the last campaign, before the old Baron Fulk had been—removed—the qualities of the Fulk heir had seized Acker's imagination and claimed his devotion.

Like most of his blood and rank, Acker was an enthusiast of the stage. He saw cannon emplacements point at the walls of Drake and thought of a curtain rising. Stogar was the director and also the principal player. Stogar's star was in the ascendant, and Acker would rise with him.

The King's Road outside Drake was jammed with brightly enameled carriages spilling the plumage of the Wheel ladies and Aristo concubines who'd come as audience to Stogar's performance. Among them was the ornate gilded equipage of Prince Roald. King Leon's absence was noted variously with approval, curiosity, or disappointment.

Elliot Drake, Chief of the Bank of Drake, sat proudly on horseback, next to the Aristo splendor of Duke Colfax. Elliot felt level for the first time with the old bloodlines. He was the essential element in the show. For all Stogar's grandstanding, he had no money to speak of. Elliot had generously opened his bank's coffers to finance Stogar's Works.

The banker watched with pleasure as his brother, Nathan Drake, the Blood Chief of Nolan's cavalry, rode his big sorrel stallion slowly about the rotten brick walls that confined the workers. Stogar's cannon were aimed as directly at Nathan's prestige as they were at Drake's walls. It was a prestige that had never been given to the banker brother, who'd financed the other's education at the Equine Academy. This morning's events would begin to change all that. Money was more powerful than warrior skills and heroics.

The light wind ruffled the manes of the war stallions that moved restively under stony-faced Guards and cavalry. The audience was becoming restive as well. Acker shifted his grip on the black banner of the Fulk barony stamped with the gold emblem of Three Trees. His black stallion pawed the surface of the Road.

It got so quiet Acker could hear the rustle of what was confined in the wicker chest fastened behind his saddle. As if on cue, Stogar made his appearance, mounted on a white stallion named Cannonball.

At a sign from his Baron, Acker joined him. Together they cantered across the wasteland surrounding Drake. Satin and leather, white and black, were the focus of attention. Though Stogar's eyes were cold, his mouth smiled. His face showed no traces that he'd lived in the saddle and barely slept for eighteen days.

"The King's Guards are muttering, Sir. They don't approve of you riding white. White stallions are supposed to be the prerogative of the Eidel throne," Acker told him.

"There's no law that only the King can ride white, or that I must ride black because my sire and grandsires did," Stogar said. "It's a time of changes."

Stogar's fair coloring and his sky-blue embroidered satin coat, as fine as any Drake master's, went well with his white horse. But his knee-high, worn boots and his long-roweled spurs were those of an old bloodline warrior. In his person he declared to Aristos and Wheels the new Nolan.

Stogar dismounted. Acker passed the wicker chest to him and took Cannonball's reins. Acker hoped the white stallion wouldn't bolt at the first detonation.

Acker leaned down and patted Stogar's hindquarters. "You've got the luck, now bring those walls tumblin' down for everyone to see!"

It had been Acker's idea. The Drake laborers' strike provided a dramatic opportunity for a public field test that would increase Stogar's fame.

Behind each cannon mount was a pyramid of cannonballs. Next to the rammer member of the gun crew was the ammunition caisson. Stogar's success depended not on the cannon, but on the charge, which had been manufactured under his direction.

The ready-to-use charge of potassium, nitrate, sulphur, and charcoal had been corned last fall in Drake, then transported down to Newport and stored. The new corning process prevented the elements' separation during the two journeys between the cities, and the wet weather hadn't dampened their firepower. Stogar had tested a little of it early that morning. It had fired.

Behind the center gun, a fourteen-pounder, Stogar opened the caisson. The ball was loaded, the charge put in place.

Every gunnery team turned their eyes to the wicker chest in Stogar's hands. Acker had coached them carefully. It was for effect and for the Fulk luck.

Stogar opened the lid of the wicker chest. A swirl of death's-head butterflies was freed. The black wings with their white skull patterning fluttered all about Stogar. Several of the death's-heads clung for a moment to Stogar's fair braided hair, then circled his uplifted hand.

Burning punk approached the cannons' touchholes. Stogar's arm came down in a short vicious jerk. The cannons fired. Dense white smoke drifted through the air like fog. Out of the gaping holes in the walls of Drake, dirty red dust drifted up and swirled in the wind to twine and conjoin with the smoke.

Cannonball reared under Stogar. The King's Guards and cavalrymen had their hands full trying to control their mounts. The women in the pretty carriages clapped their hands over their ears and shrieked but no one heard them. The carriage horses shoved and plunged in their traces, but were too closely packed to bolt and run. Only Nathan Drake's horse, Quillon, and the horse of his aide Hengst Fulk, stood solidly.

The first battery was followed immediately by the second rank of cannons. Behind them, a third unit was loaded while the first guns were cooled with water. That was the rhythm—load, fire, cool down.

Flames erupted inside the walls of the city. Screaming came out of the tenements hit by cannonballs.

The masters observed from the safety of the road, knowing their mansions on the heights of Drake wouldn't be touched. The factory hands had been warned. If they had been too stubborn to leave their filthy holes, then they were part of the lesson the workers were being taught today.

The firing was kept up until an hour before noon. Pulverized rubble was all that remained of the rotten brick walls and buttresses.

The gunners and foundry engineers, all of them Shoes,

cleaned the bores of the cannon. They swaggered about their work, taunting the young Aristo bloods on their war stallions.

"We've shot you out of the saddle, boys! We're all the same now!"

Nathan Drake, who'd said nothing all morning, touched Quillon with the toe of his boot and rode to the center emplacement. "And what will you do when those behind the walls get their own guns?"

He turned on his saddle and addressed the Fulk cavalrymen. "By the sun and my gut! It's time for dinner. Elliot's got a good table laid for us at Silkwalls. Break ranks and race you there!"

Quillon made a standing leap over the fourteen-pounder's two-wheeled, horse-drawn limber. Nathan galloped Quillon across the front of the gunnery line. Clods of dirt were thrown up by the stallion's hooves against the bodies of the gunnery crews.

The Fulk cavalrymen came tearing after him with whoops. Nathan outranked their Baron, and their Blood Chief had given them an order.

The gunners, their faces sweaty and now black with dirt, threw curses after the riders. Their own noon meal, they realized, would be field rations eaten on the cold ground by their cannon.

The rider last off the mark halted his horse for a moment. He kicked at a rammer's face with his spurred boot.

"Nothing has changed, *Shoe*. We ride and you don't!" the young Aristo gibed. He shot off both of the pistols, with their inlaid silver and fine wood grips, presented by Stogar to his own men.

The colonel of the King's Guards sent his men back to join the ranks protecting the Drake masters' mansions and factories. The courier dispatched to St. Lucien ran his horse around the jam of sightseers on the King's Road. For several furlongs, no matter what the courier did, three death's-head butterflies clung to the message pouch.

The carriage drivers untangled traces and released hooked axles. With or without invitation, everyone on King's Road followed those headed for Silkwalls.

Roald caressed the presentation musket given to him by Baron Stogar. He pressed his cheek continuously against the stock and took aim at imaginary targets among the green buds of the drive. The wheels of his open carriage twirled sweetly over the ground and Stogar, leaning down from his horse, inclined attentively toward the Prince, pretending to listen to his lecture on the use of cannon in siege. Stogar smiled and smiled.

* * *

After the ladies retired from the table in the Silkwalls hall, Elliot Drake stood to salute Stogar. "The Baron's colors are black and gold. The black of his powder, touched by the gold of fire, explodes into white smoke. And whatever stands in our way dissolves into dust. That white smoke will turn Drake into a city of gold! Hail Baron Fulk of Soudaka County and the City of Drake!"

Prince Roald stood up from his place at the head of the table. "On that white smoke my friend Stogar will ride his white stallion to Nolan's greater Dominion! And I wish to be remembered as the first to understand what he's offered us."

The Prince's voice rose in scale. "I will see that the Eidel throne continues to back the cannon foundry in Newport!"

Roald's heavy body stumbled into the edge of the mahogany table. His big hand lost its grasp on the fragile stem of the goblet filled to the brim with wine. His other hand splatted into the setting in front of Elliot Drake. The Prince regained his balance, threw back his lank hair from his wide forehead, and drank from the neck of the wine bottle he grabbed from a waiter's tray.

The men toasted again and the luncheon broke up.

The Drake textile manufacturers had done well out of the strike. Their warehoused stock had been disposed of at inflated prices, while they begged pardon. It was the fault of the hands.

The first step that proved the masters innocent of responsibility for high prices was the execution of the strike leaders. All of them were Lighters, out of the Baron's Soudaka County. That Stogar did not plead on the Alaminites' behalf proved his solidarity, Spur though he was, with the Wheels.

The death floggings paid the merchants for the strike. The floggings paid Duke Colfax for the death of his man, Volstead Gridban, and for the holding hostage of Dorn Jerick. The floggings of the men tied spread-eagle on the triangles were administered by the executioner of the Guards. The deaths were the spectacle that afternoon in the unharmed part of Drake.

As soon as the Alaminite women came to remove the remains, the stones of King's Yard were washed down. Colfax observed Dorn Jerick removing his hat as the litters bearing the dead passed by. The man had lost all of his excess flesh, and the bones of his face were sharp in the afternoon sunlight.

"You punished no one," Dorn said. "The leaders are still free, and they've a remarkable organization," he told Colfax.

Each of the dead had been a volunteer for execution out of

the ranks of Hans Rigg's followers. The first smoke to rise out Drake after the end of the strike was from the burning of Millennium martyrs' bodies.

Close to midnight the Alaminites who'd been chosen to negotiate with Stogar took their leave from the Baron's office at the Ammunition Works.

The office was a place of bleak lamplight and sharp, bare corners. Duke Colfax shifted slightly on the hard chair where he sat. "Do you think it's wise to have given in to the Lighters' demands? We had crushed the strike."

"It's wise to increase production as fast as possible. No one works better than Alaminites. Kick the Lighters and then give them a little, that's the only way to handle them. We kicked them hard today. We've been doing it up in Soudaka for generations." Stogar was loquacious from lack of sleep.

He found a jar of Mule-Kick, the rough spirits distilled by his cook on Three Trees. "This will put some life into us."

Colfax raised one elegant eyebrow. Stogar seldom drank liquor of any kind.

"What a foolish display this morning was," Stogar remarked. He poured the Mule-Kick into clumsy pottery cups. "But all of them—Elliot, the masters, the Prince, the bloody cannoneers—believe it meant a great deal."

Colfax sipped the Mule-Kick. "This stuff is as vile as Richard Thorvald's Esker." After a moment he said, "Nathan Drake knows exactly what the shelling of the walls meant."

"Nathan, no doubt, should be removed," Stogar said. "Another war with Sace-Cothberg would most likely oblige us, since Nathan's so much like my old man—the complete hero warrior, always at the front of his troops and in the thick of the action."

He got up from the barricade of his desk and looked from the broken window to the ground below. By the light of pitch torches, Alaminites labored thick as ants clearing away the debris of the explosion.

"King Leon wasn't removed," Colfax said very softly.

Stogar suddenly kicked out viciously. The four unbroken panes of glass shattered.

"That pet Lighter of my father's has always been bad luck," Stogar said, his teeth grinding away at each other. "I asked you last fall to send her back to Three Trees."

"Pardon me, Fulk," Colfax said coldly. "It was *my* bad luck. My wife was the one that saved Leon's life."

"Leon the hero!" Stogar sneered. "He was ready to throw

himself into the mob for the sake of the Ely twang until Glennys
rescued her. Once he was off the dais my man would have
brought him down!''

Colfax put aside the Mule-Kick. ''Your horsegirl's out of our
reach now. Albany's got her. But she's not a player. My Catherine did her best to cancel the girl's luck, as I instructed her.
She put her in Roald's hand. That he failed so badly is his fault
and no one else's. The Prince has no idea how to command
women.''

Stogar laughed rudely.

In the court of the Ammunition Works, Colfax's man spread
a mantle of fox fur over the Duke's back, and put fleece gauntlets
on his hands. The groom gave him the reins of a fine grey stallion.

''What happened to spring?'' Colfax asked.

The gold emblem of Three Trees, stamped on the back of the
Baron's leather greatcoat, shone brightly in the torchlight.

''Up here spring's a prick-teaser, Collie. You don't understand
the north at all.'' Stogar laughed as he mounted Cannonball.

The two men parted company on the King's Road, the Duke
for St. Lucien and the Baron for Silkwalls. They gripped hands.

''War, Collie, think about war and money. That's your job,''
Stogar admonished.

In the Alaminite quarter of Drake there was weeping and lam-
entation for the dead and wounded, and hosannas were sung for
the martyred.

Thea Bohn stated flatly to the gathered elders and deacons,
''The first time Hans Rigg or even one of his Prophets comes
into my presence, I vow to leave Drake, never to return.''

· Eighteen ·

THE JAW OF the lowliest member of Queen's Ballet Company was tightly clenched. In spite of that, her lips and tongue moved.

"Cayetana de Alba's a hoor. She's a bitch, she's a slattern, she's a filthy Gondolese twang," was the main burden of Glennys's litany. It got louder as the wait for her dress rehearsal stretched longer.

Behind her Whistle, a gelding as new to Queen's stage as Glennys was to the ballet company, let out three high-pitched notes that explained his work name. She'd matched lightly with Whistle's senses to keep him quiet and confident before running through their little interact number, *The Stalking Horse*, with the orchestra.

But in the matching, her own frustration and lack of confidence had leaked into the gelding. He tugged on his lead. Saliva foamed around the bit.

Lloyd Kerrit led Whistle back to the gates of the menagerie ramps. The horse balked and laid back his ears. He didn't know what he wanted, but he didn't want to go back and stand on the sloping stones of the dark passage leading down into the animal hold.

Glennys followed Lloyd and put some time into soothing the golden bay with black legs, tail, and mane. "Don't be confused, baby. It's only a rehearsal," she whispered into his ears.

Whistle was one of the new string of geldings brought into the Yard as replacements for the performance horses dead and missing after the Hunger Riot. He was a dashing piece of horse-flesh with all the verve she needed for her little interact. But, like her, he was a novice. Tonight was his debut in front of an audience.

Glennys corrected herself. If she were *lucky*, Whistle's debut would be in front of an audience.

This time of year the houses were often thin during the opening acts. The festivities honoring the opening of the Summer

Palace late this afternoon and early evening would make an even later audience.

Glennys went back to the stage. "Cayetana, the schedule has my dress rehearsal slated for right now. You're over your time."

Cayetana didn't answer. She kept her back turned to the horse trainer who had the impertinence to call herself a ballerina.

"Conductor, if you please, the music for the garden act duets. Again. From the entrance," Cayetana ordered.

The orchestra members who'd bothered to attend afternoon rehearsal broke raggedly into the opening bars of music they'd played five times already.

The eight male dancers, all of whom had arrived this season as a fresh innovation out of Outremere theaters, leaped out of the wings. This time they flaunted their tumbling and acrobatic skills, trying to outdo each other and capture Cayetana's attention.

They twirled in mid-air, performed double-twist backflips, and landed on their knees in front of the First Dancer. Cayetana extended her hand to the most agile acrobat to partner her in a duet that spoke more of lasciviousness than ballet.

"Cayetana should actually rehearse, instead of coquetting with her partners," Glennys unwisely complained to the stage manager. She managed to shut her mouth after these first words escaped.

The stage manager shrugged. Cayetana's *Carnival of Love* was very popular with the Wheel ladies who flocked to St. Lucien while their men stayed at home in the provinces with their works, mills, and banks, leaving the ladies free to find amusements in the urbane capital.

Would she have an audience at all, Glennys fretted. Unlike Rowena and some of the others who performed interact solos, she had no claque of her own.

Her teeth began grinding again. Cayetana was doing her best to turn Glennys's solo into a humiliation.

Joss Thack rubbed Glennys's neck. He took in the situation with a glance. "You knew what you were getting into. Want to come back and work for the Yard?"

Glennys emphatically shook her head. "I know what I'm do-ing—if I have a chance to prove it. I never thought she'd pick on me this way. I'm no rival to Cayetana de Alba. I have no ambitions for Carnivals of Dalliance. I want to work with the horse ballets."

Lloyd Kerrit hitched Whistle's blanket straight. "To Caya,

anyone, especially the horses, are rivals. With all these new horses, we're half-crippled, and she likes it that way."

Glennys blew her front hair out of her eyes. "That's ridiculous. Queen's has room for all sorts of entertainments. Without horses the Theater will lose the Spurs."

Lloyd put his hand under Whistle's blanket. "This one is restless as the deuce. His coat's damp. He should either work or be taken downramp to rest."

Glennys shook her head again. "No, not yet. I'm going to plead, beg, and offer bribes to the musicians to stay for one runthrough."

After Cayetana declared herself satisfied, the musicians packed their instruments so fast that the scores on their music stands fluttered to the pit floor. They were out the back entrance before Glennys got out one word. Most of them were racing to find a place to play for tips on the grounds of the Summer Palace on Eidel Isle. They all feared there'd be no cheap boats left to take them across the Setham River channel to the island.

Joss's boots tromped across the stage boards. "I used to bang the saddledrums for the Equine Academy's parade drills. I could give you a beat on the kettledrums," he offered.

Glennys shook her head. "Thank you, but I need a real musician."

Out of the first row of seats behind the orchestra pit a tall, slender man stood up. He strode to the pianoforte. "I'll play your music on this if you tell me which piece it is."

Chestnut-colored hair fell in waves past his shoulders. He was young, and his skin was fair. He stooped and grabbed a sheaf of scores from the floor.

"It's called 'The Bear in the Boat,' that's all I know. I wouldn't recognize it written, only when I hear it. It's out of the old opera, *Virtue and Vengeance*," Glennys said.

He laughed and shuffled through the sheets of music, most of which were without such frivolous ornamentation as titles.

"Here we go. Why ever did you pick something so old-fashioned?" he asked.

"The music director assigned it to me," Glennys replied. "He says the Queen's audience heard 'The Bear in the Boat' in the nursery, so they'll recognize it and laugh when they hear it. I hope."

She added, "My number is supposed to be funny, people are supposed to laugh. It has nothing to do with bears or boats, though."

The musician laid out the score on the pianoforte stand. His fingers ran through the melody line before she was able to collect Whistle.

"Please be emphatic on the turnarounds so that I'll be sure to notice them," Glennys called down from the stage. "They're my cues to send Whistle into his changes."

The music academy students Duke Albany had engaged to coach her ears had been worked very hard, and she had each line memorized. The students had made an arrangement for her and scored copies of it for each orchestra member and the conductor. Her cues were marked in bold notation where all the instruments were to be played in unison—loudly.

The young musician began. He was an excellent sight reader and unlike the orchestra, he was easy to follow. For the first time since she'd been working on *The Stalking Horse*, Glennys stopped struggling with the music.

The Stalking Horse was only about five minutes long. They went through it three times. The first two times were shaky; Glennys was clumsy because she spent too much of herself on nudging Whistle's changes and poses. But by the end of the third try, horse and dancer were calm and confident.

She surrendered the bay to Joss and was about to thank the musician and find out who he was.

"Sorry I'm late, but I see you've been occupied, so that's all right, then," announced Duke Albany. "The luncheon I sponsored for the Equine Academy cadets was most successful."

Glennys rapidly stored her props in what she hoped was a safe corner backstage. No one else seemed to think it was their job to do.

"You must come and rest, my dear," observed the Duke. "You're quite frazzled."

"I can't. I've got Shop before Call. The corps has a punishment class because *The White Revue* was so bad last night," Glennys sighed. "Too many new geldings, and the orchestra bored out of its mind with the music."

The young musician said gaily, "Too much spring. Everyone has other things on their mind, even at work." He began to climb the stage stairs from the pit.

Baron, who'd come into the Theater at Albany's heels, growled a warning, and then gathered himself to leap at the musician's throat.

"*Stay!*" Glennys flung herself on the mastiff.

The musician jumped back down into the pit. He laughed up

into Glennys's horrified face. She hung onto Baron's collar with both hands. The dog was silent but she could still feel his throat vibrating.

"He doesn't usually act like this. I don't know what got into him," she apologized.

"I don't much like animals, and they know it, that's what got into him," the musician said.

"I don't believe you," Glennys denied.

"It's true," he said with a wicked grin. "I don't like them and they don't like me."

She put Baron firmly to heel, but the dog remained surly.

"Animals know things that even you, my concubine, don't," Albany said. "You must always heed them."

Glennys looked at her protector in astonishment. That was the first time he'd ever claimed possession of her like that in front of another man.

At that moment some of the overhead lamps flared into brilliant life, lighted by the secrets guild. Duke Albany looked very old. The lights dimmed again and he was the same Albany she'd always known, elegant and ageless.

She blew a kiss to the musician. "My Duke is right, and I must run, or be late and fined. But another time I'll thank you properly—and find out who you are!"

Glennys couldn't see his face in the shadows, but she heard his voice clearly.

"Never fear, you'll see me again!" he said.

There were no horses in Cayetana de Alba's *Carnival of Love*. Glennys had nothing to do between Call and the first and second act interval except prepare herself for *The Stalking Horse*, which was the first of four interacts. She stared at her reflection in the dressing-room mirror. Her stage makeup looked awful in the unfiltered lights, through the film of grease and oil lamp soot on the peeling glass.

Her costume was daringly unelaborate. There were no ruffles, garlands, or furbelows into which she had to be sewn by overworked wardrobe members. It could hardly be called a costume at all. She wore an oversized coat such as stable boys all over Nolan worked in, leggings, and ragged trousers that ended just below her knees. Only her ballet slippers had been specially designed for the occasion. They had upper cuffs like those of stable boots, but with kidskin soles, and no heels. An oversized spur, constructed of stiffened felt and painted with gilt, was sewn to the heel of one of the boots. A bell hung from the rowel.

Glennys combed her fingers through her hair. Released from the tight braids, it bushed even wilder after she used a crimping iron. She put on a headband, then took it off. She couldn't decide.

The same leg that had been slashed during the Hunger Riot throbbed, pulsed, and trembled. It was her nerves that made her leg hurt. There was nothing wrong with it but a scar, invisible at a distance. It had healed perfectly, thanks to garlic poultices, Thea Bohn's skills, and good luck.

She pleated and unpleated a copy of the evening's program, which had her name in it. She got up from the dressing table and stood in the center of the common area. She limbered and stretched in a vain attempt to empty her mind.

A bevy of ballerinas ballooned into the room, led by Nan. They'd just completed the *Carnival*'s promenade scene.

"There's no one in the house, horse trainer. Everyone's still on Eidel Isle!" Nan announced gleefully. "You'll be playing to nobody, and that's just as well. You look a fright! Wherever did you get that wig?"

Glennys's stomach lurched, and her mouth filled with saliva. She wouldn't heave into the chamber pots in front of the others. It was no good being up here.

Though it was endless minutes yet before "time" would be called on her, Glennys went down to stage level, then to the menagerie hold.

Whistle greeted her with an edgy whicker. She explored what he smelled, heard, and saw, finding out what noises and odors made him apprehensive.

With him she smelled the empty cages. Traces of bear, wolf, and big cats kept Whistle on his toes. He knew none of his hereditary enemies were present, but he was aware that they'd been there. He was wary, and Glennys smoothed the wariness away. He needed confidence that nothing in this place was dangerous to him.

Vibrations ran through the timbers of the ceiling, made from the fall of backdrops on their lines and the shifts of scenery and engagement of machinery. Glennys made him believe there was no danger from above.

Taking care of her partner's apprehensions helped her forget her own. She flooded Whistle with well-being and eagerness to display. Abruptly she closed off her Horse Sense as she felt herself panic over her props. Had someone moved them?

Back up the rampgates a time girl came through before Glennys lifted the latch. The girl was surprised to see a dancer on the ramp, but rushed down to call, "Time, *Stalking Horse* time," to those below.

The curtain was down. The singers and dancers were running into the wings, racing to change costume, or to buy a drink from the backdoor keeper of Queen's. A stage secrets apprentice boy had assembled her props. Suddenly Glennys was filled with all the same eagerness that she'd encouraged in Whistle.

After a few moments she saw Joss and Lloyd across from her in the wings of stage left, Whistle between them. The interacts were performed between the first swags of stage draperies and the orchestra pit, while the scenery for *Carnival* was changed behind the curtains.

The first lumbering bars of "The Bear in the Boat" began. Lloyd released his hold on Whistle's halter. Glennys divided her awareness, one part for herself, one for Whistle's cues and signals, then merged them to make one focus, which was to do *right* what they'd come here to do.

The bay's head lowered, his jaws snapping on purely imaginary grass, his legs daintily raising in a slow trip across the pasture the stage was now to be. A ripple of amusement reached Glennys's ears out of the house as the patrons recognized the melody of the silly song they'd all learned as children.

Then Glennys was on stage.

She made her entrance, her hands in her pockets, miming the gestures of a stable boy, about six years old, sent to bring in a huge horse from pasture.

Pointe, slide, chassé, glide—crouch, when the big horse threw up his head and regarded her. Now, for the half-turn, back to the big mean horse, so he wouldn't think the stable boy was after him. All of this was done quickly, elbows akimbo.

Whoever was in the audience—and she didn't dare look out—caught her mimed boy-character, and laughed.

The boy made a startled leap backwards, his right arm reaching nonchalantly to grab the halter. The big horse's head and neck swung out of range. The horse made a short turn from his hindquarters, his head and neck twisted over his shoulders to look at the boy. The boy, off balance from his grab, belly-flopped to the grass, legs kicking up in the air, looking foolish, yet pathetic.

He scrambled to his feet. The horse kicked out with his hind legs and turned. He snaked back his head to butt the boy. In a series of leaps the boy got out of the way and disappeared into the wings. He returned immediately, making two bourrée steps to the side, offering a huge platter of oats to the horse. The boy stood, his right leg crossed behind, his left leg extended out to the front.

The horse sidled toward the platter in passage, his legs raised in alternate pairs. Now the music was a back-and-forth motion that imitated a boat swaying under a bear's weight.

The horse stretched out his neck to the oats and knocked them out of the boy's hand. His teeth snapped at the boy's fingers. The horse made another turn and kicked out behind. This was the dangerous part. She'd calculated it carefully so that from the audience it would appear that the boy she was miming was being kicked. The boy was knocked to the ground. He sat up and knuckled his weeping eyes.

Immediately the boy dashed off and returned, all of him hidden except for his arms under a giant carrot mask. He stumbled blindly about the pasture, trying to locate the horse. The horse looked back at him over his shoulder, opened his jaws, and gave a horse laugh, a real one stimulated by Glennys, loud enough to be heard over the music, which was supposed to be playing softer now—but wasn't. The horse laugh was lost.

The audience laughed anyway. The boy walked into a scenery tree and knocked himself silly.

Once more he ran off and returned, this time behind a huge equine figure constructed out of hide. This was Queen's Theater, so the stalking horse was brightly painted, with exaggerated sexual characteristics, and dripping ribbons and flowers to indicate femininity.

The horse raised his long tail, black as midnight, with a flourish. He pranced up to the make-believe filly and nosed her from tail to neck.

The stalking horse trembled and shook as the little boy's arms attempted to reach across the blind and capture the horse's halter. His contortions made the stalking horse move suggestively, like a mare in season.

The audience laughed, loudly this time. Broad humor was always appreciated at Queen's.

As the music reached its close in a dundering upset of boat and bear, an authentic Horse Skiller, wearing real spurs—the obliging Lloyd Kerrit—ambled into the pasture and took posses-

sion of the outwitted horse. The boy followed, pathetically miming that he was just this close to having him, just this close.

It was over. Glennys's makeup was runneled. Hardly anything
had gone wrong, but she was thinking of what had missed.

The stage manager gave her a little push. "Get back out
there!"

"What?" she asked, suspended between two worlds.

"Your claque wants a curtain call. Listen!" he said.

"I don't have a claque!" Glennys said.

"That's what they all say," sniped August Gardel. "But don't
go out like that." He pulled the stable coat from her back, leaving Glennys in a lacy corset, bare midriff, trousers, and leggings. He poufed up her hair.

In the Theater auditorium, nearly as brightly lit as the stage,
Glennys saw row after row of seats filled with youths wearing
the Equine Academy uniform.

She blew them kisses, and made a deep reverence. She called
for Whistle and Lloyd. Lloyd made a short bow, and Whistle
bowed over his knees. The applause remained strong.

Glennys's Horse Sense gave Whistle a little shove. The horse
reared. With one hand she grabbed his halter, as the stable boy
hadn't been able to manage, and brought him down. She encouraged the horse to show off, and to enjoy the applause.

Her Duke was in his box, stamping his feet doggedly in a
manner comic to behold. Enthusiastically, but more decorously,
Sharissa and the Baroness Ely applauded with him. Prince Roald
was in the Royal Box, a Wheel lady at his side, pounding the
edge with his walking stick.

It had worked, she thought. The cadets were exactly the sort
of audience for which she'd made *The Stalking Horse*. Every one
of them had had an early stable experience like that. Albany's
luncheon had been gathering her an audience, and it was exactly
the audience he wanted her to have.

She saw Thadee Maywood working the front rows, removing
cadets so that friends, relatives, and paid attendees would have
those crucial front seats for the next interact number. Glennys
ran off.

August Gardel said, "Not too bad. You're not much of a
dancer, but you're a good mime. I believed you were a boy—
until I took off your ugly coat. Next time wear something pret-
tier."

The Duke's advice had been on the mark, she thought. One
night in bed, discussing Glennys's presentation to Gardel for *The*

Stalking Horse, Albany had showed Glennys how she could use the director's well-known preference for men to her benefit. "Change your role into that of a boy. August will be friendlier to the idea," the Duke had said.

As soon as Gardel's critical eyes were on the second act, Glennys ran upstairs to change costume and makeup for *Carnival*'s third act, in which the corps de ballet danced an interlude. It went by in a blur, Glennys an anonymous pair of legs and arms in the formation.

It was time for the closing number, *The White Revue*. Glennys ran to join her partner, a grey gelding named Ariel.

The White Revue was King Leon's favorite, so it was always scheduled to run at the end of the night. The King did not attend every show, and often, when he did appear, arrived only for the *Revue*.

Made of schooled horse maneuvers, rigged out in white net, gauze, and flowers, the *Revue* was composed to be different in each performance, with opportunity for spontaneous variations.

Any member of the corps might become a soloist, or take part in a smaller formation within the larger perimeter. Each dancer had to think for herself and her horse, and elaborate on what another might begin.

It called above all for teamwork. But since the Hunger Riot too many of them, preoccupied with controlling their new horses, thought only of themselves, or didn't think at all. Too often, like last night, the *Revue* had fallen apart, and the King had conveyed his disappointment to Gardel.

Tonight the music sounded fresh and lively. Glennys led the entrance with Ariel and, when she had the opportunity, she looked into the orchestra pit. Instead of old Vigano conducting, she saw the same young man who'd rescued her rehearsal that afternoon.

As each horse-and-ballerina couple's march on half-toe brought them across the line of sight into the orchestra pit, they too realized why the music was better tonight.

The music was supposed to be played like this, steady and clear. The ensemble awoke as if from slumber.

Glennys arched backwards into the pose called the bridge. She returned to her feet in fifth position, her right leg forward. She grasped the arch of her foot with her right hand and slowly raised and straightened out the leg. Supported by her left hand's hold on Ariel's white-ribboned harness, she assumed an attitude of high hauteur before melting back into the pattern.

It was the most basic acrobatic pose out of the old character ballets. Glennys looked back over her shoulder to Rowena. Rowena caught her glance and grinned.

Center stage front in her turn, Rowena sank into the classical split on the stageboards. Her horse paused, his front legs reaching out in the extended walk, but in place. Springing like a ball of rubber to her feet, Rowena too adopted the foot-in-hand pose before moving ahead into the march.

The pattern shifted out of the circle march. Others had caught the possibility. These elementary acrobatics were part of the Shop's classes, and all the horses and dancers knew them.

In duos and trios, and solo, dancers surged in a wave of backward and forward somersaults under their horses. They leaped lightly onto the geldings' backs, where they stood, arms open, in a gesture of offering to the audience. After the offering the dancers dropped like dew in their filmy skirts to the boards.

Glennys's Horse Sense was at work. She caught and matched with Whistle, who was starting to lose his nerve from the rapid changes of gait and the unexpected cues calling him to mark time on the spot. Repeatedly she nudged his memory and his confidence to the fore, straightening out his hesitations so Nan, his partner, could think about her next move. Wherever there was a weakness in the horses' understanding, Glennys was there, holding them in time.

The more confident the geldings, the more spirited they became, and the more daring the corps acted.

The pattern turned into a four-pointed star, with Glennys and Ariel at center stage. The star dissolved and she and the gelding stayed there, separated from each other. Ariel's profile was to the audience. Glennys cartwheeled to him. At the bottom of the third wheel, Glennys's Horse Sense signaled courbette. She whirled safely under his raised forehand. He jumped three times on his hind legs. The audience rewarded Ariel with applause. The other dancers marked time with their geldings so Ariel could bow in return.

The corps got braver after that.

The dancers' hearts pounded from exertion and from the exquisite terror of a risky performance.

The music held their tempo. It extended and contracted with their movements. It announced clearly and dramatically the rhythmic formulas that signaled the transitions between sections.

The audience demanded more spectacular chances so that it might receive more intense thrills. But before the performers dropped dead of exhaustion the orchestra played the finale.

The ovation was led by King Leon from the royal box.

There was no encore for *The White Revue*. Like the act of love, which too, in its own way this had been, the *Revue* couldn't be the same thing twice.

The corps fell into the dressing room, and collapsed into limp piles of stained and ripped skirts. After their pulses and breathing slowed, the assessment began.

"Why didn't we think of it before?" Rowena gasped. "Glennys, what an inspiration! It's the only new thing we've done in months. And that new conductor made the orchestra support us instead of fight us! I think that was the first time the orchestra's sounded good since I've been in the company."

"Was *that* Jonathan Reed?" asked Rais.

Everyone except Glennys seemed to have heard about the young musician from Seven Universities who had won last year's Langano Prize and gone off to study at Langano's Teatro Urbino. Newly returned to St. Lucien, he'd just been named under-conductor at Queen's.

"It takes a real *man*," said Rowena, "a young *Nolanese* man, to dominate that surly pack of dogs Rambert calls an orchestra."

Like many of the others', red-haired Nan's legs and feet jerked with cramps after their prolonged, intense work. "Tonight was extraordinary in every way. I never knew the *Revue* could be like this. I got coupled with Whistle, and thought he was a goner several times, but he always steadied and ended up right. Glennys has handled him most. It's a lucky thing for us to have a horse trainer in the company."

Glennys slumped on a stool, her legs wide-splayed, her head hanging between them. Every joint, every muscle in her body hurt. Her head ached, overfilled with trackings of all the geldings' weaknesses, fears, strengths, and graces. She'd never been so tired and so awake at the same time.

She raised her head and looked at Nan through a veil of hanging hair. "*Chinga tu madre*, Nan," Glennys said, and, in a perfect caricature of Cayetana de Alba, blew the red-haired dancer a kiss.

"*Chinga tu madre*, yourself, Glenn," Nan shot back, and followed it with another blown kiss.

The ensemble took it up. Kisses were blown back and forth

across the basins of sour water, towels stained with greasepaint, laddered stockings, and broken corsets.

Rais left off massaging a strained muscle in her right buttock, the result of a wrongly positioned back-flip. "Look at *us*. All the corps are Nolanese born and bred for the first time since Queen's founding."

The dancers leaped into the air, colliding with each other in the cramped quarters. "We're the Romantics! We're Nolanese ballerinas! We're young and it's our turn! We're all related, we're all related!"

They surged together and fell into a pile of arms and legs. They flew up again and dropped into curtsies. King Leon had come in. Behind him was a flood of bloods and swells representing the patronage of Spur and Wheel families.

The triumph in the common dressing room was all the sweeter for the corps' knowledge of how Cayetana de Alba would punish them for it tomorrow in class. She rampaged whenever Leon congratulated the *Revue* in person.

Glennys eagerly examined each new arrival, but none of them was the one she hoped to see.

• NINETEEN •

TO THE GREAT delight of the cadets and dancers gathered for Albany's champagne supper, King Leon joined them for a short time. His tail was very short; only his two sons and Duchess Colfax's recently delivered daughter came with him. It was a clever contrivance of the King, Glennys thought. The baby was the object of all the cooing and kissing that otherwise would have been given to Leon.

The party broke up early, on the heels of the King's departure. The cadets had curfew, and the dancers had classes, rehearsals, and another performance night at Queen's.

Afterwards, Glennys slid down from the pillows at the head of Albany's bed. She pressed the length of her body against his. "I want to seduce you again, Pierce," she whispered in his ear.

Duke Albany raised himself on one elbow. He smoothed back her hair and kissed her forehead. "I'm sorry, my Stallion Queen. I can't manage another seduction tonight. But I can service you. I'm always at your service."

The candlelight followed the trails of smooth rapier scars that ran over Albany's chest and shoulders. The puckered one under his left breast was a memento of his only son and heir. The Duke had killed him in a duel fifty years ago.

"My son earned his execution," Albany had told Glennys, and nothing else. Yet she knew that her Duke had never unsheathed his sword since, either in battle or duel. His fascination with art and journeys of exploration had begun after his son's death. These days his occupation was his network of spiders—some called them spies and informers—and her. He supported her career on stage, he said, for what it was teaching her about managing people. He'd been very pleased tonight because she'd learned how to use the Horse Sense to knit the dancers and horses together in a common purpose.

Gently Glennys removed his hand. "This is not necessary. Your previous service was enough," she whispered. Soon the Duke was asleep.

She slipped out of his bed and belted on a robe. She concealed the little case of moss, wax, sheaths, and the foul-smelling potion of pregnant mare's urine within one of the billowing sleeves. She seldom needed the contents of the case, for Albany was an expert at withdrawal. More often he wasn't able to spend at all.

Baron's tail thumped on the floor when she came into her own suite. She stepped out to the balcony off her sitting room. For a few minutes she savored the good smells rising up out of the Duke's gardens. Lights were scattered here and there over what she could see of St. Lucien, like sequins flashing on a stage costume. When she slept, it was deep and refreshing, and her dreams were full of promises and very entertaining.

Jonathan Reed walked out of Cayetana de Alba's party at midnight. Outside the air was as soft as the silken atmosphere of the First Dancer's house. As he made his way over the Promenade he could still catch strains of Caya's gitar and her voice singing a street song from her childhood.

He hailed a cab. The driver's tongue and ears were back-country, but Jonathan and the cabbie had no trouble communicating. His father's relatives spoke the same dialect. The composer had loved those summers of his childhood spent with his dad's family. Every fall his father would insist Jonathan drop the back-country rhythms and pronunciation from his speech and speak like a proper Seven Universities scion, and every summer Jonathan would become countrified all over again.

When Jonathan broke away from his University mathematical studies and went off to St. Lucien to study music, his father had cast him off. The Langano Prize, sponsored by Lady Abigail Withy, hadn't changed the old man's opinion about music as a profession one bit.

Instead of sitting inside, Jonathan got up next to the cabbie and listened to his story. Once he'd been a small freehold farmer down south. Tonight was his first time driving the horse and wheels leased from the city. He didn't know St. Lucien's twisted routes as well as Jonathan, so the composer gave him directions to Old Harbor Hide.

Earlier George Sert had asked Jonathan to visit him after the Queen's performances had concluded. The painter had vowed he'd still be awake any time before the sun came up. He wanted to discuss a commission with the composer.

Jonathan hadn't planned a detour from Queen's to Cayetana's first. He'd expected an invitation to Albany's supper party, but had been disappointed. Cayetana professed herself thrilled that he could speak her own language, and he could no more turn down an invitation from a woman than he could turn down a free drink.

When the cab rolled over the Canal Street Bridge, the neighborhood where he'd spent his student years brought back powerful memories of his previous destitution.

"We all will jist stop right heah, sira driver. I'll be takin' me own way now," he apologized.

Before the Langano Prize, Jonathan's purse hadn't allowed any transportation but his own feet. In those days he'd sat hunched up in threadbare clothes in the winter's wet cold. He'd not dared to put a note on paper until he'd heard it and seen it a hundred times in his head, and all the relationships that note had to those already on paper and those to come after it. He couldn't afford to spoil even one sheet of good paper then.

The Seahorse Tavern stood wide open to the spring night. The friendly uproar called to him.

He'd been back from Langano only a short time but the Copely folks behind the bar greeted him like an old, valued customer, even as they'd done in the bad years. Back then they'd sometimes ask him to make music so they could dance and sing at their own private jubilees. In exchange they wrote off what he'd owed them in unpaid meals and drink.

Tonight, without asking, one of the daughters put a short tumbler of Esker in front of him, with a back of Alluv Ale.

Old Copely grinned at him through his grizzled beard. "Nice to see old friends don't forget us."

Jonathan grinned back.

"Put your name up on the tab board, why don't you, any way you like," Copely offered kindly. He cleaned the top of the board with vinegar, erasing someone who had fallen out of his good graces. He handed Jonathan a fresh stick of chalk.

A friendly, understanding tavernkeeper was a treasure more precious than a Langano Prize, Jonathan thought.

He climbed the ladder. Quickly he drew a pair of staves, substituting a "J" and "R" for the treble and bass clef. Along the lines he rapidly notated the bars of "The Bear in the Boat."

When Jonathan stepped around to the front of the bar, another drink was next to the glasses he hadn't yet drunk. "On us, Jonathan Reed, a favor returned for the favor of *The White Revue!*"

Rowena, Rais, and Nan had stopped off for a nightcap after Albany's champagne. "We were about to seek our lonely beds, until you appeared," Rowena said, with her lovely smile. "Do you know that King Leon came up after the *Revue*, and to Albany's afterwards? We all looked for you, but you never came."

Copely cleared his throat. In respect for the man whose generosity had helped all of them through more than one bad interlude, the dancers stopped flirting with Jonathan.

"If anyone asks me, what's the music up there on the board? Is it your own?" asked Copely.

Rowena laughed. "Among other things, it was Glennys Eve's interact music tonight." She winked at Jonathan. "Do I know something?"

Gallantly Jonathan said, "Well, I know something. You can read music. Not many dancers can."

"Anyone can read that!" Rowena protested modestly. "My mother and aunt used to dance to it in that old opera, what's-it's-name. They changed off as the bear. They'd borrow the costume and chase us around at home during jubilees. Me and my cousins used to go into fits, we laughed so hard."

Rowena lumbered about, skillfully missing tables, drinkers, and benches, miming a drunken bear that had stumbled into a moored skiff.

In her own fashion she was more attractive than Caya, Jonathan thought. What might have happened, he never found out, because George pushed his way through the women to the bar.

"Jonathan," he said, putting out his hand to shake. "I thought you were coming to my place, but I see you've been abducted."

The dancers gave way. Rowena kept one eye on the two men while Rais and Nan described to Copely Glennys's *Stalking Horse*, their shared triumph in the *Revue*, and Albany's supper party for them.

George and Jonathan moved to leave.

The three dancers each gave Jonathan a kiss at the door while George watched impatiently. George noticed that the composer had left a tip on the bar larger than his tab, but that he hadn't paid for his drinks. Old Copely had charged him for only one round, though there had been two on the bar when he'd come in, and another after that.

Jonathan had caught George's exact payment, and that the painter's name on the board had nothing owing behind it. He wondered where George's money came from. Probably his parents, he thought. Painting was as expensive a profession to study and practice as music.

At his lodgings, George poured out servings of Esker and ale generously. He didn't ask if Jonathan wanted any first. Jonathan liked that.

George said, "Thorvald and I were very impressed by your recital at Lady Abigail Withy's. The pianoforte is a thrilling instrument, and your music for it allowed me to think about my work, and forget about myself. I think you're a genius. Thor agrees."

"Thank you very much, both of you," Jonathan replied, not knowing what was the appropriate response to the announcement that he was a genius.

"Thor's hosting a private view of my work for invited bloods before the official Gallery exhibition. We want you to compose music for the occasion, anything you think appropriate. Thor will pay you well, and the arrangement will be left up to you and him, so that our friendship won't have to be embarrassed by money," George said.

Jonathan liked that.

Inwardly he exulted first, then sighed. Occasional music was found income. It had to be put together fast, and the occasion was over before he got sick of it. He sighed, because even other artists, who should know better, insisted on finding anything and everything in music except music. But that was why Romantic dogma gave music art's crown. Painters, poets, historians, Wheels ignorant of anything but buying and selling, all believed they understood music. Most of them didn't even know what equal temperament was, which had been the most exciting development in three hundred years! And they were all so easy to impress with the pianoforte. Bang loud, then play soft, then loud again. He cringed when he remembered how badly he'd played at Abigail's.

George fitted Jonathan with a flat-crowned, wax-laden, wide-brimmed hat mounted with candle scones. "This is how I can work after dark," he said.

The candles were lit. George fitted himself out in the same manner, and gave the composer a lamp. He led Jonathan through the ell of his lodgings.

Dust covers were pulled off nineteen easels. "This is it," he announced briskly. "Only Thor's seen them before you."

George found the long silence intolerable. He hadn't felt so negligible since last fall at Albany's dinner honoring Thor's "Three Kings."

Finally Jonathan said, "This one is what you're exhibiting, this one canvas?"

Humbly, George nodded, making the shadows cast by the candles mounted on his hat dance. "All the rest are the best of the studies for it."

Jonathan examined the nineteen offerings yet again, and very carefully. "You've certainly not put up any false bucolic Big House landscapes, full of happy lads and lasses working for their blood masters."

George cried out, "But do you like it, man? Do you think it's any good?"

Slowly Jonathan responded. "My judgment has nothing to do with it. I'm not a painter. I believe in your judgment. I'm not even a horse lover, but, yes, this picture speaks to me. I hear all kinds of things in it, though I can't tell you why."

George pointed out the effects of his technique. Jonathan didn't understand everything George told him about working with the sources of light that were created within the canvas itself, or how the light sources acted upon the representation of movement. But he believed George knew precisely what he was talking about.

The title was "Gordonsfield Horse Fair." The surround of the canvas was made up of clusters of stones, painted with hands and animals, in brilliant colors.

The central figure was unmistakably Glennys Eve. She was holding a rearing black stallion, his eyes deep pools of hostility. She and the stallion were circled by a group of elderly men, who had cut her out from a group of youths her own age, who bantered and flirted behind the elders. The lowering sun threw shadows like bars over her body through a rack of spears.

The background of Gordonsfield Heights balanced the foreground. The Gordon Big House, a Fortune House, and a Spirit House made part of the middleground. The few buildings were made of rough logs and roofed with felt. It was a Nolan groping her way out of tribalism.

The eighteen studies showed the plat of the canvas in closeup. Horses were picketed, tents raised, fires kindled among clan masks and tribal banners. The studies were in chalk, pencil, charcoal, and a few in oils.

"This canvas gives me the spooks," Jonathan observed.

"Your music does the same to me," said George, pleased.

"That's Glennys Eve, isn't it?" asked Jonathan.

George nodded, proud of his skill at portraiture, even if it wasn't the most noble of painting skills.

"I didn't know she worked as an artist's model, though I suppose that's not unusual for dancers."

"She doesn't model," George said shortly.

"What would she think about this?" Jonathan asked, indicating the picture.

George shrugged. He sat down on the floor, contemplating his creation. He bent back his head to drink from the ale jug, illuminating the splashes of paint on the floor as he did so. "She probably won't even notice she's in it, so interested she'll be in the black stallion there, and telling me how I don't know how to see a war stallion at all."

Jonathan grunted. He sank to the floor himself, and tucked up his long legs tailor-fashion. He took off the artist's night hat and blew out the candles.

This late at night they couldn't see the moon through the round windows of the room. But the glow and shimmer of moonlight reflected off the many waters of St. Lucien, making the windows circles of luminance in the dark.

"You've known Glennys Eve a long time, then, have you?" Jonathan's casual question came out of a dry mouth.

George groaned. "I don't want to talk about her." But he was off and running, concluding with the night of the Saquave stallion's death. "That night I saw a lot I'd never seen before about her relationship to bloods and horses, but if I understand any of it, or her either, I'm the deuce," he muttered at the finish.

"She's smart," Jonathan said.

George understood Jonathan well enough to know that was high praise.

"Her little interact proved she knows her strengths and her weaknesses, and how best to serve them both. Most of those dancers would have tried to imitate the Gemma or Caya, and proved that yet another fool had put herself up for display."

"Strengths and weaknesses," mused George. "What do you think my strengths and weaknesses as an artist are?"

Jonathan peered into the dimness where the painted image of Glennys's fairness glimmered between them. He considered his words. "Your strength is that what you see, you can make others see too. Your weakness—your weakness is your inability to see through any eyes but your own."

· TWENTY ·

THE SLEEK FORTUNE House officiate was a modern man, whose dress was the same as any prosperous Wheel. He'd not even considered putting on the mask, breechclout, and cape that the archives indicated as traditional for the ceremony. But his face made a mask all its own, one of considered blandness.

Smoke rolled off the burning brazier when the officiate threw on more incense and herbs. The tiny room behind the vast central chamber was stiflingly hot. There were other rooms available for small ceremonies in the Circle Gardens Fortune House, but Duke Albany wanted to keep this as discreet as possible.

The officiate caught Glennys's eye, and almost imperceptibly, he winked. He thought she believed swearing service to the Stallion Queen was as preposterous as he did.

But Duke Albany had chosen Justin Sharp deliberately to be the judiciar skiller who searched out the ritual for Stallion Queen service. He was the best at untangling the knots where ancient tribal laws and the new ones of settled Nolanese life threaded together. Equally important to Albany was Sharp's sense of humor.

The smoke made Sharp sneeze vigorously. "Duke Albany, bare your sword arm."

Lenkert Deerhorn opened a small, flat gold case. "This needle was made from the cannon bone of Storm, honored war stallion of King Albany. I attest that to the best of my knowledge this is a true relic of the Albany tribe," he said matter-of-factly.

The needle looked remarkably like a toothpick. Glennys's eyes met Sharp's and Deerhorn's, where a hint of a smile lurked.

The officiate accepted the needle and passed it through the smoke. Albany knelt. The needle punctured the crook of his elbow. Sharp's fingers squeezed the skin.

Swiftly Albany gathered the bright beads of blood on the long nail of the third finger on his left hand. The smoke swirled about them like grey silk. The faces of the other three now matched the Duke's look of intense determination. Even as little as it was, it was blood on the Duke's fingernail, and Glennys had never been amused by blood. There was nothing to laugh at here. She was part of a high ceremony, which, though long unperformed, was still binding, according to Justin Sharp's opinion.

Albany placed the drops of blood from the silver sheath on the nail of his finger on her tongue. "My life, my service, my goods, and all that is properly mine to dispose are now yours. Not as husband, lover, or father of your children, but as Companion to my Stallion Queen, I am bound until death. Sa, sa, sa."

Albany's blood merged with the other fluids in Glennys's mouth. A hot stream ran down into her body. She swallowed again and again, as one did from a fountain on a sweltering day.

She looked down at the man who had out of his own will given her the oldest, purest Nolanese bloodline as her own in the ceremony of Stallion Queen service. "I accept what you have willingly given, my own Duke, with modesty and respect. I vow to use your gift, not to my selfish benefit, but for all who are in need, whenever and whatever that need shall be."

She raised Albany to his feet. They met in an embrace which had nothing of coupling in it. It was the embrace of comrades.

The four left the stifling room for the tiled antechamber. There Justin Sharp's amanuensis stamped the record of the ceremony with Albany's seal of crossed arrow and spear, that of the Circle Gardens Fortune House, and the officiate's personal seal. Gustave, the Duke's parrot, fluttered impatiently in a corner, where he was fastened to his perch by a soft leather cuff. "Wine, wine," he croaked.

Sharp invited them up to his office. "I have a bottle or two there, one of which ought to please you, though I can't vouch for Gustave here. His judgment is of the finest discrimination."

"Thank you, Jus, but I'd best be moving along," Albany said. "Len, pass over the other things that go with the record. You'll be seeing to these yourself, Sharp, and keeping them safe until Glenn here needs them, or until my death, whichever comes first."

The Aristo, the dancer, and the eunuch crossed the marble floor of the Circle Fortune House to the door wide enough to accommodate six mounted horses abreast.

Up in his office Justin Sharp shuffled through the papers. One was a copy of a letter from Baron Fulk, demanding that by all Nolanese law, the woman calling herself Glennys Eve belonged in his service. It had been sent to Colfax's Office of Inquiry, and officially delivered to Albany's townhouse, initiating the events leading up to the ceremony of Stallion Queen service.

The second group of papers included a copy of Glennys's concubine contract with Albany, also registered with the Office of Inquiry. It was a very modest one—clothing, a small allowance, and the use of his house and stables—and binding for only a year.

The third group, with Albany's seal and signature, attested that Glennys was of Aristo blood, that she carried the lost Nolanese Horse Sense actively within her, and that therefore she was a Stallion Queen, bound to Nolan, not to an individual blood.

The last papers were declarations of legacy. Duke Albany had bequeathed his royal charter of Saquave lands to Glennys Eve. With the declaration of legacy was a locked leather and steel trunk. It was massively weighty, containing gold coins and bars, to be held in trust by Justin in the Fortune House treasury for the Saquave Land Settlement Company.

From the secretaries' room Justin could hear his amanuensis, Blaze, whispering to the other clerks about this last folly of an old blood who'd far outlived his intelligence. Sharp let loose with a volley of his own laughter, startling his staff into silence.

Crazy like a fox, Sharp said to himself. He opened a bottle of wine and toasted the Duke Albany in solitude. That man had not outlived himself at all. He'd only had the fortune to live so long that he knew the best means of hedging his dreams with the best safeguards of the past and the present. Sharp took out a sheaf of papers that were the latest draft for the Saquave Land Settlement Company. On top was a list of names of possible investors. Among them was his own.

Outside, Circle Gardens was a bustle of spring sensuousness. Albany tucked Glennys's hand within his arm and led her down the steps. "Now you're protected, and I can take up my duties as tribal elder and see what your half-sister has gotten up to. This is a bad time for her to stir up a blood feud between the Waterfords and the Lubbocks."

"Be kind to Thurlow," Glennys said. "She was never meant to be buried in the back country with such an old man before she got the chance to be young."

"I am much older than Waterford," Albany observed.

"But I am in St. Lucien," Glennys said, "and I freely chose this, and you are helping me make my dream come true." But

at this moment, still tasting Albany's blood in her mouth, his
dream seemed more real than hers.

They strolled through the Gardens. Deerhorn walked behind
them carrying Gustave's perch, though the parrot rode on Albany's shoulder. Gravel crunched on the looping carriage drive.
Lady Abigail Withy's open equipage pulled up next to them.

"Why aren't you gone to the Waterfords', Pierce?" she demanded.

A warm flush rose to Glennys's cheeks. Riding with the handsome Lady Withy was Jonathan Reed, no doubt as part of his
duties as her object of patronage. He lived in Abigail's artists'
quarters on the garden floor of her house. The Lady ignored
Glennys, but Jonathan acknowledged her with obvious pleasure.

"I'm leaving tonight on the first leg of my journey," Albany
replied to Lady Withy. "I had affairs to settle before such a
protracted absence, you know."

"Affairs indeed," Abigail sniffed. "When you return, bring
my niece back with you. Thurlow's done her duty and presented
the Waterfords with heirs, and now that the broken-down old
stud's-dead there's no reason for her to be stuck in the back
country. I suppose she'll have an empty purse. The Waterfords
don't have any money, so I'll take care of her expenses. Certainly Stogar won't. He's a worse skinflint than my brother-in-
law was."

Abigail leaned forward and rapped her walking stick against
the driver's box as an order to drive on. All the artists she sponsored were men, but her driver was a pretty girl. So were all the
staff that worked for her.

Glennys knew that Abigail had no idea that they'd met before.
Properly speaking, of course, they never had. As apprentice stablemistress to the Fulk stables, Glennys hadn't been of interest to
Abigail. Back then Glennys had hated her, but now she had a
respect for the strong-minded, independent woman who had such
good taste in music.

That evening Glennys could hear the barge horses stamping
outside of Albany's cabin. The bells on the horses' harness jin-
gled. The barge men whistled and chirruped. The long lashes
of their whips snapped in response to the pole men's signal that
the sluice gates had been opened and the lock's water level was
rising under the barge.

Gustave had settled on his perch. "Come out and take a walk

my dear,'' he croaked, preening his feathers in front of the shaving mirror.

The Duke kissed Glennys on both cheeks. ''Enjoy the summer. I know you will do nothing that will embarrass my honor or yourself. My service is to you, not the other way around. You are free, and not a fly in my web.''

The barge captain knocked on the cabin door, which stood open to the fine night. ''All visitors down the gangplank now, my lord.''

Albany went out with Glennys and Deerhorn. ''Water up, water up,'' was called down the line of waiting vessels tethered to the horses on the canal's banks.

The Duke watched Baron spring to his feet as Lenkert and Glennys walked off the loading raft.

''Most attractive, my lord. Your concubine?'' asked the captain.

''My Stallion Queen,'' the Duke answered.

''You don't say,'' the captain said. Behind his authority as a river chief it was clear the captain thought the famous Duke was a fool.

Albany bit his lip to hold back the laugh that would tell the captain he understood him very well. He stepped over to the awning erected aft that sheltered his groom, his baggage porters, and his string of horses.

The barge lifted, the barge horses pulled, and the Duke grinned like a boy. The nomadic blood of his ancestors was as strong in him as ever. To be going, anywhere, was what he liked better than anything. His life and his luck were still strong in him.

Glennys was tenacious, smart, and tough. She'd begun her rise in St. Lucien before he'd put his hand out to her, even as she'd done up in the northern march country. The young who shared her qualities were attracted to her.

She'd told him about how the Saquave Desert had fired her imagination ever since she'd learned of it in school, how she'd often dreamed herself there, with the wild horses, in that vast wasteland on the other side of the Rain Shadow Mountains. One of these days her earliest dreams would grow strong again. She'd grow into his vision of the Saquave.

''It's auction music!'' exclaimed Thorvald. He laughed so hard he popped a button over his stomach. ''Brilliant, Reed, brilliant! However did you come up with it?''

"My back-country relatives have always had an auctioneer or
two in the family. I followed them around in the summer and
made them teach me the chant. It seemed a good background
for a painting about a horse fair."

"And you ain't ashamed of your Shoe background, I see.
Neither are we, hey, George? If anything will excite the Spurs it
will be the rhythm of horses going off to money."

George was less confident. Though he knew better than to say
so, it seemed an undignified way to launch the career of a noble
artist.

But Richard Thorvald was a noble artist, and he was rolling
on the floor now, happy as a pig in his wallow. Esker was called
for and brought up by Thor's wife.

"He only does this when he's sure he's right," the old lady
consoled the bewildered George and Jonathan. "He's never been
wrong, you know, in one of these fits. He has the true Nolanese
luck of seeing fortune."

Both Thor and his wife were right. The following afternoon
the small and unconventional chamber orchestra that Jonathan
had assembled—six strings, four winds, four brass, and four
percussion—accomplished the unveiling of George's painting.
The composition, a lively fugue joining the rhythms of an auction chant to an old country melody, drew a noisy ovation. Jonathan set down his baton, swept around to face the audience,
and—to his own surprise—instead of acknowledging the applause, began to bid call.

Soon a half-circle surrounded Prince Roald, Baron Gordonsfield, and the Baroness Ely. Thadee Maywood, uninvited as
usual, stood taking notes. Glennys buried herself at the back and
pulled the veil on her hat over her face and neck, while Lenkert
Deerhorn laughed. Lark, George's betrothed, standing behind
the artist's family, couldn't keep herself from turning around and
darting outraged looks at Glennys's veiled head.

"I'm a seven, now half, now half, would'e gimme seven
fifty?"

Prince Roald was the first to drop out of the bidding, his
stinginess bringing him no honor among the old bloodline Aristos.

"I'm eight fifty, now nine, now nine, b'lieve I would! Eight
fifty, now nine. . . ."

At nine hundred fifty gold forients, Baron Gordon backed off,
making of it a gallant gesture. "I don't want to ruin you, my
love," he said to the Baroness Ely. The picture was hers.

The Baroness Ely gave Gordon a hearty kiss on the mouth. "This goes into the house Sharissa will have when she marries, for if Glennys hadn't rescued her, there would have been no wedding."

In keeping with the impromptu spirit of the auction, Thor advised George to offer Jonathan the traditional ten percent auctioneer's fee.

That night the news was galloped through St. Lucien, sent out by post riders and coach, and in ships across the Majis Sea. Sert's painting was the first wedding gift. King Leon was taking Sharissa Ely for his Queen.

George's, Jonathan's, and Glennys's names were lesser parts of the news, but part of it just the same. The popularity of the royal wedding among the Spurs and lower classes spilled over to include the three young Romantics.

What mattered most to Jonathan was that the unexpected ten percent auctioneer's fee allowed him to move out of Abigail Withy's artists' quarters and get a place of his own.

· TWENTY-ONE ·

GLENNYS LEANED AGAINST a table set on rollers. The surface was partly map, and partly scaled modeling, of the Rain Shadow Mountain Range and the Saquave lands west and south on the other side. Most men would have given a leave-taking gift of jewelry to their concubines, but the Duke had given her this.

Tiny animal figures, constructed of ivory, silver, fur, and feathers, with minute chips of turquoise for eyes, could be picked up and moved about. With a finger Glennys gently urged a herd of silver horses to the banks of the solitary Snake River. There was water in the river, provided by a system of pumps and a reservoir concealed under the table.

Jonathan sat at the pianoforte in Albany's music room. During this dark period of Queen's preparation for the fourth and last season, he had worked constantly with her on the music that would support the small solo she'd been awarded. It was part of Catherine's new piece, called *The Ghost Lover*. Catherine's role was that of a woman who returned from the grave to bring vengeance upon her lover and the woman he'd taken in her place. It was both lovely and eerie, and quite appropriate to Romantic principles.

One of the footmen came noiselessly through the gallery. "Miss Thea Bohn is here," he announced. "Shall I say you are at home?"

"You don't need to run up and down stairs for me or my friends," Glennys said. "Thea knows the way and I'm always at home to her."

"Yes, Miss Eve. But Len Deerhorn would take our heads if we relaxed the standards of the Duke's house, even at your request."

The music didn't stop, but it changed into something softer, lighter, and soothing to restless hearts. Jonathan was lost in some musical dream of his own, but still in touch with what was occurring outside.

Thea was thin and pale. She was back in St. Lucien because Glennys had bent all of Albany's resources at her disposal to do it. In the last months of her pregnancy Catherine Gemma had become sick with a low fever she couldn't shake. The delivery had been difficult.

"If it hadn't been for the strength Thea poured into me and into Lorenzo, both my baby and I would have died," Catherine had said. She'd rewarded Thea well, and begged her to stay on for the recovery.

"I'm going back to Drake," Thea announced. "Catherine's fine now, and they need me there."

"No, you're not," Glennys said softly. She gently touched Thea's cheeks, and then her forehead. "You're far too warm for such a mild day. I think you should stay here for the summer. There's plenty of healing for you to do in St. Lucien. You want to stay. You're making yourself ill fighting against yourself, and what good is a sick healer?"

Thea was perfectly willing to accept Glennys's authority.

Glennys led Thea out to a pile of cushions on the balcony. "Rest, my dear. The samovar will be brought up soon. We'll take tea and then have some beef and red wine to build up your blood."

Thea allowed herself the deep pleasure of obeying, since she didn't have the strength to resist. But first she paused at the table. "What is this pretty toy?" she asked.

"A scale model of the Rain Shadows and the Saquave lands which are Duke Albany's by charter. These highest peaks are the Spear, Fang, and Claw," Glennys answered.

Thea considered the mountains. "Is one of those peaks called the Hammer?"

Glennys opened a drawer in the table and took out maps. "Let's see, these all have labels. The Hammer would be here in this outcrop under the Claw."

Thea put her finger on the Hammer. "It's here that Hans Rigg and Reverend Tuescher are making Silver City—when the Millennium comes and Alam burns the heathen so a new world can begin."

"The poor people are full of that kind of talk. I hear it everywhere in St. Lucien these days," said Jonathan, who'd joined them.

The three of them looked up from the table. Their eyes went over the beautifully polished floor of various inlaid woods, up to the colored lights falling through the stained glass in the gallery skylights over the paintings lining the walls. "This toy alone could keep a Drake family for years, I think," said Thea. "How can I live with these things knowing how miserably those in Drake live?"

Jonathan said, "None of us are rich. None of us own these things surrounding us."

"But we have the benefit of them all the same," Glennys said. "I guess we're simply luckier."

Jonathan disagreed. "It's not luck. It's our condition. Artists and healers are as necessary as any other labor. Our work allows for a world that has more than brutish sensuality in it. We could turn our backs on the support of the rich and powerful, and go live in the Drains. These toys would still be made. But our work would die, and the world would be the lesser for it."

Thea looked troubled, and her trouble was mirrored on Glennys's face.

In a tone of mock solemnity Jonathan said, "It's a dilemma which each of us must ponder." Then his infectious grin broke out. "In the meantime, let's indulge our brutish sensuality and eat."

Even before spring was finished, the hammer of the Majis Seaboard's wet heat came down on St. Lucien. The Assembly House adjourned and the ruling classes left for the country.

Midsummer's Eve marked the end of Queen's four seasons. Marie Bonheur's school went into recess. The Academies, except for the Equine Academy, shut down.

The Shoes, men and women alike, dressed in one-piece kibbas of the thinnest materials they could afford. Women scraped back their hair and bound it on top of their heads. The markets opened at dawn and closed before noon, to resume business after sunset. The ice houses went up, layers of dirt, straw, and canvas with ice between that had been winter-cut and stored in deep pits. Mosquitos had jubilee. Skunk cabbage and wild carrot flourished. Ivies and goldover sprayed down the walls and abutments of the city.

"What are you doing?" Thea asked drowsily. "It's barely dawn and you came in only an hour or two ago." It was the morning after Queen's had closed. Thea sat up in the other bed that had been moved into Glennys's suite of rooms. The healer had agreed to live in the Duke's house, but was too shy to take a room of her own and be waited on by maidservants.

Glennys had slushed down her body with tepid water and was binding her damp hair in a tight circlet of braids on the top of her head.

"There are no Shop classes or rehearsals now, Glenn. Why aren't you resting?" Thea inquired.

"I'm going to Queen's Yard to school a string of geldings in

Velvet Ridge Park before the sun's too high. The Duke takes care of me, but he gives me no coin. I have no income now until Queen's reopens, and Mother needs money, as usual. I'm really lucky that Joss offered me work. Most of the dancers don't know how they're going to live for the next months. The midsummer benefit didn't give us much of a bonus, and the salary is so small anyway. I think Catherine's *Ghost Lover* was ill-timed, now that the King's marrying Sharissa. Lady Colfax was the only one of the Aristos who might have cared for it, and she hates Catherine, so her circle of friends didn't attend," Glennys explained.

The maidservant entered to take away the bath things. "Will you want breakfast on your balcony, Miss Eve, or downstairs on the terrace?" She looked over at Thea, who'd begun to regain some of her much-needed flesh after near starvation in Drake. "Will that be breakfast for two?"

"I'll take tea and melon in the kitchen," Glennys replied. "Thank you. No need for you to get up, Thea, just because I am."

"I'll come to the kitchen with you. I'm making rounds with the Fortune House alms beaters, to try and persuade the poor mothers to have their children scratched for smallpox. Then the afternoon begins a lecture series on infections," Thea said.

Lenkert Deerhorn, if he was surprised to see Glennys so early, concealed it. She'd hardly seen him since the Duke's departure, busy as the eunuch was about Albany's interests, one of which was negotiating her contract for the next four Queen's seasons. He saw Glennys off on Cedar Rose, her favorite among the Duke's horses.

Thea took herself off by foot, though Lenkert offered her a horse. "I can't ride," she said.

On the way to her work, done in exchange for attending Fortune House healer lectures, Thea thought about artists. Even the very fortunate ones such as Glennys, Jonathan and George—or even Catherine—worried constantly about their livelihood. As with farmers, Thea realized, a good beginning or a good year was no guarantee that disaster wasn't waiting in the near future.

When Thea returned to Albany's late in the afternoon, Jonathan was seated at the pianoforte and the house was filled with music. Shyly, Thea went in through the kitchen entrance and from the butler learned that several young cavalry officers and cadets, and some dancers, had come calling.

Thea peered out at the party on the terrace from behind the filmy folding summer doors designed to keep out the insects.

The cadets and officers were in dishabille. The dancers wore outlandish costumes that only they could dare put on. Glennys herself was in an old pair of wide, gauzy trousers, loose weskit, and bare feet.

Rowena, Thea's favorite of Glennys's "revuers," as she called them, had them seated in a circle. One by one she was hennaing their toenails a brilliant orange. That there had been horseplay between the dancers and the cavalry was evident. Several of the Duke's geldings were tethered alongside the drive with the unsaddled cavalry mounts.

Glennys popped up from her cushion. "Come out, Thea. Come and meet Hengst, our old Baron's second son. We grew up together but I've not seen him since he went off to be a cadet. Now he's an officer, and an aide to Nathan Drake to boot!"

Thea had never had anything to do with the men from the Big House on Three Trees. Hengst kissed her on both cheeks, Aristo fashion. Hans Rigg and Reverend Tuescher would call this sin and treason, she knew, to associate like this with Devil Stogar's brother.

Except that Hengst was taller, and his dress different, Thea would have had trouble distinguishing him from Glennys at first sight. His hair was the same shade as Glennys's, and pulled through a matching feather-and-bead slide. His eyes were the same blue. His build, slender at the flanks and shoulders, was much the same as hers. So were his hands, very large and long, awkward-seeming on such narrow wrists.

Thea touched the orange, blue, and red feathers of the slide confining Glennys's hair.

"Isn't it pretty? The Old Men who watch the Badlands horses made them. Hengst is just back from Soudaka, and he brought one of these as a reunion gift," Glennys said.

"What's it like up there?" asked one of Hengst's fellow officers.

"Well, you know, our nearest neighbors are so far away we have to raise our own tomcats," he joshed. "Would you say that's about right, Thea?" he asked, making a place for her to join the conversation.

Tea was produced. "Where's the brandy, Glenn?" Hengst asked. "Albany's got liters of the stuff in his cellars, I know."

"No wine, no ale, and certainly no spirits at this time of the day for you, dear boy. You always did drink too much," Glennys said fondly. She reached over to hug him. "You can't understand how glad I am to see you." And very soon the liquors came around to celebrate their reunion after all.

Hengst had appointed himself Thea's servitor, and settled next to her. "Glennys serves us cold beef," he said approvingly, "not that everlasting mutton and lamb. Sheep, everywhere you look these days, and the land spoiled for running horses and cattle. Some of your congregations have been fighting with the old men in the Badlands again, bringing sheep out there."

Thea attended to her hunger. She still wasn't used to being able to eat whenever her stomach asked for it.

"I like to see a woman with an appetite," Hengst said with a grin. He got up and refilled her plate.

When he returned he said, "Glennys has changed so much since the Three Trees days. She hardly seems to be the same person. Whenever anyone came around she used to run off and hide in the stables. Now she's even got a sense of humor. My fellow officers and the cadets think very highly of her. Quite unusual for them, to treat a pair of Legs as anything but what makes twang walk."

It was disquieting, but oddly thrilling, Thea felt, to engage in a discussion of what Alaminites never mentioned out loud.

Venturing a bold remark, Thea said, "They're men, and from what I've seen men are very attracted to her."

"That's a fact of life for sure, and that's why we have King's Daughters. Some of us don't think it shameful like the Outremere religionists, or Lighters either." Then Hengst begged pardon, realizing he had insulted one of Glennys's guests.

"For a King's Daughter like Glennys, no, the condition isn't shameful," Thea said.

Hengst began to understand why people spoke so highly of this young Alaminite woman. She had a balance about her that made anyone in her company feel comfortable enough to reveal anything. She was awfully pretty too. Yet, there was something missing in her. It wasn't that she preferred women, he thought. It was as though all her vitality that might have gone into romance was put to some other purpose. There'd be nothing doing with her tonight.

"Glennys is a bloody fine Horse Skiller," Hengst continued, "and she isn't afraid to take risks. She would have shaped up a good cavalry officer, I think, probably better than me."

"I don't think so," Thea replied. "She thinks war is the worst waste in the world."

When the soiree broke up, Thea declined to go with the others to Old Harbor Hide and visit the Seahorse Tavern. She tired easily these muggy summer days.

"When you're a little more recovered, I'm going to teach you to ride. You aren't going to be able to hide in Pierce's house all summer," Glennys insisted.

Where did Glennys get her vigor, Thea wondered. She was as blooming and ready for fun as if she'd had a long night's sleep. She watched Glennys pulling Jonathan up behind her on Cedar Rose, and at that moment, something, perhaps the way their hands met, gave Thea a suspicion of where Glennys's energy came from. Then she thought she was mistaken. She'd seen them together so often, so closely, and she was sure there'd never been anything of that in their behavior, not even intercepted secret smiles.

Two bells after the sun had set, under the noise of the Seahorse patrons, Jonathan said to Glennys, "Do you think we can escape now?"

She nodded quickly. "You first. I'll meet you in Wishing Lane by Marie's school."

In the darkness of the narrow Wishing Lane Jonathan strained to hear the tap of Cedar Rose's hooves. When it came, his breath caught in his throat. Then Glennys was there, out of the saddle, and into his arms.

"Johnny, Johnny," she whispered. He backed her against the wall, his hungry mouth on hers. She gasped as soon as he touched her. She pressed against him as he showered kisses on her, behind her ears, on her chin, over her neck. His hands opened the top of her weskit. He lifted her breasts, and she cried out.

"I've waited and you've waited, and we've been so good, but now you're mine. I love you so much," he said.

"I love you, Johnny, and now you're mine." She twined her body with his. Her head was thrown back against the wall where climbing honeysuckle vines made a cushion. Her head turned from side to side in her desire and crushed the yellow blossoms. He could do this forever.

The cup of her hips rocked against him. The sound of her was the most wonderful music ever made. His hands never left her breasts. His mouth moved down her throat to the taut skin above them. At the first touch of his lips to her nipples she released a thin wail to the silver moon sailing above them.

He sank to the ground on his knees. One of his long arms still reached to her breasts, and the other circled her waist. He rolled his face against the out-thrust mound of her pubis. The thin fabric was damp and smelled of her. He groaned, caught in the current of sound, smell, and feel in which each woman is the same and totally different from any other.

Cedar Rose swished her tail without stopping. She stamped, and shook the forelock over her eyes ceaselessly.

"Oh, Johnny, can't we go home?" Glennys whispered. Wishing Lane, so hot, moist, and fragrant, was aswarm with thousands of mosquitos.

"We're being eaten alive," Jonathan realized. "But I can't get up right this moment."

Glennys slipped one hand between his knees and sighed.

"You're not helping matters any. I'm as helpless to stop what I'm about as these bloody stingers, but I'm so happy!" Jonathan moaned.

Out of her old Three Trees saddlebags Glennys pulled a net covered with tassels and fringes and flung it over Cedar Rose to distract the mosquitos. She had a cotton-silk weave shawl which she draped over the two of them. Hand in hand, leading the filly, they walked in the deeper darkness of Wishing Lane.

"We're all alone here. Baron knows it, and so does Cedar Rose," Glennys whispered. "My dog and my Horse Sense keep us safe."

They turned into the twisting maze of what was called Hidden Hide, for without knowing it well, it was hopeless for a visitor to find anyone. It was the oldest part of St. Lucien, built on the principles of Outremere old towns. The buildings reeled, shoulder-to-shoulder, and, where the upper stories overhung, nose-to-nose. Many of those from Outremere who worked in their countrymen's businesses had settled in Hidden Hide, finding it more homelike. The other inhabitants tended to be old and eccentric, and not necessarily poor.

The Hide had been built before horses or horse-drawn equipment. Some parts were so narrow that not even the delicate filly could get through.

Jonathan had chosen to live there because he could afford it, because he could play music at any time of the day or night, and because, so far as he knew, there were no other composers and musicians there. It was out of the way, so he and Glennys were thoroughly private. The inhabitants of Hidden Hide cared nothing about St. Lucien's theaters.

His landlady was deaf. Her house was filled with dusty, mildewed, peeling splendor. His rooms were at ground level, and he had the right to use the courtyard.

His landlady dealt in used furniture, and the courtyard was jammed full of it. At the beginning of their affair Glennys and

Jonathan had cleared a reasonably safe path and stall for her filly in an old shed.

Sometime after they'd lost track of when they'd slept and when they'd made love, Jonathan put on the teakettle. The small fire sent shadows dancing over the carpet woven with figures of birds, leaves, and flowers that had never existed. An ancient picture of the Mourning Mother and her son, with expressions of suffering faded to quaintness by age and dirt, hung over the fireplace.

"Were you as pleased to meet Hengst again as you acted?" Jonathan asked. "By the deuce, the two of you look alike."

"I'm even surprised by how glad I am to know him again. Remember, he was the one who first got Fulk to bring me from Dephi to Three Trees. He and Thurlow were the only friends I had for years. But, Jonathan, I wonder if he could see how alike we look. I wonder if he's figured out that he's my half-brother," she speculated through bites of an early peach.

Jonathan leaned over the bed and licked up the juice on Glennys's breasts.

"Oh. That's one of the many reasons I love you, Johnny. Nothing matters when I'm with you," she sighed, clinging to him.

She kissed and licked his breast, where his skin was smooth, white, and hairless as a girl's. She thrust one of her legs between his thighs. Her tongue just naturally followed the rill between his breasts down to the lacing of dark hairs that began under his navel.

"Your affair is standing to attention, Johnny. Does it want some attention?" she murmured.

Her tongue made his shaft slick. It was as smooth at the base as it was along its length. She curled her tongue around the softest part of all, the wide head with its little mouth in the center. His balls were tight and hard inside their suede purses.

Outside, dawn glimmered among the leaves. Cedar Rose neighed, as if greeting a friend, and then abruptly went silent.

Glennys stood immobile in a large hole in the carpet. Jonathan could feel her leaving him, though her body was still standing right in front of him where she'd pulled out of his embrace.

Then she came back. "Lenkert Deerhorn has followed me here. How did he do that? How dare he?"

"How do you know he's outside? He'd better not make trouble for you. This is *my* house, not the Duke's," Jonathan exclaimed.

"Cedar Rose knows, and I smell his scent with her sense. And Baron never barked. He likes Len."

"And that bloody stupid dog hates *my* guts," Jonathan growled.

"Baron is intelligent in ways you can't even understand!" Glennys snapped.

Both of them melted instantly and begged each other's pardon.

Jonathan pulled on a pair of breeches and his shirt. "I'm not leaving you to face him alone."

Glennys went straight to a pile of weatherbeaten lumber in the corner of the courtyard. "You know, Johnny," she said in a loud voice that turned him cold, that he'd never heard from her before, "spiders live in this mess, and Lenkert Deerhorn is the most loathsome spider of all of them."

She saddled Cedar Rose and then whistled up her dog. She kissed Jonathan slowly and lovingly on the mouth. "I will see you as usual then, Johnny, at the Duke's and my house, later."

Lenkert Deerhorn came out of his hiding place. "Miss Eve, it is my duty to my Duke to see you are safe every moment. I came here on foot, and I'm very tired. May I ride home behind you?" he asked, every line of his body proclaiming subservience.

"You spun a web, spider, to get here. Scuttle back on that," Glennys said shortly. She rode off to prepare for her morning's work in Velvet Ridge Park.

In the library office of the Waterford Big House, Duke Albany read over several times the concluding words of Lenkert's report. It was no more than he expected. It was best that the woman in her get what no woman ever went satisfied to her burial kurgan without having. Evidently that musician was serving his purpose nobly. But much to his surprise a part of the Duke bled, because he could not provide what she needed.

"I'm an old fool after all, wanting revenge put on that Johnny-come-lately," he said to himself.

Though his role of the moment was to be peacemaker between the Waterfords and the Lubbocks over another female who took what she wanted, he found himself giving a great deal of thought to vengeance.

· Twenty-Two ·

MOSQUITO CURTAINS OVER the windows and balcony doors, and again around the bed, sucked and exhaled with the inflation and recession of the breeze. Drone of bumblebee, buzz of fly, and whump of mosquito draperies were the only punctuation in the dim afternoon silence within Glennys's bedroom. Jonathan had taught her to notice all the sounds that made up the quiet.

A flagon of mint tea, the silver pearled from the ice in it, and a platter of fruit under a damask napkin stood on a tray. Water waited in the tub. Grand dresses, or merely pretty ones, work clothes for dance or horses, all clean and tended by attention and hands not her own, waited for her choice.

Luxury. This was luxury. She loved it. She was impatient to give it up.

She and Johnny had to wait until Duke Albany returned before they could be together for all eyes to see. For the sake of Albany's honor it had to appear that he was the one to break their contract. Even in the summer city, deserted by the Duke's peers, she'd not allow his name to be bandied on derisive tongues. A fragrant cedarwood desk was part of the sitting room's furnishings. One series of compartments was given over entirely to letters from her mother. Another was for tradesmen's bills for gloves, ribbons, and other essential notions. But her contracts and licenses were kept in a strongbox in the boudoir's wardrobe, next to where she hung her capacious Three Trees saddlebags.

In the desk was water for the ink, fresh-cut quills, and dry sand. There was also wax and a seal of her own, designed by George Sert, of a horse filled with the figures of other animals.

I write to my dear Duke Pierce Albany—

Pierce, I am happier than I've ever been before.
By the time you read this you already know. Your chief spider wove himself into a web that was private to you, Jonathan Reed the Composer, and myself. Your sympathy, so much

wider than your eunuch's, may catch an echo of what is be-
tween Mr. Reed and me, and then again, you may not. There's
a gulf, forever fixed, between those who perform for the ben-
efit of others' entertainment, and those who don't.

I love Jonathan Reed the Composer. He too, like you and
me, and more than either of us, is alone in this world, with
no family and only such friends as honor him for his music.

Your honor is saved by both of us from vile gossip. Not even
Thea Bohn, the Alaminite healer who sleeps in my room,
knows. Not a breath of our connection will be public until you
return to St. Lucien and repudiate me.

Our own bond, my dearest Pierce, holds fast, but not yet.
I am too young. The Saquave is an honest dream that I share
with you—but not yet.

I have striven hard and long for another dream that Jon-
athan Reed knows with all his heart. We are not foolish, dear
Pierce. Sharissa Ely will soon be Queen in Nolan and she is
my patron, and that of Jonathan and George Sert, the painter,
as well.

Pierce, I am so very, very happy, and you are part of my
happiness.

Glennys Eve.

She folded and sealed her missive, and then put it within
another, heavier cover, directed to Lenkert Deerhorn for the
Duke's thrice-daily messenger pouch. The chambermaid would
take it to the library.

Glennys had not forgiven the eunuch. His spying upon her
was all the eunuch's own doing and none of the Duke's, she'd
decided. It was the Duke who had chosen to do the ceremony
of Stallion Queen service. He would understand everything, including how her love for Jonathan would not interfere with his
plans for her. He'd understand she deserved a normal woman's
happiness for as long as it could last. But how quickly her con-
nections had become tangled, she thought.

She dressed and went downstairs to prepare for the arrival of
Jonathan and her friends. There was no stain of any kind upon
enjoying the summer and preparing for a brilliant fall season at
Queen's for them all. With Sharissa as Queen they could plan as
confidently for success as those on the List of Artists could ever
expect.

Some days later they were all gathered under a half-tent erected on the deck below Duke Albany's watergates. Catherine Gemma had made herself so much a part of the revuers' gatherings that they all now were as comfortable with the First Dancer as if she were one of them.

"Why are you so restless this afternoon, Glenn?" inquired Rowena. "It's far too warm for you to keep pacing about." She followed Glennys in the mirror in which she was also following the course of Amalia's hands giving her a new way of doing her hair.

Taking Rowena's hint, Glennys threw herself upon a pile of cushions. She tried to interest herself in the others' prattlings about the small sloop tacking up this channel of Setham River.

"We should take this opportunity for improving conversation," Catherine began. "We should all be considering how the new Sace-Cothberg war will affect our fortune and that of Queen's."

"We should be considering how to improve our looks," Nan replied vigorously, "so we will be best prepared to catch some wealthy Chief. That's the only effect war has on our fortune."

Glennys wished Thea would come soon. She'd have conversation both improving and interesting.

Rais got to her feet. "Speaking of those for whom war is the greatest affair, I believe some of them will visit us momentarily."

They shaded their eyes and squinted into the distance where the sun's glare on the water was most blinding. The sloop was going to anchor.

Several small boats were lowered. Soon they could make out the figures of Nathan Drake, Chief of Cavalry, Hengst, several other officers, and the cadets of Nathan's blademaster class.

The dancers all peeped quickly into the mirror before it was hastily put out of sight. Catherine, however, had taken up her sleeping baby from his wet nurse. Amalia helped her take out one arm from her dress and bare a breast before arranging a light shawl discreetly over that side. What was the First Dancer up to, Glennys wondered. Cathy had dried up her breasts as soon as possible.

As greetings and introductions went back and forth, Catherine said in her low, lovely voice, "Nathan, you've not yet seen my beautiful Lorenzo."

Leaning down to gaze at the baby's sleeping face, Nathan

said, "He's a beautiful child indeed, nearly as beautiful as the place at which he's privileged to rest his head."

"Oh," Catherine gasped, and blushed prettily. "I'd forgotten." She instantly replaced the shawl, which had become disarranged.

Rowena and Glennys had caught the maneuver. "The rest of us are raw recruits next to the Gemma," Rowena whispered. "How very clever."

For the rest of the time Nathan Drake's eyes continually went back to what he'd seen for such a short moment, though now all was decent, and Lorenzo was back with his wet nurse, Nicola. Nathan spent the greatest portion of his visit at Catherine's side. Reluctantly, the Chief prepared to take the cadets back to the Academy in time for roll call, promising to return immediately.

Then the Romantics arrived. With Jonathan came George Sert, Richard Thorvald, Thor's wife—and George's own newly married wife, Lark.

Lark's eyes opened wide when she saw the company—such outrageous clothing, such banter, such an expanse of bare limbs, feet, and midriffs. The coverings cut low over the women's breasts announced clearly what sort of women these were.

"It's necessary business, sweetling," Mrs. Thorvald told Lark. "You'll be accustomed to it in no time. And such happiness for you. So many painters leave their ladies at home when they call upon these."

Glennys paced about under the half-tent, as though the deck were a cage and she an animal shut within it. "What disturbs you so much today?" Jonathan asked her.

"The geldings," was her unexpected answer.

"There's not illness in the Yard, I hope?" asked Catherine. "All of us, menagerie, stable, and ballerinas, are going to be very busy soon preparing for Sharissa's wedding festivities before the war."

"No, not that, not exactly," Glennys began. Then she was interrupted. Nathan Drake and Hengst, on horseback, had rejoined them. Catherine's charms had not lost any of their power since motherhood, it seemed.

After the Chief and Hengst were settled, Catherine returned to the topic of Glennys's uneasiness.

Glennys said, "It's a new trainer Joss has taken on trial. Another woman, named Cody Bonacker. She comes to the Yard with the same Horse Skiller license I have. And she plans to join Marie Bonheur's ballet classes when the school reopens."

Catherine smiled. "It sounds like jealousy to me. You're less of old Joss's pet now because you're one of us. But you did so well for Joss that he wants to try it again. This girl has heard you got on stage through the Queen's Yard and wants to try it for herself. You should be flattered."

Glennys smiled ruefully. That there was some jealousy, a scent of the rival unseating her in Joss's affection, she had to admit. "But even so, I don't like her. She's awfully quick with the whip, and her spurs don't just tick or prick. That's not how to treat stage geldings."

Hengst looked thoughtful. "Bonacker is the name of the Stablemaster for Baron Acker, though they never did very well with their own war stallion lines. He always bought pickets of our Three Trees stallions for his own sons. I know because Colonel Acker is one of Stogar's men. I remember Acker from the first winter Glennys came to us. I didn't like him then, and I don't like him now."

Nathan Drake said, "I know Colonel Acker." He said no more, unwilling to gossip in this group. Glennys believed he thought no better of the Ackers than they deserved.

Thea Bohn had come home. "You're in time for tea!" Catherine said. "Come and sit with us, Thea, and look at Renzo. He sleeps so well these last two days. He's not wakened once all afternoon."

"I think he sleeps too much," observed Nicola. "I said so yesterday. He usually is squirming and demanding to eat."

Thea took the baby into her arms. Unlike Alaminites, the Langanese didn't swaddle their infants into immobility. Renzo was loosely wrapped in a thin blanket and wore only a diaper. He opened his eyes and sighed a little when shifted into Thea's hold. But he didn't stretch or wriggle.

Thea jiggled him for a few minutes. Then she said, "Cathy, I'm sure there's nothing to be alarmed by, but I'd like to take him into the house and examine him upstairs in Glennys's rooms, where all my things are."

Catherine sent Nicola and Amalia, her eyes and ears, with Thea and the baby. Glennys could see the First Dancer was torn in two, because she wanted to stay in Nathan's company. But in a few moments, Catherine excused herself to follow the others.

Twilight was approaching. The other guests, with the exception of the Chief and Hengst, had left. Glennys rang the bell to have the tea things removed. "How odd," she said. "No one has come to the bell."

The three by the river heard a shriek from the house. Glennys, barefoot, ran faster than Nathan or Hengst could run in boots and spurs, across the gardens and over the terrace.

She waited at the stairs for them to catch up.

"I will *not* go with you, Hans Rigg, not for anything in heaven or hell!" That was Thea's voice. It came from Glennys's suite.

"Good girl," Nathan whispered to Glennys, "to wait for us."

She pointed to their spurs. Hengst and Nathan nodded. She looked wildly about in the poor light of dusk and found a napkin dropped on the first stair. The lamps of evening had not been lit. Where was everyone who staffed the house?

Swiftly as thought, Hengst cut off strips from the cloth and bound up his and Nathan's spurs. Then they followed her up the dark, handsome staircase to the floors above.

Gently she tried the door to her sitting room. It was locked. The key was always on a little table by the door, though she'd never felt the need to use it.

There was another way—a passage of discretion, built for dalliances and intrigues, that connected her bedroom to the master bedroom. She knew where the passage was, though she'd never had to use it. The three of them slipped into Albany's bedroom and through the passage toward Glennys's suite.

Her bedroom was dark and empty, as was the dressing room. But the sitting room was brightly lit. They could see Catherine, Nicola, and Amalia, all bound and gagged. Lorenzo lay on a large pillow in the middle of a table wearing nothing at all. He was beginning to squirm fitfully. An ugly man came toward him, knife in hand.

"A hoor's begetting, Hans. Should we give the little bastard what he deserves, and these hoors too?"

Then Glennys saw Thea. She broke free from the man who restrained her, snatched up the baby, and raced for the door. But the door was locked.

"Can none of you control a girl?" growled the one who must have been the leader. "Come Thea, angel, you know not what you do. You've been corrupted by living with hoors and witches. We won't hurt the brat, put him down. You're the only one we want, the only one worth saving in this heathen place. Alam will take care of these others soon enough."

"I'd rather die," Thea cried.

"Lighters," Glennys whispered in Nathan's ear. "Four of them. But there must be others, or else the house would have roused."

Thea clutched Lorenzo. The leader and his men closed in on her. She opened her hand. A small vial caught the light and sparked. "Foxglove, Hans Rigg. Unless you leave immediately, I will take it. I will take it the first move toward me you make."

"Let her drink it! She's no good to anyone now," one of the Alaminites urged.

The narrowness of the doorway made it difficult for Nathan and Hengst to act together against the four Alaminites.

Nathan's throwing blade hit one. Hengst passed him a second blade immediately, which Nathan threw at the next best target. Then Nathan was in the room, Hengst at his back, their swords drawn. The Alaminite Nathan had spitted second wasn't dead. Spewing blood, he grabbed Hengst. The third henchman grappled with Nathan as Hans Rigg turned and ran back from the door toward the balcony.

The mosquito curtains were a flimsy barrier. Hans vaulted off the small balcony shouting, "Prophets! We are discovered! Prophets! Out! Escape!"

Glennys had no war stallion matched to her to break out and chase down an enemy. Her own throwing knife was in the wardrobe of her dressing room. There was nothing she could do.

Nathan dispatched his opponent in seconds, but in those seconds Hans Rigg and his men escaped.

"Oh, God," Thea said, gasping.

"There's no question of you going back to Drake now," Glennys said to Thea.

"Would you really have taken poison rather than go with him?" The ungagged, unbound Catherine shivered, holding her baby close.

Thea looked down at the little vial that she still had in her hand. "It's perfume. It's Glennys's perfume. It was on the table here by the door. No. I would have pretended, and lived to escape another day. But the reason I thought to do that is I was thinking of poison already. Catherine, Lorenzo is being poisoned."

"Poisoned?" Catherine repeated.

"But very slowly," said Thea. "We've found out in time. He'll recover, but you must be very, very careful."

"Who?" said Catherine. "No one touches him except myself, Amalia, and Nicola."

"Are you sure, Catherine?" questioned Nathan. "You have a house of your own and people to care for it."

Amalia said, "None of them have anything to do with the

nursery, not even to clean it. Other than Thea, no one except us three has even held him. And the ballerinas today, of course, but they can't be responsible. Not even the Duchess Colfax took him in her arms when she came to see Lorenzo a few days ago.''

Catherine screeched more wildly than she did when the Prophets of the Millennium invaded the sitting room. ''The Duchess did it! She wants the Duke to make a eunuch of Lorenzo and send him to the Colfax horse farm! She can only give daughters, and the King has cast her off. But I gave a beautiful, beautiful son, the only son Colfax has.''

The women's eyes were all wide with horror.

''Renzo only takes Nicola's breast milk,'' said Amalia.

Nicola's pretty face was blotched by terror. ''I thought the Duchess had become kind. She gave me a salve to use on my breasts so they'd not be too tender and crack. It was what her daughters' wet nurses had used, she said. She'd asked, and I told her how lustily Lorenzo sucks.''

''Aristos,'' Thea said. ''Now I see why the Fortune House teaches a class in poisons and their antidotes. Nicola, do you have this salve with you?''

Nicola produced a pretty jar enameled with doves and flowers in pink and gold.

''I'll take this to Healer Gaffin. He'll help me determine what it is. I think not much harm has been done. See, the skin of the salve has hardly been broken,'' Thea comforted Nicola.

''My breasts are good ones. I hardly need to use such things,'' she said, looking up with a tear-wet face. ''See,'' she said. Her bodice gave evidence that her milk was running high. Much to Hengst's amusement, Nicola pulled out the great globes for Thea to examine.

''But you can't feed him now. Whatever the poison is, it's made to work slowly, to give the appearance of a long wasting away,'' Thea said.

Nathan returned with the staff of the house. Except for Deerhorn, who was away from home, they'd all been locked in the wine cellar.

''What the deuce?'' wondered the butler, seeing a woman with milk-streaming breasts standing among three dead men and on a carpet of blood.

''These Lighters must have been learning the habits of the household,'' said Nathan. ''Don't you usually, Miss Eve, go with your friends at the time of day those Prophets invaded your home?''

What a bloody tangle, Glennys thought.

Nicola was pleading as if for her life.

"Oh, nonsense," Amalia said briskly to Nicola. "We don't think you poisoned Renzo purposely. But we must find another wet nurse."

Indeed, the baby was crying, though less loudly than in previous days, demanding to be fed.

"Hengst, go to the city watch, though I think there's no need to tell them anything other than that there are Alaminites about, bent on trouble. I'll go with the women to the healer's. Butler, tell Deerhorn when he returns to organize a watch day and night on the Duke's property," said Nathan.

The carriage was ordered. While Nathan and Hengst waited for their horses to be brought up with the carriage, Catherine saw that the Chief's eyes hardly left her. There was a knowing twinkle in those eyes, and very nice green ones they were, she thought, with long lashes and winglike brows.

"Now you know," she said to Nathan. "I did it purposely, exposed myself to you to catch your interest."

"I was most interested," Nathan gallantly replied. "However, the Duke Colfax would not like to hear that."

"I tore up the concubine contract when Colfax wanted to geld Lorenzo as the price of continuing his protection. Nothing that interests me is any longer his concern," Catherine said.

The next afternoon all the dancers except Cayetana, who was in the country, were called to the Shop. One by one they straggled in, mopping their faces and brows. They met in the banquet room, an oak-paneled vastness that hadn't been opened in weeks.

Lenkert insisted upon attending Glennys. "This is business. You are still the Duke's concubine, and I'm obligated to look out for your interests."

August Gardel looked quite frail, not at all his usual well-groomed self. The ballet director showed his age in the heat.

When he had gotten them into a group around the enormous dining table, Gardel began, "King Leon is marrying Sharissa Ely in four weeks." He got no further.

The dancers leaped into the air and flung themselves into each others' arms. "We knew it! We knew it! We knew it would be an early wedding because of the Sace-Cothberg war. Now we don't have to get jobs!"

"You'll wish you were taking in laundry, Legs, when you hear the rest," Gardel shouted. "We've got to get on ships and sail down the coast to the seat of the Elys—in Yemmessee. You think it's hot here? Wait until you've been in the Yemmessee in the summer.''

"Yemmessee? Yemmessee? Why there?" they all asked.

"Because the Elys' port is a good one from which to sail Outremere this time of year, something to do with Majis Sea currents and winds. I don't know. But King Leon will sail from there with both his sons to Outremere, to teach his Dallas and Hakaan about war. What a terrible thing for those two beautiful boys," he lamented. "Outdoor living is so bad for the complexion."

Glennys was as glad of the call to action as the others. She'd already tired of spending so many afternoons and evenings doing nothing to much purpose.

She was also glad to leave Albany's house, first because of Jonathan, and second because of the Alaminites. Since Hans Rigg had tried to kidnap Thea, neither of them felt secure there.

Everyone was asking Gardel how much they'd get paid, and when they'd start getting it. "We need an advance immediately," reasoned Rowena. "We've got so much to arrange for our clothes before we sail. *When* do we sail?"

Lenkert inserted himself between the revuers, beat out Amalia, and got to Gardel first. "Glennys is working for Queen's Yard again this summer. She should get a bonus for that."

By then the stage secrets guild was at the ballet director over what properties and scenery should be taken.

"Leave me alone for one minute so I can talk. I've only been told about this last night. I haven't received a budget or a sailing schedule or anything yet!" He beat the floor with his bull's-pizzle walking cane for emphasis.

All over the Shop could be heard loud voices in altercation and inquiry. The opera, the orchestra, and the conductors would be going, so that meant Jonathan would be too. How wonderful it·all was, Glennys exulted. Somehow they'd get Thea with them. She couldn't be left to fend off Hans Rigg by herself in St. Lucien. Oh, Glennys thought, she was glad to be going somewhere, anywhere, to see something of the world outside St. Lucien.

Runners were taking off in all directions to procure the endless miles of satin and ribbon that would be needed for garlands and wardrobe.

Gardel left them to meet with the heads of Queen's different parts. The confusion was wilder even than the backstage chaos of a premiere night.

Glennys ran into Thorvald and George, who'd heard the noise from the Arts Academy. The two painters had received their summons last night. They were to be the official artists of the wedding, the coronation, and the sailing of King Leon and his two heirs.

"It still seems odd, and terribly inconvenient, to have it in the Yemmessee," Glennys mused.

Thorvald wiped the sweat off his face with a very large handkerchief. "Sweetheart, don't you understand? It's for the same reason the King's marrying a southern Aristo. This is to be a horse warrior wedding, and the last. It's a compliment to the Spur cavalry, for the Sace-Cothberg campaign itself is going to be put mainly into the hands of Stogar's ammunition and Colfax's cannon and guns, in other words, the Wheels. It's supposed to unite the Aristos in the face of the rivalry they've got from the gunners."

Glennys thought about King Leon and Prince Roald, Stogar and Duke Colfax, the Duchess Colfax and Sharissa Ely. She didn't give much chance that even another war could unite the Spurs and Wheels. The home hostilities had begun long before those overseas.

The Stalking Horse

• Act IV •

• TWENTY-THREE •

WHEATLY LUBBOCK, ONE of the three young cavalry officers playing Trump and Jester in Glennys's tent, broke out in one of the cavalry's new oaths. "Shoot it! I'm out, I'm dead, and Glenn's got the pot again." He mopped his wet face with the edge of his neck cloth.

Glennys's tent was in the gardens behind the palatial Big House of the Elys. Blue Fields was the name of their seat, either because of the indigo plantations or the color of the grass. Blue Fields was in the uplands away from the coastal country around Yemmessee Town.

Glennys's tent was an improvement over the general camp of the cavalry regiments in the fields. She also drank and ate better than they did. Lenkert Deerhorn's long experience with the gatherings of the great had brought staff, supplies, and comforts from St. Lucien. Glennys had a share in all the services provided to Duke Albany as his concubine, and also because she'd had a tiny part in Sharissa's wedding-coronation yesterday.

Glennys had had the honor of standing on her feet under the sun for hours wearing splendid, heavy clothes. The nuptial-coronal had taken place under an awning, but enormous as it was, it hadn't been large enough to reach all the way back to cover Glennys, the last hair in the Queen of Nolan's tail.

Three hours into the ceremonies Glennys almost wished she'd never sacrificed old Cognac to rescue the girl beset by hunger rioters at the Festival of Hearts. The honor had been intended to show that the new Queen, of an old bloodline, didn't forget her friends, but Glennys could have done without the privilege. Dehydrated and exhausted, she then had to lead the revuers and the balky geldings through their patterns for everyone else's entertainment immediately afterwards.

"Do we dare to deal again?" inquired Colonel Gordon.

"Not me," said Talbot Waterford. He wasn't the Baron Waterford, though he was part of the clan. The new Baron was Thurlow's young son. However, Talbot and Wheatly were as good friends again as they'd been before Tal's older brother had been killed in a duel by the head of Wheatly's Lubbock branch over Thurlow's favors. Duke Albany's peacemaking mission had been successful, though it had been helped by the royal courier calling the Aristo bloods to war, wedding, and coronation.

Talbot Waterford said, "I can't afford to play another hand, and still keep any cash for Outremere—not if I'm playing against Glennys Eve." It was said gallantly, with no trace of ill humor. He toasted her and drank down the rest of his Winebow.

"It's neither luck nor skill on my part. You all drink too much," she teased the three men.

"But you gave us the Winebow," protested Colonel Gordon. "Not to drink it would be an insult to the provision of decent wine by Duke Albany. Yemmessee is empty by now of anything to drink but that overpriced Firewater swill."

Firewater was disgusting. Fermented from rice, and infused with tobacco for a kick, Firewater was what the indentured hands who worked the Yemmessee fields drank. But the invasion of Spurs and Wheels had inflated the prices and depleted everything. Firewater was what was left—Firewater and the mess tents.

Glennys kept the wine and ale in a pit dug in the soft ground under the half-timbered, matted floor of her tent. Her cellar was intended to attract exactly this sort of visitor and to help water the idea of the Saquave Land Settlement Company in the minds of these estateless young Aristo men.

She wondered how many would return from this war.

She got up from her cushion and looked into the camp bathtub behind a screen. She'd put six bottles of the sparkling yellow Winebow into so-called cold water before the men had arrived.

"I've got a bottle left here in the tub, though the ice is melted. You all want to open it?" Glennys offered. She didn't think their heads needed more wine, but she thought their spirits did.

"Bring it out!" called Wheatly Lubbock. "It's our dummy prize, since you got all the pots."

They didn't bother with glasses for the last bottle, but passed it around. Already they were slipping into campaign habits.

Dance music drifted over from the weeping willow grove. "Jonathan Reed," Talbot Waterford sighed, "rehearsing for tonight's ball honoring the first sail of cavalry to Outremere. That's us. A salute to the luck. May she bring the same cheer to the cavalry as she's done to Stone-face Stogar and Crooked Colfax."

"So Stogar's gone already?" Gordon asked Waterford.

"As soon as the last toast to Sharissa was drunk at the banquet. Left us to Hengst, he did, while he sailed upcoast to his bloody munitions factories in Drake. He and Colfax and their whole bunch won't be back until the King sails later.'' Waterford's words were sober, in spite of the wine he'd drunk during the card game.

Gordon said, "I wish it was clear exactly who was in charge of the Fulk regiment. Hengst should be, if Stogar's not with us. But Hengst isn't in charge because he's in Nathan's service."

Wheatly Lubbock stirred uncomfortably. Unclear lines of command boded badly for the future.

Gordon tried to banish the gloom rapidly settling over them. "King Leon is going with Nathan in the third sail. Between the King and our Chief, the fornicating shooter troops will be kept in their place. We're the Spurs, and we're Aristos because we're the horse soldiers. No constance of black powder noise can change that."

He saluted with the bottle. "We're all related."

The others returned it. "We're all related! We'll show the bloody Sace-Cothbergians and the cannon a charge or two that'll make 'em cry for nursey!"

Outside the tent came the chink of war stallion spurs. Through the mosquito netting around the half-rolled walls they saw a pair of legs encased in black riding breeches trimmed in gold.

"Hengst, old boy! There's a swallow of Winebow left for you. We'd not share that with everyone come a-callin' on Glennys,'' Talbot greeted him.

"You all better move it. Staff meeting in quarters the hour before dinner in the Big House, and then it's down to the quays until we sail tomorrow,'' Hengst told them.

The three card players got to their feet. With great enthusiasm they kissed Glennys farewell—for how long? Forever? "Thanks for Albany's hospitality and your own good cheer. Our first assignment back in Nolan will be to cheer you at Queen's. Our second will be to beat the breeches off you in Trump and Jester and get back our forients. Then we'll listen some more to this Saquave idea."

Glennys kissed them back and they were gone. "I hope they do come back,'' she said sadly.

Hengst laughed. "Without war, what would the rich, old men do with all us hot, young ones riding on their tail, who've got no money or lands of our own? At least in war we'll get a share of the loot—though what loot there'll be in this one I don't know, since it seems we're fighting to hold territory and not expand."

Hengst was sweated through his clothes, and the hair falling down under his turban was wet. He was tired. There had been long days and nights of uninterrupted duty ever since the general muster began—weeks before the nuptials.

Nathan had promoted his young aide to the trusted but unenviable position as Chief of Purveyors, so Hengst was in tomorrow's first sail. He was in charge of provisions and bivouacs on the cavalry's long overland trek across Gondol, Tourienne, and up into Langano to the front lines of the Sace-Cothbergians' invasion of the Nemourian cantons. That was his reward for last year's delightful riding all over the Outremere Domains, when he'd learned their topography under Nathan's tutelage.

"What a wedding jubilee for Sharissa! A war gathering," Glennys said. "I don't think anyone's been overjoyed except Stogar and Colfax. They're making piles of money selling their powder and guns to the throne."

"We're all right," Hengst maintained, with a flash of his usual carefreeness. "We're the flower of Nolan. What can happen to us?"

"Death and maiming!" Glennys wished she could take back that needless remark. She made the sign to ward off bad luck, as did Hengst.

"Surely you can spare a little time to say a proper farewell to me? I can find another bottle of wine," Glennys bribed.

"Only if you drink with me, Glenn. You've gotten a bad habit of abstinence." He seemed glad for the offer, however, and followed her into the tent. He threw himself on the cushions with a groan.

He talked about the war, though it seemed to be a topic that compelled him, rather than being freely chosen.

The Sace-Cothbergians were making a bid to get down to Langano's port cities. The neutral Nemourian cantons in the forested mountains stood between the Sace-Cothberg states and the Outremere Domains.

Glennys listened closely, while thinking her own thoughts. She was sure the Nemourians prayed fervently for a pox to fall upon all the powers who indiscriminately razed their timber, burned their bridges, battled through their market towns, and killed their people and livestock.

"You dance good now," said Hengst, "and make great jubilee for our King, his sons—and for my Chief—when they all

take third sail. Nathan needs every support to put heart into him
for this cannon war. It's loco to make the cavalry march from
the shores of Gondol. We should be sailing directly to
Langano! We won't reach the Nemourian Mountains until
winter's set in. I don't have to tell you about winter.''

It was the first time Glennys had heard voiced baldly the foreboding in the hearts of the cavalry.

Hengst mused, staring at the bottle of Winebow. ''I understand why the King's waiting so long to join the rest of us. He's
got to give Sharissa a moon-to-moon to catch with his child. But
Nathan should have been given the first sail!''

He stood up to leave. Hengst took Glennys in his arms and
hugged her close. He kissed her, a peculiar sort of kiss. He
rubbed his lips gently over hers.

''Kiss my Chief like this before he sails. Maybe then some of
the famous Glennys Eve good luck will rub off on him. With
my brother hand-in-glove with Nathan's banking brother, I think
both Nathan and I are confused as to where our family honor
and loyalty lies. Nathan's going to need your luck, as well as his
own, to track between family and honor,'' Hengst said.

Wanting her last words to Hengst to be gay ones, Glennys
said, ''Before kissing Nathan Drake in any manner at all, I'll
have to get Catherine Gemma's permission. The two of them
have what might be called an understanding.''

Hengst said, ''There's no woman Nathan's going to care for
so much as his honor and luck. Kiss him.''

Baron leaped up to put his paws on Hengst's shoulders, nearly
knocking him over. The mastiff's tongue washed over Hengst's
face. He fondled the dog's ears. His wide-palmed, long-fingered
hand met Glennys's on the dog's head.

''Why did you name your dog Baron?'' Hengst asked in an
odd, tight voice.

''I named him after our father,'' she said.

She had said it to him. She held her breath.

Hengst captured Glennys's hand, so like his own, within his
own hands. He stared into her eyes, also like his own. He already knew.

''After our father. Yes, I thought so. Now tell me,'' he demanded, ''truly, on your family honor. Did you and *our* father's
horse execute *our* father's murderers? You were there, Glenn.
Tell me!''

''Stogar killed Fulk, with a crossbow. Deadly and I killed two
Alaminites, made to look guilty by Stogar,'' Glennys said.

Hengst wiped the sweat off his face. "It's good to know for certain. It explains so much of Stogar's treatment of me, and his command that I must have nothing to do with you. He guesses you know."

Hengst's laugh was thick and without amusement. "It's the great crime among Aristos, killing the sire. That the father might execute his son they justify. It's the curse of the old bloodlines' long life. Sons get sick of waiting to come into their own. But I'm a second son. I don't have anything to come into. Perhaps when I come back I'll be ready to talk over this Saquave land deal."

He kissed her again, this time for himself. "Till then, I hope your luck holds strong. We're all related."

He walked away between the magnolia trees, slapping his gauntlets against the wasps.

Glennys swallowed the lump in her throat. Hengst had figured it out. Their brother Stogar had killed their father. Hengst knew she was half-sister to him. He accepted that, and her.

Exhilarated with Hengst's acceptance, in spite of the heat-induced lassitude, Glennys began to clear up the card-game clutter on the floor of her tent. A sound between laughter and a sob bubbled up from her diaphragm. Hengst had walked away from a good bottle of wine, having drunk less than a glass. Nothing else could have told as vividly what he thought about the chances of this war for him and those he rode with.

Glennys considered the Winebow. She poured Hengst's wine into her own glass.

Sundown. Her tent was filled with a heavy golden glow thick as honey. It was a long walk to the mess tents. She had a badge, but no appetite. How could the air be so still, so sweltering, when the sea was so near, and the Yemmessee River ran only furlongs away?

Up in the Ely Big House dinner would be served to the entitled. They'd dine on frog legs, turtle soup, and crab on crushed ice. Up at the Big House were the giant kaftas, pulled by indentured children to fan the Aristos. The Big House's height captured whatever breeze came through. With so many ladies of the bloodlines, even her position as Duke Albany's concubine gave her no place at the Big House's table.

Glennys wanted more than anything to be out of the Yemmessee. She loved the heat, having grown up where it was freezing for so much of the year, but she couldn't stand this eternal sweating. She hated how nothing changed after sundown, except that the heat clung even closer about her body, attracting every kind of insect to feed on her.

Most of all she hated that there were four more weeks of it before going home to St. Lucien, the Theater, and her new life with Jonathan.

What was there to do? There was nothing but to join the revuers and complain about everything and gossip about what it meant that Queen's Theater had a true Queen, who was patron to one of their own. But no one had any energy to work on new routines for the fall. She could visit the Gemma's tent and listen to fears regarding Duchess Colfax and baby Lorenzo. Thea was equally miserable and afraid about the Alaminites and Hans Rigg, and very sick of ministering to cavalrymen's venereal diseases.

Much later in the evening Glennys would be summoned by Albany to join him in his rooms in the Big House to brief him on the qualities of the young men he'd marked for the Saquave. She felt more excited by Albany and his plans than ever, and less like a dancer.

She refilled her glass.

Glennys wanted Jonathan. She wanted to lie with him. She wanted how he made her laugh and think at the same time. He'd give her back to herself and make her forget Fulk, Stogar, and this strange excitement that had come with Hengst's acknowledging their kinship and their father's murder. But he was occupied, providing musical accompaniment for the Big House dinner.

"Shoot it! Fornicating shoot it!" she exclaimed, when after trimming her lamps against the insects she discovered the Winebow bottle was all, all empty.

"Shoot it! Fornicating shoot it!"

Like an indulged, half-grown cat, she raced about her tent. Her eyes glowed, and the tiny hairs downing her body all stood upright, even in the moistness of the Yemmessee air.

The moon was half full under a haze of scudding cloud cover. Baron was close to her legs, which had somehow gotten clad in thin breeches. The hem of her kibba was pulled up through the belt of her knife sheath. They were at the edge of acres of walls, hedges, and fences that divided Blue Fields' grazelands, which had been turned into a cavalry field camp for the duration.

Torches burned among the tents. The flames had halos of

moths, flying cockroaches, and mosquitos. Men, horses, and dogs lazed about in the heat of the night.

Through no volition of her own, Glennys's Horse Sense was wide open. It led her to a stallion, about nine years old. She recognized him. He was velvety black, and by the banners along the picket line, he belonged to one of Nathan Drake's own. She'd had her hands on him in his first year. She didn't know what the stallion's call name was now, but she and the Badlands' Old Men had named him Terror.

She played with his mane, already shorn against the pests that bred in the close quarters of the stallion ships. She straightened his long forelock and brushed away the flying insects. She blew into his nostrils, and stroked his neck and withers. She let him flow into her as she flowed into him. He snuffed her and the air. His ears perked with a new jauntiness. He was most willing to go for a ride.

Knowing the sort of men Nathan Drake chose to be closest to him, Glennys found what she looked for. Nathan's own were veterans of all weathers and climates. Nearby was the stallion's gear wrapped in oilskin against rain and mold. She strapped a pad woven of wool and linen to his back with the girth. She needed no bridle, reins, or stirrups. She mounted.

Cleverly they rode away behind the lines of pitched tents where men drank, gambled, boasted, and quarreled. Through the gathering mist they made their way to Yemmessee Town.

It was dark, but through Terror, she knew when they cantered over bridle trails between tobacco plantations, cotton fields, rice paddies, or indigo marshes. These crops made the Elys prosperous, so prosperous they could marry a daughter to a King. She realized why all the Fulks, whose land was in the hard, stony north, believed themselves poor. The wealth of the Elys was staggering. The thought disappeared into the joy of her ride.

Glennys thought she was going down to the beaches south of Yemmessee Bay Harbor. She sang the stallion's call name to him, turning it into *ta-rah, ta-rah, ta-rah*. Terror's hooves thudded over the timbers of corduroy roads and rattled on the cobbles of the avenues. Scenting other horses, he had gone into Yemmessee Town of his own will.

Comfortable homes and mercantile establishments were set back from the streets behind walls. Pecan trees shaded the public ways. The unripe windfall nuts crunched under Terror's hooves. The stallion was drawn by the other horses. Glennys was at-

tracted by the lighted central hide of Yemmessee Town. They
emerged into the Sale Yard. Vagrants, sent in lot consignment
into the Yemmessee, were up at auction.

"Whatem ay bid, whatem ay bid, for this fine, strong she?
Whatem ay bid, whatem ay bid for the she and the suckling at
her tits? Oo'l start, oo'l start at two? Gimme two, gimme two,
two for two. I hear three for two, three for two, a fine she and
sucker as one. Three an a half, three an a half, four, four, four
is more. Done! Next.''

Glennys measured time only by Terror's restive responses to
the other horses tethered about the Sale Yard. The auctioneer's
chant rolled, turned, trilled, and cooed, making a seductive music out of voice, rhythm, and diction. Suspended in the level
where she participated in the world partly through her own senses
and partly through the stallion's, she was charmed by the lin-
guistic virtuosity. This state recalled, though it did not resemble,
her hours with Jonathan in his bed. They could cleave to each
other for entire nights, he in her, and she in him, floating in a
world that was only sense, that flickered with shared images.

That this night's enjoyment came from the sound of human
flesh being sold gradually penetrated Glennys's wine-visioned
mind.

Holding pens alternated with sheds and barns on the Yard's
periphery. Families had been broken up. Only the youngest children and babies were allowed to stay with their mothers, to be
sold as one unit. Plantation owners bought labor here for an
indentured bondage of seven years.

People who'd lost their luck were being forced to work in a
land they didn't choose, stooping their backs for the fortune of
Aristos who gave them nothing that anyone who valued health
and independence wanted. The indigo, rice, cotton, and tobacco
they produced were wanted all over Mittania, but at a terrible
cost to the land and the people who worked on it.

She saw a lot of cavalry about. They weren't bidding, but they
were interested in something. They mainly flowed back and forth
out of a narrow street behind the central sale block. Curious,
Glennys nudged Terror among them.

She saw a row of sheds, broken into many flimsy-doored cu-
bicles. Here was where the attractive units of the consignment
were kept, all the young, healthy, and pretty ones. They weren't
being sold, they were being rented. The men were encouraged
to examine the merchandise in any manner they liked.

No doubt Baron Ely got a percentage from this sort of trade, as he did from the other.

Sharissa would never have come to be Queen of Nolan if Glennys hadn't lifted her to Cognac's back. But these had no hope of rescue, either now or ever.

This was sin. The earliest years of Glennys's life had taught her about sin. Sin wasn't a Nolanese idea, only something shared by Alaminites and the Outremere religionists. Sin could only be forgiven, not excused.

She dismounted and left Terror at a hitching post, without tying him. She and Baron shoved their way through the crowd of men around the nubiles' shed. These weren't King's Daughters, who chose to sell their favors for a night or a contract. Some of the girls flirted to the best of their starved ability; others were resigned.

There was a trio made up of a grizzled campaign veteran, a much younger man, and Cody Bonacker. Cody had shorn her blonde hair in imitation of the war stallion campaign clip. They were sharing a jug of Firewater and were much the worse for it.

The three were teasing a girl, so young and so lovely it made Glennys's clenched teeth ache to look at her. The girl's hands were tied behind her back to a stout post in the ground, unlike the others. She said nothing, did nothing, but everything about her stance screamed hate and defiance—and determination to escape.

The girl refused to focus her eyes on anything but the distance. She couldn't have been more than thirteen. The three were touching the swellings around her eyes and mouth. Glennys thought the welts were pimples at first, and then realized skin that fine would be flawless. She figured out the bumps were bug bites at the same moment she saw the girl was a boy.

He saw her looking at him. For reasons she'd never know, the boy strained toward her. "Buy me, Mistress."

He said it only once.

The veteran tried to pour Firewater down the boy's throat.

Cody, less drunk than she appeared, tracked the victim's line of sight.

"Glennys Eve! Who'd have thought the Lighter-pure ballerina would come out to find fun with the rest of us lesser mortals!"

The dealer came running at the veteran's command. "For horesmen fighting for Nolan, I'll give him to you for nothing! Only three silver forients, one for each of you, to have him all night. I only ask that you don't damage him. The twang shed's

over there.'' The dealer laughed jovially, and made a notation
on the numbered wooden tag hanging from the boy's collar.

They led him past her. The garnet-haired boy gave Glennys
one disdainful glance that said she'd failed him. Then he clenched
his muscles and refused to cooperate. Whooping with laughter,
they grabbed him by his shoulders and legs and carried him off.

Glennys had money, all of it back at the tent, most of it won
in card games. "I can't buy you. I can't buy human beings,''
she whispered, but the boy wasn't there to hear.

In her throat Glennys thought she tasted the Albany blood
from the Stallion Queen service. But she wasn't a Stallion Queen,
only Albany's stalking horse.

Behind, Terror sounded a warning bugle against some other
horse who had come too close. Her common sense faded and
her Horse Sense taunted her. She might not be a Stallion Queen,
but she had a stallion, and a trump stallion at that.

Glennys let go of herself and dived deep down into Terror. In
him there was no sin. She saw in black and white. There was
only desire and danger, and the flaring penumbras around ob-
jects backlit by the torches. Terror presented his hindquarters to
the cubicle door and kicked it in.

The boy was under the veteran already. Cody Bonacker and
the other one were holding the boy on either end. The boy had
sunk his teeth into the younger man's arm. Baron hit the veteran
with all the weight of his body and held him at bay. The boy
comprehended a miracle, but he couldn't seem to run, and he
had no clothes on. Half lifting, half throwing, Glennys got him
on Terror, and vaulted up after. He clung painfully tight to Glennys's waist.

They galloped through a dank alley, down to the quay. Terror's hooves thundered on the timbers. When the sound changed,
and the smell told them water was under them instead of sand,
Terror leaped off into the dark. He swam along the shore-
line, with Glennys holding on, clutching the boy.

When they came back to the beach, the sand made easier
going. But it was a scramble getting over the dunes, back into
higher country. The boy fell off and clambered up the dunes
himself. At the top she pulled him back on the stallion, in front
of her this time. Not once did he cry out or ask a question.

Glennys didn't know this country, and it was dark as a coal
mine. The moon had gone under a heavy cloud cover. She had
to trust Terror to find their way back to his picket line.

They loped under pecans, hickories, white cedars, and weeping willows. On the top of a levee between rice fields a deer flashed across their path, a piece of dark, darker than their way in the night.

Terror was a war stallion. His stamina and bottom were much greater than the geldings and fillies Glennys had been riding for the last years. This was nothing for him. Glennys fell into her own trance, rocking easily within the stallion's pace, submerged in that half-world between human and horse.

The boy had been groaning softly for some time before Glennys's reflexes told her Terror had run long enough and should be breathed. After he was cooled down Glennys grabbed handfuls from the swags of moss hanging off the trees to rub the horse down.

As soon as the stallion halted, the boy fell off his back. He threw himself face down on the ground. Baron sat next to him, panting.

While Glennys's hands were busy in the dark, her activity lighted only by the sure knowledge of what she was doing, she smelled blood. It wasn't hers, the horse's, or Baron's.

"You've been hurt," she said. "I suppose riding bareback has rubbed you raw," she added delicately.

"No," he said. "You know I'm bleeding because they did it to me, like a girl or a sheep or anything," he cried in grief and outrage.

"Girls don't like it against their will either," Glennys said sharply, "and neither do sheep, I'd guess. I'm sorry I got there too late. There are so many like you still there too, and I'm even more sorry about that."

She pulled off her underdrawers. "Put on these. They're only thin silk, but better than nothing."

The boy didn't move. "I'm grateful, if you want to know."

He wasn't grateful, Glennys could tell.

"You needn't ride, if you can walk," Glennys told him.

The fog was thick as curdled milk by now. It was some time before Terror got them back to his camp. The boy went with her silently. He waited without question of whether or not Glennys would return for him when the horse had been put back where he belonged.

"My name is Thorne," he said.

The wine's influence was gone. Glennys wondered how bad a mess she'd gotten herself into. She'd attacked two cavalrymen— and stolen another's stallion, though she'd given him back. She'd stolen the boy, and had no intention of giving him back. He belonged to himself. But she was responsible for him now.

There was a large gathering at her tent in the Ely gardens. Glennys took the boy's hand in hers. "There's no help for it, Thorne. I'm leading you into judgment."

Baron Ely wasn't at all pleased about the disruption of his Sale Yard.

"I understand why you did it, Glennys," Duke Albany whispered grimly. "But that was too theatrical a gesture even for a ballerina of Queen's to get away with."

A herald came down from the Big House. "Sharissa, the Queen of Nolan," he announced.

Now the Baron Ely was truly angry.

"A Queen's ballerina is certainly my business," Sharissa said, coming among them.

Glennys pushed Thorne down into a semblance of a bow, while she folded into the lowest curtsy she'd ever made in her life.

Sharissa stood silently. The herald pointedly stared at Baron Ely, until the Baron went down on one knee.

"I apologize, my Queen," Glennys said miserably. "You should be with the King at your ball."

"Ah, but Leon's dancing with all the disappointed ladies, so I'm free. You're well known by now, Glennys. A pale-haired woman on horseback, attended by a bristlehair mastiff, riding to the rescue of innocents. Let me see your prize," Sharissa commanded.

Glennys helped Thorne to his feet. His hair, so much like King Leon's, caught the flames and lit up like a crown of rubies and garnets. The blood staining the back of the thin underdrawers was nearly the same color.

"Take him to your healer friend, Glennys." Sharissa's voice trembled.

The Baron Ely objected.

"Father, I am Queen of Nolan, and you are going Outremere with our King. Trust me to guard your holdings while you and my brothers are gone. Beginning now, I expressly forbid this kind of thing," Sharissa said with queenly dignity, pointing to Thorne.

Glennys's good luck had held, and her Queen had not played her false.

• Twenty-Four •

THORNE LIVED UP to his name and became a thorn in Glennys's side. She was obligated to take care of him and find him employment when Thea Bohn had pronounced his body healed.

He couldn't get along with the indentured Ely staff of his own age group, and fought with them all. The women in Catherine Gemma's tent would have been happy to make him a page, both because of what he'd suffered and because of his beauty, but he despised them almost as much as he despised Glennys.

Thea explained it to Glennys. "Thorne was hurt in more than his body. The Yemmessee itself, and the cavalry, remind him every day of his violation. He insists on believing that the sin wasn't lack of consent, but treating him as a woman. Most of all he hates to be in your company because you witnessed it."

The only one Thorne liked was Jonathan. He tagged along to rehearsals, and asked questions afterward. He had never seen most of the instruments of an orchestra before.

Nathan Drake put the Sale Yard of Yemmessee Town off limits to the cavalry. The public pandering stopped—or at least became clandestine—but the labor auctions continued.

The night of the second sail to Outremere a strong wind blew through the Yemmessee hard and steady to the east.

The wind played havoc with the hangings, bunting, and carpets decorating the quayside. The garlands and flowers of the Queen's ballet tribute spun and bobbed on the choppy waters of the bay, a small fleet all their own, chasing after the ships. The performance geldings' manes and tails streamed along with the unbound tresses of the dancers.

"We're all related!" was torn from their lips by a great gust of wind, more powerful than any that had preceded it. The orchestra players' parts, and Jonathan's conductor's score, lifted into the air like a flock of seagulls.

Thorne leaped and ran, fighting the wind to capture Jonathan's scores.

The wind didn't drop at nightfall. The sky was a thick boil of clouds. Lightning and thunder sported majestically above them, and below the trees heaved and tossed.

Late in the night the wind had blown away the flying blood-suckers. It was too wonderful to waste. Jonathan and Glennys went to her tent and made love. They were so deeply engrossed with each other that they hadn't noticed how hard the rain was beating on the Yemmessee.

The tent strained and groaned against its moorings. Glennys started up from their bed, which was laid above the floor on a rigging of boards. The bottle of wine and the two glasses were knocked over by the force of the wind. Her bare foot found the matting over the half-timbered floor soaked. They heard the gurgle of rushing water all around.

"Johnny, your instruments!" she cried.

"They're in the Big House," he said, "but all my scores are in the orchestra tent!"

Their hastily discarded clothes lying upon the floor matting were sodden. There wasn't anything else to wear. Faintly, through the roar of wind and rain, they heard shouting.

A sheet of lightning blistered the darkness. A small figure darted into Glennys's tent, followed immediately by a thunder-clap.

"I thought I'd find you with your twang," Thorne yelled. "Mr. Reed, everyone with the Theater's gone to the Big House. It's a big southern blow. I've saved your scores, got 'em all in their portfolios, and I put 'em next to your pianoforte. Get goin', Mr. Reed. Tent poles fetch lightning."

Another sheet of lightning tore away the dark, as thunder drowned out the wilding wind and beating rain.

Glennys groped in the dark for her old Three Trees saddle-bags. They contained her copied licenses and her card-game winnings. Her clothes and boots, wrapped in oilskins inside the lockers, would have to weather the storm as best they could.

Glennys and Jonathan stumbled, hand in hand, out into the storm moments before it destroyed the tent.

Glennys and Baron were taken up into Duke Albany's rooms. Catherine Gemma, Lorenzo and his new wet nurse Adina, Amalia, Nicola, and Thea Bohn went to Nathan Drake's suite. Legs and Lungs, directors of Queen's, and conductors and musicians were put into the cellars.

Fortunately they didn't have to stay there for the entire duration of the storm. Music and dancing were good distractions as the rain and wind raged on throughout the next day.

As that day wore on, King Leon and Sharissa took the opportunity to retire together. Then the Aristos too retreated to find some privacy. Jonathan and some of the youngest opera singers and orchestra musicians were left to themselves. For once they could be as loud as they wanted to be, and no one in the vicinity would complain.

No one had thought to feed them, and they'd been drinking quite a lot. Lightning and thunder cracked the world in two for so long even the music-makers were silenced. The Big House shuddered.

The most ancient Ely oak split in half. One part still stood, but the other had crashed into the roof over the Ely Big House wing in which King Leon was in bed with Nolan's Queen.

While the servants shifted their things to Baron Ely's suite, the King and Queen came down to the hall where Jonathan was pounding the piano, trying to compete with the storm, driving the other musicians to wilder and madder improvisation.

When he saw the royal couple, Jonathan began playing a waltz. One by one, the other musicians joined in.

In the great hall, inhabited mainly by Lungs and musicians, the King danced with his Queen. They danced and they danced, back to the staircase and up the steps, and disappeared into their private cadence.

Jonathan and the others were sung and played out. So was the storm. Streaks of gold, violet and rose showed against the western horizon. The rain softened into a drizzle, and the wind sighed. Before full dark, the clouds were gone. The stars and the moon opened their lights.

The King and Queen had gone to sleep.

Glennys got up from the floor behind Jonathan. She put a hand on his shoulder.

When the Theater artists went out of the Big House to scrabble in the wake of the storm for what might be saved, Thorne asked Jonathan a question. "Is all twang like that?"

Jonathan understood that Thorne meant the King and Queen.

"No, most of the time, it's not like Leon and Sharissa," Jonathan said.

Thorne's feet and the composer's squelched through the moss and mud to the spot where the orchestra pavilion lay in ruins.

"I like it best when you make it as loud as you can," Thorne confided.

Together they raised the awning poles, and dragged the wet mass of canvas off the ground. They draped it over tree branches and beat it hard with fallen boughs. Water splashed everywhere. Others were raising the partitions of the pavilion roof.

"What kind of twang is Glennys?" Thorne asked suddenly.

Jonathan grabbed the boy sharply by his shoulders. "Glennys is not 'twang.' "

Thorne twisted out of Jonathan's grasp. He swung the bough he'd used to beat the awning wildly at Jonathan.

"Why did she wait so long until he did it to me? I asked her to help, and she waited too long! I hate her. She'd never have come at all except she thought I looked like a girl!" Thorne yelled.

Jonathan wrestled the tree branch out of Thorne's hands. He held the boy at his shoulders and allowed him to kick and flail at his body, but not to run away.

Jonathan's colleagues came to give him aid. When they saw Thorne, and heard what he was saying, they gave way to Jonathan's unexpressed demand for privacy.

"My daddy died, and mamma got a new man who hated me. He said I was too pretty to be a boy. So I ran away and mamma never went to find me." Thorne was crying now.

"Glennys's daddy hated her too, because she wasn't a boy, and she wasn't his. My daddy don't want me either," Jonathan said over and over again into Thorne's ears, until the boy finally heard him.

"She never came until he did it to me," Thorne wailed.

"If you didn't have good luck, Thorne, she'd never have been there at all. If she hadn't put the stallion to the door, you'd have been with all three of them all night. She went after you because you fought back!" Jonathan yelled. "You fought back. And right now plenty of others are suffering what you might have got, but Glennys got there for you!"

Jonathan slapped the boy across his cheeks. Then he folded Thorne into his arms and let him weep.

"Thorne, Thorne," Jonathan insisted finally, shaking the boy. "Glennys did her best. She doesn't expect you to love her. She understands how much you hate being around someone who saw you under that man."

Jonathan had put into words for Thorne the worst of it. After Thorne had no more tears to weep for this night, he clung to Jonathan.

Jonathan said gently, "Thorne, you're not alone anymore, unless you choose to be. You can't despise Glennys. Not and keep my friendship."

Jonathan put Thorne into a damp bed. The composer wanted nothing more than to be alone. He took his flute to the scenic overlook on the Yemmessee River. The river was running fresh and high after the storm.

He got to play for a short time before George Sert came to the same picturesque view with his sketching materials. The moon was moving out of full, but still lit up the sky. All about them standing water reflected the moonlight like shards of a broken mirror. Alligators lay alert on the banks of the river.

After some time Jonathan gave up making his own melody and listened to that of the river and the night. Sert asked, "So what was all that about with Glennys's boy?"

Jonathan described it sparely. "I don't need a responsibility like this, not at this time of my life. But I suppose I've no choice."

George sighed. "I'd never allow Glennys to drop an egg into my nest like a cowbird. For one thing, Lark wouldn't care for it."

Jonathan said, "Glennys didn't make me do it. This is what's happened, that's all."

George asked, "What's going to happen with you and Glennys? I know which way the wind's blowing, you know. Is she going to break Duke Albany's contract?"

Jonathan said, "They've only been waiting to get all these ceremonies over with, and all of us back to St. Lucien, to save the Duke's face. Albany knows everything. He's being very kind."

George shifted on the damp bench. "You know what Thorvald says? Put not your faith in princes, for they'll cut your throat when you least expect it."

· Twenty·Five ·

Flush tugged, then threw his head back against the lead-line. Glennys's grasp on the performance gelding's halter tightened. He gathered his haunches and half-reared, pulling hard. Her arms ached after days of this.

The geldings hated the stage, constructed of barges extending the longest dock in Yemmessee Bay out to deep water. The tide had turned, and the stage's monotonous rocking was more extreme as the Majis Sea poured back into the bay.

The glare of sun on water was blinding, though it was deceptively cool out here. Dock workers, under the direction of the stage secrets guild, hammered and sawed, preparing the flimsy arches and columns that would be draped in satin and garlanded with ivies and flowers. The dock and barges were being made into a grand arcade over which King Leon and his sons would embark for the stallion ship, *Queen's Dominion*, tomorrow night.

War stallions trumpeted and bellowed, protesting their own condition, further agitating the geldings on the barges. The war horses were being rafted out to the fleet of stallion ships anchored in the bay. The ships were unwieldy, bulky transport galleys. Their sides could be opened and let down to function as loading ramps so that the horses could be led into their cramped stalls in the lower decks. This way they weren't winched into the air and hauled over the ships by tackle and pulleys. The contrivance spared the stallions that greater misery and terror.

This was a spot rehearsal, and spot rehearsals were always hideously tedious, even with sure footing. This one was done for George and Thor's benefit, rather than for lights and scenery. The artists were sketching everyone, and putting their names on the sketches for the canvas commemorating King Leon's farewell to Nolan's Queen before he sailed off to war.

The singers and orchestra twirled about the barge-arcade in boats. They couldn't hear each other, and most of them couldn't see Jonathan's conducting. The sound of music was carried out to sea, not toward the shore where the Aristos seated in the grandstands should hear it.

It was idiotic.

Lord Clapton Roper, the Royal Master of Ceremonies who'd conceived it, was besotted by his conception. He only thought about how it would look after dark, with the water reflecting the hundreds of torches in the boats, on the beach, and along the concourse dock. The dancers were expected to toss sheaves of camellias into the water among thousands of floating candle flames, making the bay a carpet of flowers. The grand finale would be King Leon's farewell to Sharissa on the last barge, before he and his sons were rowed out to *Queen's Dominion*.

King Leon wasn't suffering the boredom of a spot rehearsal. Lord Roper, a full wig over his bald head, played the King's stand-in. Sharissa, newly wed and newly royal, had insisted on learning her part in company with Queen's Theater. She looked pale, and a little queasy.

One after another, the anchored barges heaved up on the rollers that were coming in higher and stronger as the day progressed. Once again, to be sure Thor and George had it exactly so, Lord Roper insisted they watch him ride in the guise of the King from the concourse out to the barges.

Lord Roper's horse, Bechtan, hated the footing as much as the geldings did. This time he refused to step off the dock to the first barge at all. The Master of Ceremonies resorted to spurs and crop. Bechtan bucked, came down hard on the first barge, and straightened out in a gallop. Each section of the arcade tipped and rocked, then smacked smartly down against the rollers, sending water splashing upwards.

The last section, only anchored forward and not ballasted by another barge, was hit first by the rollers, and flew up as Bechtan's weight came on board.

The Queen was on her knees, on the very edge of the stage, her head hanging over the side. Terrified that the Queen was going overboard, and would be pushed under the barges by the tide and drowned, Glennys rushed to her side. Lord Roper managed to halt Bechtan only a short distance from the edge.

Flush, Glennys's gelding partner, protested when this stranger forced himself into his spot. With no one to hold him, Flush struck out at Bechtan with teeth and forefeet.

The dancers and singers close enough to see shrieked. No one in the world could make as piercing a sound as opera divas. The other geldings, on the brink of panic from the shifting surface under their hooves, shoved and pulled against their dancers.

Glennys, for once not thinking of the horses, clung to Sharissa, pulling the Queen from the edge. "Leave me, I'm not in danger," Sharissa gasped out between surges of vomiting. "I'm only pregnant. Already."

Glennys lost her footing, as Flush and Bechtan fought in earnest, and the stage rolled under their weight.

"Fornicating ass of a dancer!" Lord Roper shouted at her. "Why did you let go of your horse?" He beat at Flush with his crop, and tried to pull Bechtan away.

Glennys threw herself between the two horses. Only Rowena and Nan had the common sense to grab Bechtan's bridle. Glennys hung on to Flush's lead, moving in on his head, hand over hand, talking to him, trying to damp his panic and rage, to coerce him into stillness.

But she couldn't find her way once inside him. Flush had no sense of position or balance. He couldn't coordinate his legs, and she couldn't either. She was being sucked into a vortex that whirled without purpose or direction and that propelled Flush in his wildness.

Then she was spewed out of him and back entirely into herself. A shock wave of pain ran through her. She couldn't see or hear or move through the fireworks of agony. She dangled from Flush's jaws as he reared and lashed out with his forefeet. The long leadline snapped and tangled around his hind legs, and he fell.

A horse had attacked *her*. It happened to others, but never to her. The world fell apart.

"Most patients would have taken pity upon the poor healer and fainted before their dislocated shoulder was reset," Thea said. "But you're so stubborn, Glennys, you spared me none of your agony."

Glennys shook and quivered inside her tent, racked with pain. At least no bones had been broken, but her shoulder muscles were badly chewed and torn. Thea feared that even without infection the injury would leave a disfiguring scar, which would mar Glennys's future as a ballerina.

"Glennys, please drink this," Thea pleaded, offering wine mixed with laudanum. "It will put a wall up between you and the pain and let you rest, so it can begin to heal."

"It will make me stupid," Glennys said between clenched jaws. "I've got to talk to Joss Thack first."

When Joss arrived, he wasn't pleased at what Glennys said.

"The geldings have gotten to locoweed, or whatever the Yemmessee variety of it is. The only time in my life when I didn't know what a horse was going to do before it moved was when one had gone crazy from locoweed." Glennys couldn't see Joss's face clearly, her pain was so great.

"Glennys, you're the one who's gotten loco, you're so shaken because a horse hurt you. I'm very sorry for your injury, of course, but everyone working with horses gets hurt sometime. There's nothing wrong with the geldings, other than their dislike of that fornicating stage barge," Joss said.

Glennys sat hunched over on her bed, her bound shoulder and arm cradled in her good one. "What are they eating these days, Joss?"

Coldly, Joss said, "In the Yemmessee, after that storm, and on the downslope of summer, find me hay or horsecake that's not been touched by mold. Find me any grain at all with the whole section feeding war stallions. You, the Duke Albany's concubine, with your patronage from the Queen, found me nothing at all. You never thought to inquire. Cody Bonacker did, and she got us our feed."

Glennys rocked back and forth, as if that way she could soothe the pain into sleep. "I thought so. Cody Bonacker believes in using whips and spurs, and she doesn't care about what the horses eat. I can't believe you kept her on with the Yard after she was mixed up in Thorne's rape," she raved.

Joss's face seemed to waver in front of her eyes. "You have to blame someone for what happened to you. That's real small, Glennys. I'm short-handed. Cody's stepped into the hole like a right one. Every stable has its own way of doing things. Because Cody's training was different from yours doesn't mean it's wrong."

Glennys's pain-dilated eyes were fixed in the direction of Joss's voice.

"I am sorry about what happened, but—don't you understand? You're not one of *us* anymore. You're a ballerina, which is what you worked for the whole time you were in the Yard. You're the concubine of a Duke. You've got the favor of Nolan's Queen. But you can't have everything, and the Yard's mine." Joss kissed the air on either side of Glennys's staring face and left.

She moaned. "What if something sets the geldings off during the performance?" She didn't know Joss had gone.

Thea, who'd discreetly gone outside when Joss had come, returned. "Will you drink this now and rest?"

Glennys clutched out at Thea's hand. "Please, please find Pierce. He's the only one who will understand."

Thea said gently, "Duke Albany's been in attendance since you were carried back here. If you're too hurt to remember you talked to him earlier, you're too hurt to talk to him now."

"Pierce! Pierce!" Glennys shrieked.

It had struck the Duke hard after the accident to see Glennys streaming blood and mumbling wildly. Though she'd been cleaned up now, she looked no better. He seated himself on a camp stool next to her bed and rested his cool, white hand on her forehead. To Thea's astonishment, the Duke was able to quiet her patient's shaking. He listened carefully to what Thea thought were fevered ramblings.

"Glennys, you're still my Stallion Queen. I do believe you. As soon as you take Thea's wine and stop tossing about, I'll go and see to it," the Duke promised.

After Glennys drank the wine and slipped into a stupor, the Duke went quietly away. To himself he thought there was nothing to be done, though for the sake of them all, he'd try. The show had been put in motion, after all, and the show would go on.

It was with a jealous pang that Jonathan took Albany's place by Glennys's bed. Why had she screamed so wildly for the Duke and not for him? She looked so broken. He kissed her lightly as thistledown.

"You're my home, my family, all I've got that loves me, and I love you," he whispered.

She shifted slightly toward him. A shadow of a smile crossed her face, and the tense lines of pain smoothed out a little.

The next night, the night of the King's sail, lower Yemmessee Town bloomed with light and jewels. A whole new batch of Aristo Wheels and Spurs had come downcoast in the tail of Prince Roald, Duke Colfax, and Baron Stogar to enjoy the final days of the festivities.

The only cavalry on shore was the spit-and-polish drill team of the Horse Guards who garrisoned the cities and towns of Nolan. The King had reviewed the team that morning. In the afternoon the team had taken on the Yemmessee Horse Guards in a swordfight.

The final farewell feast was over. Everyone was down at the quay, in the town, or gathering in the front drive of Blue Fields. Glennys was the exception. She lay in her tent, delirious, attended by Thea and Thorne.

Duke Albany sat quietly on Bolt, a stallion as gray as the streaks in his rider's thick braids. He appeared so at ease that others believed him bored.

The Master of Ceremonies was exceedingly gratified to be the motivating functionary. He himself abstained from drinking, but never spoke against those who did, which was nearly everyone. The wine and spirits had begun to flow early.

He cantered Bechtan back among the Aristos. He'd ridden over the procession road in company with Nathan Drake down to the docks. Chief Drake had been rowed to *Queen's Dominion*. Roper had seen to his satisfaction that the cheering masses had been gathered to the edge of the processional road, and that the prompters were in place to lead the appropriate cheers.

"Get some spirit of the occasion, man," Lord Roper admonished Albany. "You've still got your part to play on the docks. I know you've been honored as Chief Councilor during other reigns, but for the sake of us younger ones, appear honored and gratified."

Duke Albany shifted his weight only slightly, but it was enough to make an observant man think of a blade pulled out of a scabbard. Lenkert Deerhorn would have known, but he was off on a mission. There was no one else in this company who had lived long enough to know what the Duke Albany's mask of boredom indicated.

Without showing it, Albany's eyes were very closely upon Duke Colfax and Baron Stogar. Their places in the procession were widely separated, but to the Duke's eyes they were aware of each other's smallest gestures. Though they sat easily upon their horses, it seemed to Albany that the two men were as tight as crossbow springs, and that the least touch would set them off. They took no part in the horseplay going on around them, and had drunk nothing all day.

One of Lord Roper's aides blew "to attention" on a trumpet.

"Thank you, friends and relatives, for giving me your attention," Roper began. "I am about to bring out our King's family. This summer has been filled with cheer and enjoyments. It is now time to recollect that our King and young Princes are going off to war, the most solemn ceremony of Nolan. All of us here are staying safely behind. King Leon is the first of Nolan's Kings to go to war in his own person in three reigns. Conduct yourselves in a manner seeming to this momentous occasion.''

"Shall we weep?'' shouted one waggish Aristo.

"Of course not!'' Lord Roper exclaimed, outraged, and not at all catching the irony. "You are to cheer when the King appears. But, if Sharissa were to weep, a little, and becomingly,'' he began to mutter to himself, "that would be a lovely thing.''

The King was cheered promptly and lustily enough to satisfy even Lord Roper when he came out of the Ely Big House. First came the King and Queen, flanked on either side by Dallas and Hakaan. Behind them was Baroness Ely on Prince Roald's arm. The Baron Ely had already gone with his sons to the ship named after his daughter's position.

The Eidel grooms led up four white stallions. "His name's Loyalty. A white horse for you, brother, my farewell gift. You've no trouble with that, eh?'' Leon laughed, punching Roald in the arm.

Sharissa was a glittering statue. Her crown was heavy, and so were the many jewels she wore. Though her skirts were split for riding astride, the various layers of brocaded finery, each thicker than the last, made it impossible for her to mount unassisted. The King helped her to the saddle, giving her a kiss, initiating another round of cheers as he did so.

Dallas and Hakaan wore the heavy, quilted Equine Academy battle leathers, cut like the ones their father wore. Their own honor guard, selected from the senior cadets, was already on the ship. Simple silver coronets were set upon their rich, auburn hair, tied back at the base of their necks. The sons of the King tried hard for an impassive demeanor, but their excitement at sailing to war was too great to be hidden. They were so beautiful and full of vitality that the ladies cheered them without prompting from Lord Roper.

Prince Roald was dressed in white and crimson satin. His hair lay over his shoulders. He mounted his gift stallion cautiously.

The massive, four-tiered, jeweled crown of Dominion was on King Leon's head. A mutter about the crown passed among the ambassadors from the three Outremere Domains, who saw it as a slapping reminder of the Capitulation Articles that had made their own kings into marionettes who danced to Nolan's tune.

Albany would have preferred that the King had not worn the crown either. It weighed nearly thirty pounds, and had been cunningly constructed to stay on the ruler's head. It couldn't be removed without assistance. The diamonds set into the gold were large and of the finest water. Even when the King was in shadows the diamonds' sparkle betrayed his location.

Albany moved Bolt into his place between the young Princes and the couple made of Prince Roald and the Queen's mother. Baroness Ely's face glowed with the happiness of satiated desire. She looked almost as she had thirty-five years ago in the subdued light of many bedchambers, as Pierce Albany had every reason to recognize. She had schemed and plotted ever since Sharissa showed the first promise of her beauty and character to make her daughter Queen of Nolan.

For the sake of his own dreams and desires Duke Albany was hotly glad that Glennys was so ill from the infection that had set in from yesterday's mauling that there'd been no question she could play her role tonight. The night fog twined and crawled among their horses' hooves on the road. In it Albany scried his vision of a Nolanese colony in the Saquave, and Glennys's fitness to build it.

His last chance to be immortalized in Nolan's history was by bringing civilization to the Saquave wilderness, birthplace of his people. Why did he have to die and fall into the great nothingness of time's black pit? The longer and richer his life became, the more passionately he believed he was fit for immortality. The stronger his conviction grew, the more demandingly the Duke felt his mortality nudging him. What other use were the young, except to serve the wisdom of age? The Saquave Land Settlement Company, dependent upon the sort of skills and luck Glennys possessed, was threatened by Jonathan Reed. It was sex, the wildest sorcery in the world, that had interfered with his plans.

Duke Albany shook his head vigorously, returning to the present. It was bright as mid-day. But it wasn't day, it was night. The Duke's eyes failed him past the dock-concourse. The lighted boats, the myriad torches and candles floating alongside the barge-arcade under which the tide rolled out, refracted and splintered blindingly upon the moving water. Even ten years ago the Duke would have been able to see clearly out to the *Queen's Dominion*.

There were other craft on the bay's waters, despite the efforts to keep them beached. Those who lived by harvesting of the bay were not going to go hungry tomorrow because an Aristo fool like Clapton Roper wanted to walk on water.

The show went on. Catherine Gemma and Cayetana de Alba performed a masque in honor of the Royal Family, as the handmaids of Battle Luck. Duke Albany formally accepted the office of Chief Councilor of Nolan. The Horse Guards made a sword arch under which Dallas and Hakaan rode out alone. The dancers and geldings, with flowers and lights, preceded the Queen.

To Albany's eyes this part was very poorly done. As far as his impaired vision reached, he saw the geldings resisting and ignoring their cues. Too many of them reared, or simply refused, when they were to bow in their usual precise display of timing, one after another. But no one seemed to notice the raggedness.

The audience on the shore was caught up in the music. Fortune had favored composer and conductor Jonathan Reed. A bindlestiff current in the prevailing western movement of air herded the sound from the water back to the shore. The opera divas sang out the text, written for the occasion by Lord Roper:

Evening falls on the water
The Stars rise out of the Sea

On then Stallion Warriors
On to glory over the Sea

Led by King Leon
Warrior of Warriors
Father of many,
Lover of Stallion Queens
Who live in the Sea

Follow, Stallion Warriors
On to Glory
Behind Dallas and Hakaan
Prince Lovers of the Sea

Queen of Dominions
Let your Hawk King fly
From out of your sleeve

High in the Air
On the Breast of the Sea
Far away, far away
Let the Hawk King fly

To his Hunting Ground
Where Morning and Sun

And Glory
Rise beyond the Sea

King Leon's most experienced stallions had already been loaded onto *Queen's Dominion*. For the sake of this staged leave-taking, he was riding a young one called Serenity. As soon as Serenity's forehooves touched the ramp going down from the garlanded dock to the barge-arcade, the stallion lost the characteristic for which he'd been named.

At first Serenity's anxiety appeared nothing more than an opportunity for King Leon to show off his horsemanship and his dominance. The stallion squealed, bucked, and attempted to turn back to the more solid footing of the dock. The King, carrying the weight of the Dominion crown effortlessly on his head, insisted upon his mount's progress toward the Queen.

From the excited commentary by the Horse Guards, Albany knew that Leon had reached the Queen. "The crown hinders him not at all. Look! He's leaning down from the saddle to kiss the Queen before he dismounts!"

The Horse Guards cheered.

Then the fireworks were set off on the beaches, and from fishing boats anchored between *Queen's Dominion* and the barge-arcade.

A young Horse Guard thought the Duke's vision was dazzled by the burning spears assaulting the heavens and the whirling spurs biting into the waters.

"If you squint your eyes, Lord Albany, you can make out the crimson and starlight white of the Eidel Kings. Ain't the explosions exciting? I'd give my left ball to be in one of those gunnery teams for Colfax's cannon! It's as good as being in battle."

"Fornicating mule!" screamed Albany. "What's going on at the end of the stage?"

"Why that, Lord Albany, beg your pardon, nobody can see. That's the center of it all," the Guard replied, without taking his eyes off the roses, hawks, ships, and rampant stallions painted by fire on the great canvas of the sky. "What a wonderful surprise old Roper's given us. He never breathed a word."

Duke Albany gave up trying to see to the end of the world and looked at those around him. Colfax and Baron Stogar had flowed toward each other out of the grandstands of the Aristos as if they were passionate lovers who couldn't help themselves. They were very close to Prince Roald, who was watching the fireworks with his mouth hanging open as though he were about eight years old. Lord Roper stumbled out to the dock, and then ran back. He leaped to the beach. He was shouting, but no one could hear him. His arms windmilled wildly. His movements appeared to jerk and flicker.

Only Duke Albany had eyes for the Master of Ceremonies, or realized the fireworks weren't part of Roper's intention.

Light, dark, light, dark alternated so rapidly that no one could see anything except the patterns etched against the sky and the tracers of the afterglow. The end of the barge-stage was hidden in a wild turbulence of blazing colors and steam as the explosives fell back into the water.

A stage gelding broke away, tearing down a section of arches and columns. The horse was a silent runaway, its pounding hooves lost in the rumble and crack of fireworks. Vines and ribbons twined about its neck. The horse plunged off the dock and trampled over Lord Roper before braining itself against the stout planking and rocks that shored up a warehouse.

The dancers and geldings surrounding the Royal Family at the end of the stage were the first victims of the fireworks. The white stallions tangled with the locoweed-fed performance horses. They turned on themselves and anyone, anything else. Rowena, Rais, and Nan were the first knocked into the water, as the forward barge reeled and bucked like an earthquake. Everyone still on the barge, horse and human, scrambled to the high side. The sudden shift of their weight tipped the barge over on what had been its high edge.

The outgoing tide was at its most powerful, running inevitably out to the Majis Sea.

The water didn't shock the geldings into any sense that could have guided them back to shore. They swam madly in any direction, shoving into the light, anchored craft carrying the singers and musicians. The horses' legs tangled against the anchor lines, their necks in those of the buoys. On the water, the cries of the singers tore piteously into Jonathan's ears. Their long, many-layered skirts and petticoats dragged them down underwater, hindering any movement they might have made toward saving themselves. Blindly churning hooves that couldn't be seen under the dark waters tore open their bodies, knocked them unconscious.

Swimming wasn't a skill much practiced by anyone but coastal fishermen and country boys. Jonathan had spent many happy childhood afternoons diving and swimming in the cool waters of the swift, narrow Blackgum River with his cousins. He tore off his boots and livery of Queen's Theater and swam strongly against the undertow.

Bloody fornicating horses, he thought. How could people be so witless as to trust animal intelligence? Then he thought about his precious, personal pianoforte, the best of the three he owned. It was safe in his lodgings in St. Lucien. His second best was in the Ely Big House. The least valuable one was under the waters of Yemmessee Bay.

The course of Jonathan's struggle was at an angle, directed toward one of the local craft owned by fishermen, who had the common sense to fish out whatever bodies their gaffs could reach. Before he could grab a gaff, another body rolled over in front of him. Without thinking, he grasped it, turned on his side, and swam one-armed.

The body was that of a woman. She struggled, until Jonathan gasped his name in her ear.

"I'm Rowena," she said, and she stopped fighting him.

A hook caught her clothes, but the gauzy stuff of a ballerina's dress, which had initially saved her life, tore away. Jonathan shifted his hold upon her, and grabbed the hook with his swimming hand. He pulled her out of the water. Rowena wouldn't let him go even after they both knew they were safe.

A very small skiff rowed deliberately into the carnage around the end of the stage. It was equipped with smugglers' small, dim lamps, practical against wild rain and tax cutters. The eyes of the rowers, and Lenkert Deerhorn, who'd paid them extravagantly, were only on the black water.

Their boat was piloted against the tide with a lifetime's assurance. It made its way between the lights of *Queen's Dominion* and the dying radiance of the fireworks. It steered well clear of the royal pinnance and the other boats lowered from the flagship of the last stallion fleet. With expert eyes the crew assessed the bodies bobbing in the bay. They were all dead.

A final spume of brilliant colors exploded between the water and the night. It made a glitter against the gold and jewels fluttering softly on the tide. No wild flailing came out of the ripples surrounding the heavy shroud of precious stones, cloth, and metal.

There were only tiny, slow movements that indicated an intelligent, vitality-preserving force. That intelligence was taking all the time in the world it needed, to rid itself of its jeweled encumbrances, stay afloat, and understand the forces of the world made of water and sucking energy determined to drag it down and out to the Majis Sea.

The skiff dropped anchor. The youngest three crew went overboard on Deerhorn's orders. They respected his eyes, because those eyes had been the first to spy the only valuable wrack promised them tonight upon Yemmessee Bay.

During winter it was the wrack from storm-broken ships that kept these Yemmessee men alive. When Fortune was too kind to shippers, on occasion they'd had to nudge it to work for their benefit. The man who'd paid them tonight understood very well the necessities of life.

Lenkert Deerhorn accepted the woman's body, without a crown, from the arms of those who'd gone overboard. Albany had not been able to circumvent circumstance, but he'd managed to save a most important player out of the wreck of Spur power.

• Twenty-Six •

ALL NIGHT THE boats poled, rowed, and tacked across Yemmessee Bay to recover the drowned bodies. As the first colors of dawn spilled over the water, the news came to those holding vigil on shore. The corpses of King Leon and his sons had been found tangled together in a tight rock crevice that jutted into the southern end of the bay. One of the garlands, plaited out of tough ivy, no doubt torn out of the decorations by plunging horses, had gotten wrapped around them.

The Fortune House officiates took note of the contusions inflicted by jaws and hooves on the waterlogged bodies wherever their heavy battle gear hadn't protected them. Water had stretched the jewel-encrusted leather bands that crisscrossed the King's neck and shoulders to the four-tiered crown of Dominion upright on his head. The crown had slewed down behind his shoulders. The King had drowned before his crown strangled him.

Queen Sharissa's body wasn't found.

Duke Colfax and Baron Stogar, acting for Prince Roald, now the heir apparent, ordered the bodies displayed on the shore before the Fortune House cortege bore them away for embalming. Grieving Nolanese, high and low, rich and poor, flocked down to the sand, to see and touch the still-living hair of the King and his sons.

Aristos gave red wine, garnets, red roses, and rubies to the spirits which had merged with the water of the Yemmessee. Less impressively, though perhaps more extravagantly, Nolan's Shoes cast into the Bay rice, cotton, indigo, and tobacco out of their own little private store.

Everything was for the King, very little for the Queen. Her reign was so brief, and there was no body about which sorrow could gather.

Much further down the beach lay the bodies of those recovered from Queen's Theater. The surviving dancers, led by Catherine and Cayetana, danced their sorrow. Rais and Nan, with most of the revuers, and so many, many others had perished.

Jonathan took charge of the musicians and the music. Cimi Terrazo's magnificent bosom would never swell again in song or indignation. Old Rambert, the music director, was too shaken to view the bodies.

Most of those on the List of Artists had no resources for embalming and transport of the dead back to St. Lucien. There were no great family burial kurgans for them. Legs, Lungs, and orchestra were burned together that night on one funeral pyre.

Lord Clapton Roper, his spine broken, had died quickly. He would be embalmed and carried back to lie among his clan.

The next morning the last living performance geldings were executed on the beach by the Royal Horse Guards. Joss Thack, in company with the Yard's trainers in heavy manacles, was forced to attend. Cody Bonacker wasn't among them. She'd cut her own throat.

Glennys Eve escaped arrest. Nathan Drake, Baroness Ely, Duke Albany, and even Joss Thack testified she'd warned them that the horses had been disturbed with locoweed. But she was shunned by Rowena and the rest of the survivors. The Queen's Theater dancers, shaken and grieving, chose to blame Glennys. If she'd been with them on the barge-stage, ruin wouldn't have struck. Some said that if Glennys had never been made a ballerina in the first place, and had not formed the revuers into such a tight-knit working ensemble, Roper would never have conceived of the tragic foolishness of dancing on water.

Jonathan did his best during those days to shield her from the accusations and anger. And Baroness Ely clung to her as though Glennys, having rescued Sharissa once before, could now conjure her out the Bay, alive and well.

The King was dead; there would be another King crowned. Neither fact changed the overriding consideration. Nolan and her Capitulary Domains were threatened by Sace-Cothberg. Chief Nathan Drake and the Ely men sailed with the last stallion fleet to Outremere.

The uncrowned King's family was dead by treasonous negligence. Though Roper and Cody had passed beyond Roald's justice, Thack and the other trainers were vigorously alive. They'd provide a dramatic addition to the kurgan burial rites. The trainers of Queen's Yard would be taken up to St. Lucien and given horse execution before Prince Roald's ascendancy to the throne.

"It wasn't treachery!" Glennys screamed when she heard. "Not on Joss Thack's part, though possibly on Cody Bonacker's. But we'll never know now, will we, since she so conveniently took out her evidence with a knife. Where did she get that knife? How do we know Cody killed herself? Because she was the only female, she was incarcerated alone. No one saw her kill herself. And Roper, he was a fool, but fools generally run things and hardly ever suffer the consequences of their foolishness. It was an assassination! Under it you'll find Stogar, if not Colfax. All this smells of Stogar's touch.''

Duke Albany abruptly stopped pacing back and forth over the silk and wool knotted carpets on the floor of his receiving room in the Ely Big House. ''Shut up!''

Glennys was as shocked into silence as if Albany had slapped her.

''Womanish wailing at the top of your lungs will get all of us—death. There are plenty of your elders and betters, wiser than you, that have thoughts leaning the same way. But what have we got to back ourselves? The cavalry's Outremere. Roald's got a whole army of cannon and gun infantry that has not yet sailed,'' Duke Albany said fiercely. ''Now listen to me very carefully.''

Duke Albany was sending her back to St. Lucien on his yacht. She could take as many Queen's Theater people with her as wished to go.

''Lenkert and I are going out to the Saquave. My St. Lucien house will be closed. That shouldn't matter to you since you're going to live with Jonathan Reed. I've sent on all the documents, and now you're free of me in all obligations, except those of the Saquave Land Settlement Company. There will be nothing for you to draw on from my accounts because everything I've got left is being made liquid for the Saquave. Don't you understand yet? Nolan's changed. The Spurs are down, and the Wheels are on top. The Wheels are going to press the bloodlines hard. It will be best for me to get out of the way.''

Glennys curtsied, very carefully and painfully, to the Duke. There was something he wasn't telling her, something that would make a difference, she was sure, in how she'd play the next years of her life, if she knew. But she was exultantly glad to be free of him, and free for Jonathan.

Duke Albany lifted her to her feet. ''I am not deserting you. I'm going away to do my best for the best of Nolan's blood that survives. It will take more than a single year or even two, but I will be back. In the meantime wait for a gift, the one gift the Stallion Queen needs to know herself once and for all.''

At that moment, in physical pain, her heart lacerated by the loss of her friends and workmates, Glennys hated the Duke. "Jonathan's taught me myself in ways deeper than you ever reached."

"That's not true, Stallion Queen," the Duke said. "He's teaching you to be a musician's best audience. From me you learn your own gifts, which require a larger stage than a theater's."

The *Saquave* carried a stunned Queen's Theater back to St. Lucien. Her crew sadly brought the yacht into her slip next to the one that served the Eidel craft. The *Saquave* was to be put up for sale.

As the passengers disembarked Rowena observed, "Marie Bonheur's school must have reopened by now. It's almost a year ago I learned I was going on Queen's stage, and all of us were so excited about Cathy's *Stallion Queen*."

At first, so relieved that Rowena had finally spoken to her, Glennys hardly comprehended the words. Then she said, "Yes, that was a very important day for sure."

"This was to have been the best year of our lives," Rowena said. "Now, Queen Sharissa's dead, and most of us with her. How can this year be anything but evil?" Tears spilled over Rowena's cheeks.

Old August Gardel had caught a chill in the Yemmessee storm and remained in frail health after a bout of pneumonia. He couldn't take hold of the ballet he was to fight for and direct. The decimated revuers didn't want to dance with horses, and there were no horses, or Queen's Yard.

Catherine Gemma resigned from Queen's. Fearing Duchess Colfax's intentions about her son, believing ballet in St. Lucien had lost its eminence for the foreseeable future, the First Dancer sold her house and most of her possessions. She went back to Langano, expecting to be taken on by Teatro Urbino in the ancient city of Orza.

"Such a seductive city, my birthplace, Orza. The quality of the stone in which we build makes everything shine. Oh, to see the great castle reflected in the Sea of Rinovo again. You should see it, Glennys. My city is the nearest large one to the Nemourian Mountains. Surely the Nolanese officers will come there to find relaxation and regain their vigor. Orza is where a ballerina's fortune will be, I know," Catherine said.

What was left of the ballet belonged to Cayetana de Alba,

who'd never been friendly to the upstart Nolanese revuers. Her moment of danced pity on the Yemmessee shore was long behind her.

Queen's Theater was to reopen, though its programs would lean for the most part upon music and opera. Even though Rambert was as ineffectual these days as August Gardel, the opera company was in much better shape. The opera had young, vigorous Jonathan Reed to motivate it, work for it, write for it, and conduct.

As soon as he arrived in St. Lucien he was at work with the other composers writing the interment music for the procession to the Eidel burial kurgan. For King Roald's coronation, he recruited the best singers and instrumentalists he could find from all levels of Nolanese life. He blended all the musics of Nolan's people into a charming tapestry that veiled the doubts and rivalry dividing the upper classes. King Roald's councilors had been most grateful.

Jonathan organized a memorial concert for the members lost in the Yemmessee. Thadee Maywood flogged the occasion for days in his *Town Topics*, ensuring a large and generous audience of Wheels. The receipts were distributed among those who'd been supported by the dead artists.

There were classes for him to teach at the Academy. Unexpectedly, Jonathan liked training students in the theories and practice of modern music.

There were private concerts in one or another townhouse. All of his talents were in demand and paid for. King Roald sponsored his music.

He had a home. Thorne was a son, of sorts; Glennys was a wife, of a kind; Thea Bohn was quite like a sister. He was most proud of his new position as head of a household that he supported by his talent. Taking the lease on Walnut House for the four of them to live together was undeniable evidence that he'd accomplished what his father insisted couldn't be done.

Glennys's name was on the List of Artists still, in spite of her injury, but she had no roles to dance in the ballet's truncated season. Jonathan urged her to be patient until the new year, when there'd be no doubt she was completely healed. And in any case, one artist to a household was quite adequate.

• Twenty-Seven •

Glennys wasn't in rehearsal for anything, not as a lowly, comic mime-character interact, or even as part of the ball in the opera, *The Mad Bride*. The choice of this opera had been King Roald's, and the old bloodline Spur faction felt it a slap in the face of their short-lived Queen Sharissa.

But the Bride's role was an excellent introduction for the Nolanese soprano who'd renamed herself Rosa Bellini. Jonathan loved rehearsing Rosa. She had perfect pitch, and she could read music and learn it rapidly. Her range was astounding.

Glennys had two reasons to go with the others from Shop class to the Theater. She wanted to remind everyone in Queen's that she was still on the List of Artists, and she wanted to see Jonathan.

The complicated business of changing the stage machinery was going on that morning. With that was the chaos of costumers and seamstresses, scene shifters and properties overseers, repairmen and builders. It was the first time she'd set foot inside Queen's since summer. Everyone greeted her kindly, and asked the progress of her injury. Jonathan kissed her enthusiastically, and begged her to listen to Rosa's progress.

The diva's warm-up exercises of her voice, however, was tedious to a supernumerary, which Glennys knew herself to be. She was an outsider, as she'd not been even during her days as a horse trainer. She was missing the accumulation of daily gossip and complaint, except as she got it secondhand from Jonathan. And all Jonathan's talk was of music, not dance.

She returned to the shelters behind the Shop, where Queen's staff stabled their saddle horses and left their wheeled vehicles. She backed Puppet, a frisky chestnut pony, into the traces of her buggy. She performed her St. Lucien errands and went home to Walnut House.

To Thea's astonishment, Glennys's shoulder had healed rapidly and with little scarring. Glennys had enough strength and flexibility to drive a pony in St. Lucien's miserable daytime traffic, cook, clean house, make love, and take class.

To the ordinary, untrained eye, Glennys was a young, healthy woman of striking face and figure, ornamented with a grace and suppleness most women who didn't dance never had during their most blooming years. But in the eyes of someone trained to see the lines of ballet, Glennys was deformed.

She worked and sweated in Shop class. At home she worked and exercised at barre and with a buttoned rapier. Her torn muscles still couldn't achieve the precise, continuous line of head, neck, shoulder, back, and arm demanded by ballet. She wasn't ignorant of the whispers which declared that the horse trainer had never had the ability.

After the errands Puppet and Glennys continued their way to the outskirts of St. Lucien, over Frontage Road, and past the inn called Pig's Trotters. Puppet knew the inn as a sign that he was almost home. He picked up his pace and swung the buggy across the front drive of Walnut House to the small stable and pasture behind it.

Jonathan had leased Walnut House cheaply because the previous occupants had died that summer of smallpox. Glennys and Thea had fumigated, scrubbed, and scoured until the healer was satisfied no danger lingered.

Asters, dragonheads, torch lilies, catmint, poppies, and mistflowers threw up a cloud of brilliant autumn color around the foundations of the house. The kitchen garden, planted and well tended by the previous tenants, still yielded squashes, carrots, potatoes, and more tomatoes than all of Frontage Road Hide could eat.

The pasture sloped gently down to a channel of Setham River. It ran fast enough to keep algae and duckweed from clogging it, and slow enough that the banks were reliable footing for their three ponies.

Thea had picked up quickly the skills to harness Popcorn and drive her. Jonathan hadn't bothered, for Thorne had eagerly taken to himself those responsibilities. Thorne had changed the name of Jonathan's pony to Drumhead. Thorne was determined to become a percussionist in the Orchestra.

Unless Thea was called by her Fortune House healer officiate to work again tonight in the Drains, she'd be home about sunset. Jonathan and Thorne would return much later. Johnny had a concert tonight.

It was nowhere near noon yet.

Glennys groomed Puppet and turned him out to grass. She cleaned the harness and stowed it in the tack room. She washed off the city's dirt from her buggy's wheels, and wiped down the leather seats and folded hood. She covered the rig with a dustcloth and mucked out the ponies' stalls. It took no time at all.

She made several trips between the stable and kitchen door with market purchases and their laundry. She checked on the poultry run, and looked for eggs. She fed the two fattening pigs. They snuffled in blind satisfaction, ignorant of their fate at the first freeze. She fed Baron.

She separated the laundry and took it upstairs. The clean linen went into the passageway linen closet, Thea's clothes into her bedroom, Jonathan's and Glennys's clothes into the bedroom they shared. She hadn't shared her sleeping quarters since she was a little girl on her mother's farm. Glennys shuddered, thinking of Stogar's new tax assessment on Stella's farm. After buying three ponies, three rigs, and the harness, Glennys was desperately short of cash of her own.

Thorne's clothes she took up to the attic, where he slept. Drumsticks and small drums were carefully arranged around the boy's bed. Thorne couldn't read, write, or cipher very well, though he seemed to have no trouble learning musical notation. For part of every day Jonathan had put Thorne into a boys' school.

"You must learn arithmetic, the foundation of music. And you must learn the grammar and structure of our language in order to learn those of Langano and Tourienne. If you want to become a professional orchestra musician, you've got no choice."

There was one other room upstairs. Here Jonathan was to keep his instruments and do his work. He'd had little time to use it, and most of the work he did at home, he did downstairs in the parlor. His instruments had traveled down there too, since he'd started holding weekly dinners for their friends. It was good professional policy, Glennys knew, but more than that, Jonathan was a convivial man. He preferred company in most things he did. He got tremendous satisfaction in providing food and drink for others at his own table.

A parlor, connected by a narrow passage to the kitchen, together with an attached pantry-scullery, made up all the ground floor. Walnut House was named for the wood which paneled the walls, covered the ceilings, and made the floors and staircase.

The little house was as clean and well run as anyone might

expect, if anyone in their circle had thought that two women trained by Alaminite standards of housekeeping lived there. Glennys wondered why, when Jonathan wasn't in it, she felt the house a shell which cut her off from the world.

Glennys began a solitary barre on the side of the parlor given to her. The harder she worked, the more clearly she could see in the mirror that her shoulders were not quite aligned, and that her left arm's stretch was at least an inch short of her uninjured right side's extension.

She alternated stretch and strength exercises right and left for balance. She resisted the compulsion to put all the work on her weaker left side, to force it to compensate for an unworked right. That sort of approach in an injured horse led to new injuries. Glennys couldn't believe it was any different for humans.

Glennys rolled up the secondhand carpet that covered the center of the parlor. She pushed the dining table against the wall. She began to move to the music Jonathan had composed for Cayetana de Alba's ballet, *The Pipes of Desire*. Glennys knew that music so well she could hear it in her head, because Jonathan had played it into existence right here in this room.

When her body was as pliant and supple as it could be, when she knew she was moving at the top of her form, she watched herself in the mirror.

There was no veil of horses, acrobatics, stately public patterns, or comic mime between herself and the mirror. The mirror answered the question she'd refused to ask herself.

She wasn't good enough to be a ballerina on stage.

How could it be? She worked harder than anyone. Movement came as naturally to her as breathing. She had good timing, a good eye. She could train and ride a horse through any sort of complicated maneuver. She could handle a knife skillfully enough to bring down a small moving target from the back of a galloping horse. She could make love so skillfully that Jonathan was satisfied to keep her with him, even if she didn't earn any money.

It didn't matter. Ballet was art, not skill. Ballet deserved the best, and the new Romantic ballet was more demanding than the dance had ever been. Cayetana and Rowena had moved into it naturally.

She, Glennys Eve, wasn't even a second-rate dancer.

Glennys stooped, immobile, her right hand clutching her left shoulder. Firmly she accepted the knowledge that her injury was not the cause, but a consequence.

Then she walked slowly over the parlor floor, as if the walnut wood was ice that splintered and crackled under her and solid footing was nowhere in sight. Without a place in the Theater, what was she? She was no different than George Sert's wife. But Lark was giving George children. There had been so many occasions when she and Jonathan had forgotten pregnancy precautions that Glennys was now certain of what she'd long suspected. She was barren. Jonathan was so pleased with how Thorne was turning out. Once he'd mentioned how the other room upstairs could be a nursery.

The walls of Walnut House closed in on her. Glennys went outside to the garden shed. She attacked the rattling skeletons of dead, yellow bean rows. She pulled up the vines, hoed out the roots, and spaded up the ground under the hazy sun, in the humid heat of Shadow Summer.

Flush had attacked her. He'd been eating locoweed, and his senses were so disturbed that her Horse Sense had closed for self-protection. That was what she'd been telling herself.

Her spade hit a stone in the earth. She hadn't been paying attention to Flush, with or without her Horse Sense. Full of pride that she'd made the revuers a smooth working ensemble, she'd been overconfident. In her pride, resentful of Roper's stupid plan for the King's Farewell, she'd withdrawn her support. She'd been more interested in recruiting the young cavalrymen for the Saquave, and in Hengst's acknowledgment of their kinship.

She dug around the rock and pulled it out of the dirt. If being a ballerina was in her blood and bones, she would have worked to make the best of it, no matter how stupid the situation. She would have discovered how to put something of herself into it. She hadn't. The Saquave was more interesting.

She turned up more stones, roots, worms. Her Horse Sense simply wasn't interested enough in the geldings, or respectful enough of them, precisely because they *were* performance horses. She'd withdrawn because they'd bored her. She'd betrayed the one genuine attribute that made her a part of Queen's.

The revuers had gotten so used to her invisible coercion of the geldings that the dancers had neglected their own common sense. The ballerinas should have protested themselves that the geldings were unfit to perform. But all the revuers' business with the horses had been hers. She'd liked it that way.

Control was a double-edged weapon of power, as likely to turn on the wielder as on others. The more control over a common goal a person usurped, the less control the others had. That was bad for a community. The revuers had been a community with a common goal. Now most of them were dead.

Stogar had used Queen's Yard, just as he'd used her as an opportunity to kill their father and get control of Soudaka County. This time Stogar got to manipulate Nolan's throne for his own use. Albany had seen it coming, in the same way he'd seen, through his long experience with artists, that she would have to come to the conclusion that she wasn't one of them.

She allowed her rage to burn bright and hot. Stogar had killed her friends, and the horses she'd trained, and her life at Queen's. He was harassing her mother and sisters and all their community with taxes.

Glennys cleaned the gardening tools and put them away. The plant carcasses and weeds she burned down by the river. The seed pods popped and crackled. Stogar wasn't going to have it all his own way.

She took a sponge bath in the kitchen. The meat for dinner had been soaking in water to leach out the salts. She cut it up with vegetables from the garden for stew.

She brought down the table model of the Saquave from the attic and put it by the barre in her corner of the parlor. There was another, smaller table that had never fit anywhere. She moved it over to her area, with a chair. Pen and ink and paper were available from Jonathan's desk on the other side of the room.

Before she came to the end of reviewing the maps and accounts of the Saquave written out in Albany's hand, Glennys had to light the evening lamps.

She knew enough from her raising among farmers in Soudaka County to corroborate Duke Albany's assessment. The Saquave was vast, but the rainfall was sporadic. Farming couldn't be done in the same way it was in the well-watered valleys of Nolan. Gardens were possible around the rivers that fell out of the Rain Shadows, if they nurtured plants native to the Saquave. The settlers could have homes around those rivers, hunt, and run the large domestic animals on the grasslands. Sheep could be raised for wool, but they'd destroy the land in large flocks.

Stations, roads, and bridges would have to be built in the mountains. That would be difficult, but these days it was possible. The equine cadets were taught engineering, and the cavalrymen from earlier campaigns in the mountains of Nemour had come home with practical knowledge. Anything could be done if you had the money, the materials, and the people with know-how.

There was so much she didn't understand yet about the money. But Glennys knew the person who knew all of that. Tomorrow she'd go to Justin Sharp, the Fortune House judiciar skiller, the one who'd conducted the ceremony of Stallion Queen service. Justin Sharp already knew about the Saquave Company.

She pushed back her chair and stretched. She could do this, Glennys thought. Albany was right. Then Jonathan's image thrust into her thinking. Would he go with her? He loved her, so he must be part of her great adventure. But the suspicion came that he wouldn't. How could she leave him then?

Baron barked viciously as he tore around to the front of Walnut House. His barking got deeper. She heard him growling on the walk before the front door.

Glennys leaned over and reached for the sheathed, buttoned rapier that stood in the corner at the end of her barre. Thievery and violence of all kinds against small properties and individuals had increased again. She unbuttoned her knife sheath and took off the button on the end of the rapier's blade. Holding the rapier behind her, Glennys opened the door.

"You do remember me?" asked Justin Sharp, from a respectable distance.

"Sir Sharp, you're very welcome at Walnut House," Glennys said with happy surprise.

"My friends call me Jus," Sharp said, "and I believe we will be friends, as well as business associates. Duke Albany has sent to my care a gift for you."

Everything in Glennys was alert, reaching out, as she'd been doing all that day, for something as large as herself with which to partner. The sun was sliding down behind the trees. Farmers, their carts clattering over Frontage Road on the way back from market, had lit their lamps. The slant of sun was that of autumn, as was the overpowering smell of burning garden refuse, and the bitter tang of the flowers.

She stood transfixed by light and smell, everything around her dark, all alone. Then her mind opened, and it held an answer to all the questions with which she'd been wrestling since the tragedy of Yemmessee Bay. The gangs of the indentured, those taxed out of their holdings and their businesses—she'd take them to the Saquave, where they could start over again, free and equal, each to each, where there'd be no Aristos to oppress any of them.

Confinement, restraint in Nolan, that was all she could

see, wherever she looked. She couldn't breathe, or smell, or see, or hear anything important.

Justin Sharp asked, "Are you feeling well?" But then he was left alone. Glennys had dropped her rapier and was running up Walnut House's drive to Frontage Road.

Past the Pig's Trotters Inn she found a horse car, the kind built to transport the fighting stallions, escorted by a weather-beaten band of Albany's Saquave Rangers.

"Stop!" she cried.

She tore open the car's tailgates. Before she touched the four-legged hobbles and the lines that manacled him, or backed him out of the car, or removed his blindfold, the stallion's history was hers. From the moment he'd been foaled, it had been bondage—to men, to lines, to thick walls—to keep him away from his heritage as free-roaming king of the Saquave, to keep him away from his own kind and what they would teach him.

He wasn't crazy, but impatient almost to despair with the narrowness of his life.

Her hands went over him. In the glow of sunset the stallion's coat, ungroomed as it was, put out a silvery sheen under the thicker, longer, darker hair coming in for winter. His legs and back were straight and true, but his muscles, never allowed enough exercise, were unconditioned. His hooves, roughly shod for the Rain Shadow Mountain Crossing, needed attention, but they were healthy. He'd been held an honored prisoner.

The stallion quivered, caught between the instinct to escape when he had the chance, and the other one, which was to yield to the herd comfort of other flesh and like mind, which had been denied him since his weaning.

He was young, not more than twenty months, Glennys thought. He was an unexplored ocean, wide and deep, filled with dammed potential, never opened to a life that wasn't confinement.

Clearly he was a Saquave stallion, born out of a Nolanese mare of the Fulk war horse line. Like her, he was a half-breed, cut off in his youth from his strongest inclination toward his own kind, who could have taught him all he could be.

Glennys whispered into his ears, "Break out, break free, break, break," over and over. The litany became a sound of two syllables. "Brecca, Brecca is your name," she told him.

By degrees, rubbing his cramped legs, she led him to the pasture behind Walnut House. Brecca was soft in body, but not in instinct. A bugle call of dominance sounded out of the stallion's nostrils.

Indignantly Puppet, the pony-gelding, backed his hindquarters against the safety of his stable. Until this moment he'd been boss horse here. Protesting Glennys's treason to him, Puppet aimed a half-hearted kick at Glennys when she escorted Brecca through the gate.

The stallion stepped majestically into the little pasture. Glennys apologized to him for its smallness. It would have to do them both for a while, but she promised he'd be bound by nothing else than *her* bonds.

Brecca's ears swiveled, his nostrils opened to catch all the odors of Walnut House. It was as though a royal prisoner honorably indicated his private reservation at certain aspects of his honorable parole—even though the assigner of the restrictions was of his own blood.

Glennys listened through those royal ears and smelled through the horse's nostrils. The distinctive gait of *pop-pop-pop-pop*, belonging to Popcorn, was heard, bringing Thea home.

Shadow Summer was in its glory. Thea saw the long shadows of the river willows pulled like a drape to cover Glennys and a stranger horse in the field. By degrees the shadows retreated, and by degrees the stranger was brought to meet her.

Glennys looked like she had before Flush had torn her up and before the deaths in the Yemmessee, Thea thought. She hadn't known how much she'd missed the confident vitality of her old Glennys, until it had returned.

"Thea, this is Brecca. Duke Albany sent him from the other side of the Rain Shadows. Brecca, this is Thea, my friend, and yours."

Brecca snorted. The long shadows came reaching across the pasture to cover him. "He doesn't like being stared at," Glennys said, her eyes bright with interest. "He's been stared at since he was born." Finally Brecca allowed Thea to touch his rough, tangled mane, and then the velvet of his ears and muzzle.

Much later, when Jonathan and Thorne came in behind Drumhead, they were greeted by a stallion warning of trespass. A group of hard-looking men and a Fortune House legal skiller watched what they couldn't see. The fire in the kitchen hearth was out, and the supper stew had cooked away into a hardened lump.

Jonathan climbed down from the buggy. Glennys should be running to him, asking for an account of his day, wanting to hear about his recital. His flesh prickled. His stomach felt sick with apprehension. She'd been hurt! Nothing else could explain the broken refuge of his precious home.

Then he saw her. She was racing with Baron, tracking wisps of autumn mist and shadows down by the river.

An arrogant, aristocratic shape materialized on the bank of the river. Jonathan's breath hissed out between his teeth. In the long silver mane fluttering in the breeze, Jonathan saw clearly the silver braids of Duke Albany.

"I can guess your game, old man, but you won't get her," he vowed. "I won't let you."

The stallion stepped in front of Glennys. He neighed, a wild, silver call. It was like a chorus, singing of places far away.

What Jonathan heard was, "It has changed between you and her. It will never be the same."

The Stalking Horse

• Act V •

· Twenty·Eight ·

NOLAN'S NEW COURT, filled with hungry young men out of Seven Universities, was an eager arm of the Colfax-Stogar faction. Like the rest of their annually commenced friends, the New Court's employment came from merchants, bankers, war entrepreneurs, and factory owners. The ultimate goal for members of the New Court was a seat in the Wheel Assembly House.

After Justin Sharp filed articles of incorporation, applications for traveling licenses, and notice of intent of colonization for the Saquave wilderness, the New Court challenged the Company's right to exist. The Court failed to dissolve old Duke Albany's prerogatives, but it managed to put the Company under interdict until the Sace-Cothberg war was concluded.

The argument against the Saquave Land Settlement Company was sedition.

Justin Sharp, at the head of a regiment of Fortune House judiciar skillers, fought for two years to strike down the New Court's interdiction against the Company, with no success. The Fortune Houses understood that they were the actual target. The legal battle over the Saquave Company was a convenient pretext for the Wheels and the physicians of Seven Universities to make a grab at the Fortune Houses' accumulation of wealth and power. The New Nolanese wouldn't be satisfied until they had broken all parts of the traditional ruling class, and the Fortune Houses had always stood with the bloodline Spurs. Regardless of the Company's legal status, Duke Albany continued the development of his vast Saquave charter.

So did an independent horse dealer named Glennys Eve. Her horse handlers were an ever-changing, bitter group of mutilated cavalrymen who'd been lucky enough to get shipped home—to find their lines' land now bought up dirt-cheap by Wheels. They burned local Inquiry Offices, raided press gangs, and gave the people they rescued aid in reaching the Saquave. It may not have been the community Duke Albany had envisioned, but these were the settlers he got.

Glennys found pleasure in her new profession. It fit the times like a custom-made glove. She never could forget that the hand ultimately directing the times was that of Stogar.

"There's no luck in business, girlie Moira, only business, and that's the first and only rule of business," Mr. Cogner gloated.

These days Glennys was traveling under various names, using forged papers provided by Justin Sharp. Today her name was Moira.

"Quite a bargain you've given me, my stablemaster says. I can say that now our deal's concluded. You're too small an operator to get any profit. You're a fine-looking gal, and you wear good cloth and better lace, but your head for business isn't anywhere near as good as it is for what you chose to cover up your figure," Cogner instructed her. "You'd do better as a draper or a dressmaker, I think."

His belly was as swollen as a pumpkin under a warmly lined coat that fell to his ankles. His boots, encasing feet that, now Cogner had become rich, never walked anything but easy paths, were proof against mud or stone. He stroked his belly as if it was a darling grandchild.

Cogner's stablemaster directed his sullen grooms to take off the bunch of healthy, dashing, well-trained stock bought from Glennys. The horses were intended as part of the foundation for Cogner's racing stable.

The recently appointed young stablemaster was immaculate in the spanking new design of the Cogner livery. With pride he exhibited the horses' papers to another Wheel stablemaster who had no more experience reading breeding lines than he did. The close-drawn breeding history told a story that any bloodline child could have read. What the new stablemasters and Wheels could see were the names of studs and dams that even they had heard of. The papers were legitimate, unlike Glennys's own, and registered with Nolan's Horse Skillers Association.

Glennys was willing to fake an identity for herself, but never for horses. She didn't need to with buyers like Cogner.

She tucked away the forients between her lace-covered breasts. She thanked Cogner for his advice, and regretfully declined to have a drink with him and discuss him backing her in a little seamstress business in Cogner Town.

"I'm overdue overseeing my children's education in St. Lucien," she told him, with a motherly expression in her big innocent eyes. She'd learned that from Catherine Gemma. It worked every time. Cogner had no interest in a mistress encumbered with another man's children.

She rode off the grounds of the Horse Fair on Brecca, decorously sidesaddle, showing a great deal of the lace on her underskirt that Cogner could read better than breeding lines. Her neck and Brecca's curved downwards, as they'd have done on stage if they were miming bad luck and an unprofitable deal.

Out of Cogner's sight Glennys whooped, and she and Brecca became erect. "Ye-ah, Cogner! Horse dealing with Wheels ain't business, it's blood sport! And oh, did I kill you!"

None of the horses were as young, strong, or swift as Glennys had gotten Cogner to believe. Better yet, among them were mares who'd never thrown a foal that lived. Best of all, the two stallions had never managed to sire a foal at all. She'd picked up the string here and there, from experienced horse skillers, for hardly anything.

It was only justice, Glennys figured. If Cogner could sell shoes and coats to Nolan's armies that had only the appearance and not the function, and get an exorbitant profit for it out of the over-taxed Nolanese, it was only right that he buy horses just as spurious in function.

Cogner Town, two years ago called Sheering, had a small Fortune House that Justin Sharp had approved as safe. There she signed to have her profits credited to her account under Justin Sharp's administration in St. Lucien. That account was associated with the Saquave Land Settlement Company.

Nolan's Shoes and Aristos had used the Fortune Houses to move their money, or hold it, every since hard money came into existence. The Fortune Houses could also advance money, if they chose. It was done for graduated fees, but there was neither interest, as with banks, nor investment of funds.

The Fortune Houses' monetary practices had helped preserve the great estates of cash-poor bloodlines, and shore up local businesses experiencing difficulties. But since they didn't make their cash holdings available to manufacturers for expansion, the Wheels wanted the Fortune Houses to give up handling money entirely.

The physicians of Seven Universities lusted for the lucrative practice of the Fortune House healers who presided over the births and deaths of the royal house and the bloodline Aristos. Seven Universities didn't accept women into their courses.

Glennys had never heard of a young Seven Universities commenced physician dispensing his skills to beggars and the poor, as Thea and the Fortune House healers did. Of course, a significant percentage of the Fortune House healers' fees from their prosperous patients went into the Fortune House treasury, from which the officiates deducted a goodly sum for administration.

Glennys knew that the Fortune Houses would leave off charitable work at once if that would ensure their survival with wealth and power intact. However, charity and healing gave them the loyalty of the poor. These days, with their existence threatened, the Fortune Houses cultivated that loyalty conspicuously.

It was the end of the horse-trading season. All but two of her men had ridden off on business for Baroness Ely. Wheatly Lubbock and Tal Waterford planned to ride with her to Gordonsfield Horse Fair, her last stop before St. Lucien, where she'd promised to spend the season of Uncommon Days with Jonathan. Tal and Wheatly were waiting in the tavern called the Hammer and Saw. The owner, Tom Farlow, made horse skillers welcome, and froze out anyone who had to do with Cogner, Inquiry Offices, the Horse Guards, or press gangs.

Rising taxes and prices, loss of old employments and homes—and press gangs too—had begun before King Roald's coronation. But since Roald had come to the throne, no one unprotected by wealth and position felt secure. When an unimaginative man like Tom Farlow, whose family had held the same business for generations, felt more threatened by the throne than by the poor, King Roald was in deep trouble.

Glennys could almost find in herself compassion for Roald. Almost. He wanted so much to be popular. He'd thought as King everyone would love him. Instead his name was damned daily in company with the taxers, the Inquiry Officials, the press gangs, and Stogar. Roald's response was to insist that the unrest and misery in the country didn't exist.

Among the stumps of what recently had been a fine stand of ancient oaks, cut down by Cogner's sawyers, an Alaminite Prophet of the Millennium preached. The late autumn air made Brecca's blood fizz, and he didn't want to halt, but he obeyed her. The stallion hated standing, doing nothing, while humans conducted their senseless activities.

It was a large gathering of shivering and starving vagrants that was listening to the Prophet. Mostly they were women, some heavy with pregnancy, most accompanied by young children, but with no men at their sides. One of the Prophet's ministering angel attendants passed out loaves of bread and smoked herring. As soon as the gathering had devoured the charity, the Prophet

described Silver City, the City of God the Alaminites were building in the Rain Shadow Mountains. If this Gatherin would only
follow him there and lend their hands to the labor, then not only
would their bodies be fed, but also their souls, through all eter-
nity.

The crowd grew, even though the air was cold and the overcast sky promised a downpour. Glennys wondered how they'd
feel about the Prophet's promises when and if they arrived at
Silver City. According to Duke Albany the site of the city was
mostly bleak and bare, with far too many people for the Alaminites to feed or clothe. Mountains didn't make the best farms
or provide the best hunting either. She rode on again.

As soon as Glennys entered the Hammer and Saw she knew
something had gone amiss. The place was empty, except for Tom
Farlow himself. "Take your horse out back," he hissed, barely
showing his missing front teeth. "Your boys are waiting with
your gear behind Widow Juney's barn. This place is being
watched. The Horse Guards are asking about a dealer calling
herself Moira. She's wanted for questioning over what happened
to a presser's work gang three days back on the road."

Glennys sent Brecca around to the rear and ran out to him,
jettisoning the sidesaddle and her Wheel-baiting clothes. Farlow's mother hastily shoved a pair of her son's trousers at Glennys.

"A pity to burn such good quality and the lace and bury that
saddle in the pigsty," the frail lady lamented.

"Do whatever you must so you're not suspected of helping
me," Glennys said.

Baron and Brecca had their ears pitched for listening up the
street. Through Brecca, Glennys heard the sound of cavalry shoes
hitting the broken cobblestones. The horses were coming on
very fast.

Meeting her two men, they quickly put Glennys's working
saddle on Brecca. Then they rode hard through the rain that
started with the fall of darkness. Baron was as nervous as he
could be, constantly circling back behind them. Glimmering on
the very top of Brecca's awareness was the knowledge of a large
group of mounted men, not far enough behind, trying to catch
him and put him in restraints.

Shortly before midnight the trio rode through a village called
Hoople. The wind had died, and the rain had become a downpour. Hoople was a post stage stop so the inn was lit and manned

all night. They didn't stop until two miles further along, where a dirt road crossed the King's Highway, and even then they didn't dismount.

Baron crouched under Brecca's belly, seeking a slight refuge from the steady lines of hard rain. Glennys dropped her own feeling of discomfort and pushed her will through Brecca's irritability with so much wet. He was fighting her again. He wanted to go west, toward the Mountains, not east as they were tending. But he yielded the knowledge she sought.

"They didn't stop at Hoople for the night. They're hunting us. I can't get an exact count because Brecca can't do that, but there's at least twenty of them. There are more horses than men, so they're tailing remounts, which means they're making our capture a determined operation, and they're after us by intention, not a fluke of opportunity." Glennys's voice was smothered within the hood of her oilskins. "We're going to have to leave the Highway to get to Gordon County."

Gordonsfield had turned into a hotbed of sedition. Last winter, after the Old Gordon received the news that his sons and heirs had been killed—ending the tradition that no Gordon ever died in war—the Old Gordon had effectively seceded from Roald's Nolan. Glennys and her riders would be safe there.

Tal winced. "If we keep to the Highway we'll make the border of Gordon County about noon. Taking the back routes, we're going over fields, and we're going across the wastes where there's no bridges. It'll put hours on our time."

Wheatly said, "Our horses can't do the Highway and stay ahead of the hunters, but Brecca's another story. Why don't you ride break-for-leather on the Highway and we'll take to the waste by ourselves?"

"No. We stay together, and leave the Highway," Glennys said firmly. What she didn't say was that she feared for the two men. They'd been so badly wounded Outremere that they'd never completely recover. They had been weakened by the night's chase and she knew it. They were going to need her support to reach safety.

Their horses scrambled down the Highway's embankment. Underneath the mud slick the Highway's footing had been dependable. That wasn't the case in the rough-humped plowed fields, the fallow burn-off, and the increasing numbers of sloughs and rocky patches.

Tal Waterford's game knee, his withered leg which constantly shed slivers of shrapnel, and the stubs of the missing fingers on his left hand all ached and throbbed.

Under Wheatly Lubbock's eyepatch the empty socket had suppurated again, and wept pus over his scarred face.

Baron's pads picked up thistle stickers and burrs.

Glennys's left shoulder, the one chewed up by the stage gelding over two years ago, began to feel tender. Brecca kept grabbing for the bit, which he resented, and he pulled hard against her. Sometimes, Glennys thought, Brecca was too much like his rider. The stallion could be delicate, but often he was as obstinate and rude as the most ignorant Alaminite she'd grown up with.

A spot of pain budded in the center of her left deltoid. Rapidly it bloomed into full-petaled agony.

Brecca felt no pain, and she made herself into him. His muscles gathered and released without strain. His hard hooves with their light shoes seemed to have senses all their own over the rough ground. He didn't stumble or falter. He didn't tire, though he'd not fed properly since last morning. He hated the rain, but it didn't interfere with him. He wasn't cold or stiff.

It was otherwise for Wheatly and Tal's horses. Two hours before dawn they had to halt. Glennys untacked their mounts and turned them out into a rock-walled pasture among other horses. The two Aristos dug a cave in a haystack outside the wall. The three gnawed stale bread and hard sausage and threw themselves into sleep.

While they slept the wind freshened up among the clouds and moved them along. They awoke to a watery sunrise reflected on a slough within the pasture. In a whir of wings and chatter, a flock of migrating mallards settled on the water to rest and feed.

"Duck for breakfast wouldn't unsettle my guts," Wheatly mused. He searched in his gear and found a dry bowstring.

All summer and fall Glennys had noted Wheatly's efforts to learn how to be accurate with his impaired vision. He could handle a blade effectively by now, but she was doubtful that a small, moving target like a duck was within his ability. She was wrong.

Wheatly returned to the haystack with two brace of duck, his ruined face radiating a joy no less warming than his previous good looks.

Baron had caught himself more than one breakfast, judging from the rabbit fur and duck feathers on the wet grass.

Tal removed the soaked bark from a fallen birch tree for dry fuel and set some hay alight as poor kindling. Between the wet and the hay the ducks were more smoked than roasted, but that didn't matter.

"Now you get a bit of the flavor of what battle living is like," Tal joked. "There's nothing like any kind of food to prove you're still alive and kicking."

Baron disposed of the guts. Tal's stallion evacuated over their dead fire. They set off, horses, riders, and dog all more refreshed than Glennys could believe on so little rest and food. That too must come out of war, Glennys thought.

War. Hideous war. War had done more than teach Wheatly and Tal how to live on little sleep and food. It had destroyed their beautiful bodies and distorted their lives.

They rode with short rests all day, feeling the gradual incline of the land grow steeper under their horses as they approached Gordon County. The same hilly, coniferous palisades that rimmed Gordonsfield edged the boundary on this side.

The bridge over the rain-swollen Courser River was the only way through at this time of year. To pass through Gordon's Heights they had no choice but to return to King's Highway.

Their horses put hooves down on the Highway shortly after sunset. They were struck by the slicing rain, driven forward by a mean wind. Horses, dog, and riders were exhausted, hurting, and ravenous. Only Brecca was still alert.

He sorted the scents that came to him. He paid no attention to deer. Coyote, wolverine, and bear he heeded. Their lairs and runs had been used for so many centuries that not even a flood could have eradicated their odors.

Tal was nearly unconscious. The thigh of his bad leg hung down, his twisted foot entirely out of the stirrup. The maimed muscles had given out on the flat after his tremendous will had kept the toes at his mount's shoulder during the climb. His ruined hand was shoved into the opposite armpit for comfort and protection. The reins hung loose on his stallion's neck.

Wheatly had his neckcloth wrapped around his forehead. Part of it was pulled over his eyepatch against the assault of wind, rain, and cold. Most of his good eye was covered too, and it teared. His nose spewed mucus, and saliva dribbled out of his slack jaw. Thea could have told her, Glennys thought, why the loss of an eye had these consequences.

Glennys pulled vigor for herself out of Brecca. She squinted through the blades of rain cutting the dark. From her previous rides here, she knew what she was looking for.

She couldn't have found it in the dark without Brecca. He smelled it, the cave dug within a spruce-crowned, rocky point off the Highway. It had a pungency of many animals who'd taken refuge in it.

Brecca helped her chivvy his companions up the incline. In the cavalrymen's gear she found a small ax and cut pine boughs for them to rest on in the cave. She rubbed down their horses, for they couldn't be left to stiffen more than they already were. She heated water and threw in tea leaves. Much against their will, she told Wheatly and Tal she was going on alone.

"If the bridge is safe, you'll be fetched. If the bridge is an ambush, Brecca and I alone have a chance to get through it, find Gordon's men and drive the throne's carrion-feeding Horse Guards into the Courser. If I fall, which I won't, you'll be free to find your way to Justin Sharp and help me, instead of all of us providing the Horse Guards sport. I give you these orders both as your employer, and as Stallion Queen of the Saquave Land Settlement Company, in which both of you have enlisted your bodies and skills."

Glennys felt like an impostor, invoking Stallion Queen obligations from these men who'd been in war.

"Some body and skills I provided," Tal said bitterly, striking his game leg.

Wheatly said, "If more of those renegade bloods in Nemour had been willing to go to the front like you, more of us would be left alive. I hate to admit it, but upon my horse's honor I can't do any more tonight. I can't even see. Best of luck go with you, Stallion Queen."

She was very hungry, but denying herself food was a long habit from her days working to become a ballerina. It was the same conditioning that as a trainer she'd imposed on horses. Ignoring hunger put the body on its mettle.

She tended to Baron's paws, and left him to ward her men. Very slowly she and Brecca approached the bridge.

The Horse Guards were waiting in ambush.

Using Brecca's ears she heard them, concealed among the trees, in the lower declivities, and on the west bank of the Courser River. They had guns and swords, bows and arrows, nets and spears. They whispered about a seditious force headed by a fair-haired horse dealer called Moira.

Her hunters were on the near side of the bridge, carefully keeping their distance from Gordon's County. Old Gordon's riders saw to it that no press gangs, Inquiry officers, or Horse Guards operated within their territory.

Mist crept down from the Heights. Spray was thrown widely out of the Courser's rocky channel. Agitated by wind, the clouds erased moonlight and starshine. The rain played games with all lines of sight. And she knew it had to play snake eyes with the hunters' gunpowder, whether it came from Stogar's factories or not.

She and Brecca were nothing. He'd not fed, any more than she had. They were nothing but the soughing of the great spruce limbs, giving way to the wind.

In his own manner Brecca recognized and assessed the elements through which they rode. He knew they were hunted. The men threw off heat, smell, and sound, with streamers that led to each position and each undisciplined shift in movement. To Glennys those streamers now were bright as lantern lights.

She hung more in Brecca's perception than her own. Glennys's comprehension rode Brecca's inner certainty as her body rode on his. Her cheek was against his neck. Her fingers curled tightly into his mane. Rain drops sparkled like jewels in the stallion's sight. She went deeper.

A lacemaker made an intricate pattern out of linen and silk on a back. Glennys was the pattern maker, and Brecca was the backing which held the pattern secure. The threads were water, wind, and dark.

Glennys balanced within Brecca's responses as her body balanced on his withers. She directed him when it was appropriate and hindered him as little as possible. Together they wove a pattern within which they couldn't be seen.

It was the patterning any wild animal knew. The pattern hid the hunted from the predator, and the hunter from its prey. It was the pattern of disappearance, the pattern that allowed a wounded creature to escape under the full light of sun or moon. Those who dismissed animal intelligence would call it witchcraft.

The sounds of Brecca's hooves were synchronous with those of rain and masked by that of river water dashing against the boulders of their near side. His breath was quieter than the wind rattling the falling leaves. He melted into the vapors of the wet, cold night.

The stallion crossed the bridge into Gordon County, unseen by those who waited for three hard-riding traitors to King Roald's justice. Then, later that night, a band of Gordon's Rangers poured over the bridge and down the embankments, flushing out the Horse Guards' ambush. Outnumbered, the Guards fled from the borders of Gordon County. Tal and Wheatly were taken up and brought into the dry, warm watch kurgan tower.

After a short rest Glennys took her leave alone, heedless of the old Gordon's advice. She'd promised Jonathan she'd be at Walnut House on the agreed day, and she would not be faithless.

Glennys had barely gotten Brecca rubbed down and turned out into the Walnut House pasture when a carriage turned into the drive. Thurlow, Baroness of Waterford, sister to Baron Stogar Fulk, and an important topic of gossip in St. Lucien as King Roald's favorite companion, alighted. She was breathtakingly beautiful in scarlet velvet that set off her dark curls and eyes, and revealed the creamy perfection of her swelling bosom.

"I swear," Glennys said, after she swallowed her apprehension at seeing her companion from the days of Three Trees again, "you're even more lovely than before you were married and a mother. Whatever brings you to see a horse dealer?"

Thurlow stood, hands caressing the curve of her hips, surveying Walnut House. Her mouth curved in a tiny, condescending smile. "A humble horse dealer," she said. She turned to look at Brecca in the pasture, who paid her no attention at all.

"So, Glennys, I see you've found yourself another big troublesome stallion. And you've got yourself in deep waters."

She held her hand out to be curtsied over and kissed. "You are called to stand before the King's Justice and answer some very dangerous questions. Roald has a sentimental attachment to you, and he's very unwilling to have you injured." Her mouth curved in a knowing smile. "However, Roald doesn't have the backbone—alone—to stand against Stogar. But with my influence, perhaps you will be able to ride this trouble out," Thurlow purred, "without personal damage."

Glennys's days as a horse dealer were over.

· TWENTY·NINE ·

GEORGE SERT WAS the only one awake in Catherine Gemma's house. He'd been drinking and painting all night while his wife and their two children slept. He'd begun with wine when Catherine returned from Teatro Urbino with the latest lover allowed to contribute toward the expenses of her establishment. George had started painting before joining them at late supper, and had continued drinking after the other two retired.

Cathy had sent away her Oriental treasures merchant some hours ago. Lark and the children would sleep for at least another hour, unless the little one woke up with another teething fever. George treasured the sunrise over the blue sheet of the lagoon below the rose-walled city of Orza as much as the merchant valued his pearls. Even more, George cherished the solitude in which his soul was his own.

The more a failure he felt, the more he needed sunrises. Sunrises promised new beginnings, and George needed one desperately. His career had been assured until King Leon's death. King Roald had refused to pay for "Leon's Farewell to his Queen." The bloodline patrons had been decimated in the Nemourian Mountains by artillery, and at home by taxes. Thor was dead. George's parents, as well as Lark's, had no work for their businesses in Gordonsfield since the County had sequestered itself.

Like other artists disappointed at home, George had gone abroad to try his luck. Catherine had rescued him by recommending him to the Teatro Urbino. Now he made designs and painted backdrops and scenery. It wasn't the work of an artist. It was at best a craft. George's dependents cared nothing about how such work demeaned him.

He was miserable.

Oh, he was miserable. He'd thought in the past he'd learned all that misery could teach. He'd only begun. Now he had two children and another on the way.

Still, he painted. Something about his hostility to the patronage-charity of Teatro Urbino and Catherine Gemma made him productive. The studio below the roof where he sat drinking was filled with finished canvases that no one cared to see.

Catherine had become the benefactor of Lark and his children. They all lived in the prima ballerina's palazzo, and George was the bad-tempered pet they all indulged.

The sunrises over the lagoon that led out to the Sea of Rinovo, the noon light on the water, and the sunsets over the courtyard to the west helped George forget his failure. The wonderful, hard-crusted bread, rubbed with olive oil, garlic, and tomatoes, helped too. The more of a wraith he felt as an artist, the plumper his body became.

Orza, and all of Langano, had conquered and been conquered for more centuries than Nolan had owned a written history. In George's grand tour during his teen years he'd never come to Orza. Orza made what had happened to Nolan and her Domains crystal-clear.

George hated Nolan, Roald, Stogar, Colfax, and everything his home country had become. He preferred Langano, where the corruption was so deep that the high and low alike took bribery for granted. No one born in Langano would ever believe in justice. Nolan was a lie. She was no different from the old, corrupt world she'd conquered. The ancient regime was back in the saddle, even in Nolan, with her registry of citizens, licenses to travel outside home boundaries, press gangs, and all the rest. Like all Nolanese, he'd believed what he'd always been told. The Nolanese were free and independent, and thus superior, to the people of the Domains. Nolanese could travel wherever and whenever they wished, with no permissions, no questions asked. That wasn't true anymore.

There were only two images George carried from Nolan that kept his respect. Jonathan Reed and Glennys Eve. They'd never married. They'd never saddled themselves with children. The fools like Roald who loved Jonathan's music so much were so ignorant they didn't even recognize it embodied the ideals of liberty.

What a bloody fool he was. The Millenium was coming, and with it a new century in which the world would change, and here he was having to juggle the cost of cobalt blue against the cost of his son's need for bigger clothes.

Glennys was free to roam about Nolan with horses, doing whatever she liked. Jonathan was free to make his music. Jonathan was free to sleep with Glennys Eve, and anyone else too, no doubt. They were the true Romantics. And he, George Sert, artist of noble subjects, had been turned into a paterfamilias.

Yet, as much as he raged against what Nolan had become, he was homesick. He was sick of the beautiful sound of a language that wasn't his own. He was sick of the fabulous clarity of light that wasn't what he'd grown up with. The delicious food made him sick to his stomach.

He toasted the sunrise with a wine of the same color as the saffron rippling across the lagoon. He threw the crystal goblet off the roof after the toast.

A tiny tinkle of shattered glass followed from the courtyard below.

Catherine wouldn't even notice, George thought drunkenly. Not even her mean, grasping aunt housekeeper would complain. A broken set of matched crystal would be another pretext to get money out of Catherine, money that her housekeeper could skim in collusion with that bitch Amalia. Life was elemental in Orza, in a household supported by the First Dancer of Teatro Urbino.

"Kill everyone now!" George bellowed at the sunrise.

He threw the empty bottle of wine after the goblet. Jonathan Reed would have appreciated the sound of the thick bottle as it bumped and bounced down the tiles of Catherine's palazzo.

"I'm a failure!" George yelled. "I'm a failure!"

Lark was there. Where had she come from?

"You're not a failure," Lark soothed. "You provided food, shelter, and clothes for your family, when our parents couldn't help us anymore."

Lark's argument was less passionate, and more perfunctory, than it had been the first dozen sunrises when George had gotten himself overexcited from working, as she put it delicately to Catherine's household.

This morning, after he'd waked the baby that she'd spent all night tending, Lark reached her limit. Coolly she repeated, "You're not a failure, George. You're a spoiled brat. If I raised our sons to behave the way you've done for the last year, you'd have taken a belt to them. No wonder your Glennys Eve, that paragon of liberty, threw you over."

"That was a blow below the belt, Lark," he mumbled. George turned his back on her and what she'd said. He fumbled to open another bottle of wine, this time the thick, sticky, red Orza wine. Catherine Gemma, in her yellow satin wrapper, knocked the bottle out of his hands.

"Listen to her, George," Catherine admonished. She'd been

awakened by her son's stomach ache. When she heard the scene coming from her roof, Catherine the performer couldn't resist inserting herself.

"Lark is a perfect wife and mother. A man should give thanks on his knees every day for that. Love her, cherish her, and the fruit of your two bodies," Catherine added, playing to the hilt the role of wise madonna.

It was more than any man could take. "Women! Give any of you a chance and you'll break a man's dick and say it's for his own good. You always stick together. So stick together! Fornicate the house of both of you, and your precious children!"

He ran down the six flights of stairs to the courtyard. Finally they saw him emerge into the campo, mounted on one of the geldings Nathan Drake had boarded for messengers in Catherine's stable.

"Where are you going?" Lark screamed down over the parapet.

George flourished a wineskin grabbed out of the kitchen. "I go to war!"

Lark wailed, "You've got no clothes. It's still winter in Nemour. You're acting like a child!"

George was gone.

Catherine gathered the weeping, pregnant Lark into a theatrical embrace. "Yes, weep. What else can women do?"

Lark lifted her eyes. "How shall I live?" she sobbed, "deserted in a foreign land with children?"

Catherine kissed her forehead. "Who but you completed George's commissions from Teatro Urbino at other times when he was—incapacitated? You will continue his work, live here, and have your baby."

Lark considered Catherine's words. "But George has run off alone, unprepared, and—inebriated."

Catherine stroked Lark's cheeks. "Your man is an artist, and thus a fool, but a fool I understand. He's drunk, yes. There are special guardians assigned to fools and drunkards. George will land on his feet like a cat, and return safely, a wiser man. You'll see. I know these men."

By the middle afternoon, far up the ancient highway leading to the Nemourian cantons, George's mind had surfaced out of the grape. There were deep holes and ruts in the old highway, fresh ones, made by the heavy wheels of artillery limbers and Nolanese supply trains to the army. What the feet of a thousand

years of old-fashioned armies had not done, in three years the
wheels of the new ones had accomplished. He passed suspicious
peasants and traders, all hoping to make a profit selling something to the army's purveyors or to individual soldiers.

Through his headache, George recollected in hideous clarity
his actions and Lark's words. He regretted his hasty decision,
but refused to turn back. On a deserted part of the highway he
rode directly into disaster.

He and his horse were surrounded by a band of ragged men
with blunderbusses, rusty swords, and bright butcher knives.
Many generations ago the peasant farmers of this poor countryside had learned to supplement their poverty by brigandage.
George had forgotten to consider them, as he'd forgotten to consider everything else in his wild notion to join the war—with the
exception of his traveling case of artist's materials.

After living so long in Langano George understood the gut-
tural orders of his captors all too well. He attempted to obey
and dismount.

His thighs, stretched for hours across a saddle, unused to the
exercise, protested with a violent cramp. It hurt as badly as if
one of those swords had rammed into his body. He groaned,
remembering the purse under his coat. He'd gotten paid the previous afternoon for an opera backdrop.

The brigands pulled him off the horse. They ignored his soft,
ignominious form once it collapsed on the ground. For the moment they were too excited over having a horse in their possession. Should they keep it, eat it, or try to sell it? They were very
interested in the high quality of the tack, stamped with the in-
signia of Nolan's cavalry, and the personal sigils of Nathan
Drake. They looked dubiously between the emblems of Dominion and the incapacitated George. George knew only too well
that he didn't look like a horse warrior.

"A bandit, a thief, eh, fat one? Could be there's a reward for
returning what you've stolen?" speculated the leader, poking
George with the blunderbuss mouth.

Suddenly the chilling spring air was filled with what seemed
fluttering wings. The guardians assigned to watch over fools and
drunkards had arrived, riding under the banners of Baroness Ely.
There were Fortune House officiates and healers escorted by
several seasoned Spur bloods, judging by the missing fingers,
scarred faces, and broken teeth.

George tried to roll out of the way of the melee, but his body,
stiff as a corpse from riding, didn't obey. To the pounding at the

back of his skull, the agony of needles in his temples, and the churning of his stomach from hangover was added the terror of death during rescue.

He pulled in his head to his chest, and his arms into his body. His legs refused to curl up.

The brigands were driven off, except for those killed. The bodies were dragged unceremoniously into a ditch, where they lay for scavengers or relatives.

"Is that George Sert? The painter?" inquired one of the officers afterwards. "Pardon me for not recognizing you immediately. There's both more of you," the officer laughed, poking George's stomach, "and less," rubbing George's bald pate, "than three years ago in the Yemmessee."

"I'm afraid I don't have the honor of recognizing my benefactor," George said, as the officer helped him to his feet.

"That's because there's more and less of me as well." The officer opened his mouth and pulled back his luxuriant mustachios. "I've lost my teeth and grown these ornaments to disguise the loss. Refuge Steed, at your service. You did a quick portrait of me for a pretty girl's memento during Sharissa's wedding festivities."

George felt no less a buffoon, though a relieved one, as the healers, with many jokes, fashioned a litter for him. He couldn't walk at all, much less sit Nathan's messenger gelding.

They stopped early for the night in a prosperous hamlet that serviced the army and its followers. George wanted to spend everything he had in his money pouch to show his gratitude. Steed, however, only allowed him to buy their supper and wine.

"Now tell me why we found you on the Nemourian highway," Steed ordered as George sat down painfully at the supper boards.

After hearing the artist's story, Steed laughed loud and slapped his thighs. "Many a man who finds himself in battle can tell the same story. So you had no plan, only desire to escape wife and kiddies."

George rubbed the bristles of his beard. He hadn't shaved for almost two days, or slept either. The smoke, smell, and noise in the tavern, and his hangover, made everything unreal. "Why are you here, Steed, and under the Ely banner?" he asked.

"I don't exist, you know," Steed said, ordering another bottle of wine. "No one thought I'd live from the wounds I got last year. But I survived, though I was left on the field to die by the artillery doctors. I made my way home and the Baroness gave me hospitality. She, the Old Gordon, and the other Spur old bloods who are still big enough and powerful enough in their own counties to hold off the pillaging Wheels, sent me back here to help our own. The Crown isn't doing it. The fishermen-wreckers of the Yemmessee got the bloods a ship, which doesn't exist any more than I do. Behind us there are others loaded with food, clothing, and horses. This war is nothing but murder of the bloods and the conscripted infantry."

But the infantry was always conscripted, and torn to pieces, George thought dimly. Why were the bloods concerned now? Locked into his personal miseries he had cared nothing about war news.

George said, "Nathan Drake has managed to visit Catherine Gemma in Orza during the winter. He never spoke of the war except generally. Nathan trusts no one, I gathered, not even Catherine, to speak to specifically. But when he and I were alone he said something that hinted he believes the Stogar-Colfax spiders to be everywhere and armed with gold."

Steed's face showed nothing, but his body tightened. "If Nathan speaks to no one, why did he talk to you?" Steed demanded.

George's face flushed. "Nathan met me through Glennys Eve at Duke Albany's house. The Chief knows me for a Romantic and unsympathetic to the throne—and to Wheels. He knows I was driven into exile by the Crown's new policies."

Steed said nothing. His body yelled skepticism that an artist could have that sort of relationship with Nolan's Blood Chief.

George, indignant, used something he'd known but until now cared nothing about. "From hints in Jonathan Reed's letters to me, I think Albany, Ely, and Nathan are all part of a spider web, Albany's web of the Saquave."

Steed rapped out, "Who in fornication is Jonathan Reed?"

George said, "The orchestra conductor of Queen's Theater. He's Glennys Eve's lover, the one she took after Albany took her from—me."

Steed appeared puzzled, but believing now. "What does Glennys Eve see in your sort? You're ignorant. But if you still want to go to war, I think we could use you well, and make you into a real man. You're very quick at sketching recognizable likenesses of people and places. I'll give you a commission in the cavalry. Record this misbegotten war in the mountains. Your drawings will be sailed back to St. Lucien and seen by interested people."

Then Steed pulled back the handlebars of his mustachios and
waggled his tongue obscenely at the serving maid through the
space where his teeth had been.

She slapped him and bent over to retrieve an empty bottle on
the floor. Steed threw her skirts over her head. She wasn't wearing anything under them.

She straightened swiftly and screeched, "For a look I charge
twenty moneta. Twenty for each of you since you both looked.
Forty more moneta on your bill! In specie, not your useless
scrip!"

George's stomach lurched from the elderly chicken he'd eaten,
cooked in older oil. "I need a pot and sleep," he groaned.

"Right, Sert. Sleep on my proposal. Nolan needs your talents. What I've proposed is honorable. It's dangerous, and it's
nothing at all like playing lap dog to Legs and Lungs, or bounc-
ing babies on your knees. We'll be on the highway at five bells.
If you're with us, good. If not, well, no one can expect a painter
boy to behave like a blood for the sake of his country," Steed
needled.

George's brief glimpse up the outskirts of war looked bad.
Still, at five bells in the morning he found himself, groaning and
whimpering with pain, on the back of Nathan Drake's gelding.

It was the same as when he was six. He had to climb those
high, protecting walls around his mother's house, though every
moment he was afraid he'd fall. And the climb down was worse.
But he'd done it over and over until his mother finally understood
that he had to go outside her house.

• Thirty •

IT WAS STILL sad and weary winter up in the Nemourian field camp of Blood Chief Nathan Drake. All the trees for miles around had been cut down for shelter, cooking and heat. The stony ground didn't allow for digging proper latrines, so some of the ridges and slopes were knee-high in excrement. What little there was to eat turned a man's stomach.

The only preparation George had made for this wild venture had been to grab up his traveling case of paints, papers, inks, charcoal, and pencils. His case had a lamp, but nothing on the order of soap and razors. George gave up shaving.

Time. War played games with it. Time contracted to an eternal present which was infinitely expansive, for there was nothing to do but fill it, until the next wild rush of action. Except in his dreams George forgot there was another world in which one bathed, changed clothes, ate good dinners, drank wine, and made plans to be the greatest artist of his age.

The only visible support the cavalry received was from the bloodline estates, but those were waging another war at home. Denied the use of any but its traditional weapons of stallion, sword, spear, bow, whip, and net, the cavalry managed to acquire personal firearms. The rest of the army was equipped with cannon, pistols, muskets, and flintlocks. The cavalry was learning to disobey both orders and tradition.

George couldn't hope to handle a sword from the back of a war horse like the bloods. That took training from an early age. His painter's eye was accurate, though, and his hand was steady. First with a bow and arrow, and then with a flintlock, George became a sharpshooter during his first weeks with Nathan Drake's men. He had nothing better to do.

When the spring campaigns began, he had ample occupation. Thin tubes of his drawings were smuggled into Nolan over Baroness Ely's spider web, and printed up as engravings or woodcuts. Some were copied as paintings. He never saw the end result of his work, and he speculated on how cheaply it was reproduced.

The significant matter to the Ely spider web was that he clearly contrasted the Wheel commanders of the artillery, who gave orders from behind the lines, with Nathan Drake, who always rode at the front of his dwindling band of men. The cannoneers had full sets of uniforms, no evidence of starvation in their faces, and, always, good footgear. The supporting infantry was in rags and barefoot, but well armed. The war stallions were clearly overused, unthrifty from poor rations, and giving themselves to their riders, who were in worse condition than their mounts.

In those days George finally began to understand why the blood Aristos cared so much for horses.

George worked under fire. He ducked below the thick white fog of explosives that concealed the action from the commanders behind the lines. He recorded the incredible exploits of the cavalry, ordered to charge Sace-Cothberg artillery emplacements while Nolan fired wildly from behind. He spared nothing to the viewer of the tangled guts of horses caught in their own hooves, the riders' heads blown off, falling to ground slimy with shit and blood.

War was not a glorious enterprise as George portrayed it, but back home the cavalry and Chief Drake became heroes.

One set of his drawings was stained with his own blood. He worked madly under the spell of those caught between friend and foe. He never saw or heard, or felt until afterwards, the impact of the cannonball on the barricade behind which he was drawing. His arm bled from splinters of wood that impaled themselves in his flesh.

Now he saw through many eyes, and recorded what those eyes saw. Usually, before he could come back to himself, Refuge Steed, or one of Steed's under-spiders, would tear the sketch sheets out of his hands to send off over the web.

When he was given a little more time he put himself as a tiny figure on the paper, suggesting his location and perspective in regard to the field action. Glennys, Jonathan, and maybe even Duke Albany would see those drawings, he'd think.

Steed's web carried packs from George back to Lark in Orza. "As I was," one cartoon was captioned, which exaggerated the bloat of his body and the mean creases in his face. "As I am now," captioned the companion sketch, showing him lean and hard, wearing a beard that covered cheeks, chin, and lips. Other cartoons showed him wildly saddling a horse and whipping up to its back. Some depicted him as a shooter hitting innocuous targets on stumps. All of them were softened scenes of what it was like to be at war under Nathan Drake's command. He studied to make the notebooks of drawings sent back to Lark witty and comic, so his older son would be allowed to see them. The horses and men looked better spirited and better fed than in his other drawings.

He never recorded, even for himself, the action in which he killed a Sace-Cothbergian soldier who'd stumbled over him in the field. George had done it, clumsily, filled with bowel-loosening fear, but effectively for all that, with the man's own knife.

Lark showed George's little, hand-sewn books to their boy every night, while she spoke with him in Nolanese. She imparted great pride in the child's heart for his father. She concealed, even from herself, all other feelings she had about George, except for the constant fear that he might be killed.

Lark gave birth to a daughter and named her Gemma, in honor of Catherine. While recovering from childbed, Lark received a packet of letters from St. Lucien over the route that communicated regularly between Queen's Theater and Teatro Urbino. She cared nothing for Jonathan's gossip about Glennys and how a woman named Thurlow, related to Baron Stogar Fulk, had successfully intrigued with King Roald to keep Glennys from going on trial for treason. She treasured what Jonathan Reed wrote about George, though it was pitiful enough consolation under the circumstances.

Every one of George's fellows is passionately jealous of him. The Romantics have collected as many of George's originals as possible, and Copely has hung them clandestinely in a private room of the Seahorse Tavern. As the only St. Lucien artist to have experienced battle, George is a hero here at home.

Lark would have preferred a non-heroic husband, safe with her in Orza.

On the upper slopes of the Nemourian Mountains that divided Langano from Sace-Cothberg, autumn already glimmered yellow around the edges of the trees. Below the mountains were the Cothberg principalities, and beyond them, in one of the Sacian states, George, Hengst, and Refuge Steed were ensconced comfortably in a small hunting lodge.

The Sacian timber dealer who owned the lodge had left it in the care of an elderly couple and one young steward. For the moment, the lodge was Nolanese territory.

Hengst and George had seen to it that the caretakers were humanely imprisoned in the cellar. Hengst had been relieved there were no young women on the place. Steed's way with helpless women was not something he ever wanted to witness again.

Steed had spent years as a prisoner of war in Sace-Cothberg during the previous campaign, when he was little more than a boy. His experience had left him with a fluent command of Lorsch, the language of Sace-Cothberg, and an ugly hatred for everyone and everything Sace-Cothbergian.

Several leagues beyond the timber dealer's lodge was the Sacian city of Logroat, a center of manufacturing and trade built on the Usker River.

Dawn found Steed, Hengst, and George unwashed, still bearded in spite of the lice, dressed in peasant's gear—and walking in the company of three pigs toward Logroat's market gates. None of them knew anything about swineherding.

The muddy road was still deserted. George hurled himself upon the largest hog, who had his own ideas of where he would like to go. George had barked his shins several times already on his pig staff and his legs hurt like the deuce.

The artist looked up from under sweaty eyebrows. "I recall once Glennys remarked on the high intelligence of swine."

Hengst laughed. "If she could see us now, she'd have no reason to change her opinion."

George sat on his pig and watched happily as Hengst's knocked him into the mud.

Steed shut them up with a sharp gesture. Sacian peasants, genuine ones, with pigs, were coming up fast behind them. Part of the group had tied neat little ropes to the hind leg of each of their swine. The rest, obviously better off, had their stock in wicker cages on a cart, pulled by their wives.

The Sacians passed the disguised Nolanese. There was much laughter, pointing of fingers, and slapping of thighs.

"We've got to get some ropes, otherwise we'll never get past the Logroat gates, and if we did, the guards would know us for actors," Hengst said.

Steed growled, "Dandle the hams, babies. I'll see to it." He ran awkwardly after the peasants.

He returned with three frayed ropes, generously smeared with pig manure. In a foul temper Steed spat in the mud.

"How did you pay?" Hengst asked quietly.

"I persuaded the old caretaker to supply me with some money last night," Steed replied.

Hengst and George exchanged sober glances. They could well imagine Steed's manner of persuasion.

Once inside the city gates they turned the pigs loose. Then they lost themselves in the bustle of Logroat, the center of which was the Brugge family's ammunition works.

That two young clodhoppers should stare curiously at everything, while escorted by a somewhat older fellow, fit into their role. It was strange to be within a city of the old enemy.

It was summer, and though not as hot as in St. Lucien, it was moist from the wide Usker River. The citizens wore thick layers of clothes that covered everything.

Whores of all qualities plied their trade openly, but no matter how well dressed, they all displayed a huge scarlet badge of regulation.

Everything was built of wood, with gables and sharp overhanging roofs. The buildings were so close together they seemed to be attached to one another. The streets were dark and none of them were cobbled or graveled.

Their nerves wound tightly as Steed went about the gradual process over the next two days of improving the quality of their clothes, and the lodgings that went with them. The men of all ranks were bearded, unlike the men in Nolan. But underneath those thick clothes, George thought, the people were much the same as anywhere. Their coloring was no different from his own. The people in the Domains were often much darker.

The first night they gorged, as would anyone who had lived on tight rations for so long. But the food didn't agree. Meal after meal, it was pig flesh, pig brains, pig feet, and sausage on top of more ham. The beer, however, made up for the food.

"How do they do it?" George whispered one night up in their room, after drinking a beer so sparkling it could almost be champagne.

"A thousand years of brewing. The slops from the breweries feed the swine," Refuge Steed said. "The more beer and ale, the better fed everyone is. Without beer no one could piss. There's no water here anyone can drink."

Steed's hatred and contempt were harder now for him to control. If it wasn't for Hengst's good-natured handling, the older man would have lost everything to rage before now. At the same time, without Steed's command of the language and his fine touch for spying, George and Hengst would have been taken off by the authorities. Nathan had chosen this team wisely.

By the fourth day they looked the parts of young engineers

well enough that they could loiter in the Brugge area of Logroat without drawing attention to themselves. George could make sketches at one of the tables in a beer garden situated across from the Brugge Works because the place was full of draftsmen and engineers of all kinds.

George carefully kept what he put on paper out of sight from the other customers. He was drawing the walls and gates of the Works, and writing down the times of shift changes, and which type of workers went in and out of which gates. The dour Sacians were full of their own concerns and had no curiosity to spare.

The three spies watched comings and goings carefully. They gauged where the main office of the Brugge masters was situated. Because of Hengst's knowledge of Stogar's works in Drake, he took the risk of going into the Brugge manufactory with the third shift of laborers to learn more.

"It's so much like Stogar's part of Drake," he breathed into Steed's ear at dawn when the shift changed. "I hate it."

Steed hustled him back to their lodgings. Three drunken men leaning on each other, huddled closely, drew no attention but that of disgust from the landlord.

"It's true. My brother's working with the Brugge interest. This entire war is for nothing but both of them to get rich. I saw kegs of powder from Drake in their testing quarter, and Brugge powder ready to be taken out by the Andacac shippers to Drake. Brugge and Fulk are collaborating and exchanging what each knows with the other." Hengst spoke softly, but his tone said that he wanted to howl.

It was the vilest of betrayals. Steed exploded for them all. Hengst threw a blanket over Steed's head to muffle his bellows of rage. George and Hengst fell on his body to hold back the destruction of their room, but he threw them off.

They battled to bring him to his senses. The landlord was beating on the door, shouting at them. They didn't need to understand his words to know he was threatening them with the authorities.

All of them had bruises and what were going to be black eyes before Hengst dared open the door. Immediately Steed made an apology of the sort a landlord will accept. He proffered two gold talers for the disturbance and damage. Hunching his shoulders Steed knelt on the floor to pick up overturned pots of beer.

"Too much happiness for the likes of us," he muttered in accents of deep Lorsch gloom. "And now we pay for it. There is no pleasure in the world, no happiness."

The landlord had seen men drinking to excess before. Happy drunks weren't the usual consequence of deep drinking in Sace-Cothberg where long, dark winters took precedence over the short summer days.

Mollified, the landlord took his leave after giving them a sermon on temperance and many threats regarding their future behavior.

Hengst's face wore an expression of suffering that George had only seen before on wounded men. "My name and my pedigree are filth. How can I look my brothers in blood in the face now?"

Steed replied so quickly that Hengst's last word was cut off. "Horse warriors live by the honor codes. Your brother is no longer related. He is no longer your brother."

Only on the third shift did the officers of the Brugge masters lock up and the lowliest family members go home. "I've never seen any people work this industriously in my life," Hengst said, "as these Sacians, except for Alaminites. No wonder Stogar prefers them as laborers to any others."

The three Nolanese drifted into the Works with the other hands of Brugge. Following Hengst they slipped into the shadows around the testing quarter, which also was locked up for the night.

Inside the testing compound, explosives of all kinds were everywhere. Any spark could set them off, so most of the work was done outdoors during daylight hours. The floorboards of the storage sheds were permeated with chemicals.

Out of George's case came another of the hats he'd devised for working at night. This one was fitted, not with candles and open flames, but a shielded lamp. He was used to precautions from working with the highly flammable materials of his art, but this operation wracked his nerves. What was in the testing compound was volatile, and he was afraid of being discovered.

He sketched out the kegs, clearly labeled as being from Drake, standing next to those of Brugge. It was shocking to see, though he was expecting it. He hoped the shock he felt got into the lines he scribbled on the paper.

The three were so filled with anxiety that it wasn't until they'd replaced the window in its casement and were yards away from the testing quarter that they broke out in a nervous sweat. Their next target was the Brugge master office. A watchman was between them and their objective. Steed cut his throat.

By the light of George's lamp they ransacked the ledgers. They searched through the unfamiliar script, so different from what was used in Dominion, looking for anything that hinted at a communication with Stogar, or Colfax, or Drake. Steed could speak the language well enough, but he couldn't read much, and he couldn't write at all.

George drew everything he could see, everything that would leap off a page, in no matter what quality reproduction, and proclaim itself foreign to the Domains. One sheet showed his companions riffling through the fat ledgers carrying the Brugge criss-cross emblem. Behind them were ranged a shelf of pewter tankards, of a kind never seen in Nolan. Another page was a view of the Brugge Works from the master office window, the Brugge banner hanging outside. There was a porcelain stove with enameled tiles in a corner. None of this could have been seen in Nolan; none of this could have been drawn unless the artist had seen it.

Hengst broke open the big desk and found another ledger, much smaller, bound with a lock. "Give me that!" Steed hissed.

There it was. Even in the Sacian script, the names leaped out at them. Drake, Fulk, Colfax. Payments of exchanged cargoes between Brugge and Drake, sent by means of Andacac shippers, who sailed the North Sea by techniques no other peoples had discovered. Shipments from Brugge went up north to the Andacac colony port of Leffle where other shipments, whose origin was Drake, were picked up by Brugge.

And scrupulously Brugge and Drake divided the profits accruing from profiteering their goods to the Nolan's throne and the Thumin of Sace-Cothberg.

"Nathan's going to be as sick from this as you, Hengst. His brother's got to be mixed up in this too. Where did Stogar get his financing? Banker Elliot Drake. I bet old Brugge's got a brother or an uncle or somebody who deals money directly just like Stogar's got too," Steed said.

"We don't need anything else," Hengst said through his teeth. "We'll just take this ledger. That, and George's work, has got to be enough for anybody, even Roald."

George and Steed left with the evidence at the end of the third shift. Hengst stayed behind.

They waited for Hengst in a waste yard two lanes over from the Brugge Works. George's body was stiff with fear for Hengst's safety.

Steed's body quivered, though not from fear. "Do it. Do it. What are you waiting for? Kill the fornicating buggers. Kill them all. Do it. Do it. Do it." Steed chanted his hideous chant so continuously that George wanted to knock him unconscious. War gave one companions that otherwise a man would never even share a drink with, George thought. Steed revolted him.

After the first explosion ripped through the Brugge Works a flood of humanity came running toward the sound of catastrophe, as another flood surged away from it. Long minutes passed before Hengst slipped into their agreed lair. He collapsed under the pile of dead wood, broken pottery, and discarded furniture. The Logroat beggars who had made the place their home had been killed by Steed the day before.

Hengst rolled into a ball, his hands clasped over his ears. He still heard the screams of men, women, and children caught inside the Works during the morning shift change. Even here, their agony was louder than the roar of the flames.

George tentatively reached out a hand to Hengst's back. Hengst struck George away. He sat up. He whispered, "Stogar made me dishonor my codes. I killed laborers, not warriors."

Steed hissed, "They all deserve a long, painful death. They're fornicating Sacians, no better than mosquitos."

Then George knew that the caretakers back in the timber merchant's lodge were dead too.

In the melee, the three from Nolan slipped out of Logroat unnoticed and made for the Nemourian Mountains.

Several weeks later the coast of Langano, including Orza, was under Blood Chief Nathan Drake's martial law, enforced by fell-faced cavalry. Supplies and ships were commandeered, and what remained of Nolan's glorious cavalry sailed for Yemmessee Bay.

George sailed on the same ship that carried Nathan Drake, Hengst and Refuge Steed. Under the circumstances he had no time to make arrangements for his family. Lark, the baby, and the two small children could follow him whenever and however they could manage.

The cavalry left most of their horses behind in the Langano Domain. Never before had horse soldiers gone home without their mounts; but then, never before had the cavalry deserted a campaign.

A wife and children left behind, however—that had happened a thousand times before.

· Thirty-One ·

NATHAN DRAKE'S DESERTION from the Sace-Cothberg war was an event of such significance to all levels of society that the news of it traveled more swiftly than his commandeered ships.

Proclamations were voiced and hung everywhere that any talk by anyone, of whatever rank or condition, concerning the matter would be considered treason and that anyone repeating such treasonous lies would be subject to arrest. Rewards were offered for information leading toward such arrests.

Those who lived in the streets and hedgerows of Nolan cared nothing for the proclamations. The mob seized upon Nathan Drake's coming as their deliverance from misery and the mob's convictions fed the pre-Millennial frenzies that were sweeping through the Domains. The Alaminite Prophets of the Millennium fueled the idea by all means at their command. Nathan Drake's desertion was the great revelation that on St. Lucien's Eve Alam was to visit destruction upon a thousand years of heathen dominance.

Glennys and Thea spent the next months in a state of anxiety. Glennys's family had been burned out of their farm by members of their own congregation.

Stella had received a revelation which had cost her everything and given her everything. Alam was in reality Alma, God the Mother. It was secret knowledge, she said, that the Reverends had hidden away and twisted in order to rule the congregations. Neither her daughter Deborah, nor the Bohns, Stella's only friendly neighbors, had been able to keep her locked up and silent. Stella frequently escaped to bear witness to the wonderful tidings of Alma.

After the long disturbances in the wake of Hans Rigg, the Soudaka congregations had no patience for another batch of Prophets, much less Prophetesses. Not even the Bohns would take in Stella, though they had given her and the two sisters money and clothes, and had gotten them passage papers to

St. Lucien by post coach. But Stella, Debbie, and Becky had never arrived. Glennys wasn't allowed to ride in search of them, since she was under city arrest for selling inferior horses to Wheels.

At the first change of the post coach to St. Lucien, Stella had wandered off to preach among the vagrants. She'd lost their tickets and given away their money, leaving them destitute.

Sixteen-year-old Deborah, with no preparation for such an ordeal, was left with all the responsibility of getting them to St. Lucien. Becky, now thirteen, hadn't spoken since the night of the fire that destroyed their farm. Stella was uplifted into the cloudy realms of divine exaltation.

On foot, begging, and, far too seldom, exchanging work for food and shelter, Deborah got them to St. Lucien after months of travel. But she had no idea how to find Thea or Glennys. St. Lucien was immensely larger than any place Deborah had ever imagined. Her first day of wandering in this city defeated her, as it had defeated so many others.

Hunter's Moon rose red on their first night in the capital, as red as the anger that had pushed Deborah this far. Now that she was here, not even that was left. Her bare feet were raw, her stomach as empty as her purse, her heart as cold as her arms and legs.

Dimly she remembered that Glennys was the one who'd first stained their family as different from everyone else in Dephi congregation, that Glennys had driven away their father because she made home so bad. Because Glennys was different, their mother was a babbling lunatic. Glennys never suffered the consequences of her sins, but ran away and left the sins to be visited upon her innocent family.

The morning dawned warmer but with it came a transparent, incessant rainfall. So many people, so much filth, so much noise, and such great wealth made it impossible for Deborah to see anything, much less understand what she saw. The three women took refuge in doorways and were driven away. Urchins pelted them with street dirt. Beggars grabbed for their meager packs. The noise never ceased.

Finally the lost and frightened girl gave in to her despair. She sat in the street and wept. "What can we do?" she wailed.

Focus came back into Stella's eyes. Bit by bit the old Stella reinhabited her body.

"You want Thea Bohn, well then, find her! Do I have to do everything myself? I have so much to do that I'd think you could help me a little, Debbie. Alma is telling me the most joyful and important things! Thea Bohn is a healer. Therefore she works through the Fortune Houses. Go to any Fortune House and tell them you're looking for Thea Bohn, the healer. They'll know where she is, and she'll know where Glennys is. I remember from the old days when I was here that a Fortune House is only three streets away from the flower market. Now can you do this little thing yourself, or do I have to?'' And Stella's eyes went cloudy as she slipped back to her Mother Goddess, Alma.

After Deborah found a Fortune House and timidly requested assistance in finding Thea Bohn, everything happened very fast.

A young healer novice asked eagerly, ''There are three of you? You come from Soudaka County? Oh, why didn't you stop and identify yourselves in a Fortune House before now? Thea has had Fortune House alert for you three for weeks and weeks!''

Then the healer novice slapped his head. ''Oh, she'll be so distressed to see you like this! We'll get you cleaned up before she comes.''

''Is Glennys coming?'' Becky whispered to Deborah after they'd eaten, bathed, and changed their rags for ill-fitting, though clean, clothing.

It was the first time she'd spoken. ''Thea is coming,'' Deborah answered. ''Then we'll find Glennys,'' she added.

Becky persisted. ''Glennys will pay the taxes, won't she? Then we can go back to the farm and not be afraid anymore?''

Deborah pulled her baby sister close. Becky had never understood the forces that had sent them away from home. Stella had fretted and prayed and feared over the taxes owed on her farm all year, every year, until Glennys's remittances to pay them arrived. Then Stella would start the old litany again. Becky's understanding of what had happened to them was that the taxers had burned them out, not their own community.

Thea came among them so simply that she'd given out the Alaminite kiss of peace all around almost before Glennys's relatives realized their old friend was there. Instinctively Thea's arms reached out to Deborah first to hug her, for the healer had understood immediately that all of the burden of their ordeal had fallen upon the sixteen-year-old.

Thea patted Debbie's shoulders. She murmured soft praise into her ears, and repeated how worried Glennys was about them all. While Deborah poured out the history of their trials, Thea, without appearing to do so, observed the mother closely. Stella sat in a corner of the room, rocking back and forth, holding her arms around her chest, humming unintelligibly.

Later, while engaged in the nasty process of de-lousing, Deborah stated, not asked, "Mother's not going to recover, is she?"

Thea said, "Some might not think anything's wrong with her at all."

Deborah's lips were a tight line. "To say God is female is the worst kind of blasphemy. It's downright heathen."

Thea steadily continued the sad business of cutting off Deborah's hair and rubbing her scalp with a foul-smelling salve to kill the nits. "God cares nothing at all about blasphemy or heathenism," Thea said with conviction. "God is God, neither male nor female. That's why it's impossible for us to understand the nature of God, because we are limited by our human condition of dividing all beings into male and female."

Deborah looked around at Thea with an expression of horror. On Stella, Thea's pronouncement had another effect. With a pleased smile she plunged into a debate with Thea on the nature of God.

In the middle of it Thea hugged Stella. "It's so good to have my old friend with me. There's never been anyone else with whom I could talk of these things but you!"

Stella cocked one shaven eyebrow at the young healer. "And in St. Lucien, the heart of the heathen, we can say whatever we like, hey?"

Thea stood wide-eyed, staring at Stella.

"Oh, yes, I may be loony, but I'm not stupid, and Alma has given me her special protection." Stella stood up, elbows akimbo, hands on hips. "So where is my first-born daughter who I've not set eyes on in years?"

Thea took a deep breath. How could she quickly explain a situation that had taken all those years to create? "Glennys is hunting in the royal preserves with King Roald and his entourage. She didn't want to go, but she had to because it was a royal command." That left out much, but Thea knew Glennys's family wouldn't understand more than one part of the story at a time.

"Glennys won't be home for another few days. That's good because we'll be able to get you rested, put a little meat on your bones, and have some decent clothes made up before she sees you. I'd like to spare her the worst for the sake of her temper striking out at the King. She's begged him over and over to allow her to ride out with the guards he's put on her tail and search for you, but he's always refused," Thea said.

"Glennys has been spared too much," Deborah weakly spat

out. "She should have seen us as we were when *I* got us all here alive and safe, through no one's help, especially not *hers*."

Thea's face puckered into lines of foreboding. "When you've recovered from your terrible journey and you've been in St. Lucien awhile, you'll understand. She had no choice. Baron Stogar and Duke Colfax sued Glennys for treason. The King, for the first time ever, I think, defied them both. King Roald got the charges against your sister changed to a lesser one of dealing poor horses as breeding and racing stock. Her punishment has been city arrest under his recognizance. That means she must be in attendance to the King whenever and wherever he chooses, and she can go nowhere alone."

Thea could see that her information meant nothing to those who had begged their way on foot from Soudaka County to St. Lucien.

Thea's face brightened. "You're exhausted. Let me take you home. I'm dreadful at explaining politics but Jonathan Reed is very good at it. He'll be able to tell you everything so that you can understand. You'll love him, I promise. Everyone loves Jonathan, even King Roald."

"Who is Jonathan Reed?" Deborah asked, bewildered. There were so many names and she had nothing to bring to any of them.

Thea decided to get the shock that Glennys was living in sin over with immediately. "Jonathan Reed is Glennys's sweetheart. We all live with him. He's a conductor and composer, and a fine musician. He's a favorite of King Roald's, who often has Johnny play him to sleep. Those are the ways Johnny pays for the roof that will be over your heads," Thea concluded. She ignored Debbie's gasp of dismay.

Long before Thea's Popcorn put his hooves down on Frontage Road, Glennys's sisters and mother were deep in exhausted sleep.

Walnut House had changed. By strict Alaminite belief Thea was counted a heretic, but she was an Alaminite for all that. Little by little she'd persuaded the Fortune Houses to buy up the leases on either side of Walnut House as those leases became vacant through death or neighbors moving away. The hedges and fences were knocked down to expand the pasturage. The houses became orphanages with schools, and hospices for men disabled in the Outremere war.

These days, when Glennys was gone with the King's entourage, Jonathan slept in a suite of rooms in a hotel on the Promenade. He also retreated there after singing and playing the pianoforte in the King's palace on the nights Roald's sleepless-ness kept the composer captive. The hotel was convenient to Queen's, and the rooms were private for composition. When Glennys and Jonathan could both get away from the king at the same time, Jonathan came home to Walnut House.

Thea sat up uncharacteristically late thinking about every-thing.

Should she send word to Glennys, in the midst of the annual Royal Great Hunt, that her relatives were safe at home? The King wouldn't release Glennys, Thea knew. Despite Roald's pro-tection when Glennys was accused of treason, the King was no gentleman. He recognized no one's convenience but his own.

Thea hadn't needed to ask Jonathan's permission to house three new inhabitants under his roof. They were Glennys's fam-ily and Jonathan would welcome them. Jonathan was a gentle-man.

That was the problem, Thea thought. She had believed her father to be a gentleman. But sending off a penniless congrega-tional woman, disturbed in her wits, with no better guardian than an inexperienced sixteen-year-old girl, was not the action of a gentleman.

A gentleman, Thea believed, was someone who helped, with no hope of gain, those less fortunate that came in his way. Glen-nys's actions with Thorne, and Jonathan's acceptance of the dif-ficult boy simply because Thorne asked him to, made both of them gentlemen. Even Jonathan's rapport with the unpersonable King came about through compassion, and was a gentlemanly action. Glennys risking, and then losing, her privileges as an independent woman in order to help those captured by press gangs was gentlemanly too.

I am not a gentleman, Thea decided. I am a healer because I want to save the entire world and make it love me the way my pa loved me when I was little. I have a gift, given by God. I use it more for the pleasure it gives me than in gratitude that God gave it to me.

Hooves and wheels rattled in the drive. Jonathan came into the parlor through the kitchen passage. There was a look of satisfaction on his face. "I got your message at the Theater. How are they doing? Are they safe and sound?"

Thea said, "They're here, barely safe, and not what I can call sound, particularly the two sisters. I put them to bed in your old music room."

"Good, good," Jonathan said.

"I am so ashamed of my family!" Thea blurted. "To turn them out like that!"

"Was it a good performance tonight at Queen's?" she inquired next, having learned she should always ask.

"For once, fornicate the Theater and the opera. It was good enough. Show me her mother and sisters," Jonathan demanded.

"They're asleep. Some of the older girls from the orphanage helped me carry them up and undress them, and put down the beds." She led him up the stairs and opened the door. A faint beam from her lamp glimmered over the worn, thin faces of Glennys's family.

Thorne had brought up a bottle of wine and left it open in the parlor, before going to bed himself.

"Now Glennys will settle down," Jonathan declared, pouring out the wine. "Her family's unfit for the wilderness. She'll have to stay here with them."

Gently Thea said, "Jonathan, it doesn't make any difference. Glennys has put so much of herself into the Saquave project, and now civil war's coming. Glennys and Brecca are going out to the Saquave, and I'm going too. That her family is here only makes it easier for her. We'll take them along, as we had always planned."

Jonathan seated himself at his pianoforte. He now owned five. He counted them, to avoid believing Thea's words. One was in King Roald's bedroom. One was in the Shop, another at Queen's, and one more in his suite on the Promenade. The first one he'd ever owned, the one most precious to him, was here.

"Come with us," Thea said.

"There's no place for me there," Jonathan said quietly.

This wasn't the first time they'd had this conversation. Each time it seemed more hopeless.

"It's that bloody stallion Albany sent her, and the string of half-blood Saquave mares he brought back with him this summer to St. Lucien. Without them gnawing at her mind she'd stay with me," Jonathan said savagely.

He turned his face to Thea. "There's going to be enough damage for you to heal right here when the war begins. If you tell her you'll stay here, and her family stays here, then Glennys will stay too!" Jonathan pleaded.

A spectral figure tottered down the stairs into the parlor. "I don't know what you're talking about, but if my oldest daughter has decided to go somewhere, nothing will change her mind. I suppose we'll have to go with her, for there's no one else to take care of us. It's horses again, isn't it? Glennys was always like that, even when she was a tiny child. Are you her leman, then?'' Stella asked.

She approached Jonathan and twined a ringlet of his chestnut hair around her finger. ''She picked a pretty one, and a good one this time,'' Stella said, examining Jonathan's face. ''My daughter's a great fool.''

Stella sat down next to Jonathan on the bench. She put her arms around him and began to croon.

> *Lullaby and sleep my pretty boy*
> *Alma, most lovely mother,*
> *Alma, our mother of all*
> *Loves you best and keeps*
> *Watch over all you do down below*

As Stella released one line after another from her lips, she folded her hands in her lap, and her eyes slowly rolled up under her lids.

Jonathan and Thea exchanged glances. The composer began to pick out chords on his pianoforte and softly accompanied Glennys's mother.

· Thirty-Two ·

UNDER THE HUNTER'S MOON torchers and beaters galloped on mounts protected by thick leather padding. They rode round and round the perimeter of a circle filled with snarling, bellowing animals driven out of the forests to the sward of the Royal Preserve's Killing Ground. The beaters shouted and hit their saddledrums.

With the fall of night on the fifth day, the Great Hunt began its great finale.

A she-wolf snaked herself through one gyre of animals after another, using the swirling force of ceaseless, circling movement to get herself spun to the outer limits of the vortex. With a spring she flung herself free, past the beaters and torchers. She came to ground directly in front of a handsome stallion and his young rider, a Wheel swell caught up in buck fever.

The stallion's forelegs ran into the wolf mid-stride. The horse lost his footing and he went down on the blood-slippery grass, pinning his rider beneath twelve hundred pounds of writhing flesh.

The wind expelled out of the wolf's lungs in a hoarse bark. She somersaulted from the force of the collision and landed on all four legs, already crouched for another leap to freedom.

Brecca sprang smoothly over the downed rider. Glennys raised her spear arm to strike. The she-wolf ran low and fast, her tail and ears down. She slithered between the legs of other hunters' horses converging upon her. Their spears tangled with Glennys's. The horses kicked and bit. The wolf escaped into the darkness of the trees.

It was dangerous for the hunters, but worse for the unarmed torchers and beaters, who had to gauge the moment when the prey would break out of the circle and bolt past the hunters. More than one beater went down, caught between rider and quarry.

Out of the holding circle charged a magnificent bull. His heavy body, crowned by a three-foot span of horns, raced in a blur of speed for the edge of the Killing Ground.

Glennys and Brecca, like most of the younger hunters, went after him. A bull was the big score of the Hunt, for, due to their scarcity, only one of them was allowed as kill.

Brecca wasn't as big as the other stallions, but he was more handy in close quarters, and his strength was a match for the bull's. He was as great a male animal of his kind as the bull was of his. Brecca shot past the other hunters' mounts, using his wide shoulders and chest to shove them out of his way when they didn't give him room.

He outraced and outflanked the bull, turning him from the trees. The bull stopped. His tail lashed his flanks. He charged, aiming his head for the stallion's chest.

Brecca pirouetted sharply out of the way on his hindquarters. Baron rushed in and fastened his teeth in the bull's nostrils, pulling him around so the bull was again facing away from the trees. The bull followed the weight of the dog until he could toss Baron away with several violent shakes of his thick neck.

Brecca and Baron had given Glennys another chance to plant her spear between the bull's shoulders to make the lung kill. Her arm wavered against the bull's tough hide. The point of her spear tore down the beast's shoulder. Brecca volted about to face the bull. Baron distracted him, while Glennys recovered from her poor strike. A man's stronger muscles would have made it successfully.

The huntmaster held off the rival hunters. Glennys's team had engaged. They'd won the right to take the game alone if they could. The others pulled up their horses in a circle around them. More torchers came to light the scene.

The bull lowered his horns and charged at Brecca. The watchers in the circle howled in anticipation of blood.

Brecca leaped high in the air, all the way over the charging bull. His belly barely cleared the bull's lowered horns. He came down with his hindquarters so close to the bull's that he felt the lash of the bull's tail on the flesh under his own, tied up in a net out of the way.

In the moments it took for Brecca's recovery, Baron's fangs slashed the bull's chest in a darting in-and-out run. Stallion and bull alike turned rapidly to face each other.

Brecca stood until the very last possible moment. Obeying his rider's knee, he volted left, presenting Glennys's right arm to the bull's face. The bull's left horn hooked the stallion's chest. Brecca solidly added his weight to his rider's thrust.

"Yee-aahh!" Glennys's spear penetrated into the point between the bull's shoulders. Brecca's forward impulse carried her out of the way of the noble kill's crash to earth.

Still pouring bright blood, the bull was tagged with Glennys's name and dragged off. The spear carrier lifted another shaft and offered it to Glennys. She waved it away. She'd proved herself to her horse and dog. That was enough. In fact, it was probably too much. No doubt King Roald had seen the kill with his spyglass, and no doubt he remembered all over again that she had been accused of other activities as dangerous as killing bulls. But if the King insisted she hunt, she had to hunt. And in a hunt, the rider owed her best efforts to her mount and her harrier.

Glennys dismounted and motioned a torcher close so she could examine Brecca's wound. A groomsman hurried up with a chest of specifics most likely needed on a night of slaughter.

There was a puncture where the horn had hooked Brecca, and a laceration following the progress by which the stallion turned away. Cold water was dashed upon the wound until the bleeding stopped. Glennys applied a lotion made of a cantharide tincture, cholide of zinc, and water, and bound it all with a wet cloth.

Thurlow dismounted from her white mare in a swirl of velvet, fur, and lace. She'd delayed congratulations until the messy part was over with. She and Glennys kissed on both cheeks.

"Finished risking your neck then, Glenn? Come to the King's box and make him forget you took the Great Hunt's prize. He's speculating that you must have learned to hunt from the sort of men who burn Inquiry Offices and free impressed vagabonds."

In a louder, gayer voice Thurlow said, "So tedious! Five days of chase and one night of dancing is the wrong way about, I think. Not even Roald can leave until the carnage is complete."

Confidentially she continued, "Roald wouldn't find it so tedious if he took part himself. I thought the King of Nolan *led* the Great Hunt. But then, Kingship isn't what it used to be, is it?"

Though Thurlow voiced a common opinion, it was dangerous to do it. But Thurlow always took the more reckless path. That was what made it possible for Glennys to put up with her.

The two women, one dark and the other fair, drew eyes after them, in spite of the excitement on the Killing Ground. They chatted softly, and, it appeared, intimately, while leading their horses slowly along the edge of the Ground to the King's comfortable Honor Box at the top of the field. Not for one moment did Glennys forget how dangerous Thurlow could be. She talked of something other than her feat and how the King might interpret it.

Glennys asked, "Please, Thurlow, can you plead for me to King Roald? Ask him to let me off from the Predator's Ball tomorrow night. My family can't understand why I haven't come to greet them."

"Oo-la-la!" Thurlow laughed dismissively. "They haven't seen you in years. Another few days don't signify. What I'll do is get the King to remove your guards. I need you free to come and go myself. I can't be left with no one at my back in company with Cayetana and that Wendala. And the other women around the King are even worse. They hate me. It's exactly like when we were growing up and we had no friends other than each other."

Part of Thurlow's power over Roald consisted in seeing to it that the King enjoyed himself. Part of that strategy was surrounding him with the most desirable women in St. Lucien. Stogar had never thought to do that, intelligent as he was. Another part of her strategy was urging the King to defy Stogar and Colfax for the fun of it.

Thurlow volunteered, "I may have to marry Roald." She giggled wickedly. Stogar's increasing frustration over Thurlow's ascending influence over Roald gratified her hugely.

Glennys was weary. She'd been in the saddle for days. Her left shoulder hurt, and her right arm was still numb and tingling after the killing thrust. She attempted to be light. "There's no end to Roald's troubles, is there?"

Thurlow shivered slightly. "Fortunately, due to his 'little trouble,' Roald has no daughters, legitimate or otherwise, tucked away. Stogar would surely get himself married to her, if she existed, and that would be the end of Roald. I've been ever so gently suggesting this to the King. Instead, I think, *I* shall be the one to hold the key to Nolan's rule in my expert hand."

Disgust passed briefly over her lovely face as Thurlow looked down at her free hand. "The King is *very* fond of this hand, and its many skills, since he's incapable of enjoying another part of me that possesses greater."

It was Glennys's turn to shiver. Her family showing up was a terrible stroke of bad luck. They, like everyone close to her, could be used against her. They didn't understand what they'd walked into. She was going to have to send them out again, to wait out the winter at the foot of the Rain Shadows, in the High-lands at Goats Run. They weren't going to understand that ei-ther.

And Glennys would have to stay behind. The King's Guards tracked her every movement, even following her to latrines and to Jonathan's suite at the hotel. She, who treasured liberty, was effectively a prisoner of both Thurlow and Roald. Sometimes she thought she'd prefer a dungeon. That way she wouldn't have to listen to either one of them and witness the endless boredom of their lives.

"Where have you gone, Glenn? You look as though someone stepped on your grave. Don't show Roald anything but a face full of fun and flirtation." Thurlow touched Glennys's shoulder with the hand of which King Roald was so fond. "Remind him of the reasons he was willing to listen to me and keep Stogar from executing you for treason."

That meant, you are in my debt.

Glennys said, "Justin Sharp had something to do with it."

"Don't turn too far, worm," Thurlow warned. "One of these nights you must join us and again help Roald to overcome his 'little trouble,' " Thurlow said, revealing the claws that seldom retracted completely. "After I become Queen in Nolan you may have a great deal of occupation."

That meant, you are my slave.

In the Honor Box Glennys borrowed a spyglass and devastat-ingly caricatured the Wheels' poor sportsmanship and worse handling of the traditional Aristo weapons. She flirted with the King through her lowered eyelashes. When he attempted a pon-derous witticism about the blood on the skirt of her riding habit outshining the blood of the Wheels, she impudently ripped off the skirt of her hunting dress, showing her figure to fine advan-tage before wrapping her hips in one of the King's fur mantles.

The Wheel women clucked to each other over Baroness Wa-terford's success at fencing the King off from their daughters by surrounding him with such low-born women.

Acting from spite of their own, Cayetana and Wendala asked, when the King could hear, whether Jonathan would be conduct-ing the musicians playing at tomorrow night's Predators' Ball. That made the King swell with satisfaction. He may have loved Jonathan's music but his convenience kept Jonathan and Glennys apart more nights than they spent together.

Glennys whipped herself to ever more delirious heights of

broadly lascivious conduct. The humiliation of it colored her cheeks more brightly than any wine could have done.

Thurlow was mightily amused at seeing the bull-killer losing the last shreds of dignity Glennys had always clung to in the presence of herself and the King. Cayetana's unaffected low manners and lewd behavior suited her. Glennys's awareness of how she was perceived made her actions merely obscene.

But the King was so entertained that he rewarded Glennys's request and publicly called of the guards who'd followed her for so long wherever she went.

"Very good, my Stallion Queen," Duke Albany said softly. "You're free to move again as you like," he said. He reached out to embrace her.

Glennys pushed him away violently. "Don't touch me. Don't call me Stallion Queen. I don't have left even the honor of King's Daughter. Among all of you I've been turned out a whore in earnest!"

"That may be the least price you pay," Albany said. "A Queen does what she must for the sake of her people."

• Thirty-Three •

"WHY WON'T THIS bloody piece of junk stay in tune?" Jonathan exploded. He banged up and down the keyboard in frustration.

"Please, Johnny, I'm trying to match the last manifest of supplies with what the inventory from Goats Run states actually arrived," Glennys pleaded.

"I'm sick of getting from you only the leavings of horses, the Saquave, Albany, and Thurlow!" Jonathan burst out.

Glennys's own lacerated heart erupted, and their fight drove everyone else outside to the cold winter morning.

When Jonathan took a fire poker to his pianoforte, Glennys tried to stop him from turning the instrument on which he'd learned to play into a wreckage of ivory, ebony, strings, and splintered mahogany. They were both sobbing, and they made up their differences—again. Very late Jonathan went off to the Shop and Glennys settled down, drawn and spent, to help with the final packing.

Thea and her family were taking the barge tomorrow. Two of Glennys's men devoted to the Saquave settlement would accompany them to the bleak town of Kahia beyond the Setham River. In Kahia the party would be met by Albany's rangers and conducted on horseback during the long trip to Goats Run.

Glennys sorted through her personal belongings, deciding which things would go into the small trunk she was sending with them. Deborah began her litany again. "Give me the money you're spending to send me away and I'll rebuild Mother's farm myself!" she demanded.

Thea, determined to keep peace in Walnut House during these last remaining hours, jumped in. "Civil war is coming, sweetheart, no matter how oblivious to it the masters of St. Lucien appear to be. Soudaka County won't be safe. It's Baron Stogar's own holding. The Old Gordon will target Soudaka and Drake to avenge his sons' deaths. And the Shipper King of Andacac will likely send an army to Soudaka in a grab for the Badlands coal mines. Even with friends, Dephi couldn't keep you safe.''

Deborah began to lament. ''I am a member of the Dephi congregation in good standing. I didn't sin against them, Mother did. I got us all here without money or help. I could rebuild the farm!''

''You think so?'' Glennys snarled. ''In a time of war? Your journey was bad, but it's nothing, nothing at all, you hear, compared to setting yourself up as a woman alone in a war. I'm not going to fool with you anymore. Get on your outdoor gear and come with me!''

Deborah, weeping in earnest now, was quickly bundled into a sleigh hitched to Puppet. The icy air bit through their wind masks as Glennys drove them to the Seahorse Tavern.

Copely's face lit with welcome when he saw Glennys pull off her mask. Before he could dive into a discussion of Nolan's political situation Glennys asked, ''May I have the key to the upstairs room? Here's someone who should see George's drawings.''

George Sert's drawings of what he'd seen in the Outremere war were too disturbing to hang downstairs in the cheer of the tavern. But Copely opened the upstairs room to anyone he judged wasn't from the Office of Inquiry, and the pictures were visited frequently.

Though cold, the room was well lit. At the far end, in the center, was the largest picture. ''Look at it,'' Glennys commanded, pulling her sister's hands away from her eyes.

Soldiers fought over little caches of plunder. Houses were in flames, and used as centers of hideous actions. Horses rode over the bodies of children. Women were torn out of hiding places to suffer what women always suffer in war. Animals were slaughtered for the lust of it.

''*This* is sin,'' stated Glennys. ''This is what will happen all over Nolan soon. This is what will happen in Dephi. In the Saquave we have a chance to escape this. Look! Look at everything in this room, and tell me again you want to rebuild a past dead to you instead of birthing a place where all can live with liberty and justice.''

She locked Deborah in where all was terrible to see and stood guard outside so no young Romantics would intrude, raving over the potency of George's lines. When enough time had passed Glennys put her arm around Debbie and led her down to the

public room. She seated them in an isolated corner, ordering
food and drink.

Glennys leaned over the board between them and took Debbie's hands in her own. "If you want to go back to Dephi," she
said slowly and very gently, "I'll find the money somehow and
send you off tomorrow. But that's the last support I can give.
You'll be alone. Neither Thea nor I will allow you to take Stella
and Becky."

Deborah stared in silence at her food, though long months of
hunger had left her always ravenous.

Glennys tried again. "Family isn't necessarily those you love
or understand. Family's simply what the luck gave you, and you
can't escape your family. A family must stand together."

Deborah put down her mug of mulled wine on the board so
hard the dregs leaped out. "Everyone knows that Glennys Eve
can do anything she sets her mind to, even rebuilding a farm,
war or no war," she spat out. "Liberty and justice indeed! You're
going out to the Saquave to queen it over everyone. But Hans
Rigg and Reverend Tuescher are out there too, and I don't think
they'll let you have it all your own way. It will be worth my
while to be there and see just how long you last!"

The next afternoon Glennys wasn't at the barge to see Thea
and the others off on the first stage of their winter journey. She
made her farewells early and rode off alone on Brecca. When
the waters of the lock rose, Glennys was in the subterranean
storage chambers of the Fine Arts Academy with Duke Albany,
Blood Chief Nathan Drake, Hengst, Justin Sharp, and George
Sert.

George watched jealously as Glennys shook the tears out of
her eyes and touched Hengst's withered, pinched features. He
burned with outrage when Justin Sharp politely requested that
the artist leave them in privacy.

In the little room where Thorvald had stored the relics of
Nolanese tribalism, George batted the dust-shrouded horse
masks. No one had been down here in years. He thought about
the drawings he'd risked his life to make, which he'd thought
had made him a peer with the bloods. It had been his idea that
the Fine Arts Academy basement would provide a safe refuge
for the rebels' meeting. And now he was discarded like a used-
up crayon.

He sat down at the rickety table and fingered the dust-dimmed
painted stones that had taught him pride in Nolan's own art. The

great players on the world's stage were putting great events into motion and claiming their roles. They were assigning him no part at all. He wasn't even deemed loyal enough to be an audience to what would happen next.

In the largest storage chamber Nathan Drake, backed by the mammoth bones of some curious beast that no modern man had laid eyes on, exhibited the Brugge Works ledger to Albany and Sharp. "Get this translated at once so Roald can read it. This ledger must convince him that Stogar, Colfax, my brother Elliot, and all their faction have to be put down for treason. He must understand that the King's Justice executed upon them is the only acceptable response to the dishonor they have done to Nolan, my men, and most of all, to Hengst and me, made pawns in their money-games. Only their blood will cleanse our lines of their blood betrayal."

Sharp grabbed the ledger with greedy hands. He could read the Sace-Cothberg language and write it too.

Strangely, Albany didn't even look over Justin's shoulder at the ledger's evidence. He declared, "Oh, we can do more than that!"

An expression of more purely sensual pleasure was on the Duke's face than Glennys had ever seen on the occasions of their bedding.

Albany announced, "Roald must resign the throne in favor of Leon's legitimate heir and son."

His expression of pleasure deepened as the shock of dawning comprehension began to show on the faces of his companions. It was the deepest, most sustained release the Duke had ever known.

Glennys fought feeling sick and furious while the Duke recounted the events that led to Lenkert Deerhorn fishing Queen Sharissa out of the catastrophe of Yemmessee Bay. How differently she, and so many others, might have chosen their actions during the last years if they'd known that Nolan's legitimate Queen and heir were waiting in the wings.

Nathan's voice was cold. "Have you kept Baroness Ely and Old Gordon ignorant of this, as well as myself?"

With swelling pride Albany said, "Mother and daughter should be reunited in a matter of hours. How I wish I could witness the Baroness when she sees her grandson! I kept Sharissa and young Leon, a fine healthy boy, the image of his sire, closely secreted in the Saquave until I was sure he'd survive infant mortalities. If there'd been any whisper that Sharissa and her precious burden had lived, Baroness Ely wouldn't have been able to keep quiet about it, and surely Stogar would have found a way to kill Queen and heir.''

There had to have been a better way. Albany's secretiveness smelled dishonorable to Glennys. Her mind raced, and then filled with a brilliant conviction of insight that Nathan and Hengst felt the same. There had been too much blood of their companions poured on Outremere ground for nothing.

''You fox!'' Justin Sharp crowed. ''So, you will marry Sharissa to Roald, make him step down to the place of regent until young Leon is of age as the price of Roald's life, and thus avert civil war, while putting the Spurs back in the saddle of Nolan with all the reins in our own fingers again!''

There was no thought given to Sharissa's feelings about being coupled with Roald. Glennys's heart bled for her. But if such a marriage averted Nolanese going to war against each other, Sharissa would do it bravely.

Sharp laced his fingers together and considered. ''Further, Albany, this will ensure your immortality—the man who with quick wit and foresight beyond that of any other, saved us from disaster without shedding blood himself!''

Nathan Drake glowered at Albany. ''There has been blood shed already, lakes of it, and for nothing! My men, my comrades, my brothers-in-arms might be alive if you hadn't kept this secret.''

Albany looked down his long, narrow nose. ''Your Wheel heritage is showing. You're measuring blood as though it were bolts of cloth or gold coins you can hoard in a warehouse for a rainy day.''

Glennys asked, ''And the Saquave settlement? What part has that in your plans?''

Justin Sharp turned on her. ''The heir and the Queen assure the Spurs' dominance immediately. It will take years before the Saquave can give us the same, or any profit, populated as it is with the weak-kneed Shoes you took out of the press gangs.''

Glennys said bitterly, ''You encouraged my actions because it made the Fortune Houses look good to the Shoes. I think the only way you'll stop this war is to shout the news of Sharissa's survival and Leon's son from the housetops now. Proclaim it in every hamlet and village. Stogar's party won't have time to regroup their forces and set up protection for St. Lucien. Have you forgotten the Alaminite Prophets? They've promised the people that the city will burn upon the Millennium!''

Albany sighed and kissed Glennys's hand. "Nolanese, whatever their rank and condition, will never side with Lighters. The Prophets, if they do attempt anything so foolish, will be no more than an action for the city guards."

Glennys argued against him, pouring out her knowledge of the streets, hedgerows, and back counties. But Albany and Sharp were elated. The other Nolanese counted for nothing in their minds, she realized, other than counters in the games the Spurs and Wheels played with each other.

She tried another tack. "Even if Roald agrees to step down, the Wheels may still resort to war. Where are the Spurs' ammunition factories, cannon foundries, and mills? How many able-bodied, fighting-age bloods are left alive? Not even the Ely wealth can finance a war unaided. Will you, Justin Sharp, sacrifice the Fortune House treasury for the Spurs?"

In the headlong career of her words she'd misstepped.

"Count your needles and thread and bolts of cloth and packets of seeds, Glennys, out in the Saquave. Leave war and its finances to those who aren't afraid of it," Justin Sharp snapped.

Nathan Drake gave Sharp a hard, long look, then got up and stood before Glennys. "Albany has called you Stallion Queen of the Saquave. I have deep reservations about leading Nolanese Spurs against Nolanese Wheels. If you are right about events, Glennys Eve, I may go with you into the Saquave."

Before Albany or Sharp could react to this unexpected declaration from Nolan's Blood Chief, Hengst spoke. "However events go, Stogar's betrayal must be cleansed from our bloodline. Until then neither you nor I, Glennys, have honor. As you and I are related, I call you to aid and assist me. Once Stogar's blood is shed, I am your man, but not before."

There was bitter argument but a truce and a plan of sorts acceptable to all parties was hammered out. On St. Lucien's Eve when Roald took the auguries for the coming year in the Circle Gardens Fortune House, the other three would stand at Albany's back, when Sharp informed Roald and the world that Roald was no true King.

Nathan quickly took charge while Sharp and Albany departed. George was called back, and to his increasing delight informed of what had passed. While Glennys made up a list of people George should call on with warnings of St. Lucien's Eve, the painter began to knock together lumber for rough stalls. Glennys had to get her men some horses. The basement of Nolan's Fine Arts Academy seemed the safest hideout in the city.

In a mood of despair Glennys climbed the stairs in the hotel where Jonathan had his suite. She undressed and huddled in a ball on Jonathan's bed.

Nathan Drake had asked Glennys for a boon. "Do your best through your influence with Thurlow to get me a private interview with Roald before St. Lucien's Eve. It puts us both at risk, I know, but for the sake of the lives that might be saved, I am honor-bound to try."

It was very late when Jonathan came in. During this season of Nolan's Millennial festivities he was worked almost beyond endurance. He thankfully took Glennys into his arms, kissed her and caressed her.

For the first time in their life together she denied him.

He said nothing at first, only looked at her with such a terrible expression of pain she wished she had never been born. "Why, Glenn? When our nights together are numbered?"

"I'm terrified." She spilled out everything of the day's events, including the existence of Sharissa and Leon's son. "There will be civil war. It began long ago. Look at us—we're divided. My own sister hates me." Her voice trailed off, for Johnny wasn't listening.

He said quietly, "War is a part of life that no one escapes. It's not the fear of war that leads you to reject me. It's *me* you reject. I'm in your way. You'd rather be rousing all your friends to lead them safely away from St. Lucien. You want to give to large numbers, but the one who loves you best is too much trouble to consider. Albany's fed it by calling you 'Stallion Queen!' "

Her weariness of heart was so great she could hardly protest. "But you are the first, the most important of those to whom I owe warning, and I've warned you. Johnny, what will you do when the war comes? How will you live? Come with me!"

Jonathan pulled on his dressing gown. "I will fight the war with the weapons of an artist—exile, cunning, and silence. I'm taking a leave of absence from Queen's to accept an appointment from Mathematics at Seven Universities. The Universities have the Wheels' favor, and Roald's favor of me has placated even my father. I'm to lecture on the Foundation of Mathematics and Musical Theory. You could come with me, but you can't, can you?" It wasn't a question.

"I owe the people I sent to the Saquave my skills," she said.

Jonathan said, "I was never happier than I was with you and

Thea in Walnut House until Albany divided you from me with that bloody horse, sending you off recklessly around the country, endangering all of us. An end comes to everything, Glennys, and I've reached it. I'd prefer that you leave and not come back."

He went into the adjoining room and sat down at his piano. When Glennys dressed and came out, his back was to her. Though she stood there for a long time, he didn't turn around.

Glennys brought Brecca and Baron out of the hotel stable. On the street she looked up at the windows of Jonathan's suite. He was playing. She'd never heard the music before.

She turned Brecca's head toward Albany House, for though divided she and Albany were still allies. Brecca's mind reached out and captured hers. He bolted through the streets to the west. She wrested herself back from him, though it took long minutes for her to gather the strength. He turned his head and nuzzled her knee as though nothing had happened.

All along the Promenade fireworks were going off against the velvet sky.

The day before St. Lucien's Eve was the same as those of the last weeks. No government business was conducted. There was a play, an opera ballet, and a banquet, followed by another ball.

In his costumes encrusted with gold and jewels King Roald swelled, strutted, and preened like a jackdaw. Treasures flowed in a river to him from ambassadors, plenipotentiaries, and fellow sovereigns. Praise and compliments burst over his four-crowned head like fireworks.

Glennys had her assigned place in the vast, finely choreographed dance of St. Lucien's masters. She was Thurlow's chosen companion, and Thurlow's place was close to the King. Duke Albany, the bloodlines' elder, had a central role, along with Duke Colfax, Baron Stogar, and the members of the King's Wheel-dominated council.

The ceremonial places left empty by old bloodlines that had ended in the Nemourian Mountains were filled by manufacturers, bankers, and merchants. They'd bought themselves in by judicious gifts to the council. The surviving bloodlines prudently refrained from commenting on the absence of the Old Gordon and Baroness Ely.

After midnight every other musician in the orchestra gallery of the Winter Palace fell out to rest. The remaining half played softly, alert for the signs to pick up full strength as soon as the breathless revelers had recovered. Jonathan's arms, weary from a long day and night's work of conducting, drooped low, though he kept beating time.

Glennys couldn't help herself. She stood below in a position where she could catch Jonathan's reflection in the mirror centered among the black and white plumes of her fan. Her black-and-white dress was a somber note in the brilliant colors of the others.

She saw a waiter bring Jonathan a cup of coffee. In the mirror Glennys's heart recognized the pretty features of Rowena, her curls under a wig, her lovely body in waiter's livery.

She saw Jonathan and Rowena kiss.

Thurlow's ringed fingers pushed aside Glennys's fan and her flirtatious face replaced the vision in Glennys's mirror. "Tonight you will be with the King privately."

Carefully, Glennys said, "Nolan will bow to you, Thurlow, in gratitude. A meeting between Roald and Nathan Drake will likely prevent bloodshed."

Thurlow frowned. "Still singing that old song? I've told you that Roald would run to Stogar with the news that Drake's in Nolan. You'd find yourself in the interrogation dungeon."

The fear Glennys had resolutely pushed away for days closed in. "Thurlow, please! There's still time!"

Thurlow stopped Glennys's mouth with her hand. "I've promised Roald that tonight he'll have you, me, and whomever else has caught his eye most, in bed together. Help me pick the right one, do right by him—and me—on that field, and then you can take your life into your hands."

She shoved a glass of champagne at Glennys. "To St. Lucien's Eve. We're all related!"

Glennys couldn't understand how she'd ever been fond of the wine or of Thurlow. "We are not related," she said calmly.

Thurlow's lips thinned. "King's Daughter, you'd be wise to leave certain matters up to the stupid men whose business it is."

Glennys whispered in the perfumed, hot ballroom air. "No."

Thurlow spoke low. "You owe it to me."

Glennys's voice, though a whisper, was passionate. "I've done my best to enlist your aid in a deed of honor and courage. But you refuse. All I owe you is the warning of a reformer. There's another part of Nolan outside this ballroom that is also related, and it's been abused. If the throne won't ease its burden, that part of Nolan will join with others to break the throne," she finished fiercely.

Thurlow dashed her wine in Glennys's face. "You ungrateful whore! That's the return you give me for lifting you out of the stable manure to the condition of a lady, and saving your life to boot. Reform is another word for treason. Stogar was right about you!"

Glennys dabbed at her dripping face with her tight satin glove. Thurlow's bare shoulders retreated from her across the floor. She was on her way to seek out Stogar, Glennys knew.

She dared to look up to the musicians' gallery in her mirror. Jonathan was presenting Rowena to Roald. Then Roald sat down at Jonathan's pianoforte.

Though they'd been unable to hear anything, those who'd witnessed the scene edged toward her, avid for gossip. Glennys stepped back to hide behind two massive silver vases of flowers. The light that reflected from the swollen vases blinded anyone who looked there.

She pulled her hair out of the upsweep in which she'd styled it, and let it hang limply on her shoulders. Her dress she couldn't disguise, but there were so many remarkably dressed women that it took more than clothes to be noticed. She rounded her shoulders. She slumped out of her pliantly erect posture, took off her heeled dancing pumps, and lost inches from her height. She walked heavily, her mouth twisted, her eyes squinty. No one paid any attention to one more despondent wallflower at the King's ball. She made her way to the relative safety of a servant's wall passage. The quality of her dress left the servitors unquestioning. Many incidents, more bizarre than this, during Roald's entertainments had taught them silence.

Out of the palace she matched her Horse Sense with Brecca. Her own instinct of survival rippled along his silver-grey body. She showed him how to slip his tether. He shifted stealthily downwind from the carriage teams and mounts waiting for the King's guests.

She pulled one vaporous thread after another from her fear. Her weirding fingers tugged on the strands connecting her to Brecca, bringing him to where she stood on numb feet in the frozen garden grounds. She mounted, tucking her feet up high under her ruined skirts. They flowed through the ever-shifting deeper darkness cast by the shadows of the palace over the upper city. Darkness was their mantle, warding off all eyes, concealing them from a hard-riding troop of King's Guards who tore past them following Stogar's uncovered bright hair.

On the marble floors of the Fine Arts Academy and the hastily thrown-up ramp leading down into the storerooms, Brecca's shod hooves announced he was a true horse and no ghost at all.

Nathan and Hengst doused the lights and pulled their weapons to the ready, even though Baron stood eagerly at the ramp's bottom, wagging his tail. When Glennys announced herself softly they put their swords aside and relit the lamps.

"I've failed, Nathan," she said flatly. "Thurlow's turned against me and told Stogar everything. He's searching for all of us. You were wise enough to go to ground early, Duke Albany. Now be wise enough to get out tonight and start for Goats Run."

"Stallion Queen," said Albany, "I'm too old for a winter's break-for-leather escape. The Saquave governorship is entirely yours."

She strode to where she had stowed her old Three Trees saddlebags some days ago, along with a working saddle, bedroll, and whatever else could be carried without interfering with long, cold, hard riding. As heedless of their eyes as if the basement were Queen's dressing room and she off the boards from an arduous, thankless performance, she stripped off the rags of her ballgown, kicked it aside, and laced herself into her work gear.

After caring for Brecca and checking on the horses she'd obtained for Albany and Hengst, she squatted down by their brazier. Commandeering the sand tray, she began drawing from memory various routes from St. Lucien to Goats Run. "This is in case something happens to separate us tomorrow night after confronting Roald in the Fortune House," she said.

"Well, see to it that nothing does separate us," Hengst declared, "for it's clear you know Nolan better than I."

Nathan Drake drummed his fingers against his thigh. Every inch of his Aristo body proclaimed that skulking in cellars was unfitting behavior for a Blood Chief.

"May I attend when you interrogate Glennys, please?" Thurlow wheedled in a voice Roald would have heeded.

Stogar slapped her hard on one side of her face. "No one's been in Albany House all day. There's nothing at Walnut House but puling orphans, and mewling cripples, and the fools who take care of them." He spoke without inflection, but punctuated every few words with another open-palmed slap on Thurlow's face.

"Why did you delay telling me Glennys knew Nathan Drake was in the city?" He shook her so hard her teeth rattled.

"You'd have had her arrested and tortured, and then she'd have been of no use to me!" Thurlow screamed.

"Didn't you even try to learn where Nathan Drake's laired?" Stogar demanded, shaking her again.

Thurlow snarled, "I didn't care, and if I did know, now I'd never tell you!" She sunk her teeth into his forearm.

"You stabbed me in the back so you could have someone with whom you could boast of the love affairs you conduct behind Roald's back. I'm astounded that even you could be such a stupid piece of twang!"

"Stop hitting me! You've already ruined my face for the Eve of St. Lucien!" Thurlow attempted to snatch his dagger.

Stogar threw her across the room. Thurlow crashed into the wall. Her impact brought down a massive tapestry depicting a woman pushed high in a swing, showing her legs far above the point of discretion while the swells below simpered in adoration.

• Thirty-Four •

ROALD SHIVERED UNDER his gold-washed furs. The St. Lucien's Eve procession wound through a dark city beset by a heavy southeast wind. Time and order would return when the Fortune House bells had tolled off the Millennium, and chimed in the new year. Then fires and light could blossom again in St. Lucien.

Roald dismounted inside the Fortune House, his white stallion's reins given over to Stogar and Colfax. So far, that was the only pleasure he'd received today. He enjoyed seeing his imperious council chiefs perform lackey duties for him.

The flames burned high in the fire well of the central chamber, providing an illusion of heat. According to St. Lucien's Eve custom, the fires had been out all day in the Winter Palace, as well as the city, and Thurlow, whom he'd been counting on to keep him warm and amused, had disappeared last night, pleading a woman's indisposition.

Cords of prepared torches were stacked high in preparation for the new year. After the midnight auguries were announced the people would rekindle their doused fires from the brands lit at the fire well. Roald strode quickly to the flames. He was King; he didn't have to wait until the new year to be warm again.

Feeling for the first time a kinship with all the people of Nolan, because he himself was so cold, Roald opened his arms before the fire well. The sooner he completed the ceremony, the sooner people could get warm.

"May the auguries for the new year give the ruler of Nolan's tribes and her Dominions a safe and prosperous road. May our luck be strong and our union undivided. Reveal the path I must ride," Roald intoned.

The shadows surrounding the fire well were illuminated by the same devices used by the stage secrets guild. Vents concealed in the floor brought up swirls of incense. Justin Sharp walked on a path of fire and smoke to meet Roald.

The King touched his crown uneasily, for the High Astrologer and the dirty, ragged diviners from the nooks and crannies of Fortune Houses all over Nolan normally presided over the new year's ceremonies.

Sharp was dressed in the white brocade of his office as High Judiciar Skiller. "All the omens for this year, and those tailing it, are ill, my Prince. There is only one road open to peace and prosperity, and it is open only if you, the younger brother of our slain King, will ride on it with your full consent," Sharp said.

The fire well's flames twirled and bowed, maneuvered by the bellows hidden in the overhead dome's catwalks. The fire leaned toward Roald, and he flinched away.

"This is not what I came to hear," Roald protested.

Stogar advanced and pushed Roald aside. "What do you intend, Sharp, with this travesty of the new year's auguries? How dare you address our four-crowned King of Nolan and the Dominions without his coronal rank? You can be executed for this!"

Justin Sharp held his ground, and crossed his arms across his breast. He said, "The Prince is the Prince. He is not King. Queen Sharissa lives, and with her, King Leon's legitimately begotten son and heir."

Colfax's laughter was saw-edged. It grated painfully on Roald's ears. "Sharissa's so long drowned that the crabs of Yemmessee Bay have crunched her bones."

Albany revealed himself from the other side of the fire well. He was followed by Lenkert Deerhorn, carrying the Duke's parrot on his shoulder. The Duke gently pushed Deerhorn into the light before him. "Tell them, my man, of your feat on the waters of Yemmessee the night our beloved King was assassinated."

Deerhorn spoke to the point. His conclusion was, "Both my Duke and I were witness when Sharissa safely birthed young Leon in the Saquave." Lenkert smiled fondly. Much of the infant's care had fallen to him. "He's a healthy and whole manchild."

In the darkness of the off-side gallery Glennys's heart softened into her early sympathy for the eunuch. There had been an unaware pathos in which the gelded Deerhorn had announced the heir's equipment of an entire male. It had to convince any hearer of his truth-speaking.

Albany ignored Stogar and turned all his attention, body and voice, upon Roald. "The road you must choose, Prince, for the sake of all of Nolan and the Domains, is marriage with your brother's widow. We need you to stand as regent for young Leon until he's of age for coronation. Your consent to the marriage will preserve Nolan's unity among the tribes and between Spur and Wheel.''

Glennys saw the gleam of sweat shining on Roald's face, which worked in hideous grimaces. He struggled to speak, but his tongue failed his need.

"You see the right of it." Albany stretched out his arms to embrace Roald. "We are all related! You will be acclaimed in history for your wisdom, generosity, and compassion.''

Roald pushed Albany from him, able to speak at last. "Tell them, Stogar, tell them, Colfax, *I am the King!*" Roald's hands fluttered up and down his body, seeking to convince himself of his existence, looking for a support to hold him up, and that denied the truth he'd heard with his own ears.

Then two men, masked in the executioner's red vizard, came out of the shadows, treading the path of fire and smoke. Between them they carried a large book.

"Prince, your bloodline always insisted that even Shoes should learn to read and write. They can read in this translated ledger of the Brugge Works in Sace-Cothberg an accounting of the treason done against Nolan by your councilors, Fulk and Colfax."

Stogar and Colfax froze for long moments. They knew the men under the red executioner's vizards to be Nathan Drake and Hengst.

Sharp said, "Copies of the Brugge ledger have been sent throughout Nolan. But tonight, my Prince, read it to the people of St. Lucien; honor them by giving them the knowledge first. Then show the people the heads of these two who have betrayed us all," he urged.

The central chamber lit up, as did the stage when all plots are revealed and confounded. A host of the Fortune House's youthful officiates, well armed, were ranged about the central chamber.

Roald believed with every fiber of his being that it was his choice at this moment of fortune that mattered. He pulled the King's Blade from its scabbard. "To me, everyone, to *me!*" he shouted to the armed officiates. "I am the King, and no other. I am surrounded by idiots and traitors at every turn. Take them all to the dungeons in the Fortress Kurgan!"

The officiates made no move to obey.

Justin Sharp turned his palms down to the floor—the earth—and his face to the sky; the dome's stained-glass panels were open to the night for the sake of the fire well.

"My Office speaks. Duke of Colfax and Newport, Chief of

the Office of Inquiry, is assassin of his true and loyal King Leon, a traitor to his brothers-in-arms. Baron Stogar Fulk of Soudaka, killer of his father, assassin of his true and loyal King Leon, a traitor to his brothers-in-arms. This treason was performed, not in mistaken zeal of serving Nolan, but out of dishonorable avarice. Your lust for wealth has wantonly destroyed Nolan's unity. We condemn you to execution. Duke Colfax and Baron Fulk are cast out from the tribes. Their bodies given, not to the burial kurgans, but to the rats and crows. Colfax and Fulk are not related! Take their swords and break them!'' Sharp commanded.

The first roll of the Fortune House's massive bells rang out sonorous and deep. On the cue of the Circle Gardens bells the other clappers in St. Lucien began ringing theirs, initiating the thousand peals of Millennium. The chamber filled with martial clangor, the marble amplifying the crash of metal on metal.

It was an hour before midnight. It would take that long to ring down the Millennium and bring in the new year.

The chiming vibrated their bodies. It writhed around them. It climbed in hair-raising tendrils from the soles of their feet and the shod hooves of the horses, up ankles and legs. Everyone felt it, and instinctively looked down. Giant plumes of incense smoke vented up from the floor, filling the room.

Gustave lost his sense of direction. He squawked, but no one could hear him. His partially pinioned wings flapped frantically. The parrot launched himself from Lenkert's shoulder to Albany. His wings didn't support him properly to land. He clawed for purchase against Roald.

Roald struck out against the parrot without thinking. The King's Blade caught the bird's body. Gustave flopped to the floor in a soft patter of blood and feathers. Roald slashed again and again at the parrot.

Albany tried to stop him. Astonished, Roald pulled back the King's Blade from out of Duke Albany's eye.

Albany sank to his knees. One hand went out to ward off death, which to his disbelief, was reaching out to claim him at last.

Immediately, Colfax's blade cut through the Fortune House officiates before the ceremonial doors. Colfax escaped, bellowing unheard through the bells for the King's Guards. At the same moment Stogar grabbed Roald, whose four-crowned head and fur-girthed body made an effective shield for the slender Stogar clad in close-fitting gear. ''Protect me until Colfax comes

with your Guards. They won't harm you! They need you!'' he
shouted into Roald's ears.

Roald batted out at the officiates with his Blade. Stogar guided
him from behind with words, warning of attacks, and with hands
toward the entrance and the protection of the Guards.

The bells had pealed one hundred times.

Glennys counted them, a reflex left over from her days with
Queen's when she struggled to keep action in time with sound.
Then the shock of Albany's death took over.

Baron crouched against her legs. His ears were flattened tight
to his head. The bells hurt him.

Brecca, in company with Hengst's and Nathan's horses, quivered with the desire for escape from the racket pounding against
their hearing and their bodies. Glennys held them in place.

The traitors' horses plunged and struck out. They were in the
way of the ceremonial entrance. Nathan was attempting to get
around them to close and bar the doors.

Hengst pursued Stogar. The executioner's vizard had been torn
away. Hengst's own face burned with a terrible determination.

Officiates tumbled over each other to get out of his path. Justin
Sharp yanked down hard on Hengst's sword arm, before he could
thrust at the terrified Roald. Hengst kicked the Judiciar in the
belly. Sharp went down, vomiting.

A courageous officiate circled behind Stogar. The crack from
Stogar's primed pistol, fitted with pan and striker, added another
congestion of noise to the chamber. The officiate writhed on the
floor, spewing blood and excrement out of his gut-shot.

Stogar's second pistol drew aim on Hengst.

Roald tore himself free from Stogar. He ran for the protection
of the officiates, burying himself in their comforting flesh, which
now stood between him and weapons wielded by those who gave
him no honor.

Glennys ran out from the gallery to the floor, her throwing
knife unsheathed. The beats of the bells kept her in command
of her actions. She aimed on the strike of one bell. When the
next bell rang, Stogar's left hand clutched the hilt of the knife
buried in his chest, and Hengst whirled around from the impact
of Stogar's ball in his shoulder, and slammed face first to the
floor.

Five beats later, Glennys had hauled Hengst from the floor to
the horses in the gallery.

Long before a thousand peals had been struck, Glennys became aware of a thinning of the clangor, as though bell ringers

all over the city were being removed. Then the Fortune House bell overhead stopped too.

Her ears kept counting rings that weren't struck. From tending the unconscious Hengst's wound, she looked up. Nathan still hadn't gotten the front entrance barred.

The mounted King's Guards were backing into the Fortune House. They were fighting a tumbling, shoving, pounding mob led by Alaminite Prophets. The Prophets had knives, guns, and fire. The mob had whatever weapons it could lay hands on. They had come to loot the treasury, which the unentitled commonly believed to be in the Fortune House.

Glennys got Hengst's horse to fold down upon its legs. With her other knife she slashed off fringes from her over-jacket and used the thongs to secure Hengst's ankles to his stirrups.

A man, one black tooth in his howling mouth, leaped into her gallery. He paused, surprised to run into horses there. Then, long knife extended in both hands before him, he lunged at Glennys.

Baron, all his senses unbalanced by the bells, misjudged his attack and leaped straight at the attacker to close his jaws on the man's throat. The knife went into the mastiff's guts.

The dog yelped. He howled, twisting in circles, biting at himself. Quickly, Glennys cut his throat, and a part of herself died.

The armed officiates gathered up Justin Sharp before the embattled King's Guards could trample him. Colfax, mounted now, rode through the officiates around Roald, and pulled him up behind on the horse.

Nathan had taken command of the King's Guards. Rallying the officiates, he made a line of defense, using the fire well as their center.

The bellows in the dome bent the fire well's flames over the Prophets and the mob. As the fires fountained down to the floor, tapestries and banners hanging above the chamber ignited.

Glennys lashed Hengst's hands to the pommel of his saddle. She led his horse and Brecca into the passage that ended with the ramps that led to the service gardens in the back.

The service entrance was closed. The timbers were jammed inert in the warped runners. The ramps felt hot against the soles of her boots. The cellar coal bins fueling the fire well were down below. Evidently they'd ignited.

She feared Brecca would injure himself if his strength were put to the cross-grained doors. But she had no other choice. She backed him up.

Panicked clerks swarmed into the passage from the upper levels. They pushed on Brecca, pounding on him with their fists, slamming against the jammed doors. Glennys was separated from her stallion. She hung on to Hengst's horse, shielding the injured man as best she could from the clerks.

Smoke trickled through the planks.

Brecca attacked the clerks.

Her mind was completely taken up with keeping Hengst from being torn from the horse and from her.

Instead of using the more powerful force of his hindquarters, Brecca pounded on the doors with his front legs.

Pressed all around by the clerks, Glennys fell to the smoldering boards, losing the reins of Hengst's horse.

The force of Brecca's blows had straightened the warp of the runners to some extent. More terrified of fire than of a loco stallion, some of the clerks pried the doors apart. Fresh, cold air streamed through the narrow aperture before the doors stuck again.

The clerks climbed over each other, their bodies choking the opening. Brecca was stronger. He rammed through them, breaking their limbs and heads. He shoved through the door, scraping his shoulders, catching on his saddle. He kicked fore and back. The doors broke out of the moorings.

Behind the last of the clerks Glennys got Hengst's horse through, hanging on to his tail.

Fires leaped to the sky all over the city, driven by the wind, making the back gardens bright.

Brecca called to her.

He wanted her. She'd had nothing to spare for matching with him, keeping him under her control, while protecting Hengst. Brecca trembled, frightened of the fires. He needed her, and he'd waited.

There were a lot of people who needed her and were waiting for her to come to them. She'd better get going, though she no longer knew exactly why that mattered.

She mounted and pointed Brecca's head to the Fortune House's river gates. There was a path of sorts along the Setham River. It was the safest one she could think of. Sparks flew on the wind. Behind the garden walls came the swelling crescendo of fighting and looting.

* * *

Rotted, fallen trees, grasping vines, mud slips, and rivulets of icy drainage made for slow and difficult progress. At least the winter had put the snakes into hibernation.

Her eyes played tricks on her. Glennys caught sight of Baron loping up from behind, or circling back from foraging ahead, or leaping down the banks. Glennys could still smell the blood on her hands that insisted her dog was dead.

At some point she found her face was wet with tears. Crying for her dead guardian mastiff led her to weep harder. She sobbed for the star-crossed lost love of Jonathan. She wept for Joss Thack and her dead companions at Queen's, and all their destroyed bright dreams. She cried for Albany, and even for Gustave. At the moment that she realized she was weeping for Stella, who had been given so little in her life that she'd nestled herself into the arms of a divine mother, Glennys took herself in hand and dried her eyes.

An overhanging dead branch snapped off against her face. Splinters of bark dusted her eyes. Tears had some use then, washing her eyes clear.

She dismounted and put Brecca in front while she led the other horse, whose footing slipped and slid on the narrow trail. Hengst continued to loose blood, judging from the slickness on her fingers. The blow to his head worried her. He should have regained consciousness by now.

The river looped around here, sending her back in the direction from which she'd come. There was no further purpose to follow the Setham. The stink of shambles and tanneries was more pungent here than the bitterness of smoke blown out of the city. Hengst needed attention.

Brecca neighed. He smelled the faint evidence of horses. Glennys had her bearings. The old Queen's Yard was close, and the area being what it was, it had not attracted the mob plundering the rich upper and middle city.

The Yard was dark and shut up tight. She pounded and shouted. Only the elephant handlers came to the ramparts. All the other men had deserted the place. She had a job convincing them of her identity and that she was seeking refuge without intent to harm. The elephant men understood Nolanese poorly and preferred the easy converse of their enormous charges. Finally, they opened to her.

A set of keys to Joss's office still hung in the stables. Because the Stablemaster's fate had been such evil fortune for Queen's, the menagerie side had left the geldings' part of the Yard untouched. In Joss's old office, jars of applejack ranged undisturbed next to canisters of tea and coffee.

The elephant keepers talked to each other in the liquid syllables of their native language while they aided Glennys with Hengst. Under the lamplight she laid her brother out on Joss's back-office bed. Brecca, who generally refused to let anyone but her handle him, quietly accepted the elephant men's attention to cuts and scrapes. They examined the dusty fodder and bedding in the geldings' stable and brought fresh from their own supply.

Glennys boiled water and searched through the farrier supplies to choose what she could use on Hengst. There was ample material for bandages and slings. The ball was still embedded in his shoulder. She found a grim humor in the fact that they both would have shoulder pains until the end of their days. That reflection took her by surprise. It meant that some part of her expected a future for them both.

Using farrier tools she dug out the ball. Gently, she probed Hengst's skull with her fingers. There was a big lump over one eyebrow where his head had slammed to the Fortune House floor. There was no way she could tell if underneath was a fracture.

After bathing Hengst's upper body she dressed the wound and fashioned a sling to bind his arm close against his chest. She draped one of Joss's old, soft shirts around him. Hengst's eyelashes fluttered, and he groaned.

Roars, coughs, and growls from the menagerie's restless predators put Brecca and the other horse to stamping and neighing. Glennys felt so flattened that it was hard for her to summon out any energy to soothe her horses' misgivings. She couldn't remember why she was doing any of the things she was doing.

The elephant men brought her some of their food. She made coffee. It was old but it smelled right. The aroma stimulated a welter of memories about Jonathan. Until she went to live with him, she'd preferred tea. The brew did cure the ache in her temples, but it made the heartache worse. She was able to sleep for awhile.

With a start she came awake. It was still dark. Hengst was not in bed. In her dull, miserable state, Glennys decided that Hengst had died and the handlers had taken him away. Like the animals they served, the brown men honored the dead.

The elephant men did have him—but he was cheerfully sucking on the southern sugar cane the gray beasts generously shared with him. He had been eating bread and carrots. At his feet was an open jar of applejack.

At the sight of him on his feet, eating, drinking, and joking, Glennys felt a tiny rill of vitality trickle into her frozen veins.

He got up from a bale of straw and joined her outside. "I feel great," he said, "except for hurting like the deuce."

"I was afraid you'd died," Glennys said.

He gave her a pastel version of his old laugh. "I'm an old blood. We're seldom sick, our injuries heal fast, and we live long if we don't die soon. Now tell me what happened."

"What parts do you remember?" Glennys asked.

"That you stood at my back and did what needed to be done when I failed. Stogar's betrayal is washed clean from our blood. This is a negligible price to pay," he added, pointing to his bandages, "for his death at the hands of his own blood. I've the right to live again."

That was why *she* felt dead.

I've killed, Glennys thought. With my hands, with my own skills, and by deliberate intention. She couldn't shift the responsibility for this kill upon her stallion or her dog.

Hengst had felt like this after Brugge. He'd rejoined humanity at the price of her separation from it. Well, she was more able to carry the weight of being an outsider than he. She was used to it.

She spoke of what had occurred in the Fortune House. At the end Hengst poured out applejack on the frozen ground. "To Baron," he said, "the only Baron in our family to live up to his duties faithfully, until he honorably fell," he finished shortly.

Glennys said, "You're the Baron Fulk now. You'll be wanting me to release you from the Saquave so you can take Soudaka in hand."

Hengst bristled. "You'd insult me so? I gave you my vow for the Saquave. And you're all the family and friends I've got. I'm not letting you get away from me that easy."

The heat of his words lit a little flame of warmth in Glennys's guts. He handed her the jar of applejack.

Hengst tried to shrug, and grimaced in pain. "What have I got to be Baron with anyway? I've not a forient to my name. My blood-bond men are mostly dead in the Nemourian Mountains, and the survivors enlisted under Ely and Gordon. If the Alaminites could manage fires in St. Lucien's chief Fortune House, they certainly can manage to burn Three Trees."

All the time they spoke the wind blew hard and cold. Behind the walls was the distant thunder of a city attacked from within.

Glennys and Hengst looked up to the sky. There was too much

smoke under the cloud cover for them to read time or weather.
But their shared Soudaka-trained senses told them what they
needed to know. Dawn was three bells away.

At the same moment they announced, ''A big snowstorm,
comin' in purty fast,'' in Soudaka farmer dialect.

That struck Hengst as very funny. To Glennys's surprise, she
was laughing with him. Hengst could place his own cheerfulness
into her, much as she could put her feelings into horses. That
was no small power to have, she realized. It might be essential
in the Saquave wilderness. . . .

Hengst said, ''We've forgotten in the last year or so, Glenn,
darlin', that we're young. Thanks to your luck and foresight
we've horses, a home, and an adventure. We're goin' to have
fun!''

She looked at him sideways. ''It'll be a lot of work, that's
what I think.''

He began to tease her. ''That's what the old Alaminite part
of you needs, Glenn, in order to have fun. Good, hard work,
from dawn until after dark. Otherwise you get unthrifty and sour
in the belly.''

He lifted the applejack jar to drink deep. Glennys took it
gently from him. ''For the sake of your head,'' she said, touching the lump over his eye, ''we've got to ride soon.''

Hengst surrendered the jar. ''That's right. It's a deal. You
keep me from becoming a useless souse, and I'll keep you from
becoming a dismal old lady.''

They rested and ate. Glennys baited the horses. The last thing
she did was persuade the elephant men to sell her strings of
garlic bulbs.

''You've already poulticed me so thick with that stuff,'' Hengst
complained, ''that I smell like a Langanese mountain whore.''

For the second time, Glennys laughed.

They rode out of the Yard's private gate into Velvet Ridge
Park. Brecca's body between her legs sang into her senses anticipation, attention, and the deep, deep pleasure of moving. She
wondered about the fate of Nathan Drake.

Hengst said, ''It's bad luck to ride over the ground where
you've been, once the journey's begun. If the Chief's alive, if he
wants, he'll find us.''

Hengst was right. It was good not to be alone. And ahead
was Thea.

Dawn broke gray and dreary. They halted so Glennys could
pad Hengst's shoulder with more layers of fleece as a shield

against the icy wind. The countryside sloped down to the Alluv Bottoms and the Setham valley. In distant perspective they could see St. Lucien.

The King's Highway and the smaller roads were clogged with refugees fleeing the burning city. Another sort of folk rushed toward the city, attracted by easy grabbing. Out-and-out brigandage obstructed the way in both directions. Glennys hoped the Copelys, Jonathan, and the others had taken her warnings, proffered through George Sert, to heart and had left before the great dispersion.

The wind howled straight out of the east, streaming the horses' manes and tails. The first pellets of snow stung their cheeks through their wind masks.

Swags of snow clouds came down on St. Lucien like the curtains that dropped over the stage at Queen's Theater.

The wind at their backs pushed them hard to the west.

• EXEUNT •